W9-ANE-912

# $\mathscr{L}$OVE
## AFTER ALL

OTHER BOOKS AND BOOKS ON CASSETTE BY
MICHELE ASHMAN BELL

*An Unexpected Love*

*An Enduring Love*

*A Forever Love*

*Yesterday's Love*

# LOVE
# AFTER ALL

A NOVEL

# MICHELE
# ASHMAN
# BELL

Covenant Communications, Inc.

Covenant

Cover illustration by Anita Kim Robbins

Cover and book design © Covenant Communications, Inc.

Published by Covenant Communications, Inc.
American Fork, Utah

Copyright © 2000 by Michele Ashman Bell
All rights reserved. No part of this book may be reproduced in any format or in any medium without
the written permission of the publisher, Covenant Communications, Inc., P.O. Box 416, American
Fork, UT 84003. The views expressed herein are the responsibility of the author and do not necessarily
represent the position of Covenant Communications, Inc.

This is a work of fiction. The characters, names, incidents, places, and dialogue are products of the
author's imagination, and are not to be construed as real.

Printed in the United States of America
First Printing: October 2000

07 06 05 04 03 02 01 00    10 9 8 7 6 5 4 3 2 1

ISBN 1-57734-731-5

**Library of Congress Cataloging-in-Publication Data**

Bell, Michele Ashman, 1959-
  Love after all / Michele Ashman Bell.
    p. cm.
    ISBN 1-57734-731-5
    1. Mormon women--Fiction. I. Title.

PS3552.E5217 L69 2000
  813'.54--dc21                                                            00-058981

I'd like to express my gratitude to my
dear friends Lisa Payne and Shelley Thompson
for always believing, encouraging, and supporting me.
Thanks for never letting me give up.


I'd also like to thank my husband, Gary, for his
tremendous help and loving suggestions with this story.


And last, but not least, thanks again, Val,
for being a great editor and friend.

This book is dedicated to my grandmothers,
Norene Ashman and Viola Bauer.
Thank you for everything.
I love you.

# PROLOGUE

It was over.

Danielle Camden's stomach churned and twisted. She had to tell him. This couldn't go on a day longer. It wasn't fair to Todd or, frankly, to her either. Mentally she kicked herself for not having the courage to tell him before it had come to this.

"Isn't the temple beautiful this time of year?" Todd asked, as they strolled hand in hand around the temple grounds, which were brightly lit up and sparkling for the Christmas season. Giving her a warm smile, he let go of her hand and slid his arm around her shoulders, pulling her close. Danielle returned his smile, but her mind was racing. She had to tell him tonight—but what would she say?

"They must use over a million lights on these trees," Todd said, turning his gaze toward Danielle, his dark brown eyes hinting at a secret.

Danielle looked up into his face, remembering how handsome she'd thought him when they first met. He had glossy chestnut-colored hair and thickly lashed eyes. Dreamy eyes, she'd thought at one time. But even though she still thought he was handsome, she didn't love him.

She sighed. It just wasn't there.

"Danielle? Don't you think the lights look pretty?" he asked.

Danielle nodded absently. She was thinking about the last time she'd ended a relationship. It had been one of the hardest things she'd had to do, because that time she'd been in love. And she still remembered how wonderful it felt.

Karl had been almost everything she'd ever wanted. He was handsome, adventurous, spontaneous, funny, and romantic. A ski instructor from Austria, he'd rescued her on the slopes one afternoon when she'd taken a particularly bad fall. He wasn't a member of the Church, but he'd been respectful of her beliefs. Occasionally he'd ask her a question about the Church and then listen carefully as Danielle did her best to answer.

When the ski season ended, Karl planned to go back to Austria for the summer. Since Danielle would be graduating from the University of Utah about the same time, it had seemed written in the stars for them to go to Europe together. Danielle was confident that Karl respected her values, and that their trip, while strengthening their relationship, would not put her in a compromising position. Her family had not approved, but they would not forbid her. They did, however, warn her to consider this step very carefully.

Danielle's two sisters, Miranda and Rachel, also tried to discourage her from traveling to Europe with Karl, but she thought she knew Karl better than they did. He was nothing like either of their husbands. Both of Danielle's sisters had struggled with their marriages, and while Danielle never wanted to experience the heartache they'd each gone through, she couldn't imagine Karl and her disagreeing on anything.

Miranda had married someone who was inactive and her life had been miserable. They'd had different ideas of happiness, different priorities, and she'd felt lonely and neglected. A year after his death, Miranda had married Garrett in the temple and the two were blissfully happy.

Rachel had also endured her share of challenges with her marriage. But she and her husband had worked very hard on their relationship, and Danielle had never seen them happier.

While preparing for the trip, Danielle had felt the little niggling voice of the Spirit warning her, but she hadn't wanted to listen. Fortunately, Heavenly Father hadn't given up on her. Sitting next to Karl at the Salt Lake International Airport, waiting for their flight, Danielle had seen a missionary returning home to his family. At that moment, the crying, laughing, hugging, and joy had penetrated her heart, and the Spirit had given her a glimpse of her future if she went with Karl. She had been horrified. Even though they weren't married, and even though he knew her standards, she knew that over time he would expect more of her than she was willing to give. Without the blessing of marriage, she couldn't, she wouldn't, take their relationship to that level.

When the call to board sounded over the loudspeaker, Karl stood up and stretched, grinning at her. That was when she'd told him she wasn't going with him after all. He had stared at her blankly, obviously mystified at her sudden change of heart. She wasn't sure she understood either. But she'd been raised to know better, and when push came to shove, everything she'd been taught had surfaced.

Even now she shuddered, remembering his reaction when she'd told him she'd changed her mind. She'd been shocked to see the bewilderment on his face change to irritation and anger before he finally grabbed his carry-ons and stomped toward the gate.

Danielle had felt a curious sense of calm leaving the airport that day, and from that moment on she had made a conscientious effort to change her life. She decided to put her life in order and to only date members of the Church. Then she had met Todd.

"Dani," his voice broke into her thoughts, "I asked if you're getting cold. You looked like you were shivering." Danielle looked up at Todd's concerned face and shook her head silently. She'd met Todd at a Young Adult New Year's dance six months after she'd broken up with Karl. She had noticed him right off because he was limping around with a cast up to his knee. She also noticed him because his dark coloring, contagious smile, and good looks made him stand out from the other guys.

Later that evening they happened to meet at the punch bowl, and Danielle asked how he'd broken his leg. When he'd said "skiing," that was all she needed to hear. They'd talked the rest of the evening, and the next day Todd had called her for a date. Luckily Todd's injury wasn't bad enough to keep him and Danielle from hitting the slopes a few times before the end of the season. Both of them loved outdoor sports and had enjoyed many activities together.

But as much as they had in common, Danielle realized something was missing. Todd was a wonderful person—strong in the gospel, goal-oriented, and committed to their relationship. Her parents and her sisters thought he walked on water. But, still, there was a problem. A big one. Todd had fallen in love with her, but she hadn't fallen in love with him. She'd tried to. As she'd accepted each date with Todd, she kept ignoring the little warning signals she'd felt, hoping she would start to share the feelings he evidently had for her. But she just couldn't convince her heart.

With Karl, she'd been in love, but he wasn't the right guy for her. Todd was the right kind of guy for her, but she didn't love him. He wasn't the first thing she thought of in the morning and the last person she thought of at night. She didn't long for him when they were apart or feel butterflies when they were together.

*Why didn't I end this sooner?* She should have. Especially when she'd begun to suspect he might give her a ring for Christmas. But she'd kept hoping her heart would eventually agree with her head. It hadn't and now she knew it never would. Nor did it help that Todd's feelings and actions toward her had become possessive and stifling. He wanted to be with her every moment of every day. She had no space, no breathing room.

Danielle noticed that she and Todd had stopped walking and were standing in front of a life-sized nativity scene, a scene so real Danielle half expected one of the sheep to "baa."

"Are you okay?" he asked, peering into her face. "You seem to have a lot on your mind tonight."

"Oh, sorry," she answered quickly. They needed to have a serious talk, but now was not the time or place to tell him. She wanted them to be alone when she gave him the news, not in the middle of Temple Square surrounded by swarms of people. She tugged at the brim of her hat, her blonde hair curling about the bottom, and laughed lightly, her voice sounding hollow and awkward. "I'm fine," she said. "Really."

When he'd asked her to come to see the lights on Temple Square, she'd been afraid that he was going to propose. She tried to avoid this possibility by telling him that she and her mother were decorating the family Christmas tree. Unfortunately, her mother had overheard the conversation.

"Go ahead with Todd, dear," she'd said brightly. "We can finish the tree later."

She'd reluctantly agreed to go, and if he sensed the lack of enthusiasm in her voice, he didn't say. Perhaps he was too excited about proposing to notice. But inside she was in knots.

Todd leaned forward to give her a kiss on her forehead, and she fought the urge to pull free from him. Todd was a very "touchy-feely" kind of guy, and as his affection had grown stronger, so had his need to touch her. In fact, at dinner one night, she'd actually had to ask him to let go of her hand so she could eat. Maybe she would have been flattered had her feelings matched his, but they didn't. She'd endured his kisses, waiting for a spark to take hold and grow into something more. But nothing had happened.

He wrapped an arm around her shoulders and pulled her close. "I'm glad you decided to come with me tonight." He led her to a cement bench overlooking the nativity scene, near the tabernacle.

"Danielle," he spoke softly. "I have something to give you. I have something for you."

Danielle stiffened. *Please,* she prayed, *not the ring. Not here.* "It's kind of cold out here, Todd," she said. "Maybe we should just go. You can give it to me in the car."

"It won't take long," he said.

They sat down, Danielle's heart thumping wildly in her chest. *This isn't happening,* she told herself. *He's not giving me the ring. He can't be!*

Todd smiled at her, with a gleam in his eye. It was obvious what he was about to do.

"Todd, wait—" she began, forcing herself to speak.

"In a minute," he interrupted her. "Just let me say this first." He paused, as if gathering his thoughts, then said, "Danielle, I think you know how I feel about you. I love you and I've prayed earnestly and fasted over this many times. And, well . . ." He slid from the bench and perched himself on one knee. Danielle shut her eyes, suppressing the urge to cry out.

He pulled a ring box from his coat. "Danielle, will you marry me?"

Danielle felt faint. She closed her eyes again and drew in several deep breaths, trying to get some oxygen to her brain. The last thing she wanted to do was pass out and attract a crowd. But when she opened her eyes, she realized it was too late. A crowd of people, noticing Todd on his knee, proposing to her—on the temple grounds, no less—had already gathered.

Opening her eyes, she looked at him, kneeling before her, wishing with every fiber of her being that she cared for him, even half as much as he cared for her. *What is wrong with me?* she wondered. *Why can't I just love you like everyone else does?*

"Oh, Todd," was all she could say as tears quickly collected in her eyes and trickled onto her cheeks.

Taking that as a "yes," Todd took the ring from the box and placed it on her finger as her tears came faster. The crowd clapped and cheered, thinking they were watching a happy couple become engaged. Most likely they would go home and tell others about the "proposal" they'd seen at the temple that evening, beneath the sparkling Christmas lights and falling snow.

Little did they know that an hour later Danielle would return the ring.

"I can't do it, Todd," Danielle told him as they sat in the car in front of her house. "I can't marry you." She shut her eyes and prayed that he would understand and that the Lord would give her the right words to say.

"But the ring . . . ," he stammered, "the temple . . . , you said yes." The pain in his voice, the hurt in his eyes, nearly broke her heart.

"No, Todd, I didn't." Danielle knew this was the last thing he expected from her, but she couldn't go through with a marriage out of obligation or pity. She slid the ring from her finger and looked at it again. It was dainty and elegant, simple yet beautiful. Again she searched deep inside for any shred of love for him. But it just wasn't there. When it came down to being honest with her feelings, she knew she just couldn't marry him. She didn't love him as a woman should love her future husband. But she sincerely hoped that he would find a woman who did.

Still, he said he'd fasted and prayed to get an answer. Had Todd really received a confirmation that she was the right one for him? If so, why hadn't she been informed?

She wasn't the most spiritual person in the world, that was true, but she felt that her spirituality was growing. She'd stopped dating nonmembers and had become more involved in the Church and more dedicated to the gospel. She'd gulped down her fear and accepted a call to work in the Primary teaching the CTR 6 class. The call had surprised her, but she had quickly come to love "her children," as she called them, and they had filled an empty place in her heart. Even though the Primary lessons were simple, they'd had a profound effect on Danielle. As she'd prepared her lessons and taught them, she'd felt the power of the Holy Ghost and had decided to do everything in her power to keep it with her always.

But she'd never felt any promptings of the Spirit urging her to marry Todd. As often as she herself had prayed and fasted, never once did she get that message. But Todd had. Again she wondered, how did that happen?

"I'm sorry, Todd," she said as she handed him the ring. "I can't marry you."

"But why?" he asked, his words etched with pain.

Wasn't it hard enough already? Was he actually going to force her to say it? From the look on his face, Danielle realized that she needed to tell him how she felt. But how did she tell him that even though she'd known all along that her feelings hadn't been as strong as his, she'd honestly thought her feelings for him would grow deeper? But they hadn't. It hadn't helped matters that her family and friends all told her repeatedly what an incredible catch Todd was and what a great couple she and Todd made. That, along with her own desire for a meaningful relationship, had made it confusing and difficult to recognize what she really felt.

Other people managed to figure out who to marry. Why couldn't she? What was she doing so wrong that the Spirit couldn't get through to her? Or was she just too dense to recognize that still, small voice? She knew the minute her family, friends, and even ward members heard that Todd had proposed and she'd turned him down, she was going to get looks and lectures that would chill her bones. *How did I get myself into this?* she asked herself once more.

"I just don't love you, Todd," she said, the words feeling heavy and awkward as she spoke. "I'm sorry."

Todd stared at the ring a long moment before shoving it into his shirt pocket, then he slammed the steering wheel with his fist. Danielle jumped at his unexpected display of anger.

"So this was just a game to you?" he said bitterly. "You were just out to play with my head, is that it?"

"No, that wasn't it at all," she said defensively. How dare he accuse her of that!

"I cared about you," she said, "and we had fun dating. Then you started talking about marriage, and I . . ." Her voice trailed off. How could she tell him she had hoped she would eventually fall in love with him, but she hadn't?

"I've told everyone I was going to give you a ring," he said, looking out at the falling snow. "I had no idea you would say no. How could you do this to me? What am I going to tell my friends and my family?"

Was that all he was worried about? Wounded pride? This wasn't going to be easy for her either. She was the one who called off their relationship. He would receive sympathy and support; she'd only get curious stares and harsh judgment. She could hear her family now. *I can't believe it. You broke up with him? What is wrong with you? He's perfect.*

She swallowed, not looking forward to telling her family. "Maybe you should have talked to me first," she said. "I mean, you only told me last week that you loved me. And I didn't say it back, remember?"

His eyes narrowed. "Why didn't you say something then?" His words were sharp and cutting.

"At the time I was so surprised, I didn't expect it," she replied, choosing her words carefully, trying to calm him down. "I guess it kind of scared me. I didn't know what to say."

"Well, that's just great," he muttered. He glared at her for a moment. "Tell me something, Danielle Camden. What exactly are you holding out for? Perfection?" He laughed without amusement. "I don't know exactly what you think you deserve, but you're never going to find it. Do you think you're ever going to find anyone as good as me?"

Danielle wasn't sure she'd heard him right. "Excuse me?" she said.

"Face it, Danielle," he laughed harshly. "It's not like you have guys lined up at your door. You're going to end up marrying some loser down the road just because you're desperate. Or you'll end up alone for the rest of your life."

She knew she'd wounded his ego, but now he was making her mad. Her first impulse was to tell him exactly how she felt, to knock him down another notch or two. But she knew it wouldn't do any good, and frankly, she didn't want to sit there and be his verbal punching bag.

"Maybe so," she said calmly, "but I wish you the best, Todd. I really do." She opened the car door and climbed out. "I'm sorry—"

Without warning, he punched the gas and took off like a rocket, spraying Danielle from head to foot with slushy snow.

"And a Merry Christmas to you, too," she said as he fishtailed down the road and out of sight. Wiping the icy mess from her face, she steeled herself to face her parents. "Might as well get it over with," she muttered. Taking a deep breath, she took a step, lost her footing on the icy concrete, and nearly fell. She steadied herself as Todd's words echoed in her mind—*"You'll marry some loser because you're desperate or you'll end up alone."*

"That's what you think!" she yelled after him. "I'll show you." Marry some loser indeed!

# CHAPTER ONE

---

*One year later*

Christmas carols played over the intercom, filling the busy office with holiday cheer. But Danielle didn't feel one iota of Christmas spirit. If anything, she felt like Ebenezer Scrooge.

For the last several months, she had started to feel as if her life was going nowhere, like a hole in a sweater that kept unraveling, getting bigger and more raggedy, until it would be impossible to repair. At one time Danielle had loved being single—dating great guys, going on incredible vacations and outdoor adventures, having the time of her life. But lately, the guys didn't seem so great, the adventures weren't so incredible, and she was too tired from working all day to have the time of her life.

*Dating.* She thought about some of the dates she'd been on in the last year and winced. She didn't have enough fingers or toes to count all the freaky, creepy, and "bore-you-to-death" dates she'd been on since she broke up with Todd. She could write a book on bad dates and relationships. Like the time she went out with the guy from the sales department. He had seemed harmless enough. He was a bodybuilder, kind of cute, and drove a nice-looking pickup. But what was it, she wanted to know, that made seemingly normal people at work turn into absolute psychotic lunatics on dates? The guy had been

"Mr. Road Rage, Mr. Chip-on-the-Shoulder, and Mr. Want-to-Make-Something-of-It" all rolled up into one muscle-bound hunk of testosterone. All she could figure was that maybe he'd taken so many steroids he'd altered his personality. Like some kind of "Jekyll and Hyde" syndrome.

Then there was the guy she met at *Dino's*. Her good friend at work, Roberta Westmoor, had talked her into going to the dance club "just for fun," and it had taken only a few minutes for Danielle to decide that the "club scene" wasn't for her. Just as she was about to leave, a young man had cornered her and coaxed her out onto the dance floor. His name was Brad Fox, and he turned out to be a great dancer and a lot of fun. He, too, had seemed harmless at first. He'd been so charmingly persistent that she'd agreed to go out on a date with him. He'd taken her to a fancy restaurant for dinner and to a movie, then offered to show her his condo near the mouth of the canyon. Big mistake. He'd been aptly named and was determined to live up to his name. Danielle was grateful she had quick reflexes and a strong upper body from her years on the high school swim team. That had been the most aerobic date of her life. After fighting him off, she'd actually walked three blocks to a gas station and phoned Roberta to come and pick her up.

With a dreary dating life, a job that was rapidly becoming a drudge, and an empty-appearing future, Danielle felt unfulfilled and restless. Empty. Something was definitely missing in her life.

When she'd first started working at Turner Consulting after graduating from the "U," she'd enjoyed the challenge of a new job. She'd liked being in charge of accounts and thrived on the competitive corporate spirit. She'd worked her tail off to be the best account manager she could, and for two years in a row she'd actually won that honor. But in the last year, her position had lost its appeal. She'd lost her edge. She had a job instead of a career. She felt stuck.

In the cubicle next to her, her best friend and office neighbor, Roberta, hummed a Christmas carol. She didn't appear to be lacking in Christmas cheer, Danielle thought sourly. *And I've turned into a full-blown Scrooge.*

Leaning back in her swivel chair, Roberta whispered, "Hey, did you hear the boss's son is in town?"

Danielle looked up from her computer monitor, annoyed at the interruption. She had more pressing problems right now than Mr. Turner's snobby Harvard son. "So?" she shrugged, not taking her eyes from the facts and figures that were putting her stomach in knots.

"You wouldn't say 'so' if you saw him." Roberta's swivel chair creaked as she rolled herself into Danielle's office. "He was wearing this gorgeous Armani suit and he has the most incredible smile." She spun her chair around, which sent her long, curly red hair swinging with the motion.

Roberta and Danielle had started at Turner Consulting at almost the same time. Roberta was younger, by a year and a half, and had an associate's degree as an administrative assistant. She worked as an Account Service Rep and doubled as the department activities coordinator. Every holiday, every employee birthday, every special occasion, there was Roberta, giving out food assignments, collecting money for gifts, bringing in balloons. Without her, Danielle acknowledged, work would be even worse. But at the moment, she didn't feel like chatting.

"Roberta," she said, sliding a pen behind her ear, "right now I can't think about anything but the Chase/Dixon account."

Roberta stopped twirling. "What's wrong?"

"They're talking about changing consulting companies. Seems we've been undersold by another consulting company out of Los Angeles."

"But you've had that account for years." Roberta scooted forward to see the information on the monitor. "Chase/Dixon is one of the biggest accounts we have."

"You're telling me?" Danielle pulled the pen from behind her ear and chewed on the end nervously. "I think I need to fly to San Francisco and talk to them personally."

Roberta gave her a warning glance. "You know Mr. Turner has put the kibosh on all air travel until the first of the year."

"I'm afraid if I don't go, we'll lose them." Danielle's head began to ache.

"Well, good luck, girlfriend," Roberta said, giving her chair a push and gliding back to her cubicle. "You're going to need it."

"I don't need luck, I need a miracle," Danielle muttered. She dropped her pen on the desk and rubbed her temples. Somehow she had to talk the department manager into this trip without alarming him. No matter what Chase/Dixon's reasons were for changing consultants, she would be blamed for the loss.

"Might as well get it over with," she groaned as she pushed herself to her feet. As she walked by the window, she glanced outside at the falling snow. She dreaded the drive home after work; rush hour traffic was bad enough without a blizzard to make it worse. The only good thing about the bad weather was that she would be able to try out the four-wheel drive on her new Outback. She'd been saving for months to buy a new car and hers still had less than a thousand miles on it. It made all the stress and headaches at work worth it.

Well, almost.

She wondered how she'd gotten herself into an eight-to-five job like this. She'd been a recreation management major in college, but her advisor at school had recommended she study business instead. Jobs were scarce in her chosen major, especially for women. Plus, many of the positions required extended trips—running rivers, backpacking in the mountains, and working as on-site park management. In contrast, the business field was broad and full of opportunity. It provided more options and security in the event she had to keep working after marriage and children or in case she ended up as a single mom, as so many women did these days. A business major would give her a better chance of finding work with more flexible hours—perhaps even work she could do from home.

When Danielle had first started at Turner Consulting, she loved her job. It was challenging and exciting, and she still had her weekends free to ski and hang out with friends. But lately her life had started to feel "off-center." Her enthusiasm for work was gone, and just having fun with friends wasn't enough. Fun didn't compensate for the lack of a good relationship.

She was also starting to realize that she wasn't cut out for an eight-to-five office job. Sometimes being cooped up inside all day made her feel like a caged lion. Why hadn't she stayed in recreation management, or maybe gone into the travel industry? Or art. At least she'd be doing something fun and creative. Maybe she wouldn't be making as much money at any of those jobs, but at least she'd enjoy what she was doing.

But an office job? It seemed like a fate worse than death. Weekends just weren't enough anymore. On sunny summer days she'd look out her office window and long to be water skiing. In the fall she ached to be up in the mountains, hiking and picking wild-flowers. In the spring she loved biking and playing tennis. And on snowy winter days she wanted to be up skiing more than anything. But to do all these things, she needed money, and to have money, she needed a job.

Resigned to her fate, she sighed and tried to summon up all her courage as she approached Jack Harris's door. Jack had been her boss ever since she'd started at Turner Consulting; he'd given her a chance at a job she wasn't quite qualified for because he liked her people skills. Her business degree from the University helped her grasp the essence of her new job quickly, but it was her drive and personality that made her one of the best account managers in the firm. At least, until now.

The door opened and out stepped a coworker, Jenny Marshall. Her eyes were red-rimmed and swollen. Danielle knew Jenny was going through a divorce that had turned very ugly. It had taken a restraining order to make her husband leave her alone, and she wasn't rid of him yet. He'd become involved with pornography on the Internet and had gone from being a considerate, nurturing husband and father to a cold, selfish stranger.

Jenny rushed by quickly, not giving Danielle a chance to even say "hi."

By the strained expression on Jack's face, Danielle knew something was wrong. Even though he was her boss, Jack and Danielle had a friendly relationship. Both were avid skiers and Utah Jazz fans. Danielle shut the door behind her and took a seat across the desk from Jack. Sensing that her timing wasn't good, she was tempted to leave and come back later.

"Boy," Jack finally said, shaking his head sadly. "That wasn't easy." He raked his fingers through his hair and grimaced.

"What is it?" Danielle asked, suddenly concerned. Was Jenny okay?

"Sometimes I wish Turner would do his own dirty work, you know?" Jack scowled. Danielle knew Jack had had to do some things for Mr. Turner that he'd been uncomfortable with, but he'd never seemed this upset before.

"Is something wrong with Jenny?" she asked.

"As if that poor woman hasn't got enough to deal with, I had to let her go," Jack admitted.

"You fired Jenny?" Danielle burst out.

"I didn't fire her. Turner fired her," Jack countered.

"You've got to be kidding," Danielle blurted, rising restlessly to her feet and pacing to the door and back. "I know she's been missing a lot of work lately, and she's had a hard time keeping up with everything, but it's only temporary. Once her divorce is final, she'll do a lot better."

"I know," Jack agreed. "Believe me, I tried to convince Mr. Turner of that, but he wouldn't listen. He doesn't have time for a 'dead-beat employee,' he said. I was supposed to fire her two weeks ago, but I just couldn't. Finally it came down to me firing her or him firing both of us. I just can't risk losing my job right now. Not with Melissa at BYU and Ryan on his mission."

Danielle nodded her understanding. "You did what you had to do," she tried to comfort him. She understood his position—but poor, poor Jenny. "What's she going to do?" Danielle asked.

"She said that without steady income, she'll lose her home, and she'll have to move in with her parents, which will be hard because her father is completely bedridden."

Danielle clenched her eyes tightly shut for a moment. Darn that Mr. Turner. Who did he think he was anyway? "That man has no compassion," Danielle said. "He doesn't care about anyone but himself."

"He's still the boss, and what he says goes whether we like it or not. Now," Jack said, changing the subject, "what did you need? I've just been going over some budget figures for Turner's senior management meeting. I'm afraid he's not going to like it."

Danielle's heart hit rock bottom. Why bother asking? She had about as much chance of getting the trip approved as a snowball's chance in the Sahara.

Jack began to explain how critical the situation was. Slumping back into her chair, she tried to listen to what he was saying, but all she could think about was that she should have called in sick and gone skiing today. And taken poor Jenny with her.

⋙ ✿ ⋘

"So, did you see him?" Roberta asked when Danielle returned to her desk.

"Who? Jack?" Danielle absentmindedly double-clicked the mouse, and the Chase/Dixon account vanished. She needed a break for a few minutes. She couldn't get her mind off Jenny and the heartless way Mr. Turner had fired her.

"Not Jack. Turner's son," Roberta said, offering her friend some crackers from a box she kept in her drawer. Even though Roberta was rod thin, she had an appetite like a pro-football linebacker. Her metabolism was probably on high, even in her sleep.

"Why would I see him?" Danielle asked, taking one of the wheat crackers and nibbling on the corner. She hadn't eaten breakfast and it was well past two o'clock now. "I went to see Jack about the San Francisco trip." She chose not to tell Roberta about Jenny, since she'd promised Jack. The news would spread through the office soon enough. "He said there was no way a trip for an existing unprofitable account would be approved. Unless the trip generates new business and revenue for the company, it's not considered important right now."

"Yeah, well, things will change around here after Old Man Turner retires and turns the business over to his young, smart, and—might I add?—very handsome son," Roberta smirked.

"I hope you're right," Danielle said as she popped the rest of the cracker into her mouth and gulped it down. Then, grabbing her sack lunch out of her desk drawer, she stood up. "I think I'll go eat my lunch now."

"I could've brought you something back from the deli," Roberta said.

"That's okay. I'm still brown bagging it." Danielle held up her lunch sack. "I need to start saving. I've decided it's time to move out of my parents' house and get an apartment."

"Whoa," Roberta said, taken by surprise at the news. "That's great, Danielle."

Danielle had been thinking about it for a long time and had decided she'd waited long enough. It would still be another few months before she'd have enough money saved for a deposit and first and last month's rent, not to mention all the extra expenses, like getting the utilities hooked up.

"So, what's up with all of these big changes in your life?" Roberta asked as she licked salt off her fingers and closed the lid to the cracker box. "First, a new SUV and now you're moving out?"

"I feel like I'm in a rut," Danielle said wryly. "I'm almost twenty-six and I think it's time I figured out what I want to do with my life. I mean, what did you think you'd be doing when you were our age?"

Roberta shrugged. "I don't know. I guess I thought I'd do what everybody else did. Go to college, meet a guy, get married, have kids. I never worried about what I'd do if it didn't happen that way."

Danielle, too, had thought her own life would unfold in the traditional way, but somewhere along the way, she'd taken a detour without knowing it—one that had put her on a different course, an uncharted course.

"Well, I don't know about you," Danielle said, "but I'm not going to spend the rest of my life waiting around to get married. I'm going to do something productive with my life. I want to go places and do things. I want to travel and see the world." She spread her hands in front of her, reaching out, as if to grasp some tangible object that could help her dreams come true. But with nothing to grab onto, she let her hands drop helplessly into her lap. "Do you know what I mean, Roberta?"

Roberta inclined her head slightly, thinking. "I guess so. But it's not like we're *that* old."

"I know," Danielle agreed. "But it seems like most of the guys my age are married—at least, all the good ones are—and all that's left are the weird ones. Believe me, I know because I've dated every one of them. There's not a lot of choice left. I don't want leftovers, Roberta."

"Gosh." Roberta sat back in her chair. "You make it sound so dismal."

*Because it is,* Danielle was tempted to say. Instead she said, "I'm just saying that I'm not going to sit around any longer. Everyone acts like marriage is the beginning and the end for women. But marriage is no guarantee of happiness. I need to find out what makes me happy on my own and not expect some man to provide it for me. I guess the bottom line is that it's time to take charge of my life. And I think the first step is getting out on my own."

Roberta nodded. "Sometimes I think about moving out of my parents' house, but . . . I don't know, it's so much easier there. No bills, no headaches—heck, my mom even still does my wash."

Danielle looked at her friend with dismay. "That's just the problem, Roberta. Aren't you ready for independence? Don't you want to make your own decisions? Have your own space? Live your own life?"

Twirling a lock of hair around her finger, Roberta spoke slowly. "Well, yeah. It makes me feel like I'm back in high school when my parents give me a curfew or want to know where I'm going or who I'm with." She paused, thinking. "You're absolutely right," she said at last.

Danielle was glad to see she was finally getting through to her friend. She needed Roberta's vote of confidence. Somewhere along the way she'd lost the confidence she used to have. And as she thought about it, it seemed as though she lost control of her life every time she dated someone seriously. Karl had turned her world upside down, and then, just as she'd gotten it right side up again, she'd met Todd, who pretty much turned her inside out. And from that point on, she hadn't been able to regain control. And the more she dated, the more bewildered she'd become.

She'd done a lot of soul searching and self-evaluation lately. She knew she was a good person, and she was trying her best to do what was right, make good decisions, and get her priorities straight. She had an education, a good-paying job, a loving, supportive family, and some good friends. But she needed more.

Of course, she didn't dare complain to her family or friends. All of them thought she'd made a horrible mistake breaking up with Todd, and that was why her life was off-kilter now. But Danielle knew that turning down his proposal was the right thing to do. She'd prayed more over that relationship than she'd prayed about anything in her life, trying to figure out why the Lord would lead her to break up with Todd, just to leave her stranded. What did the Lord want her to do with her life?

Logically, it seemed to make sense for her to focus on her career and grow as an individual. That was the reason behind her new vehicle and the decision to get a place of her own. In a way, she thought, she needed some tangible proof of her hard work and independence. She'd watched her older sister Miranda struggle to get her life back together after her husband died. Danielle had spent a lot of time with Miranda that awful first year. And as Danielle had struggled herself this last year, Miranda's support in return had been invaluable. Still, no one else could tell Danielle what she had to do. She had to figure it out by herself.

Deep in thought, Danielle walked to the cafeteria and found a table in the corner with a view of the parking lot blanketed in white. She pulled a bagel, some yogurt, and an apple out of her bag, looking through the window at the people who scurried in and out of the building as the snow grew deeper.

Except for herself, the lunchroom was empty and she appreciated the quiet. She kicked off her shoes and wiggled her toes. Nylons were torture and so were dress shoes. She owned the right wardrobe for a business career, but she didn't enjoy wearing it.

As she picked at her bagel, she continued her previous train of thought. She didn't regret breaking up with Todd, but it seemed as though everyone felt they needed to constantly ask her if she really thought there were so many available men her age better than Todd? And if not better, at least as good?

If one more person in her ward came up and asked her if she was dating anyone seriously yet, she swore she'd get up in fast and testimony meeting and let them all have it. Maybe that was another reason she felt like she needed to move out of her parents' home. She could start fresh somewhere else without having everyone around her knowing her past.

Giving her half-eaten bagel an irritated look, she glanced up as someone else entered the room. A tall, broad-shouldered man with golden brown hair, wearing a deep olive-green suit, stood in front of a vending machine. Coins clinked as he fed his money into the machine.

Something told Danielle it was Carson Turner.

He certainly was distinguished-looking, as Roberta had said, like his father, but his features were softer, not sharp and strained.

He turned, took a bite of the apple he had just purchased, then examined it closely. She knew the apple was soft. They always were. They sat in the machines so long they were never fresh. He pulled a face and tossed the apple in the trash, then looked over at her.

"I should've warned you," she said apologetically. "The apples are soft."

"That's okay," he said, with a lopsided smile. "I guess you couldn't know I was going to get one." Behind his professional manner, she saw a friendly sparkle in his green eyes. She couldn't take her eyes off of him. She knew she was staring but she couldn't pull her gaze away.

*Snap out of it, you dope!* she scolded herself. And even though she told herself she didn't care about impressing him, she was suddenly grateful she'd worn her slim black skirt and favorite grey sweater.

She looked down at the piece of fruit in front of her. "I've got one here you can have. I'm not going to eat it." Despite her feelings about his father, she found it easy to be nice to Carson. Of course, it didn't hurt that he was extremely good-looking and surprisingly friendly.

"Oh no." He waved away her offer with his hand. "That's okay."

"I'll probably just throw it away if you don't eat it." She picked up the apple and offered it to him. "Honest."

"Are you sure?" Carson hesitated, then approached her table, holding out his hand. "I'm Carson Turner."

Danielle reached out, then realized she was holding the apple in her right hand. Both chuckled as she quickly slipped it into her left hand and accepted his handshake. "It's nice to meet you. I'm Danielle Camden."

"Mind if I have a seat?" He smiled, motioning toward a chair at her table. He must have had years of dental work to have such straight, even teeth, she thought.

"No, of course not," Danielle said, her heart beating fast. *Roberta would die if she walked in right now.*

"Busy day?" He glanced at her food. "Kind of late for lunch."

"Yeah, you could say that." *Busy running your father's business into the ground.*

"So what do you do here at Turner Consulting?" The apple crunched loudly as he took a bite. "Mmmm," he said. "Much better."

"I'm one of the account managers."

"How's it going?"

She didn't mean to, but she rolled her eyes in frustration.

"Not good, huh?"

"Oh, no," she tried to cover up her reaction with a quick response. "Actually, everything's fine." *Would that be considered a lie?*

"I know my dad's having a big meeting about all the accounts with the senior management team. He wants me to sit in on it."

*Well, that's just dandy!* Danielle thought. *He's going to hear all about Chase/Dixon at the meeting and know I wasn't telling the truth.*

"Well," she amended her reply. "I'm having a few challenges, but that's to be expected occasionally."

"Is one of your accounts giving you a hard time?"

She hated going into details, but short of being rude, or lying again, she didn't know how to dodge his pointed question. "I'm having a bit of a problem, but I'm sure I'll get it worked out. I just want to get things taken care of before Christmas. I don't want to let it sit over the holidays." She put the empty yogurt container and the rest of the bagel back into the brown paper bag. Fearing that he'd ask for details, she quickly changed the subject. "So, you go to Harvard?"

"Right," he answered. "I'm getting an MBA there."

"How do you like it?"

He nodded before he answered, giving him a chance to swallow. "It's okay. I enjoy the East but I really miss the mountains."

"I'll bet your father is happy to have you home." She liked his hands. He had long, strong fingers with neatly trimmed nails.

He shrugged. "Yeah, I guess. He's so busy with work, we haven't spent much time together. I mainly came home to do some skiing. A friend invited me to his family's cabin in Deer Valley for Christmas."

"You're not going to be with your dad on Christmas?" Danielle asked, surprised.

"He'll probably come in to the office like he usually does." Carson shrugged again, as if used to his father's absence. "Anyway," he said, neatly changing the subject, "tell me about your account."

She didn't know why but she found herself explaining her concerns about the Chase/Dixon account and the amount of competition the company had been feeling lately. Carson listened intently, rubbing his chin thoughtfully, nodding in understanding as she spoke. After listening to the history of the account up to the present, he said, "Would you mind if I offered a few suggestions?"

Danielle expected herself to feel defensive about his offer or offended that he would presume she needed his ideas. But she didn't feel threatened at all. It was obvious that he sincerely wanted to help solve her dilemma, not criticize her work or take her account from her. As he sketched out his ideas, Danielle's mind clicked and whirred. She quickly grasped his way of thinking and felt a surge of excitement at his suggestions.

"The only problem I can see," she said, "is not having the authority when I speak to them to guarantee that we will not only meet our competitors' price, but undercut it."

"But it's more important to keep the account, even if it means cutting our profit." He leaned back in his chair, satisfied that the solution was clear-cut and inarguable.

That was her thinking exactly.

"Who is your department manager?" he asked.

"Jack Harris," she answered, hoping she wouldn't regret getting the boss's son involved.

He nodded. "Jack's a good man. He's been a great friend to me for years, almost like a father. But I get the feeling you want to handle this yourself first, right?"

"Right," she said, grateful that he understood.

"Would you mind if I offered to help you on this? I think it would be valuable for me to see some of the inner workings of the company. Besides," he said, one side of his mouth lifting in a smile, "I'm not very excited about sitting in on that boring meeting."

Danielle couldn't help but smile back. It made it twice as hard to resist his offer because he was just so darn cute!

"I guess," she answered. "If you really want to."

"Good! We won't get Jack involved until we absolutely have to. First, we have to find out what we're up against and then hope that a possible four percent margin isn't going to kill us. But one way or the other, we're keeping that account. If we don't take care of our clients, someone else will."

Finally! she thought. Someone who thinks more about people than money! Carson might look like his father, but Danielle could tell that their hearts were completely different. With Philip Turner, the buck was the bottom line.

"My father's out of his office right now, so why don't we arrange a conference call to Chase/Dixon there?" he offered.

Danielle couldn't help feeling nervous going into Philip Turner's office and prayed he wouldn't return until they were through with their phone call. She rarely encountered him face to face, but he always intimidated her with his cold gray stare. Now she was in the lion's den.

With her stomach churning and a prayer in her heart, Danielle placed the call and got Chase/Dixon's representative, Ned Goodall, on the phone. Introductions were made and the process began. Carson let Danielle do most of the talking, nodding in approval as she discussed terms and fees, but she was grateful for his input and the air of authority he lent to the discussion.

Since Ned himself was a Harvard graduate, he and Carson were able to make a connection and for several minutes enjoyed chatting about professors and campus memories. Danielle sat back and watched Carson interact with Ned over the speaker phone and felt her admiration for him grow even stronger. Clearly he had a keen business mind, but there was no question, Carson was a people person. He was warm, friendly, and sincere. A complete package.

Just as they secured an agreement, saving an important business relationship and account, the door to Mr. Turner's office opened. Danielle's heart jumped into her throat. It was Mr. Turner himself, and by the look of displeasure on his face, he wasn't happy about finding them in his office.

# CHAPTER TWO

Danielle said a quick good-bye, ending the conversation just in time.

Seeing his son behind his desk and Danielle in a chair nearby, Philip Turner scowled. "Son? What is going on?" his voice boomed, rattling Danielle's bones. "You were supposed to be in the senior management meeting."

"I've been helping Ms. Camden here with a phone call to one of her accounts," Carson explained calmly.

"Which account is that?" His eyes narrowed as he looked at her appraisingly.

She had to remind herself to breathe. "Chase/Dixon . . . sir."

"Why do you need my son's help?" he demanded. "Can't you handle that account on your own?"

She felt her defenses fly into attack mode.

"I've managed that account now for three years, sir," she said, her chin held high, grateful he couldn't see her knees knocking wildly together.

"It was my idea, Father," Carson jumped in. "I wanted to see the working relationships between your account managers and the clients."

Mr. Turner looked at both of them for a full thirty seconds, then said, "I assume you've finished with the use of my office . . ."

"Oh, yes, sir," Danielle said, leaping to her feet. "I'd better get back to my desk."

"And I'm meeting with the legal department at three-thirty," Carson said. He stood up from his father's chair and skirted the desk in one quick motion. Danielle could tell even he was intimidated by his father, but was obviously more used to dealing with it.

Outside Mr. Turner's office, Danielle drew in a lung full of air and blew it out slowly. Carson immediately apologized. "I had no idea my father would be back so soon or that he'd be so hard on you. I'm sorry."

"No problem," she shooed his concern away with her hand. "At least we saved the account, right?" She smiled brightly, truly relieved that together they'd managed to convince Ned to stay with Turner Consulting. "You did a good job in there on the phone."

"So did you, but you didn't need me. You would have been fine on your own." He dipped his chin to look directly at her. He stood nearly six-foot-three, a good eight inches above her five-foot-seven frame.

"Thanks, but I think Ned liked the fact that you two stayed in the same dorm back at Harvard. He seemed to back down after you mentioned that." She looked into Carson's incredibly deep green eyes and found her thoughts drifting.

"I'm just glad I could help," he answered.

"There you are!" Roberta's voice echoed from down the hallway. "I've been looking . . ." Roberta rushed toward her, then stopped when she realized who Danielle was talking to. "Oh, my goodness, Mr. Turner, uh, um . . . ," she stammered.

Before she could curtsey or address him as "Your Highness," Danielle quickly introduced them. Roberta melted as Carson shook her hand. When her brain engaged again, she remembered her errand. "Danielle, Jack is trying to find you. He needs to talk to you."

"Oh, dear." Danielle was flooded with guilt. She was supposed to have had an account summary prepared for him to take to his meeting. "I forgot all about the report. I gotta go. Thanks again, Carson," she called over her shoulder as she sped for her cubicle, hoping Jack wouldn't have a heart attack wondering where she was.

Roberta waved a hesitant farewell to the handsome young heir to the Turner fortune and followed her friend back to her office. She could barely contain her surprise until they were out of earshot. "Have you been with Carson all this time?" she demanded.

Danielle tried to lower the volume of the conversation. "He helped me with the Chase/Dixon account. I managed to renegotiate with them. They're staying with us."

"Carson Turner helped you?" Roberta was flabbergasted. "You are the luckiest girl I know."

"I'll tell you about it later. Right now I've got to print out that report. Come on."

⋙ ⚜ ⋘

That night as Danielle relaxed in front of the television with a bowl of popcorn and a diet soda, she thought about going to the gym and working out her frustrations on the treadmill, but she was just too tired. Her mom and two older sisters, Rachel and Miranda, had gone Christmas shopping. Her dad was at league night bowling. She'd opted to stay home. It felt good to be alone and unwind after the hectic day at the office.

Did all full-time jobs suck out your life and energy like hers did, she wondered. If it weren't for the good friends and great people she worked with, her job would be unbearable. She used to have ambition and drive, but she'd lost them along the way. Work just wasn't enough anymore. Where was the fulfillment? How did she find contentment? Was it even possible?

She thought about her boss, Mr. Turner Sr. and his son. They were as different as night and day. She would have never expected someone as nice as Carson to even be related to a man like Philip Turner.

Then she had a thought that gave her a glimmer of hope. Things around Turner Consulting would definitely change once Carson took over. Yes, working for Carson would make her job *much* more enjoyable. With Carson at the helm, she wouldn't mind going to work as much. She just prayed she could last that long.

Sinking into a zombie-like state, working the remote with one hand while the other hand emptied the bowl of popcorn, Danielle was barely aware of the phone ringing. "Dani, it's Roberta."

Danielle looked at the clock. Almost nine. "What's up?"

"You know Marilyn from the office? Mr. Turner's secretary?"

"Sure."

"I ran into her at the grocery store this evening. We had quite an interesting talk. I could hardly wait to get home and call you." Long ago Danielle had realized Roberta was in the wrong business. She would have made a perfect detective. She could sniff out a story a mile away and thrived on finding out every detail she could.

"Why?" Danielle put on a front of disinterest, but she couldn't deny that she was, in fact, very interested.

"First of all Marilyn told me that old man Turner has been a real beast lately."

"That's nothing new. He's always a beast," Danielle grumbled.

"Well, he's even worse than usual. She doesn't know if it's because his son's here for the Christmas holiday or if it's because the business is having serious financial trouble. It could be both."

"Okay, so Turner's a regular sourpuss. Tell me something I don't know. Maybe the holidays bring out the Scrooge in him." She'd felt pretty "bah humbug-ish" all day—except for when she'd been with Carson.

"Actually you're right. The holidays are hard for him, but it's because Mrs. Turner died on Christmas about six years ago. While Carson was on his mission."

Danielle sat up and put the bowl of popcorn on the coffee table in front of her.

"Except for a few distant relatives, there's no one in the family but Mr. Turner and his son. Mr. Turner was an only child and Carson's mom's only sister passed away recently. And what's even more sad is that those two aren't very close."

"I'm not surprised," Danielle said. She was well aware of how different they were.

Roberta went on to reveal that even though Carson was apparently doing well in business school, he really didn't want to take over his father's business. He wanted to be a doctor.

"I guess going into medicine has something to do with his mother dying. He wants to help people who are sick," Roberta said, "but his father has always expected him to take over the family business and follow in his footsteps. Marilyn said their relationship is very strained and that if Mr. Turner keeps pressuring Carson, he just might lose him."

Danielle didn't speak for a minute. Was the situation that bad between father and son? She thought Mr. Turner ought to be thrilled that his son wanted to be a doctor. How could a father be anything but proud of a son who wanted to help other people? Her heart ached for Carson. "I can't imagine how hard this is for him," she said.

They spoke a few more minutes, then Roberta said, "Hey, I gotta go. My dad needs the phone. I'll see you at work tomorrow. We can talk more then."

"Wait a sec," Danielle exclaimed. "You said Turner Consulting is having financial troubles?"

"Yeah, but no one's supposed to know just how serious. Marilyn said something is going on but she doesn't know any details yet."

"Wow," Danielle breathed, wondering just how bad it really was. "No wonder they've stopped all travel and unnecessary expenses."

After Danielle hung up the phone, she thought about Carson and his father. Was the reason the two were so different because Carson was like his mother? She went over the events of the day in her head, replaying the time she spent with Carson. She could still feel the fluttering in her heart as she looked into his eyes. She could easily fall for someone like Carson, but she doubted that he'd ever be interested in someone like her. She wasn't elegant or classy enough. She loved the outdoors and hiking and camping. She played football in the park, went jogging in the rain, and had never even been to an opera. She lived on the ski slopes in winter and enjoyed playing tennis in the summer. They weren't each other's type. Still, she couldn't deny the attraction she felt for him and the fact that they'd had some kind of connection that afternoon.

With a sigh, she grabbed a handful of popcorn and tossed it into her mouth. Nothing could ever come of it, she knew. But, still, a girl could dream, couldn't she?

The sound of voices at the back door let her know her mother and sisters were back from shopping. Why didn't her sisters just drop their mom off, she wondered. Why did they have to come in? She wasn't in the mood to talk to them.

"Dani, honey, we're home," her mother called from the kitchen.

"I'm in the family room," she hollered back.

Footsteps headed her direction. "Hey," her oldest sister, Miranda, said when she entered the room, "what're you doing?"

"Not much." Danielle pulled her feet toward her so her sister could sit on the other end of the couch. "How was shopping?"

"Oh, you know." Miranda put her hand over her mouth and whispered, "Rachel was as bossy as ever."

"She drives me nuts when I go shopping with her," Danielle whispered back. "I'm glad I stayed home."

Another set of footsteps came their direction.

"Dani, we missed you tonight." Rachel entered the room briskly. "You should've come. We found the best sale at Nordstrom. You would've gone nuts."

"I'm sure I would have," Danielle said, flashing a wicked grin at Miranda.

"Also," Rachel emphasized the word, dragging it out, "we ran into an old friend of yours." She plopped right down in the center of the couch between Danielle and Miranda. Danielle didn't ask "who"— she didn't need to—as Rachel went on to recount the incident whether Danielle wanted her to or not.

"We were just coming out of Nordstrom when we ran straight into Todd Hardaway."

Danielle shut her eyes briefly and prayed for strength. Rachel just couldn't let it die—along with everyone in the entire world who thought she was an idiot for breaking up with Todd. It didn't help that he was nice-looking, strong in the Church, and focused on his education. But Danielle had been about as attracted to him as she was to vinyl siding. There was nothing. Nada. Zilch. When he'd held her hand, it felt clammy and hot. When he'd kissed her, she had to hold her breath like she did when she ate meatloaf as a child. She'd wanted to have feelings for him, but she didn't. And besides that, it was over. Why couldn't everyone just let it go?

At least Miranda had tried to understand her feelings for Todd. Once again, Danielle was thankful she had at least one person in her family who supported her. Other than Roberta, Danielle didn't have anyone else she could really confide in.

"Anyway, his wife is as lovely as ever and—" Rachel looked at her like she was about to tell her the secrets of the universe "—they're expecting their first child in March. Isn't that wonderful?"

"Yeah," Danielle said flatly. "Wonderful." She waited for her sister to go on.

"Just think," Rachel said, not disappointing Danielle. "That could have been you." Sitting on the other side of Rachel, Miranda leaned forward slightly and rolled her eyes at Danielle. "Seeing her pregnant, well," Rachel took a deep breath, "it just reminded me how much I would like another baby. They just looked so sweet." Rachel and her husband had been trying for over a year to have another baby. She had three darling daughters, but they wanted to have one more child.

"I think Danielle would rather not talk about it," Miranda said in her sister's defense. "Someday Danielle will find the right man for her. You'll see."

Danielle sent her sister a smile of thanks, grateful for her support. When she'd refused Todd's proposal, she had thought she'd felt a confirmation from the Lord, but now she wondered why her life didn't seem to be coming together. What was she doing wrong?

That night before she went to bed, she opened her scriptures and began to read. She'd searched for answers, for wisdom and guidance, but she still couldn't clearly see the path she should take. As she read, she kept a prayer close to her heart as she pleaded with the Lord to help her. She was ready and willing to do anything to make positive changes in her life, she decided. Anything to have the peace and happiness she craved.

She continued reading, forcing her thoughts to stay focused on the words written on the page. Then, as if a blindfold had been stripped from her eyes, she found a scripture in 3 Nephi 13:33. She read it once, then again, then once again, slowly, internalizing every word, feeling its power and promise penetrate deeply into her soul. "Seek ye first the kingdom of God and his righteousness, and all these things shall be added unto you."

Was it that simple? If she put the Lord first, would everything else truly be added unto her? Would things in her life finally fall into place?

She'd been trying to live righteously, go to church, read her scriptures, and say her prayers. But right then, right there, on her knees, she made a covenant to the Lord to do better, to put Him and His righteousness first. She would do everything in her power to be worthy of this promise. It took all her faith to do it, but she knew she had nothing to lose. The Lord had never let her down before. She knew without a doubt, He wouldn't let her down now.

For once, she fell asleep peacefully, without a worry about her job, her life, or her future to keep her tossing and turning all night.

⊱ ❦ ⊰

"What are you looking at?" Roberta asked when she walked into work the next morning. She hung her coat on a hook in her cubicle and tossed her purse into a desk drawer. She handed Danielle a small brown paper sack.

"What's this?" Danielle looked up from her magazine.

"Chocolate chip cookies. I made them last night."

Roberta was always doing stuff like this. Some guy would be lucky to get Roberta for a wife, Danielle thought, thanking her friend. Roberta loved to cook and her specialty was baking. Her brownies were to die for.

Peering at the magazine in Danielle's hand, she read the cover: "Apartment Guide." Looking up at Danielle with a surprised expression on her face, she said, "Wow, you're not wasting any time, are you?"

"You know, last year at this time I was almost engaged. I could have been married and had a baby by now," she said, remembering her sister's chance meeting with Todd and his wife.

"But Todd wasn't right for you," Roberta countered.

Danielle was grateful for a friend like Roberta. She'd been loyal and true and had stood by Danielle when she'd broken up with Todd. Danielle had leaned on her friend a lot during that time.

Roberta continued. "My mom always tells me, 'Don't give up what you want most for what you want now.'"

Danielle thought about that advice for a moment, then said, "Maybe that's my whole problem. I don't know exactly what I want most. All I know is that I need something more. I just feel so empty inside."

"You'll figure it out," Roberta said encouragingly. "I know you will."

Danielle smiled her thanks. She didn't know what she'd do if she didn't have her friend to talk to. "I hope you're right." She tossed the magazine onto her desk and asked, "What are you doing for lunch?"

"Nothing. I thought I'd just grab something out of the vending machine." Roberta clicked on her computer and adjusted the monitor.

"You want to come apartment hunting with me? I found a couple of places that sound good."

"Sure," Roberta agreed. "Sounds fun."

⚜

The first apartment was located in a part of town Danielle wasn't sure she dared live in. Graffiti covered the fence around the complex, and most of the cars in the parking lot were broken down or wrecked.

They drove to another complex that had about five hundred units, was recently built, and seemed reasonably priced. But it did nothing for Danielle. She wanted a place with some character. A place she could look forward to coming home to at night.

They drove down the I-215 belt route that wrapped around the city and wound its way beside the foothills of the Salt Lake Valley. Seeing some restaurants, they exited to grab a bite to eat, and as they drove around some of the streets, Roberta suddenly cried out, "Stop!" Danielle slammed on the brakes, half expecting a deer to come bounding across the road.

"Back up," Roberta cried.

"What?" Danielle demanded. "You scared me half to death."

"Turn down this road. There's a 'For Rent' sign back there."

Danielle followed her directions and they pulled up to a cute cottage nestled against a backdrop of cottonwood trees and pines.

"I could never afford to rent a place like this," Danielle told her.

"Hey, it doesn't cost anything to ask," Roberta said, undaunted.

She was right, so Danielle pulled the car into the driveway and they got out. A woman answered the door right away.

"Hi," Danielle said, "We were wondering about the 'For Rent' sign you have out front."

"Oh, hi," the woman said, "Let me grab the key. The house is out back." Danielle and Roberta looked at each other with raised eyebrows. The woman joined them quickly and led the way around the house to the backyard.

"We built this place for my mother-in-law. She lived here almost five years until she passed away recently." In the corner of the spacious yard was a darling little bungalow, with flower boxes underneath the windows and a wishing well in front.

She led them inside and showed them around. There was a comfortable living room, a small but adequate kitchen, a nice-sized bathroom, and a surprisingly spacious bedroom. Danielle immediately fell in love with it and could tell by the look on Roberta's face that she felt the same.

"Why don't I let you girls have a minute to yourselves? Drop the key by the house on your way out and you can tell me what you think." The woman gave them a warm smile before she left.

As soon as the front door closed, the girls turned to each other and squealed with delight.

"This place is so great," Roberta said. "I love it."

"I do too," Danielle cried. "It feels like home already."

"I wonder what she's asking for in rent. This is kind of a pricey neighborhood. Maybe you should take in a roommate to help you with expenses," Roberta offered, her intentions completely obvious.

"You think so, huh?" Danielle teased.

"C'mon, Dani, this place is so cute. We could have so much fun. Barbecues in the summer," she twirled as she talked, "fires in the fireplace during the winter."

Danielle smiled at her friend. "Actually I did think about taking in a roommate to help meet expenses." Danielle's skin prickled with goosebumps. If Roberta split the cost of the place, she knew she could make it. "Would you consider moving in with me?"

Roberta clapped her hands with delight, "Yes!"

The girls looked at each other and laughed gleefully, then hugged and danced around the room. "Let's go tell Mrs. Richmond we want it," Danielle said. This little house was meant for her, she just knew it. She was making a choice that would be good for her future and for her life, and it felt great. She was finally taking charge of her life.

# CHAPTER THREE

"Sister Camden?" Little Olivia raised her hand and wiggled her fingers anxiously to get Danielle's attention. "Teacher?"

Danielle could tell it was going to be "one of those days" in Primary. The children in her six-year-old class were full of wiggles and couldn't seem to stop talking. It had taken fifteen minutes just to get the opening prayer said. She knew she'd never get through the lesson.

"Yes, Olivia," she said patiently.

"How many kids do you have?"

"Kids?" Danielle asked, wondering if she'd heard the child correctly.

"Yeah. Where are your kids?" repeated Stewart "the Wildman," as Danielle referred to him.

"I don't have any kids," Danielle explained.

"Why not?" Stewart demanded.

"Well, because I'm not married," she said, then quickly changed the subject. "Who can tell me who this is a picture of?" She put the picture of Nephi up on the board and looked at the children expectantly.

"How come you're not married?" Stewart persisted. "You're supposed to get married when you get old."

"Uh . . . , um, I guess because . . ." she stammered beneath the gaze of several six-year-olds staring back at her, all of them waiting for her answer. How did she explain that at her age all the good guys

were already taken, and that the only ones left were confirmed bache-
lors, guys with serious emotional problems, or flat-out losers, and that
she had enough people in her face about not being married at her age
without a bunch of six-year-olds giving her grief about it?

"You know what?" she said abruptly, jumping to her feet. "We
can talk about this later. Right now we're going to play a game and
then we'll have a treat. Who wants a treat?"

"I do," Stewart yelled. "I want a treat!"

"Me too," the other children shouted.

They ended up playing Duck, Duck, Goose for the remainder of
the class, then eating fruit snacks and pretzels until the bell rang to go
to sharing time. When the children were all seated in the larger
Primary room, Danielle asked one of the counselors to sit with her
class so she could go home. She had a headache and needed a pain
reliever.

On the way home Danielle thought about the children's question
in class. Of course they had no idea that they'd brought up a very
painful, sensitive subject, but nevertheless, Danielle couldn't help
feeling bruised by their words.

*You're supposed to get married when you get old.* Stewart's words
rang in her ears. Was he implying that she was old? She was only
twenty-six, for crying out loud. How old did he think she was? She
was getting sick of people bugging her about marriage. What did
people want her to do? Was being married just for the sake of being
married more important than marrying the "right" person?

She pulled into the driveway and put the car in park.

She couldn't imagine being married to someone she didn't love.
Before she broke up with Todd, she could barely stand to hold his
hand. How could she have married him? How could that be good
and right?

It couldn't! She was convinced of it. She'd rather be alone than
marry the wrong man.

⋇⋇ 🦢 ⋇⋇

"Mom, I need to tell you something," Danielle said, taking a deep
breath. She had been waiting for the right time to tell her parents

about her decision to move out. She knew they'd be supportive, but she just wanted to make sure they knew she was moving for her, not because of them.

Her sisters and their families were also there for their regular Sunday evening family gathering, and she would be able to let them all know at the same time. This would save her phone time and having to explain over and over what she was doing and why she was doing it.

"Just one second, dear." Her mother slid the last dinner plate into the dishwasher, shut the door, and turned back to Danielle who sat with her sisters at the dinner table. The men and the children were in the other room either watching television or playing computer games.

Miranda and Rachel looked at Danielle with interest.

"I just thought I should tell you that I . . ." she began, then stopped. Everyone was staring at her, waiting for some great revelation.

"What is it, Dani?" her sister Rachel insisted.

"Honey?" Her mother's expression grew worried.

Danielle released a long breath of air. "Never mind. I can tell you later, Mom."

"Just tell us," Rachel prodded. "What is it?"

Miranda didn't say anything, but by the look of interest on her face, Danielle could tell she wanted to know, too. She squared her shoulders, lifted her chin, and said, "I've decided it's time for me to move out on my own."

She wasn't sure what kind of response to expect, but she was pleasantly surprised when her mother's face broke into a smile.

Danielle relaxed. "I thought the news might come as a surprise to you, but obviously you're okay with it."

"Actually, now that you mention it, I remember something I forgot to tell you." Her mother's smile broadened. "Some woman called—a Mrs. Richmond. You got the apartment."

Danielle closed her eyes and groaned. "I'm sorry, Mom. I wanted to tell you first. I didn't think she'd call so soon." Then it dawned on her what her mother had said. "I got the apartment?" Her mother nodded. "I got it!" she exclaimed.

"Vonda and I had a nice talk," her mother said. "We haven't spoken for years."

"Vonda?" Danielle asked, wondering who her mother was talking about.

"Vonda Richmond. They lived in our ward fifteen years ago. I guess you don't remember her?"

Danielle's memory came up blank. "No, not at all."

"She was happy to know you were our daughter and said she feels good about letting you rent the house behind them. She was worried about having a renter in her backyard, but now she's not worried at all. She mentioned you had someone else there with you. Was that Roberta?"

"Yes, she wants to move in with me," Danielle told her.

"Gosh, Dani, that sounds really fun." That was Miranda, bless her heart. Always the positive, supportive sister. "The place sounds really cute, too."

Danielle looked at her sister. "How do you know?"

"Mom told us earlier, while you were at your Primary board meeting," she explained.

"Are you sure you're ready for this?" Rachel asked, making Danielle feel like she was a teenager again. "It's a big step."

"Yes, I'm sure," Danielle said, trying not to roll her eyes. "In fact, I'm positive." *I'm twenty-six*, she wanted to add. *How much longer do you think I need?*

"As much as we'll miss you, dear," her mother said, "I want you to know your father and I support you."

Danielle appreciated her mother's pledge of support. She knew she would need it. "Thanks, Mom. That means a lot to me."

Her sisters asked a few more questions about the bungalow and offered some of their spare furniture to help furnish the place. As they figured out a day when they all could go see it, Danielle felt a surge of excitement growing inside of her.

Finally things were falling into place for her.

⁂

Monday morning Danielle drove to work with high spirits. She couldn't wait to see Roberta so they could talk about moving in together and discuss how they were going to fix up their place.

Danielle had spent a great deal of time praying the night before, hoping that the changes she was making in her life would help her move forward on to bigger and better things. She hadn't done such a great job of handling her life on her own, she thought ruefully; it was definitely time to let the Lord in and have Him take over.

Pulling into the parking lot at her office building, she felt her stomach quiver with anticipation and she wasn't sure why. Perhaps it was the excitement of finding a place of her own. One thing she knew, there was going to be a change in her life. She could feel it.

It didn't take more than a few seconds to realize something was terribly wrong when she walked into the office. No one was talking or walking around getting their morning cup of coffee or quibbling about the game on TV over the weekend. A heavy, somber cloud seemed to hang over the room. Expressionless faces met her gaze as she walked to her cubicle. She said, "Good morning," but no one returned the greeting.

Roberta wasn't at her desk when Danielle looked in the cubicle next to hers. Sitting at her own desk, Danielle checked her phone for messages and saw that the message button was flashing wildly. Her stomach clenched into knots. Even before listening to the message, she knew it wasn't good news.

The message was from Jack, asking her to come to his office as soon as she got to work.

Retracing her steps, she walked back to Jack's office and tapped lightly on the door. He said, "Come in," and she opened the door and stepped inside. His face mirrored that of the other workers in the department.

"Jack," she exclaimed, "What is going on around here? Did someone die?" She was kidding, but she was also serious. They acted as if they'd received the shock of their lives.

"Close the door behind you and sit down, Danielle," he instructed.

Then it hit her. It didn't take long to figure out the problem. She took her seat and faced him. "We aren't getting our Christmas bonus this year, are we?" Rumors around the office had circulated quickly about the company's financial struggles, and with only two weeks until the big holiday, it seemed obvious.

"Actually, it's worse than that," he said, not meeting her eyes. Instead, he stared at the pen and pencil set on his desk, a gift from the company for outstanding service.

"Worse?" She swallowed, wondering how much worse, but not wanting to know.

"I received the news early this morning. Turner's downsizing his staff. We're losing seventy percent of the employees in our department alone."

The news hit her like a fist to her stomach and left her gasping for air. She dreaded what his next words would be.

When he spoke, she could hear the pain in his voice. "I'm sorry, Danielle. It's not my decision."

It took a moment to sink in. "You mean he's letting *me* go?" She jumped to her feet. "I don't believe this! How can he do this?" She smacked the back of the leather chair with her hand, making it rock back onto two legs. "I've been the top account manager for two years in a row. Why me?" She spun around and faced Jack. "Why, Jack?!" she demanded.

"I don't know. Mr. Turner didn't specify his reasoning."

She reached for the doorknob. "Well, I think I at least deserve to know why! I'm going to talk to Mr. Turner right now."

"I doubt you'll find him. After our meeting this morning, he left the office."

"Oh, great!" She threw her hands up into the air. "I shouldn't be surprised. The slimy weasel. He can't face what he's done to us. What a coward!"

Jack scooted his chair back and stood up. "Danielle, you need to calm down. Getting upset isn't going to help any."

Visions of her apartment faded as her anger grew. All the big changes—getting out on her own and rooming with Roberta— seemed to evaporate right before her eyes. This was the worst thing that could have happened to her. Why did this have to happen now?

"I can't believe this is the thanks I get for over three years of hard work and loyal service," Danielle said, not even trying to hide the bitterness in her voice.

"There was no other choice," Jack tried to calm her. "If he doesn't make some drastic changes, he could lose his business."

"Good!" she spat the words. "I hope he does!" Then it dawned on her that Jack was handling all of this rather well. "You still have your job, don't you?" she asked directly.

Jack looked down at his shoes and cleared his throat. "Don't think I don't feel guilty about this, even though I had no part in the decision making process—" he looked at her, "—and don't think this is going to be easy. With only a few managers left to handle all the accounts, it's going to be like trying to put out a forest fire with a water gun."

"How could he do this just before the holidays? Couldn't he have waited at least until Christmas was over?" She rubbed her temples and clenched her eyes shut, feeling a stress headache coming on. "What about those who have families?"

"He tried to keep as many of those workers as he could. At least he did pay attention to those employees who support a family."

It didn't make it easier to take the news, but it made it easier to understand why she was on the "let go" list. But still . . . she thought of her apartment, her charming little cottage with its own stream. Now it would never happen.

"Is there anything else you needed to tell me?" she asked, feeling a need to get out of his office and get some air before she passed out.

"No, that's all. Danielle, I'm sor—"

"I know, it's not your fault," she said. "You've been great, Jack. It's just that . . ." A lump formed in her throat. How did she tell him that for once she had felt like things were finally falling into place? And now this. She shrugged. ". . . Oh, never mind." Opening the door, she hurried to the ladies' room, nearly knocking over some fellow employees on her way.

After a good cry in a bathroom stall, she stopped in the employees' lounge for a pain reliever. Her head throbbed viciously.

With a defeated sigh, she sat down wearily and rested her head in her hands, waiting for the medication to take effect. Jobless. Where would she even begin looking for a new job? She had to find something that paid as well as the money she was making now so she could afford her car payment and the rent each month.

*Heavenly Father,* she prayed silently. *Why did this have to happen? Just as I was getting control of my life I lose everything. I don't under-*

*stand. Please, Father, You have to help me. I don't know what I'm going to do now.*

She paused, sensing another person in the room. Looking up, she saw Carson Turner standing in front of her.

"What do you want?" she said caustically.

"I've been looking for you," he said, his concern evident in his voice.

"Why?" She knew her mascara was smeared down her cheeks and her nose was running, but she didn't care.

"I wanted to see how you were doing. I feel bad about what's happened."

She sat up straight and squared her shoulders. "How bad do you feel, Carson? How bad *can* you feel?"

"Danielle, I feel awful about what my father did to all of you. I didn't even know this was going to happen until I came in this morning."

There was an angry edge to his voice, sharpened, Danielle sensed, by an even deeper pain.

"I wish I could change what's happened," he said, "but the company is having serious financial problems right now. I just never thought it would come to this."

"It's not your fault," she found herself saying, regretting that she'd lashed out at him.

"I'd try to change it if I could, but my father won't listen to me. Not that he ever has." Carson shrugged. "I've seen him do things like this my entire life. The way he does business, he's made a lot of enemies. He puts money in front of everything." He shook his head and looked away. "Even me," he said softly, his emotions just below the surface.

"I don't know what to say." Danielle's heart ached for him. She'd always thought he'd been born with a silver spoon in his mouth, but it sounded like the spoon had become tarnished.

"He wants me to take over this business when I finish school," he continued, "but I don't want it. I don't want any part of his life. When my mother was alive, she managed to keep my father in line. He's always had a tendency to be a workaholic, and she had to remind him to spend time with our family. After she died, he completely immersed himself in the business."

Danielle could tell Carson missed his mother desperately. "Your mother must have been a wonderful woman," she told him.

"She was incredible. I've never known anyone with her love for life and other people." His thoughts seemed to drift for a moment. "She wanted a large family, but I was the only child they were able to have. Since she didn't have other children, she spent a lot of her free time volunteering at the children's medical center and working in the temple."

Danielle had a hard time picturing Mr. Turner going to the temple with his wife. The image just didn't fit.

"When she was alive, my father had friends and went to church and spent time with me. Since her death, he's become inactive and he's lost track of any friends he ever had. Well," he clarified, "any real friends. The only people he knows are afraid of him."

"Do you think he's lonely?" Danielle asked, suddenly aware that the pain of losing a loved one could cause anyone to behave as Mr. Turner had, and surprised to find a wisp of sympathy in her heart for him.

"I think he's trying to bury the pain under all the money. My father's a smart man when it comes to business, but he's not very smart when it comes to people," he told her honestly. Then, as if he suddenly realized what he'd just said, he quickly added, "I'm sorry. I shouldn't be telling you all of this. It's just . . . I haven't really had anyone to talk to about this since my mother died."

"You don't need to apologize, Carson." She gave him a reassuring smile. "I'm glad you feel comfortable talking to me. But I do have one question for you."

"What's that?"

"If you have such strong feelings about your father and his business, exactly where does that leave you?"

He studied her for a moment, making her conscious about her mascara-streaked face and puffy, red eyes.

"I don't really know," he confessed. "I've spent my entire life trying to do what my father wanted me to do, trying to please him, to make him proud of me. But I've never heard him say, 'I'm proud of you, son.'" His voice was steady, resigned. "I'm not sure I'm ever going to please him, unless I become exactly like him, but I can't do that. I can't become something I'm not. I will never be the kind of businessman my father is."

"What do *you* want to do?" Danielle asked.

"I've always wanted to study medicine. After my mother died of cancer I became fascinated with biology and physiology. I hated the feeling of helplessness I had after she died, and found comfort in learning all I could about the disease. I felt like the more I knew, the more control I had over my own chances of developing cancer, since my risk increased having a parent die of the disease. My interest in medicine hasn't changed. I'm still fascinated with it, but I would probably do obstetrics or pediatrics. I really love children, babies especially. Maybe because I never had any brothers or sisters of my own. My mother hoped I would become a doctor and spend my life helping others. But my father insisted I get an MBA and take over his business when it was time." He looked at Danielle with a look of helpless resignation.

Danielle thought his dilemma was far worse than her own. He knew what he wanted to do, but was being forced to go in a different direction. She didn't even know what she wanted to do. "So what are you going to do?" she asked.

For a moment, he looked lost, then he admitted, "I don't know. I am going to look into medical school while I'm here, though. I've got an appointment to meet with one of the counselors up at the University this week."

"Carson, if medicine is what you truly want to study, then you should pursue it," Danielle said vigorously.

Carson's voice was tired, as if he'd been through all of this before. "My father refuses to support me or pay my tuition if I go to medical school." He looked down at his hands, then back up to her face. "After my mission to Thailand, I went back to the country with some companions to visit. We ended up spending six months there, living with members and helping them. We volunteered our time to work and help them and in return they gave us food and housing. It was the most incredible experience of my life."

Danielle looked at him with admiration. He'd gone out in the world. He'd made a difference. She'd done nothing like that. Her efforts had been spent earning enough money at various jobs to support her lifestyle—ski passes, spending money, clothes, her SUV. Aside from graduating from college, she hadn't achieved anything, let alone helped anyone else.

"I hated coming home. I could've stayed there forever. But I'd put off going to school as long as I could and I risked losing my scholarship. So I came home. It's amazing how much you can grow to love people you serve. I felt as if I was one of them. They became a part of me. After I get my medical degree, I want to go back and help them. They need medical care so badly. Not just in Thailand either. There's India, Africa, other parts of Asia—just to name a few. There's such a great need for doctors in developing nations and I want to do something about it."

Danielle could imagine how much the experience meant to him just by the longing in his voice and the expression on his face. She thought of him traveling to far-off places, changing people's lives, helping and making a difference. What a great and noble goal.

Which confused her even more. How could a father be so controlling and unsupportive—especially when Carson wanted to do such a wonderful thing for others? "What exactly does your father think is wrong with the medical profession?" she wanted to know.

"It's not that my father doesn't think medicine is a good profession," Carson explained. "It's just that his dream is to have me follow in his footsteps."

"But what about your dreams and what's important to you?"

Carson shrugged again. "That's something I need to decide. I guess I'll be able to make a better decision after I talk to a counselor and see what is involved in getting into medical school."

A group of voices were heard coming down the hallway toward the employee lounge.

Danielle glanced at the doorway and said quickly, "For what it's worth, Carson, I think you'd make a wonderful doctor, and what you want to do is really incredible." Before the others came in, she added, "I'm glad we could talk. I hope you have a Merry Christmas."

"Thanks," he said, "You too. If there's anything I can do, I hope you'll give me a call."

As the group of employees entered the room and saw Carson Turner, they became suddenly silent. Eyeing Danielle oddly, they gathered around a table in the corner of the room and one employee threw a bag of popcorn into the microwave.

Sensing their hostility, Carson rose from his seat. Danielle joined him as he left the room, and they walked down the hallway toward the elevator together.

"It's been wonderful meeting you, Danielle," Carson said, looking deeply into her eyes.

"You, too," she said, wishing she'd met him in another place, in another time, that he wasn't Philip Turner's son.

"I'm going back to school after the Christmas break," he said. "But do you think . . ." he paused, searching for words, ". . . you might consider going out with me . . . before then?"

She smiled at him, flattered and pleased—even surprised—that he would ask. He wasn't really someone she'd consider her "type," and nothing like other guys she dated. Her ideal date was fun-loving, athletic, out-doorsy, and a little on the crazy side. Carson was business-like, serious, even a bit stuffy. Still she had to admit she was attracted to Carson. "Yes, I would. In fact, I'd like that."

He grinned, obviously pleased at her answer. "Thanks again for listening," Carson said. "I'll be in touch."

Danielle's smile broadened. "Okay. See you later, then."

She watched him disappear down the hallway. He was a good man and a good son. If only his father could see that and appreciate his son instead of forcing him to be someone he was not.

The elevator doors opened and to Danielle's surprise out walked the boss himself.

"Mr. Turner!" Danielle exclaimed. He was the last person she'd expected to run into.

He looked at her, his expression strained and tired. The look in his eyes halted the scalding words she'd wanted to hurl at him earlier. But for a split second, her eyes locked with his and she saw past his stern demeanor into a deeper, hidden spot. Briefly, she glimpsed a look of pain and anguish. The look was fleeting, quickly replaced with the familiar coldness that his eyes usually reflected.

It was quick, but Danielle believed she saw behind Turner's facade into the real person inside. All her anger died. Her sharp-edged words and stinging barbs fell aside.

He paused, as if expecting her to say something to him, but when she said nothing further, he turned and strode down the hall, leaving Danielle behind. She stood for a moment, wondering what to make of it, then shook her head, puzzled by the brief encounter.

With a sigh, she headed for her desk to start packing her things.

# CHAPTER FOUR

Christmas came and went, and Danielle, along with many others from her department, left Turner Consulting in search of new jobs. She never heard from Carson. Once, while she was out shopping with Roberta during the holidays, her father had received a call for her. Unfortunately, the caller hadn't wanted to leave a message. About a week later, her mother had taken a call for her while Danielle was at a movie. Her mother had thought the young man was calling long distance but again, he hadn't left a message. Danielle wanted to think it was Carson, but when she heard nothing further, she gave up hoping.

It nearly broke her heart to tell Vonda Richmond she couldn't take the bungalow after all. Vonda held it as long as she could, hoping Danielle would find a job, but finally had to rent it to someone else when Danielle's job-hunting efforts were slow to pay off. Slowly but surely Danielle felt her life begin to crumble around her.

Roberta took a job at her father's insurance firm but except for flexible hours, she didn't enjoy it much. She and Danielle had lunch together every Wednesday. They spent their time talking about traveling. They both wanted to see the world, so they spent their Wednesday lunches planning trips and dreaming about the fun adventures they could have.

One cold, windy March day, after one of their lunches, Danielle got into her used Honda Accord and headed home. She'd had to sell her Outback since without a job, she couldn't afford the payments any longer. As she negotiated the busy roads of downtown Salt Lake City, she drove past a large building with a "Help Wanted" sign in the window. The sign on the building said "Creative Display," and it appeared to be a decorating and design firm. On a whim, she pulled into the turn lane and entered the parking lot. Figuring she had nothing to lose, she jumped out of the car and went inside, seeking the manager.

In high school she'd worked in a small flower shop. She'd also taken several classes in interior design in college. With that background and as much enthusiasm as she could muster, she met with the owner. They chatted for a few minutes about her background, experience, and education, then he took her on a quick tour of the facility. Aside from the large showroom, where dozens of displays and different types of floral arrangements were displayed, there were stock rooms, work rooms, and storage rooms. She saw somewhere between ten and twelve workers busily doing their jobs, and she retained about one-tenth of all the information the owner told her during their tour. A half hour later, she found herself walking out with a part-time job.

At least it was something, she reasoned, and smiled with anticipation at the prospect of working somewhere that would allow her to be creative instead of being analytical and intense, like her job at Turner Consulting. And, she thought wryly, she wouldn't have to get dressed up in nylons and heels.

That night at dinner, Danielle told her parents about her new job.

"That's wonderful, dear," her mother said. Danielle's father was busy reading the newspaper and didn't appear to hear her.

"Earl?" Dorothy Camden prodded him.

"Holy smoke, listen to this," he exclaimed. "'Turner Consulting Forecasts Negative First Quarter Earnings.'"

"What?" Danielle exclaimed. "Are you sure?"

He showed Danielle the article in the Metro section of the paper. There, above the headline, was a picture of Mr. Turner, gray-haired and stern-faced as he left the building. As Earl Camden read the article out loud, Danielle couldn't believe it.

*"Turner Consulting share price falls 82% in heavy trading on Wednesday, March 13th, after senior management announced forecasted*

*negative earnings for the first quarter. Industry experts estimate earnings to continue a negative trend, making Turner Consulting a prime takeover target. Philip H. Turner, Sr., admitted poor market conditions, terminating accounts, and employee turnover as the reason for the sharp decline in profitability. Turner Consulting was founded in 1976 by Philip H. Turner, Sr. The company saw its glory days in the early nineties, but in the last three years reported flat earnings."*

"Whoa," Danielle exclaimed, "this is unbelievable. After all this time he finally gets what he deserves. He always took credit for everything, so he can take credit for this!"

Her father looked at her. "I'd say that's a pretty harsh statement."

"Well, it's true," she defended herself. "He never realized how valuable his employees were in finding and taking care of *his* accounts. I will give him credit for starting a great company with a lot of great ideas. But it was the employees that made it all happen. Too bad he didn't know how to take care of them."

"That poor man," Dorothy said. "This must be so hard for him."

"What do you mean, that poor man?" Danielle replied incredulously.

"To lose everything like that," her mother sighed. "To spend your whole life working and then have nothing to show for it."

"Mom, he didn't lose everything." Danielle had learned all about corporations in her business classes. "He'll have to sell his business for nothing, but his personal assets aren't at risk. I'm sure he still lives in a mansion and has a whole staff of help waiting on his every need," Danielle explained with distaste. "In fact, he's probably already started a new business by now. Believe me, it would take more than this to bring that man down."

Dorothy didn't reply, but began clearing the table. Danielle helped her mother with the dishes then went to her room. Hearing about Turner Consulting reminded her about Carson, and she wondered why he hadn't called as he'd said he would. She'd thought of him constantly over Christmas, but in the months that followed, her thoughts had turned to him less and less until she'd finally forgotten about him. His memory was stored along with that of her cottage and her Outback, those things that had represented a new life that had never had a chance.

Since then, Danielle had slipped into complacency. She still wanted out, she still wanted to change her situation, but everything hinged upon a job and money, both of which she didn't have. Still, things could begin to change now with the start of a new job.

She noticed the apple tree outside her window sprouting tiny blossoms that would soon explode into fragrant color. It had been over three months since she'd lost her job, and even as winter was evolving into spring, she'd done nothing but sit around and feel sorry for herself.

She wondered how Carson was doing. Was he still in business school? Had he decided to pursue his dream of studying medicine? She hoped that he'd followed his dream. She envied him having such a passion in life.

But for her there was no passion. No driving force waking her up at night or pushing her to her limits each day. Nothing to get her out of bed in the morning, or to reflect on when she went to bed at night. Nothing to talk about with friends or family. For her to be headed anywhere would take a quantum leap from where she now stood. Even though she knew she had no right to complain—her life was good, she was blessed—she just wasn't fulfilled.

And it was all her fault, she acknowledged. She knew that sitting around waiting for something to happen wouldn't bring about any change. She had to make things happen. She was responsible for her own happiness. But when she'd tried something new and thought things were finally starting to fall into place, everything had seemed to suddenly go wrong.

She had tried to put the Lord and His righteousness first, but for some reason, the rest of the scripture—"and all things shall be added unto you"—didn't seem to be happening.

⁂

"What do you think Mr. Turner's up to now?" Roberta asked between bites of her oriental salad. They had decided to meet for lunch on Tuesday since Danielle's first day at Creative Display was Wednesday.

"I don't know," Danielle answered with a shake of her head. "The way Carson explained it, Philip Turner burned a lot of bridges as he built his empire."

"I bet he's wishing he'd been a little less cruel and a little more kind along the way," Roberta said.

"Philip Turner, kind? Please," Danielle countered. "Those two words don't even belong in the same sentence." She pushed away the rest of her meal and said, "But I agree with you, maybe things would've turned out differently for him had he treated people better. Maybe he'd still have his business."

"I'm sure he was a nice man at one point in his life," Roberta came to his defense. "Don't you think?"

Danielle dabbed at her mouth then placed her napkin on her plate, "Beats me. Carson sure didn't speak too highly of his own father."

"Speaking of Carson," Roberta said, lifting an eyebrow teasingly, "did you ever decide if he was the 'mystery man' who called while you were out and wouldn't leave a message?"

Danielle shook her head. "No. I'd like to think it was him, but it could have been anybody." She still felt a twinge of pain in her heart when she thought about it; she'd thought they really connected. "If it was him, he sure gave up easily. I don't expect I'll ever hear from him again."

Roberta shrugged. "That's too bad. He was such a babe."

"Yeah, I guess," Danielle said, not wanting to feed Roberta's fire in the least and trying to dampen her enthusiasm. "Obviously he wasn't interested. Could we please talk about something else?"

"Okay," Roberta agreed easily. "You know how we always talk about going on vacations and traveling around to different places?"

Danielle thought about it all the time. "Sure, what's up?"

"I'm thinking of calling some of the airlines and some travel agencies to see what kind of job opportunities there are."

"You are?"

"Sure, why not?" Roberta said frankly. "It sounds like a fun career, plus the benefits are incredible. You can practically fly for free and go anywhere you want."

Danielle looked at her friend with amazement. Six months ago Roberta wouldn't have even considered something like this. Now she was talking about starting a whole new career.

"Wow, that's great," Danielle told her.

"It would be even better if you would do it with me," Roberta told her.

Visions of them taking off for a weekend to the coast or an extended trip to Europe got Danielle's heart racing before it suddenly skidded to a stop. "I'm starting a new job tomorrow. I can't just walk in and quit."

"Oh, yeah," Roberta replied, disappointedly. "I guess not. But wait—" she had an idea, "You can always quit if it doesn't work out. I mean, maybe you won't even like this job. Besides, I still need time to find out about all this other stuff."

Danielle thought for a minute. "It's not like I'm not working full-time. I could take some travel courses at the community college or something."

"Sure," Roberta said excitedly. "It will all work out. You'll see."

They ended up spending an extra half hour shopping at the downtown mall. They were both excited about the prospect of seeing the world together, of getting out and actually doing something fun and adventurous. And with new spring fashions out in the stores, Roberta and Danielle couldn't resist all the bright new colors and styles. Roberta found a kicky tropical print skirt and aqua-colored cotton top she had to have and Danielle ended up with a cool cotton jumper and t-shirt to wear for work. It was comfortable and casual yet looked nice and professional.

When they finished shopping, Roberta hugged her and wished her luck in her new job. "But don't like it too much," she reminded her. "We have big plans."

Throwing her packages in the back seat of the car, Danielle headed for home, with the window rolled down and the fresh, crisp spring air filling her lungs. With renewed hope, she turned up the radio and sang along with the music. Things were going to work out. She just knew it!

❈

The next morning Danielle woke up before her alarm went off. Today she rejoined the work force. A thought that made her both happy and sad. She'd been bored doing nothing, but she'd enjoyed having a life of leisure. Still, she'd become the family "backup." If her sister Rachel needed a last-minute baby-sitter, she called Danielle. If someone needed a ride to pick up a car in the shop, Danielle was the one to call. It was well known that she had no life, so the family took it upon themselves to give her one—the life of their personal servant. Unfortunately, the pay just wasn't that great.

Danielle didn't see herself making a career out of her job at Creative Display, but she was sure it would be fun working there and she was excited to try something new and creative.

Forcing all negative thoughts from her mind, she jumped out of bed, determined not to let her fears and doubts get the best of her. Things were going to work out. She didn't know how, but somehow everything was going to be okay.

⚜

"Now, Danielle, darling, there is so much to learn, so many possibilities," Vincent Sinclair, the owner of Creative Display, said with a flourish, "but we will start you over here with Cassandra making beautiful arrangements. She will teach you everything you don't already know."

Danielle already liked Vincent. He was a thinly built man, with short-cropped hair that was lightly gelled and stuck out in disarray all over his head. Sometimes he wore wire-rimmed glasses; other times they hung from a band around his neck. He was forever putting them on and taking them off. And even though he was born and raised in Utah, he had developed an aristocratic accent and spoke with a flair, giving an impression of importance as if he were the final word on design for home and business.

Danielle had also met his wife, Abby, who had stopped in to have lunch with Vincent. She had long brown hair and wore cinnamon-colored pants that were loose and flowing, with a matching tunic. She was nice looking in a quiet way, Danielle thought, which might account in some way for the attraction between them. He needed someone calm and steady to balance his flamboyance and dramatic flair.

Abby brought Da Vinci, their pure white Persian kitten, with her, and Vincent introduced them.

"What a beautiful cat," Danielle said, stroking underneath the kitten's chin. He closed his eyes and purred contentedly.

"Thank you," Abby said. "We have another one at home—Chauncey. He's a Himalayan. But Chauncey doesn't like to ride in the car, does he, Da Vinci?" Abby said in a sing-song voice as Da Vinci stretched and yawned. "No, Chauncey would rather stay home." She nuzzled her nose up to the cat's face and kissed him affectionately.

At Vincent's signal, Danielle and Abby followed him up a short flight of stairs into a large room filled with every imaginable article to make floral arrangements, baskets, wreaths, or any other type of arrangement possible. The choice of silk flowers alone was staggering. Vincent introduced Danielle to a woman not much older than herself named Cassandra, who was busy making centerpieces for an upcoming wedding.

"Welcome aboard," Cassie said, with a warm smile. "I sure hope you can make centerpieces because I'm never going to get these finished in time."

"With you teaching her, I'm sure she'll be splendid," Vincent said with enthusiastic praise. "Now," he said, taking the cat from his wife and showering it with kisses before he cradled it in his arms. "I'm going to have lunch with my wife. I'll check on you later."

Danielle watched as Cassie showed her how to assemble the arrangement, then, relying on her past experience, did her best to copy exactly what Cassie had done. Pleased with Danielle's skills, Cassandra moved onto another project, leaving Danielle to finish the centerpieces alone. By closing time, Danielle was just completing the last arrangement. She hadn't stopped for a break the entire day and could hardly believe how quickly the hours had passed.

"Darlings," Vincent called, ascending the stairs, "we are closing."

Cassandra had been creating a massive wall hanging with driftwood and an assortment of rustic objects, including gourds, mushrooms, and twigs. Splashes of color came from silk flowers and different types of greenery. It was exquisite, Danielle thought admiringly. In his delightfully dramatic way, Vincent gasped and placed his hand on his chest when he saw the creation.

"Magnificent!" he cried, fairly swooning with appreciation for its beauty. "Cassie, you have outdone yourself on this one. It is truly breathtaking." He shook his head with disbelief as if such beauty was impossible by human hands.

"I'm glad you like it," Cassandra said, smiling proudly at her work. Deeply impressed with Cassandra's work, Danielle echoed Vincent's praise.

Next, Vincent turned and looked at the twenty centerpieces Danielle had done and quickly found words to shower her with compliments. She knew her work was nowhere close to that of Cassie's, but Vincent's warmth made her feel that her contribution was still very important.

"Thank you," she said with a smile. "I'm glad they turned out all right." His response was so positive that already she was looking forward to coming to work the next day. She also felt a determination to try harder to do even better.

⊰⊱ ❀ ⊰⊱

For once, Danielle monopolized the talk around the dinner table that night. Her parents were amused and excited about her enjoyable day at work and both expressed their delight that she liked her new job so much.

Before she crawled into bed that night, Danielle took a moment to kneel down and pray. Although she was consistent with her prayers at night, she often offered more prayers from underneath the covers than on her knees. She apologized for being lazy in her prayers and recommitted to do better. Her heart was full of gratitude and she poured out her feelings to the Lord.

Then she added something that surprised even herself. She asked the Lord to bless Carson, wherever he was, whatever he was doing.

She drifted off to sleep with faded memories of Carson teasing her mind.

⊰⊱ ❀ ⊰⊱

The days flew by after that. Even though Danielle's job was supposed to be part-time, she ended up putting in full-time hours and then some when the occasion required it. She enjoyed her job and the people she worked with so much she didn't mind staying longer to finish up projects or learn something new.

As she and Cassandra worked together she learned that Cassie was only three years older than Dani herself. Cassandra had majored in interior design in school with an art minor, and it showed in her work. Danielle paid close attention to everything Cassie showed her, trying to absorb her knowledge, skills, and talents. It was Cassandra who first suggested to Danielle to consider going back to school for a degree in interior design.

The thought of going back to school did not appeal to Danielle. She'd struggled enough just to get her business degree. But as Cassandra talked to her about the classes and vast array of subjects she would learn about, Danielle found herself actually considering it. Maybe school wouldn't be so boring if she were actually learning about something she loved.

"Ladies," Vincent announced one afternoon late in June, "I would like you to stay after work tonight for a half an hour or so for a short staff meeting. It's time to start thinking of the Jubilee of Trees and our Christmas displays." The Jubilee of Trees was a fund-raiser held every year to help the local children's medical center.

Later as Danielle restocked shelves with different shapes of Styrofoam, she questioned Cassie. "How long have you worked for Vincent?"

"Oh . . ." Cassie's lavender-blue eyes were thoughtful, "I guess about seven years. He hired me fresh out of college."

Cassandra was naturally pretty with smooth, creamy skin and wavy jet-black hair she wore in short curls all over her head, which accentuated her gorgeous eyes. In fact, except for a little mauve-colored lip-gloss, Cassie didn't wear any makeup at all. She didn't need it.

"I think I learned more from him in the first year I worked for him than I did in school. He's amazingly gifted," she said with admiration.

"I feel lucky he even hired me," Danielle said, realizing her good fortune.

"Vincent recognizes talent when he sees it. He wouldn't have hired you if he didn't think you had it in you to be creative and work hard." Cassandra stacked empty boxes together. "We're just entering our busy season, and until Christmas is over, things around here get pretty crazy."

"But Christmas is six months away," Danielle said with some surprise. She was still paying off her credit card from last Christmas.

"Vincent and Abby are in charge of the Jubilee of Trees held every year," Cassie explained. "It's very involved and requires months of planning and organizing. He's already been working on this year's Jubilee since January. Plus we're always swamped with orders from homes and businesses who hire us to decorate for them for the holidays. Abby takes time from her law practice and helps a lot during the holidays. She keeps Vincent grounded or he'd definitely fly off into orbit."

"Do Vincent and Abby have any children?"

"No," Cassie shook her head. "Just their cats. But they're practically like children to them."

"They seem to really love each other," Danielle observed.

"I hope I can have that kind of a relationship when I get married," Cassie said, thoughtfully. "They both have their own lives and interests, but they still make time for each other. Even with their schedules, they'll take off for some little bed-and-breakfast just to be together without distractions. She loves antiques and he collects first editions of old books, so they comb antique stores all over, looking for treasures."

Danielle tried to picture herself combing antique stores with her beloved, but the image wouldn't come into focus.

"You'd better fasten your seatbelt," Cassie said as she lifted the boxes to take to the dumpster, "because the ride's about to get bumpy." Then she grinned, "But that's what makes it so exciting."

# CHAPTER
##  FIVE

Cassie wasn't kidding when she said the ride was about to get bumpy. Danielle found herself putting in longer and longer hours at Creative Display as the months wore on, which didn't give her any time to socialize or date, not that anyone interesting was asking. Of course, she never got out to meet anyone new anyway. But she wasn't complaining. She loved her job and the people she worked with. Vincent was a creative catalyst at work who propelled his employees to work and stretch their imaginations. It was his feeling that as much could be learned from failure as from success, so he was always supportive of anyone's desire to try something new. Everyone seemed to feed off his enthusiasm, and Danielle wondered where the man got his energy.

She was continually amazed at the creations the employees came up with and was convinced Vincent was a true genius. He challenged any of his workers to create their own contribution to the Jubilee of Trees and was willing to let them use anything from Creative Display at cost to decorate the trees. Several of the employees gathered donations from different organizations to fund their Christmas trees and the excitement and spirit of the fund-raiser was contagious. Danielle contemplated doing a tree herself, but as yet hadn't come up with a theme or a way to raise the cash to decorate the tree.

One Saturday morning in early September, Danielle was busy opening boxes of inventory and stocking shelves when she came upon a box of new hand-painted items they hadn't carried before. The box was full of small wooden tole-painted people ranging between four and six inches tall. The figures were of men, women, and children of every different nationality and race. Danielle was immediately taken by the happy smiles and the array of variety before her.

Instead of putting the items on the shelf, she quickly put them back in the box and carried it to the back room. An idea for a Christmas tree began to spin and form in her head.

That night she presented her idea to Roberta when they met to go to a late movie.

"I'd like to take these wooden people and make a family tree—I guess you could call it a genealogy tree," she told her friend. "I could start with a husband and wife at the top of the tree, then have their children around them on the branches below and then continue on down the tree with each family line branching out and becoming more varied and far-reaching to represent people from all over the world. I could even put extra ornaments to represent each culture, like drums and wild animals to go with the people from Africa, little gondolas and statuettes to represent Italy, kangaroos for Australia—"

"How big is this tree going to be anyway?" Roberta asked her.

"It's going to have to be pretty huge to do this, isn't it?" Danielle figured, wondering if she was biting off more than she could chew.

"But, hey, I love the idea," Roberta said. "How are you going to pay for it?"

"I haven't figured that part out yet," Danielle admitted as she and Roberta took their place in line to buy their movie tickets.

"You know what?" Roberta's eyes lit up. "I bet some of the people at work would be willing to donate. My dad's always got some kind of service project or community effort going. I'll e-mail everyone in the morning and see what kind of response I get," she promised. Danielle's heart glowed, grateful to have a friend like Roberta.

Putting an arm around her friend, Danielle gave her a firm squeeze. "I'm so excited to do this tree. I just hope I can find the time. I'm putting in overtime at work as it is."

When Roberta observed that Danielle appeared happier than she had in a long time, Danielle nodded. "I've never had more fun in my life," she confessed. "But it's not just that. I finally feel like I'm doing something that stimulates my brain and is rewarding. And even though it can get hectic and stressful at times, it's just not the same as when I was working at Turner Consulting. The stress there nearly killed me. Even though I lost my Outback and we didn't get to move into our little bungalow, I'm happier than I've been in months. I hate to admit it, but getting 'let go' from Turner Consulting was a blessing in disguise."

Roberta didn't respond and Danielle could tell something was bothering her. "Roberta, what's wrong?" she asked. Had she said something to hurt her feelings?

"It's just that I talked with Sister Armstrong in my ward today," she said quietly. "She's owns Worldwide Travel."

Danielle knew what Roberta was going to say and she felt terrible. They'd planned on pursuing this travel thing together for months now.

"She has an opening for a receptionist and said that she would be willing to train someone on the job. She wants us both to come in and talk to her."

Feeling like a heel, Danielle searched for something to say and could think of nothing.

"I guess I just assumed you were still interested in the travel industry." Roberta couldn't hide the disappointment from her voice.

"I am . . . ," Danielle began. "I mean, I kind of am. It's just that . . . well, I didn't think I'd like my job so much. I mean, I really love what I'm doing. And Vincent told me that if I wanted to go back to school and get a degree, he would let me work as a design consultant. It's a great opportunity, and the pay is even better than I would have expected."

"Wow," Roberta said, sounding a little lost. "I'm glad you like your job so much. It's just that . . . I was looking forward to doing this together." The two friends were quiet and then Roberta spoke up. "I guess I'll just talk to her myself—if you don't mind," she asked tentatively.

"Of course not," Danielle responded quickly. "And who knows? If things don't work out for me at Creative Display down the road, maybe I can come and join you."

"Okay," Roberta answered with a nod. "I'm sure Sister Armstrong would be glad to help you. And I'll definitely put in a good word for you."

Purchasing their tickets, they rushed into the theater, foregoing their usual large bucket of popcorn and drinks, since it was time for the movie to start.

"So, are you really thinking of going back to college?" Roberta asked as they took their seats.

"Hard to believe, isn't it?" Danielle answered. "Vincent says I can cut back on my work hours and go to school part-time. I really think I would love learning about interior design. I mean, at work, I can't get enough, you know. I look forward to going every day, because I know I'll learn something new."

"I'm glad it's worked out for you," Roberta removed her coat and set it in the chair next to her. "For a while I was getting worried about you not having a job for so long, but now you're ready to conquer the world. And speaking of getting on with life and getting married . . ."

"Who said anything about getting married?" Danielle looked quickly at her friend and saw the smile waiting to burst onto her friend's face. "Are you and Lenny getting that serious?" she blurted out loudly. The talking around them stopped and people looked in their direction. Danielle and Roberta sunk down in their seats and lowered their voices.

"We were at the mall last night," Roberta whispered. "We walked past a jewelry store and started looking at rings."

"I can't believe it. You've only known him a couple of months," Danielle reminded her, sitting up in her chair to see better as the lights in the auditorium darkened.

"Yeah, but when it's right, it's right. I knew after two dates with him that he was someone special. I've prayed about it and I think he's the right one," Roberta whispered as the previews started. "And you know what?"

"What?" Danielle cupped her hand over her mouth.

"Someday when you least expect it, Mr. Right is going to waltz right into your life and knock you off your feet, and you'll know it, just like that."

The person sitting two rows in front of them turned around and shushed them.

"Sorry," Danielle said to the lady. They stopped talking while the lights dimmed and the previews started. But Danielle couldn't quit thinking about what Roberta had said. Would it work like that, with Mr. Right showing up out of the blue? She doubted it. Of course, that would be about the only way it could happen since she didn't go out of her way to meet guys. She didn't have time now, and when she started school again she'd have even less time to date.

She just prayed that if and when her future husband did waltz into her life, she wouldn't be too busy to dance with him.

# CHAPTER
## SIX

By October it was time for Danielle to get serious about her Christmas "geanealogy" tree, and she recruited Cassie's help in tole painting a larger, ten-inch-sized man and woman to go at the top of the tree. Even though Roberta was now working at Worldwide Travel and loving it, her father's company had pulled through and donated more than was necessary to cover the expenses for the tree. Danielle had been thrilled to receive the money. Still, she wondered how she was going to put in the time necessary to do the decorating. Her answer came unexpectedly one day after church when Brother Matthews, a counselor in the bishopric, caught her coming out of Primary.

"Do you have a minute, Danielle?" he asked.

"Well," Danielle said, drawing out the word while she tried to come up with an excuse. What did they want now? She was happy with her current calling and she was coming to church regularly. What else could they possibly need to talk to her about?

"Danielle?" he asked again.

"Oh, uh, yeah, but just a minute, though." She didn't want him thinking she had free time to spare—just in case he wanted to add her to the activities committee or something. She paused to rearrange her Primary things in her oversized book bag, then followed him to an empty classroom where they unfolded two chairs and sat down facing each other.

"So, you've been teaching the six-year-old class," he said. She nodded. "How's it going?"

Breathing a sigh of relief that he was just checking on how her calling was going, she answered brightly, "It's going great. Those kids sure keep me on my toes. Talk about full of energy."

"I'll bet," he laughed. "And I understand the kids really love having you for a teacher."

"They do?" She was pleased at his comment.

"Oh, yes. Some of the parents have told me how much their children enjoy Primary. At first they were a little nervous, you know, with some of your teaching methods."

When she had first been called to the Primary, she'd been determined to make their class time enjoyable and educational. She wanted them to learn the gospel lessons, but she wanted it to be fun. So, remembering how bored she'd been at church when she was a kid, she pulled out all the stops. They had crafts and they acted out stories from the Book of Mormon. It wasn't uncommon to see Sister Camden's class parading around the building, dressed like Stripling Warriors, or covered in her father's old dress shirts, finger-painting the nativity at Christmas. It was Sister Camden's class who set up a teepee in the parking lot at Thanksgiving, and it was Sister Camden's class who presented the bishopric with decorated sugar cookies on Valentine's Day.

Danielle waited for Brother Matthews to go on, wondering if that was all he wanted to say. But as he spoke again, she felt her heart lurch.

"That's why we're hesitant to release you as the six-year-olds' teacher," he said.

"Release me!" she blurted. "Why? Did I do something wrong? The paint came out of the carpet, didn't it? But if you want, I'll pay to get it cleaned by a professional."

"No, no, it's not that at all. You've been wonderful; the carpet is fine. It's just that we'd like to extend you another calling."

Her heart sank. She didn't want another calling. She wanted her class. Taylor and Amy, and the twins, Kiley and Katie. And even "wild man" Stewart. They were *her* kids.

"I know how much you'll miss the children. But you know, in a few months the children will be moving to the older class anyway."

She nodded her head slowly. She'd cried the last time her class had graduated to the older class.

"But we feel very good about this new calling. As a bishopric, we have fasted and prayed, and we know that your talents are needed somewhere else at this time."

"Where?" she said flatly.

"You've been called to be the second-year Laurel Advisor."

"What's a Laurel?" she asked with some confusion. Wasn't that something in the Scouts?

His eyebrows narrowed with mirrored confusion. "In Young Women. It's the oldest age group, the seventeen-year-olds."

"Oh, yeah," she remembered. Then she pulled a sour lemon face. "The seventeen-year-olds?" That's all she needed. To deal with a bunch of giggling, self-centered teenage girls with PMS and raging hormones.

"I can tell you'd like some time to think and pray about it," he chuckled.

*Yeah, like the rest of my life.* "I most certainly would," she answered.

"Why don't you give me a call on Tuesday or Wednesday and give me your answer?" He spoke kindly and with understanding, without judgment or pressure. Which was wise on his part since Danielle knew herself well enough to realize that if he'd put any pressure on her, she would've said "no" without even blinking.

The rest of the day she stewed and fretted over the new calling. Why in the world would they want her to be with the seventeen-year-old girls? She was a rotten example. She hadn't even known what a Laurel was; she'd never gone to Young Women activities when she was seventeen.

"What are they thinking?" she said out loud, as she lay on her bed staring up at the ceiling. Wasn't she supposed to have a temple recommend so they could go do baptisms for the dead? Then she remembered, if the girls could get a recommend to do baptisms, then she could, too.

Oh, wait! She thought excitedly of another excuse. Wasn't she supposed to have a van or a Suburban to work with the youth?

No, there were only five Laurels, and they would fit in her mother's Chrysler.

"Shoot!" She whacked the bed with both hands. "What am I going to do?"

She knew what she was supposed to do. She was supposed to pray.

But she didn't want to pray. Because if she did, she'd probably get an answer. And she didn't want to get the answer because it would probably be "yes."

She put off praying until she went to bed that night. Over and over in her mind she thought about what it would be like to be in charge of all those girls. They'd probably drive her insane with all their talk about makeup and boys and school dances. Hesitantly she got on her knees and shut her eyes, trying to summon up the courage to ask the Lord, torn between praying and climbing into bed. She knelt, took a deep breath, and finally decided to just get it over with.

*Okay, Lord, I guess I don't have much faith. I mean, if in fact I am supposed to accept this calling, I can't see any earthly reason why. I mean, I'm a horrible example to these girls. I didn't go to church much during my teens, and even though I go to church now, I wouldn't say that my testimony is the strongest. I mean, I believe the Church is true and I know that You love me, but I don't think I'm the right person to be teaching these girls. I mean, at least with the six-year-olds I could fake what I didn't know. But with these guys I won't be able to do that.*

*I guess I'm scared. Why can't I just stay where I'm at?*

She took another deep breath before going on.

*You need to grow.* The words came to her mind, clearly and distinctly.

*I need to grow?* she repeated.

Why? Why did she need to grow? What was that supposed to mean?

Another thought came. *This calling is as much for you as it is for the girls.*

She shook her head. Was she dreaming up this conversation, or was it real?

"Heavenly Father, am I making all this up or are You really speaking to me?" she asked out loud.

*I love you. You need to grow.*

Tears came to her eyes. She had no response. Her mind and heart had a clear understanding. She knew the answer. Whether or not she wanted to, or understood why, she knew she was supposed to take this calling. Her mind had stopped whirling, and her heart was at peace.

"Okay," she said at last. "Thanks for the answer. But I'm going to need a lot of help—a lot!" With that, she closed her prayer and pushed herself onto her feet.

She sure hoped the Lord knew what He was doing.

⁂

Danielle looked at the three faces in front of her, staring at her. Almost as if they were daring her to make them like her or to care about anything she had to say.

"My name's Danielle Camden. As you know, I'm your new advisor. You can call me Danielle, if you want."

They didn't even blink.

Danielle swallowed, wishing she was back in Primary with Stewart and the others. At least with them she knew exactly where she stood; they didn't hold back their feelings. She almost wished these girls would just blurt out how much they hated her.

"So, why don't we take a minute and have you introduce yourselves so I can get to know you."

The three girls looked at each other, then one finally spoke up. She was a beauty, with tanned skin—probably "fake bake"—thick, wavy blonde hair, perfect makeup, and neatly manicured nails. "My name is McCall. I'm a cheerleader at Mountain Ridge High School. I'm a senior and I work in the mall at Teasers."

Danielle knew that was a hot place for kids to buy trendy clothes and shoes. It was high-priced and probably very "cool" to work there. So, to make points with McCall, she acted extremely impressed. "Wow!" she exclaimed, nodding her approval.

The next girl, who had creamy skin, light blue eyes, and gorgeous red hair cut in a stylish short bob, introduced herself. "I'm Chloe. I'm a senior at Mountain Ridge, too, and I'm on the debate team and in the choir."

"That's great, Chloe," Danielle said.

The last girl wasn't as striking as the other two. She had brown hair, clipped back, wore no makeup, and spoke quietly. "I'm Lucinda, but my friends call me Lucy. I'm a senior with them."

Danielle waited for her to go on, but she didn't say anything else.

"Okay," Danielle finally said. "It's nice to meet each of you. Like I said, my name is Danielle. I work at Creative Display and I like sports and being outdoors. I'd rather snow ski than anything else in the world and I love Italian food."

She looked at the girls. They were still there and they were listening. She took that as a good sign and went on.

"I went to Lakeview High School and was on the swim team and ski team, and I ran cross-country my senior year. I graduated from the 'U' with a degree in business, but I didn't really enjoy working in that field. I love my job at Creative Display and am working on a Christmas tree for the Jubilee of Trees."

"Our choir sang at the Jubilee of Trees last year," Chloe said. "I think we're singing again this year."

"Good," Danielle nodded, feeling the ice melt just a little.

"They had some really awesome trees there last year," Chloe said. "What's your tree like?"

Danielle almost told them, then she had a different idea. "How about instead of telling you, I show you."

They had forty-five minutes before church was over. Creative Display was only ten minutes away. For some reason a lesson just didn't seem the right thing to do, so Danielle decided to follow her heart.

"Where is it?" McCall asked, impatience lacing her voice.

"It's down at Creative Display," Danielle answered.

The girls looked at each other, not seeming to know whether or not they should go.

"Come on," Danielle said. "I'd like to show you."

Fifteen minutes later, Danielle was turning on the lights inside the store and leading the girls to the back room. As they made their way through the building, the girls commented on all the gorgeous decorations and creations in the store. They even pointed out a large Christmas wreath they thought was pretty, and when Danielle told them she'd done the wreath they appeared impressed.

"Here it is," she said as she swung the door open to the back room.

The girls looked at the tree with blank expressions. It had taken hours and hours to attach the brilliant white lights just right so all the wiring was hidden, but otherwise, the tree was bare.

"Oh, wait." Danielle reached down and plugged in the cord. Suddenly the tree lit up the room.

"Wow," the girls said in unison.

Danielle spent the next fifteen minutes sharing her ideas about decorating the tree, then showed the girls the ornaments and explained the idea behind the "family tree." To her delight, the three girls actually seemed excited about the idea.

"My only problem is—" Danielle looked at each of them as she spoke, "—the only time I have to work on the tree is in the evenings. I have until Thanksgiving to finish it, but I only have a few spare hours a week to put in on it."

"I'll help you," Lucy volunteered immediately.

Danielle smiled at the young girl. "Really? That would be great. Thanks."

Danielle had quickly noticed that McCall and Chloe seemed to be friends, but Lucy didn't quite fit in. Her heart went out to her. Danielle hadn't always felt like she fit in at school either.

"I could help a little after rehearsal," Chloe offered.

Danielle felt a growing warmth inside at their willingness to help.

"I know how busy you are," Danielle said. "Thanks Chloe."

McCall said nothing, and not wanting her to feel uncomfortable or pressured, Danielle showed the girls some beautiful gold and maroon ribbon for the tree. "I just can't decide if I want to dress it up with this ribbon, or make it more folksy with the plaid," she said, inviting their opinion.

"I like the plaid," Chloe said.

"Me too," Lucy echoed.

"What about you, McCall?" Danielle asked.

She shrugged. "I don't know." It was obvious she didn't really care.

"Well, we can decide later," Danielle said. "I guess I'd better get you back to the church."

On the way back, they planned a night that week to work on the tree. Danielle said she'd take them out for pizza afterward. To her surprise, McCall said she'd think about joining them.

All in all Danielle felt their first class went okay. It wasn't great, but it could have been worse. She remembered the words that had come to her the night she prayed about the calling and realized that she would definitely grow from this calling. She didn't really have a choice!

# CHAPTER SEVEN

Even though the shop closed early on Halloween so employees could be home with their children, Danielle decided to stay and finish replacing a strand of lights that had gone out on the tree. It was a headache but it had to be done. Chloe and Lucy had been a great help decorating the tree, and Danielle thought they would soon have it done. McCall hadn't come to help after all, and although Danielle had invited the other two girls in her class, both had had to work.

Lucy had come as she had promised and had revealed noteworthy creative and artistic abilities. Danielle had difficulty getting her to speak, however, because she was so very quiet. For that reason, Danielle was surprised to learn that Lucy was very involved in drama and was in an upcoming play. Interested to see Lucy on stage, Danielle promised to attend with the other girls.

Chloe had also been a great help. She was friendly and a lot of fun to have around, and Danielle could tell that she was the type of person who had a good time no matter what she did.

Danielle studied the tree as she ate her dinner, which consisted of a veggie sandwich from the deli next door, then set to work. It took her a good half hour just to unwind the string of lights from the branches, and her neck ached from having to crouch over while she worked.

*Oh well, I didn't want to sit home and answer the door for trick-or-treaters anyway,* she sighed. A faint pounding caught her attention and she realized someone was knocking on the side door. Hurrying to the door, she found Roberta and her boyfriend, Lenny. And Lenny's friend, Bart. Roberta was constantly raving about what a great guy Bart was, and had been trying to line Bart and Danielle up for weeks, despite her friend's protests. Roberta went on and on about Bart so much, Danielle sometimes wondered if it was Lenny or Bart whom Roberta liked.

"Trick or treat," they yelled when she opened the door.

"Looks like the three stooges," she said. "What are you guys doing?" The trio laughed and stepped inside.

"We came to see if you wanted to go to a dance at the institute up on campus with us," Roberta said, looping her arm through Lenny's.

*Which means I get stuck with Bart,* Danielle grumbled to herself. *I don't think so.*

"Gee, I wish I could but I've kind of got plans for tonight," she told them, trying to ignore the disappointed look on Bart's face. It wasn't that he wasn't nice, and he was sort of attractive in a scholarly type of way, with his wire-rimmed glasses and wavy dark hair. It was just that he was a psychology major, and the few times he and Danielle had exchanged a few words, they seemed to be on different wavelengths.

"Danielle, you can't stay here all night working on this Christmas Tree. It's Halloween, for Pete's sake. Let's go have some fun," Roberta begged.

"Yeah, Danielle," Lenny chimed in. "We're going over to Bart's house after the dance to sit in the hot tub and have pizza. Right, dude?" He looked at Bart.

"Right," Bart echoed, with a pleading look her way. "I just got the new End Zone CD we can listen to. We'd love it if you'd come."

End Zone was Roberta's favorite music group. Danielle thought they were okay, but she didn't like their music enough to spend an evening with Bart. Looking at her unexpected visitors, she felt like a cornered animal, trapped with no way out.

"Oh, all right," she gave in at last. "I guess I can work on this another time. But I didn't bring anything to change into, just what I wore to work." She was wearing jeans and a deep blue sweater that brought out the blue of her eyes.

"You look nice just the way you are," Bart said, his cheeks flushing.

"Thanks, Bart," she replied, wishing she found him more appealing. It was obvious he liked her.

"This isn't a costume party, is it?" she asked as she turned out the lights in the back room.

Lenny answered. "It's just a dance, but some people will probably wear costumes. We could dress up if we wanted."

"We didn't bring any costumes though," Roberta reminded him.

Danielle thought for a minute. "Hey," she suddenly remembered, "we did an oriental window display a few months ago. I'm sure we could find something from that to use for a costume."

They sorted through some boxes and found an oriental jacket and hat for Lenny, and two silk robes for the girls. They twisted up their hair and stuck several chopsticks through to finish the look. All that was left in the box was a dragon's head and flowing fabric body for Bart. They all busted up laughing when he put on the dragon's head and growled. Danielle thought he was a good sport about it.

Walking from the parking lot to the institute, she pulled in a deep breath of the crisp evening air scented with smoke from a nearby chimney. It had been an unusually warm and late fall, and the leaves were just starting to change, painting a palette of remarkable reds, oranges, and yellows. The colorful leaves crunched under their feet, and the distant sound of music and laughter spilled out of the open doorway.

The dance in the gymnasium of the institute building was in full swing when they arrived; the place was crowded and alive with music and dancing. Seeing that most of the people were in costume, the foursome was glad they'd dressed up after all. Danielle looked around, unable to remember the last time she went to a dance. But the atmosphere and music were contagious, and she found herself eager and ready to hit the dance floor. Since Bart wasn't able to dance wearing the dragon's head, he took it back to the car.

Lenny and Roberta decided to dance, leaving Danielle to wait for Bart and wonder what was taking him so long. As she watched couples out on the dance floor, laughing and having fun dancing to the song "Monster Mash," she heard a voice with a Transylvanian accent behind her, "Excuse me, but I vunder if you vould like to dance?"

She turned to see a tall Dracula standing behind her.

"Oh, well, you see . . ." she stammered.

"Perhaps you vould rather have a 'bite to eat' then," Dracula said, flashing his fangs.

Danielle laughed. "How nice of you to ask, Count. But I'm here with someone else."

"Dat is very sad," he answered gravely, then gave a sinister laugh. "But then, ve haf vays to take care of him . . ."

"Wait a minute," Danielle said. There was something very familiar about this guy. A smile warmed her face. "I know you, don't I."

"Your neck did look familiar to me," he grinned back. "What blood type are you?

"Carson!" she exclaimed. "It's you behind those fangs, isn't it? How are you? What are you doing in town?" She couldn't mask her excitement at seeing him again.

"Just a second." He removed the plastic fangs. "I don't know how vampires stand these things."

Danielle giggled. It was so good to see him, and he looked so funny with his hair black and slicked back with a widow's peak.

"You'll be proud of me," he said. "I quit business school and moved back to Salt Lake. I'm in my first year of medical school at the University, and I work a few hours a week at the children's hospital."

Without thinking she threw her arms around his neck and hugged him. "That's wonderful," she cried. "How do you find time to do both?"

"It's not easy. I have plenty of schoolwork to keep me busy, but on weekends I have time to put in a few hours. Next year I won't be able to work at all."

"I am really proud of you," she said.

"Thanks," he smiled. "I can't believe you came to the dance. It's good to see you, Danielle." He sounded sincere, Danielle thought, but then again, she wasn't sure if he'd ever tried to call her last Christmas when he said he would.

"Is it really?" she said doubtfully.

"Yes." His answer was emphatic. "It is."

"Well then, it's good to see you, too," she said, looking up at him. Their gazes locked and she felt her heart race, speeding faster than the beat of the music.

"Would you like to dan—" Carson began, but Bart arrived at that moment.

"Danielle, there you are," he said, taking her arm. "Are you ready to dance?"

Her heart sank. She'd forgotten about him. Knowing the proper thing would be to turn down Carson and dance with Bart, she turned to Carson. "Bart brought me to the dance."

"Oh, I see," Carson answered, his disappointment obvious in his voice.

"Maybe we could dance a little later," she said, hoping to salvage the opportunity.

"Yeah, maybe," he said with a courteous smile. "I'll see you later, then." He disappeared quickly into the crowd of people, and Bart claimed her hand, leading her to the dance floor. More than anything, Danielle wanted to talk to Carson, to find out about his decision to go to medical school and see how he was doing. To find out if he had tried to call her like he'd said he would. Inside she prayed that he would indeed "see her later."

After several fast-paced dances, a slow song started. Bart slid his hand around Danielle's waist and pulled her closely. Danielle stiffened under his touch, wishing she could find a way to get away from him. She wasn't exactly his date, but he was acting very possessive of her. Maybe the best thing to do would be to leave. Her eyes scanned the crowd for Roberta and Lenny. Her mind focused on an escape plan as she tried to come up with an excuse to get away from Bart. His warm breath on her neck was making her skin crawl. She had to get out of there and away from him!

The next song came on, an upbeat tune that brought the crowd alive again. Just then another couple, dancing a little too energetically for the crowded dance floor, collided into Bart and Danielle. Bart lost his footing and started to fall, but instead of going down alone, he kept a tight hold on Danielle, pulling her down with him. She landed on top of him.

"Ugh! Get off me!" he groaned. "My ankle . . ."

As someone helped Danielle to her feet, she saw who had collided with them. It was Carson and a black-wigged Cleopatra wannabe, who knelt down beside Bart, her regret and concern evident.

"I'm so sorry," she cried. "Are you okay? Don't move. We'll have someone carry you off the floor."

Danielle had to admit she liked how Cleopatra took over the roll of protector and nurse maid and willingly let her do so. In seconds, Lenny and Roberta had also arrived at the scene.

"Hey man, are you okay?" Lenny exclaimed when he saw his friend on the floor.

"Let's take him out in the foyer," Carson suggested.

Carson and Lenny carried Bart to the foyer where they laid him on a couch. Inside the music continued. Carson knelt down beside Bart. "Mind if I take a look at it?"

Bart looked at him with uncertainty.

"He's a medical student," Danielle assured Bart.

When Bart nodded, Carson removed Bart's shoe. "Can you move it?" he asked.

Bart flexed his foot tentatively, then rotated it around. Letting out a sigh of relief, he said, "Yeah, but it hurts like heck."

"It's probably just a sprain. You need to get some ice on it right away and get it elevated. Wrap your ankle in an Ace bandage and stay off of it as much as you can for the next few days. Take Ibuprofen for the swelling," he instructed. "Where's your car?"

"We're parked just around the corner of the building," Lenny said.

"I'll help you carry him to the car," Carson offered.

Danielle and Roberta followed the men out to the car. It wasn't easy but they managed to put Bart in the back seat, with his foot elevated.

"Hey, thanks for your help," Bart told Carson as Lenny went around to the driver's side and got in.

"No problem.  Sorry about the collision," Carson said with a wave of his hand. "Hope it feels better soon." He walked over to where Danielle and Roberta had been standing out of the way and said, "If you want to stay longer, I can give you a ride home."

Danielle was strongly tempted, but she hated to do such a flaky thing—come to the dance with one guy, stay when he left, and go home with another. She looked at Roberta, who was staring at her curiously.

"You want to stay?" Roberta was clearly confused. "Do you even know this guy?"

"Actually, I do," Danielle answered. "This is Carson Turner. You remember him, don't you?"

"Carson!" Roberta exclaimed, turning to the black-caped figure in astonishment. "Carson Turner? What a surprise. How are you?"

"Roberta worked with me at Turner Consulting," Danielle told him.

Just then the passenger window rolled down. "Roberta," Lenny called out. "I think we better get Bart home." In the back seat, Danielle's injured date looked like he was about to pass out.

"Oh, yeah, sorry," Roberta said apologetically. She turned to Danielle. "Looks like it would be a tight squeeze in the car, anyway, with Bart taking up the back seat. I'll tell the guys you were offered a ride home by a friend." She stepped closely to Danielle and said quietly, "You'd better call me when you get home, though."

With a wave good-bye, Carson and Danielle watched as the three in the car drove away, then together they walked back toward the building. "You feel like dancing?" he asked.

"Sure," she said with a smile. "Just keep your fangs off my neck."

The place was still hopping, and Danielle could see that even more couples had crowded onto the dance floor when they got inside. A slow song started to play, and Danielle found she didn't mind this time in the least. Carson was a smooth dancer and kept perfect rhythm with the beat. He didn't breathe down her neck, and she loved how great it felt having him hold her close.

"How come you're such a good dancer?" she asked.

He looked down at her as he spoke, not missing a beat. "My mom. She taught me how to dance."

Danielle laughed in amazement. "Really? Your mother taught you?"

"She thought it was important for me to learn how to dance. So she taught me how to slow dance, polka, and even waltz."

Danielle raised her eyebrows in appreciation, then her eyes widened as Roberta's words flashed through her consciousness. *Someday when you least expect it, Mr. Right is going to waltz right into your life and knock you off your feet, and you'll know it, just like that.*

There it was, plain as the chopsticks in her bun. Carson had actually waltzed into her life tonight, literally knocking her off her feet. Not to mention practically breaking Bart's ankle, but that was beside the point.

Tingles swept over her, making her shiver. Of course, logically, she knew it didn't mean anything. But to think that Roberta had practically predicted it in the first place. And then to have Carson fulfill it so literally.

"Danielle." Carson's voice broke into her thoughts. "The music has ended. The dance is over."

"Oh!" She snapped back to reality. "Sorry. I was thinking of something else. I didn't notice."

"Are you worried about your friend Bart?" Carson asked, his brow furrowed with interest.

"Bart? Oh no." Danielle started to laugh, then realized how cold-hearted she must sound. "I mean, of course, I hope his ankle's okay, but I wasn't thinking about that. Actually I was thinking that you and your mother must have had a wonderful relationship."

A sudden sadness crossed his face and he exhaled slowly. "We did," he nodded. "She was great. I really miss her."

"How about your father? How's he doing?" Danielle asked.

"I don't know," he answered matter-of-factly.

She could tell by the tone of his voice that this wasn't a topic he wanted to pursue. Despite her curiosity, she was determined not to pry.

"I could use a drink of water," she said, quickly changing the subject as they left the dance floor. "Are you thirsty?"

"I sure am. If you're not in a hurry to get home, we could go somewhere and get something to drink, and maybe a bite to eat. I'm starving."

"That would be great," she said, trying to stay calm while her insides were turning cartwheels. She couldn't believe she was actually going out on a . . . kind of, well, sort of, an almost close enough to count date with Carson Turner.

⋈⋈ 🕸 ⋉⋉

They ended up grabbing a hamburger at a Wendy's, then stopped for ice cream at a popular ice cream shop. As they waited their turn, they contemplated their many choices, trying to decide which flavor to have.

"Find one you like yet?" Carson asked her.

She'd been eyeing the mud pie sundae with mint chocolate chip ice cream, fudgy caramel sauce, and Oreo cookies crumbled on top, but she wasn't quite positive yet. "There are too many to choose from," she answered. "What are you having?"

"Mmmm. Well, I was thinking about pralines and cream, or the rocky road, but what I really want is a mud pie sundae," he said. Her face must have registered her surprise, because he stared at her.

"What is it?" he asked.

"That's what I wanted," she confessed. "But they're so big, I didn't want to seem like a pig, you know, after just eating a hamburger and fries."

"Let's share one then," he suggested.

"Okay," she agreed.

They placed their order then found a booth to wait in. For a moment they didn't speak; they just looked at each other, smiling. Danielle couldn't get over how great his smile was and how green his eyes were. And he was with her! "I still can't believe we ran into each other tonight," he finally said.

"I know," she said, wondering if he could read her thoughts. "I'm glad we did."

"Me too," he said.

"Here you go," the girl from behind the counter announced as she placed a large mud pie sundae in front of them. Mounds of whip cream slid down the sides of fudge-laden scoops of ice cream.

"Whoa," Carson said. "I'm sure glad we're sharing this."

Working from opposite ends, they dug in and began eating. It was every bit as good as it looked. Danielle wanted to ask why he'd never called when he said he would, but decided it would be better to keep things light for now. She waited while he licked a drop of sauce from his lip, then she asked, "So, what's medical school like? Is it what you thought it would be?"

He sat back in his seat for a moment, collecting his thoughts. "It's been quite an adjustment from business school, but I really love it. Don't get me wrong," he said with a laugh. "I've got hundreds of pages of reading some nights, but I'm finally learning stuff I want to know about. I picture myself actually practicing medicine—working with sick children, helping them get well again—and I get so excited. I think working at the hospital really helps because I can see exactly where my schooling is taking me."

"That is so great," she told him. "I'm really proud of you."

"Thanks," he said softly. "That means a lot to me, you know."

Danielle felt herself melt beneath his gaze, just like the ice cream in the bowl in front of her.

He glanced at his wristwatch. "Uh-oh," he said, tapping the face of the watch, "I don't think my watch is right. What time is it?"

Danielle glanced at her own watch. "Almost eleven."

"I've got to get going. Speaking of homework, I've got a ton. Have you had enough?"

*Of the ice cream, yes. Of you, no.* "More than enough," was all she said.

"Sorry," he said. "I wish it wasn't so late."

"That's okay," she said, wishing she could have spent more time with him. She wanted to find out everything there was to know about him.

"Do you think we could go out again sometime?" he asked.

She managed to smile and say, "I'd love to," despite an impulse to shout, "You bet!"

"Come on," he said, reaching for her hand. "I'll take you home."

Hand in hand, they walked out of the ice cream shop. Danielle wasn't sure if her feet touched the ground the entire way.

# CHAPTER EIGHT

"What's up with you today?" Cassie asked Danielle at work the next day. "Your body is here, but your head is definitely on vacation."

"Sorry." Danielle looked at the candy cane border she was putting up around a bulletin board. It was upside down. "Did I just do that?"

"Yes. And you did the elves, too. But I wasn't going to mention it."

Sure enough, Santa's elves were on their heads; one was even floating above the Christmas tree.

"Oops." Danielle couldn't help but laugh. "Guess I'm not concentrating."

"So, who's the guy?" Cassie asked, removing the elves.

"Guy?" Danielle asked innocently. "What guy?"

"Danielle, please." Cassie rolled her eyes. "There's only one thing that causes people to have such a goofy expression on their face and turn their mind to mush. You're in love."

"No, I'm not," Danielle quickly denied, aghast. She'd only met Carson twice; how could she possibly be in love with someone that quickly?

Cassie snorted, "You are so in love with this guy, you're loopy-eyed. But then—" Cassie studied her closely, as if she were reading a subconscious message behind Danielle's eyes, "—it is possible that you didn't know it yourself until now."

Feeling herself blush, Danielle shook her head. "Really, Cassie," she said, not daring to meet her coworker's eyes.

"Fine, don't tell me." Cassie shrugged. "But you can't hide how your heart feels. It's written all over your face." She handed Danielle the cardboard elves, leaving her alone with her thoughts.

Was it written all over her face? she wondered. Then why hadn't she seen it that morning in the mirror?

In love with Carson? Impossible.

***

"I'm so excited to see Lucy in this play," Danielle said as she led the girls in her Laurel class to their seats. "I can't believe she has the lead. Why didn't she say something?"

"That's Lucy," Chloe said. "She never talks about herself." Chloe waved to a friend who was already seated. "I'll be right back," she told Danielle, which left Danielle with McCall, who, even though she was with them, wasn't very excited about it. Danielle thought she even seemed a little embarrassed about it. In contrast, the other two girls in her class, Erin and Allie, were nice, regular girls. Girls Danielle could relate to and carry on a conversation with.

"I'm going to the bathroom," McCall announced as the others took their seats.

Danielle looked at her pained expression, wondering if it was really so awful to go somewhere with people outside her popular circle of friends. "The play's about to start," she reminded the girl.

McCall left without answering, and Danielle sighed. As far as she knew, McCall was a good girl, didn't get into trouble, and was liked by her peers, but her attitude of superiority really bothered Danielle. She really enjoyed the other girls in her Laurel class. They were fun, sweet, and friendly. But McCall didn't even try to give her a chance.

"Danielle." Erin nudged her with her elbow. "See that guy over there by the stage?"

Danielle looked over to see a boy adjusting the speakers for the performance. "Yeah."

"That's who Lucy likes. His name is Jake Gibson," Erin explained.

"He's cute," Danielle remarked. The kid was tall and kind of skinny, but he had a nice smile. "Does he like Lucy?"

Erin shrugged. "She'd die if he knew she liked him. But the Christmas dance is coming up, and it would be so cool if he'd ask her. She's never been to any school dances before."

Danielle's heart went out to Lucy. She was a senior and had never been to a school dance?

The lights dimmed and music played as the curtain opened.

The play was a light musical comedy, almost like a fairy tale with a Cinderella spin, but without the fairy godmother and magic. Danielle watched in awe as Lucy's stage presence held the audience captivated. Her comical timing was impeccable and she delivered every line with the perfect punch designed to make the audience laugh. Her speech and carriage on stage were those of a confident, self-assured person, one whom Danielle had never seen. She couldn't believe this was the same girl. Did Lucy have a twin?

At the turning point of the play, when Lucy's character was completely down and out, feeling as if the world had forgotten her, Lucy stopped the show by singing a song about the night being cold, dark, and lonely. Her words of loneliness and heartache filled the room. With all the power of a Broadway star, she belted out the lyrics, singing like there was no hope of tomorrow. Then she collapsed dramatically into a heap on the stage.

The audience exploded with applause. Even McCall, who'd finally joined them during the first act, was on her feet with the rest of the crowd, cheering and whistling their astonishment and approval. Lucy was brilliantly talented and musically gifted. Danielle was blown away.

Near the end, two male leads tried to decide who *had* to take Lucy to the ball. Because she wasn't the prettiest girl to choose from, neither of them wanted to take her. They ended up paying one of their friends to ask her.

Finally the scene arrived when Lucy and her date entered the ball. The entire audience gasped in surprise. In *My Fair Lady* fashion, Lucy stepped through the door looking as stunning as Audrey Hepburn herself. Again the audience, rooting for Lucy, went crazy. The look on the two male leads' faces said it all . . . why hadn't they asked her to the dance?

Of course, everything worked out in the end. Lucy's date gave the money back to the two other boys, declaring that his prize was Lucy and that those who deserve happiness get it. Those who are selfish live with regret for their actions.

A simple story, it nevertheless contained true principles. Danielle thought the play was boring in spots and for the most part, an amateur production. But Lucy's performance made it an unforgettable night. She received a standing ovation and a large bouquet of roses at the end.

As soon as it was over, Danielle and her four Laurels went back stage to find Lucy. Danielle was glad she'd brought a bouquet of flowers to give Lucy from all of them. But she wished she had more. Lucy had been spectacular and Danielle wanted to let her know it.

It took nearly twenty minutes for the crowd around Lucy to die down enough for Danielle and the girls to get near her. Flushed from the excitement of a performance well done, Lucy looked positively radiant.

"Lucy, you were wonderful!" Danielle exclaimed when she finally got close to her. Danielle gave Lucy a hug and held out the flowers. "I had no idea you were so talented. I'm so impressed and we're all so proud of you."

"I'm glad you liked it," Lucy said, obviously pleased. "Thanks for coming."

The other Laurels crowded around, telling her how much they loved the play. Happy to see them so friendly and supportive, Danielle stepped back to give some other well-wishers a chance to congratulate Lucy. Then, noticing someone standing off to the side, she looked over to see Jake Gibson watching the commotion. She inched her way over to him, hoping she didn't regret what she was about to do.

"Aren't you one of the stage hands?" she asked.

He looked at her, a little surprised that she'd spoken to him. "Uh, yeah, I am," he answered.

"You guys did a great job tonight. The play was wonderful."

"Thanks," he said shoving his hands into his pockets and looking down at his feet.

*No wonder they aren't together,* Danielle thought. *He's as shy as she is.*

"Lucy sure did a good job, didn't she?" Danielle commented, watching his reaction.

He looked over at Lucy, still surrounded by a swarm of people. "Yeah, she's awesome."

"I'm her Laurel advisor," Danielle continued, watching him closely. She had to word things just right. "She sure is a sweet girl. It's hard to believe someone as wonderful as Lucy doesn't have a date to the Christmas dance."

"She doesn't?" he said anxiously, then quickly looked away.

"Nope," Danielle said, shaking her head as if she just couldn't believe it. "Hey, your name isn't Jake, is it? Jake Gibson?"

"Yeah," he said. "It is Jake."

Nodding, Danielle said, "She's talked about you." *Not to me, but that doesn't really matter.*

Startled, Jake looked at Danielle. "She has?"

"Oh, yes," Danielle said, letting the words settle for a moment before she asked. "So who are you taking to the dance?"

"Me?" He nearly choked on the word. "Uh, no one. I haven't got a date."

Danielle wanted to shake him. *Well, what are you waiting for, stupid!*

"You know," Danielle said, "some lucky boy is sure missing a chance to take a really nice girl to the dance." *Do I have to spell it out for you, Jake?*

"Gee," he said, seeming to finally get the drift. "Do you think she'd go with me?"

Danielle looked surprised and thoughtful. "You know," she said, "I think she would."

He looked over at Lucy again, his face full of longing.

"But I wouldn't put off asking her," Danielle warned. "You wouldn't want someone to beat you to it."

"You mean, tonight? Ask her right now?" He looked like a deer caught in a pair of headlights.

"I would, if I were you," Danielle tried to inject a hint of warning in her voice.

He nodded, suddenly understanding. "Okay," he said, still nodding. "Hey, thanks."

He pushed his way into the crowd, and Danielle said a quick prayer for him that he wouldn't lose his nerve. Lucy would really feel like Cinderella if she was asked to the dance tonight.

The next day was Earl Camden's birthday and Danielle's mother always made a huge fuss over him. In the past, Danielle used to see her parents' relationship as cheesy and annoying. But lately, she found herself yearning for the same tender, nurturing kind of love in her own life.

Miranda and Rachel and their families came for dinner as did the Camden's new neighbors, Dieter and Hilde Vollman, an elderly couple from Germany, who had spoken in church the week before. Danielle recalled that Brother Vollman was a retired doctor and his wife had taught English in Germany. Their daughters had married Americans and settled in the Salt Lake Valley, so the Vollmans had decided to relocate to Utah to be closer to them and to their grandchildren.

After dinner, the men adjourned to the family room to watch a ball game on television, and the women talked as they cleared the dinner dishes. Miranda worried aloud about her daughter, Ashlyn, who was going to school in southern Utah and studying journalism.

"She's having a hard time deciding what to do with her life," Miranda said honestly.

Boy, if anyone could relate, Danielle could. "I need to give her a call," she said. She wasn't all that much older than Ashlyn, and the two girls had been close growing up.

"She'd like that," Miranda said. "She can tell you all about her new boyfriend. She says things are getting serious between them."

Danielle didn't say anything but couldn't help thinking what it would be like to have her younger niece get married before her.

Miranda turned the conversation to include the Camden's German guests. "How did you and your husband meet, Sister Vollman?" she asked.

"Ach, my dear, many years ago, before the war, I was a young schoolgirl, and Dieter was getting ready to begin his studies at the University. Our brothers were good friends. Then war broke out and he was called into the service. I wasn't sure I'd ever see him again."

"My goodness, it's hard to believe you lived in Germany during the war. That must have been awful," Dorothy Camden exclaimed.

"I saw my entire neighborhood leveled by bombs," Sister Vollman told them. "We lost everything. But my family survived and we knew the Lord watched out for us. We had each other and the gospel and that was all that mattered. The Lord protected my Dieter, too. He came home to me after the war and we were married. Now enough about me," she said, looking at Rachel. "You are expecting your baby soon, *ja?*" she asked.

Danielle loved the woman's cute accent and had especially liked the German chocolate bars they'd brought as a gift for her father's birthday. She made a mental note to make sure they somehow found out when her birthday was.

"December twenty-second," Rachel answered. "But I'm hoping this one comes early, like my other three did." The mother of three adorable girls, Rachel was happily expecting her fourth baby. She was so excited she even enjoyed morning sickness because she knew that meant the baby was growing and healthy.

"How did your ultrasound go?" Miranda asked. "You went in yesterday, didn't you?"

"Yes. It went great. Everything looks good," Rachel said, resting her hand on her stomach.

"Did you find out what you're having?" Miranda asked.

"No. We still want it to be a surprise," Rachel said firmly. Her sisters had badgered her constantly to find out what she was having so they could shop for the new baby.

"I don't understand this," Danielle said. "What's the big deal? Think of all the great sales you're missing just because you don't want to find out the sex of your baby."

"Doug and I decided we don't want to know until the baby arrives. I don't know why exactly, but we just feel that way. I'm sorry if that inconveniences you," she said pointedly to Danielle. "Besides, it doesn't matter. We'd be thrilled to have a son, especially Doug, but I would love to have four daughters, too. We're happy either way."

"What names have you been thinking about?" Miranda asked.

While Rachel ticked off a list of names, Danielle's thoughts drifted as she continued to clear the table. She wondered what Carson was doing. Was he too busy with school to think of her? When would she see him again?

"What do you think, Danielle?" Rachel asked.

Danielle looked up from rinsing dinner plates and silverware. "About what?"

"About the name Bradford," Miranda said.

"For a boy," Rachel added.

"Uhhh," she shrugged. "It's okay."

Rachel shook her head. "You've been acting funny all night. What's going on?"

"Nothing," Danielle replied, knowing she had to put on an Oscar-winning performance. Her sister Rachel was as nosey as they came. If she sensed something was up, she wouldn't stop digging until she knew the whole story. "I've just had a lot going on at work, that's all." It wasn't a lie, she thought. She did have a lot going on at work.

Temporarily satisfied, the other two sisters listened as Sister Vollman explained why they didn't have German chocolate cake over in Germany like they were having for her father's birthday tonight. Danielle finished loading the dishwasher while her mother wiped off the table, then set the lavishly decorated birthday cake on the table.

When Danielle called the men in for cake, her nephew Adam jumped to his feet. He was at least six foot three and all stomach. She'd never seen a human put away food like he did. Right behind him came Garrett, his stepfather, then Rachel's husband, Doug. Brother Vollman and Earl Camden brought up the rear. Rachel's three daughters, who had been playing a board game, ran to the kitchen like a shot.

As family and friends sang happy birthday to him, Danielle's father beamed with pride at his lovely wife of forty-four years, his three lovely daughters, and their families. Everyone applauded as he blew out the candles, and Miranda started scooping ice cream while her mother served the cake.

The doorbell rang in the middle of the celebration, and Rachel answered it.

"Danielle," she called in a syrupy sweet voice. "It's for you. It's a boy."

Danielle wanted to die. Why did Rachel of all people have to answer the door? Quickly she went to the door, wondering who it could be.

"Carson!" she exclaimed when she saw him standing on the porch. "Hi."

"It sounds like I came at a bad time," he said, embarrassed.

"Not at all. We're just having a birthday party for my dad," Danielle explained, not wanting him to leave but not knowing how to put him at ease with her sister Rachel looking curiously at the both of them.

Carson stepped back. "I'll let you get back to it then," he excused himself.

"Why don't you invite him in?" Rachel asked, then belatedly left them alone.

Danielle looked at him, trying to read his expression. Would he be uncomfortable? Would her family do anything to embarrass her? Her father liked to tease, and Adam had been known to burp without warning. Rachel always managed to embarrass her, as she'd already so aptly done. Nevertheless, she decided to throw caution to the wind. "Would you like to join us?" she asked.

"I don't want to impose," he said hesitantly.

"Carson, it's no imposition at all. I'd really like it if you did." A burst of laughter came from the other room, punctuating her invitation, then, hearing Miranda scold her son for taking such a big piece of cake, Danielle grinned. "C'mon," she said persuasively. "My mom makes a killer German chocolate cake with the best coconut pecan frosting."

She saw the look in his eye change. "Coconut pecan frosting?" he asked, licking his lips hungrily.

"She doubles the recipe so it's really thick," Danielle added.

"Okay," he agreed. "If you're sure I'm not imposing."

Everyone looked up when Danielle and Carson entered the room.

"This is Carson Turner," she introduced. "And this," she pointed to her father, "is my father, the birthday boy, Earl Camden."

Carson stepped forward and shook Earl's hand. "Nice to meet you. Happy birthday, Mr. Camden."

"Nice to meet you, Carson. Pull up a chair," Earl invited him easily.

Danielle was delighted to see how her family pulled him right into their circle. Dorothy gave Carson a giant piece of cake with frosting oozing down the sides and an enormous scoop of ice cream. After savoring a bite, he complimented Danielle's mother, saying that his mother had made him German chocolate cake for his birthdays when he was growing up. Rachel, of course, felt it her duty to explain what Sister Vollman had said earlier about their not having German chocolate cake in Germany. Though Americans might use chocolate from Germany to flavor the cake, Germans never made coconut pecan frosting.

Between Rachel, Miranda, and her mother, Carson was forced to tell his life story, from birth to the present. Danielle knew more about Carson after fifteen minutes with her sisters than she'd learned in the hours she'd spent with him.

"What did your mother die of, Carson?" Dorothy asked him.

"Ovarian cancer," he answered.

"How awful," Dorothy said. "I'm so sorry."

"Thank you." He shifted uncomfortably in his chair.

Coming to his rescue, Danielle decided to change the subject. "Adam's waiting for his mission call. His birthday is January twentieth."

"That's wonderful," Carson said. "I'll bet you're getting excited."

"Carson went to Thailand on his mission," Danielle told him.

"How did you like it?" Earl asked.

"I loved it," Carson said. "I plan on going back after I get my medical degree. I want to find a way to help them improve their current health conditions."

The conversation split as part of the group talked about Adam's mission call and the other part talked about the University's football team. Miranda's husband, Garrett, was an English professor at the "U" and Miranda was working on her bachelor's degree in English.

When everyone had finished, Rachel gathered together her three daughters, Hillary, Holly, Hailey, and her husband. It was getting late and the girls had school in the morning. Adam and Garrett wanted to see the end of the ball game, which naturally pulled her father back into the family room.

"Would you like to watch the ball game?" Danielle asked Carson.

"Sure," he said, then excused himself to use the bathroom first.

The Vollmans announced that they needed to be getting on home. They were "early to bed, early to rise" type of people and it was getting late. By the time all the good nights had been exchanged and the Vollmans had left, Carson had returned, joining Danielle and the others in front of the television. In the final seconds of the game, one team pulled from behind, scoring a touchdown as the buzzer sounded, and the room exploded with cheers.

As Garrett, Miranda, and Adam grabbed their coats and said their good-byes, Carson said he needed to get home as well since he still had some studying to do. Danielle walked him to his car, an older model Jeep Cherokee.

"Thanks for the cake and ice cream. You have a really great family," he said. "But next time I'll call before I just drop in like that."

"I'm glad you came by," Danielle said. "You're welcome anytime, Carson. I mean it."

"Really?" His expression, in the glare of the streetlight, seemed one of surprise.

She tilted her head and studied him for a moment. She had never been known for being shy or keeping her feelings to herself and she wasn't about to start now. She wasn't the type to play games and guess someone's intentions.

"Can I ask you something?" she finally said.

"Sure." He leaned against his car.

"Last Christmas you said you would call me, but I never heard from you. Why not?"

"Well," he said slowly, "I actually did try to call you. I called once while I was still in town, but you were out, then I called from school a few weeks later. You weren't home then either."

*So those calls had been from him.*

"I wasn't sure you really wanted to talk to me, especially after my father let you go. And when I never caught you at home, I just thought maybe you were just too busy dating and stuff. So I gave up."

*Dating and stuff. Was he joking?* She laughed out loud. "Dating and stuff?" she repeated.

He looked both surprised and amused at her outburst. "Yeah. I'm sure you don't sit around much."

"Oh, no. Not me," she laughed again, thinking, *If you only knew.* Then she added, "Carson, it was your father who let me go from my job, not you. I wasn't mad at you," she said emphatically, "although I sure wasn't thrilled with your dad."

"I wasn't either," he admitted. "In fact, my father and I had an argument and I ended up going back to school before Christmas. I tried to call you those two times, but I picked up the phone to call you a lot of times after that. I'd dial the phone but hang up before it started to ring."

Danielle smiled. "You did?"

"Yeah," he smiled, a little embarrassedly. "I did."

"I'm glad to hear that you tried to call me," she said. "Because I felt bad we didn't get to see each other again."

His eyes softened. "I'm sorry. I didn't mean to make you feel bad."

His words caused Danielle to consider the previous Christmas in a new light—from Carson's perspective. "That must have been a pretty crummy Christmas for you," she said, "all alone at school. You two must have had some argument." She was curious what they'd argued about.

"It was," he said, nodding, "but I couldn't sit by and let my father do what he did without at least telling him what I thought."

"You mean, for laying everyone off?" Danielle thought that was pretty decent of Carson, since, after all, it didn't affect him personally.

Carson's voice was even. "I couldn't believe he actually did that right before Christmas. All the feelings and resentment I'd been holding in for years finally broke the surface and I told him exactly what I thought. We haven't spoken since."

Danielle was shocked. "You haven't talked to your father since then? That's almost a whole year."

Danielle remembered Carson saying his father wouldn't support him if he chose to study medicine and she wondered how he had made it so far. "How are you able to do it financially? Where are you living?" she asked, concerned.

"I'm living with the family of an old mission companion. They have a room in their basement they're letting me use for now. Plus I had some money of my own from my mother." He shrugged.

Danielle studied his face, trying to uncover Carson's feelings about his father. "You know he's having to sell his business, don't you?"

"Yeah, I know," he said, with no discernible expression.

Danielle couldn't believe it. "Don't you want to call him, just to tell him what you're doing, and see how he is?"

Carson shook his head. "No. It's better this way. He controlled my life for twenty-six years, and I'm finally free of that. He's a bitter, cruel, old man who thinks that money will make him happy and that he can buy friends and loyalty and even family. I've seen him crush people beneath him like ants under his shoe. I don't want to have anything to do with a person like that. He tried to turn me into something I don't want to be, someone I could never become."

Danielle didn't know what to say. She sympathized with his pain, but had no words of wisdom, no answers or solutions for him. His emotions were strong and complicated, and she'd never known anyone like him or experienced anything like this.

She looked at him, wanting to say something, and as if he could see her helplessness, he said, "I know it's hard for you to understand, but I feel no need to call him."

The hard edge in his voice didn't sound like him, she thought, looking at him as if seeing a stranger. She believed that Carson was genuine and kind. But talking about his father brought out a harsh, cold side of him.

"I've tried my entire life to gain his approval," he went on, sensing that she didn't know what to make of his coldness. "I did everything he ever asked of me and still, I didn't measure up. I've finally figured out that he'll never think I'm good enough, no matter what I do. You can't imagine how much pressure that's taken off of me. I don't have to worry about being first in my class anymore, about measuring up to some impossible standard. My life is so much better without him constantly hounding me to try harder and do better."

"That must have been awful," Danielle agreed. "It must make you miss your mother even more."

He nodded slowly. "We were very close. If I have any good qualities, I got them from her."

"She must have been a pretty incredible woman," Danielle told him sincerely.

Carson looked at her, a smile growing on his face. "Thanks," he said. "I think you're pretty incredible yourself."

Now it was Danielle's turn to smile. "Thanks," she said.

A chilling wind kicked up, and Danielle shivered and crossed her arms in front of her to keep warm.

"You're freezing out here. You'd better get inside," Carson said.

She hated to see him go. There was so much she wanted to know about him still, so much she wanted to learn. He'd finally opened up to her, and she didn't want it to end. But he was already fishing his keys out of his pocket. The moment was gone, for now. "I'm glad you came by tonight," was all she said.

"Me too," he said. "The cake was really delicious." He reached out and took her hand. "And thanks for listening, Danielle. You must think I come from a pretty messed-up family."

"Not at all," she murmured, enjoying how his long fingers wrapped securely around her hand.

"I'll call you sometime," he offered. "Maybe we could catch a movie or something."

"I'd like that," she said, trying not to sound too eager.

"Good night, then," he said, giving her hand a squeeze, lingering just a moment.

Their gazes connected and they inched in closer together. Danielle's heartbeat sped up. Would he kiss her? Then a car drove into the cul-de-sac, its lights shining on them like a spotlight on a stage. Both stepped back, watching as the car drove around the circle before pulling back out onto the street and turning the other direction.

"Well, I'd better take off," Carson said. "Thanks again."

"G'night, Carson," Danielle said as he opened the door and climbed inside the Jeep. She waved good-bye and watched him drive off into the night.

Even though the wind was icy cold, Danielle felt warm inside.

# CHAPTER
## ❦ NINE ❦

It was all Danielle could do to walk back in the house. She didn't want to face the barrage of questions from her parents she knew would come. But to her relief, the only thing her mother said was, "Carson's a nice boy. I like him."

"Thanks, Mom." Danielle wanted to hurry to her room before her mother decided she wanted a few more answers, but Dorothy Camden's next words stopped her cold.

"He passed the test, you know."

Danielle looked at her mom with surprise. "What test?" she asked suspiciously. Criminy, what had her mother done to test him?

"When he used the bathroom."

What? Had her mom flipped?

"He put the lid down when he was finished," she explained. "I think there is nothing more inconsiderate than for a man to leave the seat up. I know it's a small thing for most people, but to me it's important. It says a lot about the person. Carson's mother must have taught him well."

Danielle shook her head in disbelief and laughed. "I've never thought about it."

"Of course not," her mother said. "Your father puts down the seat and you grew up with sisters."

All that night the wind howled. Tree branches beat against Danielle's window, but that wasn't what kept her awake. She couldn't get Carson off her mind. She couldn't deny she was strongly attracted to him. He was warm, witty, and intelligent. His testimony was strong and he knew exactly what he wanted out of life and had the drive and desire to go after it.

But how could he completely cut off all contact with his father? The only other living member of his family? Granted, it wasn't any of her business. Still, she couldn't stop thinking about it. Maybe it was the fact that he could be so cold. If she ever made him mad, would he be unable to forgive her as well?

She had no idea what it had been like for Carson growing up. But as awful as Philip Turner was, he was still Carson's father. Carson said he had no grandparents, no aunts or uncles or cousins. Distant relatives, yes, but Philip Turner had managed to offend or alienate them from their lives. They were all each other had.

Danielle had never walked in Carson's shoes, but she knew that his resentment and bitterness would eventually canker his soul. He would have to work this out.

Maybe he just needed time. Time to distance himself and soften. But it had already been nearly a year, and his feelings seemed so strong and unyielding.

She knew it wasn't her place to interfere, but she also knew Carson's relationship with his father wouldn't heal unless he made some attempt to build a bridge between himself and his father. Even if that bridge were only one of courtesy.

In some strange way Danielle felt as though she and Carson had been brought together again after so long for a reason. But what reason could that be? Was she supposed to help Carson?

Yes, her heart told her.

But how?

⚜

The next day everyone at Creative Display was in a festive mood. Spicy cinnamon-scented candles burned and Vincent played Christmas music nonstop, singing along with it at the top of his lungs. Even the customers left humming Christmas carols.

After work Cassie and Danielle worked on the Christmas tree. The Jubilee of Trees was scheduled to open the day after

Thanksgiving, which gave them three weeks to finish their project. Her Laurels had helped a great deal. She didn't know how she could have done it without them.

"These wooden people you painted are perfect," Danielle said, referring to Cassie's creations that crowned the top of the tree. In addition to the tole-painted family members, there were little hand-carts and pioneer items. Moving down the tree, depression-era items like phonographs and vintage automobiles were hung, then memorabilia depicting each era until, at the bottom of the tree were modern-day items. The tree told a story, showing how the couple at the top, a husband and wife, were responsible for an entire family tree, filled with history. It was also filled with love, represented by shiny red hearts interspersed throughout the rest of the ornaments.

"Makes you want to dig out your grandfather's journal and read it, doesn't it?" Cassie said as she stepped back to admire their work.

"Darlings, darlings," Vincent said as he entered the back storage room where they worked. He gasped when he saw the tree. "Oh my goodness, I had no idea you were almost done. It's brilliant, stunning, breathtaking," he praised, laying one hand on his chest as if his heart would stop. "I'm moved to tears." He wiped at his eyes.

Cassie and Danielle looked at each other. They were used to Vincent getting choked up. He was passionate about everything. He was also sincere and Danielle was touched.

"I'm so glad you like it," Danielle said, hanging one last tiny picture frame containing an antique photograph.

"Like it?" he said, "I love it." He embraced Danielle and kissed her on the cheek, then did the same for Cassie. "This tree will steal the show. Abby's coming in later; I know she'll want to see it."

"It's nothing fancy," Danielle said. "I mean, it's not as fancy and glittery as some of the other trees."

"But this one speaks to you. It reaches out and grabs your heart. Mark my words, it will get the highest bid of the evening, I've no doubt," he promised.

"I hope so," Danielle said. "It's for a great cause." She knew the money could help a lot of sick children and that made the time she'd spent on the tree worthwhile. She'd already received so much enjoyment just working on it.

Her mother and father had always set an example of service for her and her sisters. They'd recently completed a full-time mission at Temple Square in Salt Lake City, which had given them a chance to further their opportunities to serve. Stories of the many people they'd reached out to, and the lives they had changed, had helped Danielle understand the importance of giving to others. Before, she'd always rationalized to herself, that it was easier for an old retired couple to serve. They didn't have anything else to do. Danielle, on the other hand, was busy trying to carve out her life, trying to make sense of this set of circumstances the Lord had given her, and make a worthwhile and fulfilling existence out of it. There never seemed to be time for service projects.

But she was learning. If it was important enough, somehow she would make time.

As closing time came and went, Danielle was left to work on the tree alone.

"Hey, Danielle," Chloe announced their arrival as she and Lucy walked into the back room.

"Hi, you guys. I didn't know you were coming." Danielle stopped what she was doing to greet the girls. One look at Lucy's face and she knew something good had happened. She hoped it meant what she thought it did. "So, what's new?" she asked, looking at Lucy, who smiled, but didn't say anything.

Finally, Chloe couldn't stand it any longer. Nearly bursting at the seams, she blurted, "Lucy got asked to the Christmas dance!"

Lucy's face shone nearly as bright as the Christmas tree.

"You did? That's great." Danielle hugged her. "Who's the lucky guy?"

"His name is Jake Gibson. He's in the drama club with me," Lucy explained.

Danielle smiled inwardly. "Well, congratulations. I'm so happy for you. When did he ask you?"

"This morning. He borrowed a pair of my shoes and left them on the doorstep filled with Hershey's kisses, with a card that said, 'I would kiss your feet if you'd go to the dance with me,'" Lucy giggled as she told them.

"Well, that's clever," Danielle commented, though she was upset with Jake for putting it off and risking having someone else ask Lucy.

Still, she was glad he'd fussed over Lucy, who was obviously beside herself with excitement over it.

"Danielle?" Lucy asked timidly. "Do you think, um, well, would you mind helping me get ready for the dance?" Lucy's mother had passed away four years earlier, which perhaps explained why the girl didn't have a real polished way about her with no sisters or a mother at home to help her.

"I'd love to!" Danielle exclaimed. "Not that I'm much of a beauty specimen myself."

"I can help," Chloe said. "I haven't got a date for the dance. And I've got a dress you could borrow that would look so pretty on you, if you want to come to my house after we're finished here and try it on."

"Chloe, really?" Lucy beamed. "I'd love to."

Danielle guessed money wasn't abundant at their home either.

"My sister Rachel can help us with your hair and makeup," Danielle offered. "She loves stuff like this. You should see her girls when they have dance recitals."

"Thank you, Danielle," Lucy said, with a tremor of emotion in her voice. "I'm so glad they made you my advisor." She hugged Danielle.

Growing warm inside, Danielle patted her on the back. "You know what? I'm glad they did too."

Chloe and Lucy left at seven-thirty since both had homework and Lucy wanted to stop at Chloe's to try on the dress. Danielle left shortly after that since she'd made plans to meet Roberta at eight for a late dinner.

The November evening held the promise of a morning frost. Danielle nudged the heater to high inside her car and headed for the Hard Rock Café in downtown Salt Lake City.

Roberta was full of news about her job at Worldwide Travel. "Sister Armstrong says I'm ready to start training, and she wants me to start doing some traveling," she announced proudly.

"Gosh." Danielle couldn't help feeling a tinge of jealousy—not so much for Roberta's job but for the opportunity to travel. "That's really great, Roberta."

As if she could read Danielle's thoughts, Roberta suggested that a receptionist would be needed soon and she could recommend Danielle to Sister Armstrong. Danielle shook her head, appreciative as always of Roberta's thoughtfulness, but she knew she was where she needed to be.

"I'm not ready to make any changes yet," she said, "but I have to admit, I would love to go on some of those trips with you." She tried to remember the last time she'd gone anywhere fun, but she couldn't.

After the waiter had taken their order, Roberta asked how Danielle's tree was coming.

"It's pretty much done," Danielle explained. "Doing this tree has been such a great experience. Just the thought of helping those little kids who are too poor to pay for medical care . . ." She looked at Roberta, inarticulate for a moment, then continued simply, "It's just neat to know I can help them. I don't know how to thank the people at your dad's office for their donations. Without them I couldn't have done it."

Roberta's eyes lit up. "Listen," she said. "Here's another idea. Every year my dad's company helps sponsor Thanksgiving dinner for the homeless. I just talked to my dad today, and he wanted to know if I would volunteer to help. We could go together."

"Help? How?" Danielle was skeptical. Giving aid to sick children was much different than hanging out with vagabonds and crazy people.

"Like helping prepare the meal, then serving, that kind of thing," Roberta explained. "I told him I would. But it would be even more fun if you were there."

Danielle was hesitant. Her family ate Thanksgiving dinner early because Rachel always had to go to her in-laws' house that day, too. But Roberta assured Danielle she'd be home by two o'clock.

"There aren't very many people signed up. We could really use your help," she said in her most persuasive manner. "I talked to a couple of girls who went last year, and they said it was a really neat experience."

Danielle was quiet, thinking. Then she had an idea. She could get her Laurels to come, too. Maybe if she had spent a little time herself as a youth serving others and giving her time and effort to others, she might have learned this lesson a lot sooner. And she could think of one Laurel especially who needed a good experience with service. This might be exactly what McCall needed to help her count her blessings.

The waiter came with their food, and as the two girls ate, they moved on to other topics of discussion. First Bart's sprained ankle, then Lenny and Roberta, and finally, Carson Turner.

"You really like him, don't you?" Roberta said slyly.

Danielle shrugged. "I think he's nice."

"Nice schmice. You are *so* flipped over him," Roberta insisted. "You should see your face right now. It's as red as that marinara sauce on your plate."

"Okay, so I like him," she confessed. "That doesn't mean anything."

"Maybe not, but it's still exciting. I mean, Carson is gorgeous and smart and rich. He's a complete package—everything you could ever want. He's like the a whole meal deal, supersized!"

Danielle grimaced as Roberta dramatically described Bart's devastation upon learning that Danielle's heart was otherwise engaged and he hadn't a prayer with her.

"He's going to be so disappointed," Roberta concluded. "He wanted to invite you to go skiing with us in Sun Valley. His dad rented a condo and said he could bring some friends."

"Skiing? Sun Valley?" Danielle was torn. She loved Sun Valley. "Well, maybe I'm being too hasty about Bart," she hedged. "We were only at the dance together for a little while."

Roberta nodded sagely. "I see. So you *would* be interested in going out with him."

"No, I'm really not," Danielle was honest enough to admit. "I'm interested in skiing at Sun Valley. I think Bart's a nice guy and that we could probably be friends. I'm just not attracted to him."

"But he's such a neat guy," Roberta insisted, "and I think he's so cute. I bet once you get to know him, you'll think so, too."

"Roberta, I said I'd go already," Danielle said, smiling at Roberta's enthusiasm.

"Good!" Roberta smiled. "It'll be a lot more fun if you come. And Bart will be thrilled."

They shared dessert, then left the restaurant. Danielle hoped she wasn't making a mistake by going with Bart, but it wasn't as if she and Carson were going steady, she told herself. She didn't even know when she'd see him again. Certainly she wasn't about to sit around by the phone twiddling her thumbs, waiting for him to call.

But every night after work, that's exactly what she did.

# CHAPTER
## ❧ TEN ❧

It was nearly two weeks, on the Saturday before Thanksgiving, before Danielle finally heard from Carson. He apologized for not calling earlier, but he'd been swamped with school. Now he was utterly burned out from studying and wondered if she wanted to go do something with him. They decided to go ice skating.

It was early enough in the day that the rink wasn't crowded. Hand in hand, they skated around the oval rink, laughing at Danielle's wobbly ankles and lack of experience on the ice. He'd played hockey in high school; she'd only been skating twice before.

"So, what are your plans for Thanksgiving?" she asked. She'd already asked her mother if it was okay to invite Carson to their house for the holiday, and of course, Dorothy was all for it. But then, she was all for anything that brought Danielle closer to a relationship with a man that might lead to marriage.

"The family I live with invited me to have dinner with them," he said, holding her tightly as they rounded a corner. "They have family in Ogden and asked me to go with them."

"Oh," she said, disappointedly. She'd been looking forward to being with him that day. At the same time, she was tempted to suggest that he and his father should be spending the holidays together, but she restrained herself.

"Why? What are you doing?" he asked, steadying her when she wobbled.

"We're just having dinner at our house, but I wanted to invite you to eat with us," she tried to speak casually.

"You were? Gee thanks, but I've already told them I'd be coming with them. Thanks for asking though." Was that a note of regret in his voice? Danielle hoped so.

"Well, if anything happens, you've got a backup invitation . . ." Danielle's voice trailed off as she tried to concentrate on keeping her ankles straight. The rink was growing increasingly crowded as swarms of kids arrived, darting across the slick surface. A trio of boys zoomed by nearly knocking Danielle to the ground.

"You in the mood for some hot chocolate?" Carson offered.

"I'd love some," she said with relief. "Besides, I feel like I'm going to be used for a hockey puck out here if I don't get off the ice soon."

Over hot chocolate and a bag of Cheetos from the vending machine, they talked about Carson's classes and his school work. He asked how her Christmas tree was coming, and she invited him to come see it.

⁂

"You can open your eyes now," Danielle said as she plugged in the Christmas tree. She'd turned out the lights in the back room so the only light came from the tree. Carson stood inside the darkened room with his eyes closed. With the door to the room shut, they could barely hear the Christmas music and the voices of the those working out front.

"Oh, wow," he said. "Danielle, this is incredible." He stepped up closer and studied the tree for several minutes. Danielle watched his reaction, her chest swelling a little with the pride of a job well done. It wasn't going to be the most spectacular tree in the lineup but it was meaningful to her.

He shook his head, "I can't believe how much work you've put into this."

"I've had a lot of help." She stepped up beside him and slipped her hand into his. They stood together in the twinkling light of the Christmas tree and remained silent for a moment.

"It's wonderful. You've done a great job." He turned toward her and took her other hand in his. "I didn't realize you were so talented."

"That's understandable," she smiled. "Because I'm not."

"Obviously, that's not true," he chuckled and pulled her a little closer.

Her heartbeat quickened its pace. "But it's okay if you want to believe that."

"I feel bad I can't have Thanksgiving dinner with you," he apologized. "Would you want to get together that evening? We'll be back around six o'clock or so." He looked down at her upturned face, the gap between them gradually narrowing.

Danielle's eyes lit up. "I'd like that. I'll save you some of my mom's pumpkin pie. She makes the best."

"Thanks," he murmured. There was barely a whisper of space between them.

Danielle could barely breathe. "You're wel—"

His kiss cut her off in mid-sentence, but she didn't care. It was sweet and delicate, and sent her pulse soaring. And when the kiss ended, he held her in his arms a moment longer.

"Mmm," he said softly, his chin resting on the top of her head. "I don't think her pie could be any better than that."

"Not even close," Danielle said. "Even with whipped cream."

A commotion outside the room caught their attention. Something was going on, and Vincent was clearly excited. The mood was broken, the moment gone, but the memory of Carson's first kiss lingered in Danielle's heart and mind and on her lips. When they emerged from the back room, they found Vincent beside himself with glee.

"What's going on?" Danielle asked Cassie, whose face was also bright with the excitement.

"The governor's office just called and asked Vincent to decorate the mansion for the holidays. They had someone else lined up, but they had to cancel at the last minute, and someone recommended Creative Display for the job."

"Isn't it wonderful?" Vincent danced about gleefully. "Me, decorating the mansion." He threw his arms in the air and spun around. "I have to get to work, and I'm going to need you girls to help me. I'll work on the plan this weekend, and we'll get started first thing Monday morning."

"What about the Jubilee of Trees? How are you going to do both?" Cassie asked, her brow furrowed with concern.

"Abby's got everything under control," he assured her. He paced back and forth like a wind-up toy, thinking. "I need a theme, something different, something new. Cancel all my appointments for the rest of the afternoon, Cass, and reschedule them for next week. I'm going to need some time to work on this."

"I'll get right on it," Cassie said.

Vincent stopped in mid-stride. "And who is this?" he asked, looking at Danielle and Carson.

"This is Carson Turner. He's a friend of mine," Danielle introduced the two men.

"Very nice to meet you, Carson," Vincent said, shaking his hand. "You've got a good girl here; they don't come better than Danielle. I expect you to take good care of her."

"I plan to, sir," Carson answered.

"Good. Now—" he looked at them all one last time, then said, "—to work. I'll be in my office."

Breaking into song, Vincent headed for his office. "Deck the halls with boughs of holly . . ."

Cassie, Danielle, and Carson burst into laughter.

"These next three weeks are going to be a killer," Cassie groaned. "He's bad enough each year with the holidays and the tree show, but now this—*aye-yi-yi!*" She rushed off to make the phone calls, leaving Danielle and Carson in the chaos of Creative Display.

Because he had a study group at the library that night, Carson had to take her home, but as far as Danielle was concerned they'd had a perfect afternoon.

"Thanks for taking me ice skating," she said. "I enjoyed it—well, except for when I fell down. I hope I can sit in church tomorrow."

The day was beautiful and clear. Except for a few flurries, there hadn't been any snow yet in the valley that year. The city sidewalks swarmed with holiday shoppers.

With the snow-covered mountains to the east in plain view, Danielle couldn't help but think about the winter ski season ahead. When she voiced her thoughts, Carson shared her enthusiasm. "Maybe we could go up together sometime," he said.

"I'd like that," Danielle said, thinking how much fun it would be to go skiing with someone she really liked.

As Carson drove her home, they happened to pass the building that had once housed Turner Consulting. Although he seemed not to notice, Danielle looked over at the building and wondered how her coworkers had survived the downsizing and eventual takeover of the business.

"I'm sure this is going to sound crazy to you," she said, bringing her gaze back to the road as they followed an on-ramp to the Interstate and merged with the traffic, "but I'm actually kind of glad I lost my job at Turner Consulting."

Carson took his eyes from the road briefly to stare at her. "You are?"

"I really am," she stated. "I'm not glad the business fell apart, but I enjoy my job at Creative Display so much more. I doubt I would have ever made the change on my own. In fact, I've been thinking of going back to college to get a degree in interior design."

"Really?" he said with surprise. "I think that's great."

"It's worked out well for me," she admitted. "I just hope everyone else has managed to find work. You haven't spoken with Jack Harris lately, have you?"

Carson shook his head. "Nope, no one."

Danielle was surprised. "I thought you two were pretty close."

Carson didn't answer. Danielle dropped the subject, but was then faced with an uncomfortable silence between them. "So," she said brightly, changing the subject, "you liked my tree, huh? I wasn't sure it was going to work out, you know, the whole 'family tree' idea."

"That's what I like about it," he smiled, glancing at her.

"Are you into genealogy?" she asked.

"Me?" he snorted. "Hardly."

"How about your mom? Did she do genealogy?" Danielle asked, curious.

Carson shrugged. "I don't know."

Danielle was surprised, but remembered that young boys are seldom aware of their parents' interests. "Has your family always been LDS?"

He shrugged again. "I'm not really sure."

"Carson!" she said with some surprise. "Are you serious?"

He looked over at her but didn't answer.

"Don't you want to know about your ancestors?" she pressed. "Learn about your heritage? Aren't you curious to know who joined the Church and what they went through so you could be born into the Church?"

"Not really," he said shortly.

She hadn't expected him to be so apathetic. Why wouldn't a person be interested? How could they not be at least mildly curious?

"Does this have something to do with your father?" she asked delicately, aware that she was entering a sensitive area.

"Why would it have anything to do with him?" he asked, his tone taking on a cool edge.

"I don't know. I just wondered." This was obviously a personal issue for Carson, but she wondered how he could cut himself off from his only living family member? She didn't understand it. Even if her family got on her nerves at times, she still loved them and wanted them around. He didn't seem to have any sense of family at all.

"Do you have any other relatives?" she asked, watching his face carefully.

"My father was an only child, and my mother's sister died. All of my grandparents are dead and I think most of their siblings. I'm sure I'm related to someone, somewhere, but I don't know. And I don't care," he added as he took the exit to her house. Stopping at an intersection waiting for the light to change, he turned to her and said, "I didn't grow up with aunts and uncles and cousins so I don't know what it's like. I'm sure you have fun at your family gatherings, but it's just not that big of a deal to me."

She stared at him with wonder. Although she felt sorry for him, she didn't believe him in the least. She couldn't. It wasn't possible for someone to be all alone in the world and not care.

"I still think you ought to call your dad," she said recklessly. "I'll bet you'd be surprised how happy he is to hear from you. I'll bet he's changed a lot since all of this has happened."

"It would take a whole lot more than my father losing his business to change him," he said curtly. He turned the corner and pulled up in front of her house.

Realizing that she'd ruined a perfectly wonderful day together, Danielle opened the door to get out. But she couldn't let it go. Not yet. "I'm sorry, Carson. I didn't mean to make you mad."

"You didn't," he answered, looking straight ahead.

"It's funny, though," she said as she swung her legs out of the car. "I've never seen any resemblance between you and your father." She stood up. "Until now." She shut the door firmly.

Pulling away from the curb, Carson drove down the road and turned the corner.

*Well, that's that,* Danielle said to herself. She wondered if she'd ever see him again.

# CHAPTER
## ❧ ELEVEN ❧

"Danielle!" Roberta shrieked over the phone. "Lenny proposed. I'm engaged!"

"Roberta, that's great!" Danielle exclaimed. "I'm so happy for you. When? How?"

Roberta was happy to elaborate. "He asked me last night. You know how Lenny likes to bowl? Well, he put my engagement ring in one of the holes in my bowling ball." Roberta's voice cracked with emotion. "The whole bowling alley gathered around to see him get down on one knee and propose."

Danielle didn't tell her friend that getting engaged at a bowling alley wasn't exactly her idea of romance, but if Roberta was happy, that was all that mattered. She only asked if they'd picked a wedding day yet.

"We were thinking about Valentine's Day, but that seems so far away." Roberta was breathless with excitement as she spoke. "I'm going to talk to Liz about Lenny and me going on a cruise for our honeymoon. Wouldn't that be romantic?"

"It would be perfect," Danielle said wistfully. She knew it was selfish, but part of her was sad to be losing Roberta. Sure, they'd still go to lunch once in a while, but there would be no more movies or Friday nights hanging out. All their plans to go on vacations together, to travel—they wouldn't happen now. And she certainly wasn't about to tag along with Lenny and Roberta.

"What time do you go to work?" Roberta asked her.

"Not till one, why?"

"I don't know. I feel like celebrating, shopping, going out to lunch. Something. Are you free?"

"Sure," Danielle said. "I'm dying to see your engagement ring."

"It's really stunning," Roberta said. "He spent more than he should have, but he wanted me to know just how much he loved me and was willing to sacrifice for me."

The two friends made arrangements to meet, and an hour later they met at Crossroads Mall in downtown Salt Lake. When they saw each other they couldn't help but hug and giggle, squealing like a couple of high school girls on prom night.

"Oh, Roberta, that is the most beautiful ring I've ever seen," Danielle exclaimed. The ring wasn't extravagant, but the diamond was clear and sparkling and looked beautiful on her friend's finger. Danielle hugged her friend. "I'm really happy for you."

"Thanks. I hope you're next."

"Well, don't spend too much time hoping, because I don't even have any prospects."

"What about Carson?" Roberta asked.

"I don't know," Danielle said with a shrug, as they rode the escalator up one floor. "We had such a great time together on our last date, but when I mentioned his father, he just kind of shut down on me. I don't think he was very happy with me when he left. I just hope I hear from him again."

"He'll call," Roberta assured her. "How can he resist you?"

"I'm sure it takes every ounce of willpower and strength he has," Danielle replied sarcastically.

"C'mon. You need to do some serious shopping. That ought to lift your spirits. Besides, I want to talk to you about this ski trip with Bart. We're going next weekend."

If there was an Olympic event for marathon shopping, Roberta would be a gold medalist. Her solution to everything was shopping, and she could go for hours. Sniffing out a bargain was her greatest strength, and no one could negotiate a sale with as much strategy and expertise as Roberta. Danielle had learned some pretty shrewd shopping techniques, thanks to Roberta.

After several hours of browsing, going in and out of dozens of stores, Roberta and Danielle ended up on the bottom floor where the food court was located. Danielle needed to get some lunch then head to work.

"So, should I tell Bart to go ahead and invite you?" Roberta asked, shifting her packages to the other hand. She'd scored on some great deals for jeans, sweaters, and shoes.

"I guess." Danielle couldn't pretend any enthusiasm she didn't feel. "But wouldn't I be leading him on if I did go? I'd only be going for the skiing."

Roberta promised to explain to Bart that she was only interested in "being friends" but that she'd enjoy going with them. "I'm telling you, Dani," she said, "I think after you spend some time with him you might find he really isn't so bad after all. He can be quite funny, in his own way."

Danielle looked at Roberta, raising her eyebrows as if challenging her last statement.

"Okay, so he's not a barrel of laughs," Roberta admitted. "But he's good for a few chuckles. And it would be so much more fun if you go." Her voice was laced with just a hint of whininess. "We could play cards, go out to eat, go dancing—"

"Dancing?" Danielle interrupted her. "Are you kidding? Last time I danced with Bart, I nearly broke his ankle."

Roberta looked startled. "Oh, yeah, I forgot. Okay, forget the dancing. I'm sure we'll find plenty to do."

Going skiing with Bart sounded a lot better to Danielle than staying home and wondering if Carson was ever going to call again.

"C'mon Danielle, it will be fun," Roberta pleaded. "Bart's a great guy, he really is. Hey, if I weren't engaged to Lenny, I'd go for him. I would, honest. I think Bart is easy to talk to and very warm and generous."

Danielle gave her a "yeah, right" smirk. "Okay, enough already. Tell him to call. But make sure he doesn't get the wrong idea. I'm not going to be holding hands or kissing on the ski lift or anything like that."

That afternoon at work, Danielle felt like her head was spinning. Vincent had her and Cassie and the rest of the crew on the go the entire afternoon. He'd decided on a traditional Christmas theme for the governor's mansion and had them building a life-sized sleigh, which would be loaded with gifts and put in the entry of the mansion. Danielle's job was to wrap the gifts and make them look authentic, with dried flowers, calico and gingham bows, and raffia ribbon. Cassie was working on a wreath that was five feet in diameter to go in the mansion.

Abby came in that afternoon to help out. She wore a soft tan-colored top with a long, loose skirt in some type of African print. Her long hair was braided down the back. Around her neck was a necklace of hand-carved wild animals and chunky, bright colored beads. She told Danielle it was an outfit she'd gotten when she and Vince had gone to Africa last summer for their anniversary.

"Everything looks wonderful," Abby exclaimed as she looked around. She watched Danielle wrapping gifts, then said, "Danielle, why don't we try tying some berries and a little stem of pine with the bow to see how it looks?"

Danielle tried one and showed her. "Like this?"

"Perfect!" Abby exclaimed, giving her a warm smile.

Danielle liked Abby, a lot. Like Vincent, she was intelligent, yet warm; hard-working, yet generous. Abby seemed more practical and down to earth, while Vincent was more creative and passionate, but Danielle realized that their differences were exactly why they were so right for each other. He needed someone to stabilize him, and Abby seemed to enjoy her husband's enthusiasm and creativity.

Efforts to prepare for the holidays, the Jubilee of Trees, and the governor's mansion kept everyone working nonstop. Danielle was grateful for the "busy-ness" of the season and for the endless hours her job demanded. It helped her keep her mind off Carson.

But as she stood in her quiet corner of the store, wrapping gifts, her mind replayed their last date—the ice skating, the visit to see her Jubilee Christmas tree, the kiss. And of course the conversation that ended everything.

Part of her wanted to kick herself for being so outspoken. She could have easily kept her mouth shut and everything would have stayed the same. But the other part of her knew she couldn't have kept her feelings in. Carson needed to make peace with his father, and Danielle was convinced that if he didn't, he would eventually become the same type of bitter, unhappy individual his father was, and she cared too much for Carson to let him do that.

It was a no-win situation. If she truly cared about him, she needed to help him see that he *had* to make peace with his father, but in the process he would need to confront some painful, personal issues that obviously he wasn't ready to face.

With a sigh, she added another present to the stack. She missed him, darn it! Just being around him made her heart race and made her happier than she'd ever been before. Even her parents had noticed a change in her since they'd been dating. They'd also noticed that she'd been ornery and moody as she sat moping around the house, waiting for Carson to call.

"Danielle," Cassie hollered from the doorway, "Line two is for you. It's a guy."

Her heart jumped. Could it be? *Please, let it be Carson,* she prayed.

"Hello," she said brightly into the phone.

"Danielle? It's Bart," the voice on the other end said.

*Boy, it sure didn't take you long,* she thought. She tried to cover up her disappointment. "Hi, Bart. How are you?"

Just as she suspected, he invited her to go to the condo in Sun Valley with his parents, Lenny, Roberta, and him. They would go up Friday morning, ski that afternoon and all day Saturday, then go to church up there and come home Sunday afternoon.

"That sounds really nice," she said. "I'd love to go."

"We're all going in my parents' Suburban. We'll pick you up at seven o'clock Friday morning."

She thanked him for calling and went to talk to Vincent about arranging her schedule to take the time off. By next Friday her tree would be finished and the decorations for the mansion would be ready. She wished there was some reason she needed to stay, but, sadly, there wasn't.

The Thursday night before they left for Sun Valley, Danielle was frantically trying to find her ski clothes and equipment stored away from last season. She had just started to pack but couldn't find her ski gloves. Then she remembered she'd misplaced one in a friend's car last year after a trip to Snowbird. They'd torn the car apart looking for it and still couldn't find it. She needed new gloves. Hoping she could get to Sports World before it closed, she quickly drove to the store to get another pair.

"We close in five minutes, lady," the boy at the checkout said as she burst through the doors.

Ignoring him, Danielle raced to the ski department and looked over the wide assortment of outerwear. Sorting through several rows of gloves, she finally found a pair she liked, rolled her eyes at the outlandish price, and dashed to the checkout counter.

Handing the boy her Visa card, she waited while he completed the transaction. He acted like it was the worst torture anyone could bear, having to wait on a customer at one minute to nine.

"Nice gloves," a voice behind her said.

"Thanks," Danielle answered without looking up. She scribbled her name on the receipt the boy handed her, then turned to see who had spoken to her. "Carson!"

"Hi, there. Going skiing?" He held a cannister of racquetballs in his hand.

"Yeah, in the morning, and I forgot I needed new gloves." The boy behind the counter shoved her gloves into a bag and thrust them toward her.

Taking the bag, she stepped out of the way so Carson could make his purchase. Her palms grew sweaty as she wondered whether she should stay and talk with him or just tell him good-bye and leave. She didn't want to seem overanxious by staying, but she didn't want to seem uninterested by leaving.

"Is that everything?" the boy asked Carson.

"Yeah," he said, digging some bills out of his jeans pocket.

"Carson," a female voice called, "I have one more thing."

"Hold on," Carson told the kid.

Danielle's heart dropped. She looked to see a girl with glossy brown hair and pretty brown eyes rush up to him and throw a pack of

Life Savers on the counter. Danielle took a couple of steps toward the end of the counter. Who was this girl? Why was she with Carson?

"Now is that everything?" the boy asked, his voice reflecting the same annoyance Danielle felt in her heart.

Realizing she was setting herself up for a very awkward meeting, she clutched her gloves to her chest. "Nice seeing you, Carson," she said, unable to keep herself from looking over at his companion.

"You too," he said. "Have fun skiing."

"C'mon," the girl said, grabbing him by the arm and hustling him toward the entrance. "The others are waiting for us at the gym."

"Bye," Carson said over his shoulder and then was gone. Danielle stood, gaping as the door swung shut behind him.

"Lady, we're closed," the kid behind the counter said.

"Oh, yeah," she mumbled. "Sorry." She walked out into the night and watched as the tail lights of Carson's car turned out of the parking lot.

※ ✿ ※

Convinced and partially determined that she wasn't going to have any fun skiing, Danielle rode in silence as the Suburban made its way up the winding road past rows of condos. The whole condominium village was alive with tourists and skiers. Sun Valley was one of the first resorts to open this season, and skiers from all over Idaho and Utah had flocked there.

Bart's dad finally pulled into a parking stall. "Here we are," he announced.

Danielle liked Bart's parents. They were a handsome couple and very nice. Bart's dad was very distinguished looking, yet youthful and physically fit. He was an avid tennis player and jogger. He ran 10K's and had run the St. George marathon twice. Mrs. Russell also played tennis and jogged, but not competitively. She was a tiny, petite thing, with silky black hair that she wore in a short bob.

Mr. Russell was a successful orthodontist. His wife was busy with three other children, all married, and two grandchildren; she was also their stake Relief Society president. Meeting his parents gave Danielle a different, more open-minded opinion of Bart. He had "cool" parents, so there was a better chance that somewhere inside of him was a "cool" guy. Wasn't there?

"What do you say we get our stuff unloaded and hit the slopes?" Mr. Russell asked the group. He received an enthusiastic reply, except from Danielle. She just couldn't shake the image of Carson with that other girl, and she was mad at herself because she couldn't. He had no reason not to be with the girl; there had been no understanding between Carson and Danielle, no commitments. But it hurt that he hadn't called. She'd told herself that he was busy, but apparently he had time to play racquetball.

"Danielle, aren't you coming?" Bart asked.

"Oh, yeah," she said, unbuckling her seatbelt. She had been in a depressed trance-like state since seeing Carson the night before. When someone asked her what was wrong, she told them she had a headache, which she did have, but it wasn't the pounding in her head that hurt. It was the ache in her heart.

"Wow," Roberta exclaimed when she walked into the condo. "This place is incredible."

"You girls can share this room." Mrs. Russell opened the door to a bedroom. "It's right next to the bathroom. You boys can sleep in the loft upstairs."

The next twenty minutes were spent unloading suitcases, while Mrs. Russell put together some sandwiches. After lunch they went directly to buy lift tickets and get in a half day of skiing.

The sky was gray and overcast, but no snow fell. The mountains crawled with skiers in bright-colored parkas, and the crisp mountain air revived Danielle's senses. In spite of everything, her limbs finally began to tingle with the excitement and exhilaration of getting back on the ski slopes.

"Is your head feeling any better?" Bart asked her as they stood side by side in line to catch the chair lift.

"Yes," she smiled. "Thanks. How's your ankle?"

"Feels okay right now," he said. "I'll let you know after the first run, though."

Danielle wasn't sure she wanted to be paired off with Bart for the whole weekend, but so far he'd been pleasant and understanding. And because of him she was at a beautiful ski resort staying in a beautiful condo. She couldn't complain.

Lenny and Roberta waited for them at the top of the run.

"Which run do you want to take?" Lenny asked Bart when they'd skied off the lift. The two of them had both skied for years, and Bart moved with a smooth, fluid style even with his stiff ankle. Roberta had the hardest time keeping up even though they had decided to stay on an intermediate run. Danielle didn't have as much style as Bart, but she was strong and able to keep up with the men. She and Bart had finally found a common ground, their love for skiing, so they never lacked for conversation as they rode the lift. He even gave her pointers to help improve her form, and as much as Danielle hated to admit it, she was having fun.

That night the girls helped Mrs. Russell make delicious chicken fajitas. Then she made a gorgeous salad to go with it. The woman was a gourmet in the kitchen, and Danielle was even further impressed with how classy Bart's parents were.

In this setting Bart was a completely different person. He was relaxed, witty, and self-assured. He actually had them all laughing as he recounted some of the events up on the slope that afternoon, including his heroic efforts to rescue a woman who somehow wound up skiing down the hill backwards and couldn't get herself stopped long enough to turn around.

They finished off the evening with a rousing game of Rook. Bart was a keen player and couldn't be beat. Once again, Danielle saw a side of Bart she hadn't seen before. A side, she decided, she kind of liked. In their room that night as they got ready for bed, Roberta asked Danielle how things were going with Bart.

"You know," Danielle said, pulling her sweats out of her suitcase to wear to bed, "I have to admit, I really misjudged Bart. He's a pretty nice guy."

"See, I told you," Roberta said. "I'm glad you're having fun. I was worried, you know, after what happened with Carson. Are you still upset about that?"

Danielle shrugged. "I just don't know what to think about why he stopped calling. I guess either he didn't like me as much as I thought or I really ticked him off when I talked with him about his father. It would sure help if I knew what he was thinking."

"Maybe you should call him when you get back in town," Roberta suggested.

"Maybe I should just forget about him." Danielle grabbed her toothbrush and toothpaste.

"I think you should call," Roberta said. "You deserve an explanation. In the meantime, have fun with Bart. Who knows? Maybe something will happen between you two after all."

# CHAPTER
## TWELVE

The next morning they awoke to fresh powder. Snow had fallen through the night and turned everything into a winter wonderland. The aroma of hot chocolate and maple syrup greeted Roberta and Danielle as they climbed out of bed.

Danielle suggested helping Mrs. Russell, and after a quick trip to the bathroom to freshen up and look presentable, Danielle found Bart's mom in the kitchen making stacks of pancakes and scrambling eggs.

"Good morning, Mrs. Russell. Need some help?"

Danielle was put in charge of the eggs, and the two women talked as they prepared the meal. Danielle found out that Mrs. Russell had a nursing degree and had served a welfare mission in the Philippines when she was younger. She had met her husband while they were on their missions although they hadn't initiated any sort of relationship while in the mission field. But she made sure he had her address when she left to go back home to Salt Lake, and they'd married six months after he returned from the Philippines. Since they'd been married, they'd returned to the Philippines twice, both times in a medical capacity. She taught the women how to have more sanitary living conditions and he had helped with dental needs in underprivileged areas. Danielle couldn't help thinking about Carson and his months in Thailand, serving, helping, changing lives.

"Something sure smells good," Bart called as he climbed down the stairs from his perch overhead. "Is that homemade syrup?"

"Of course," Mrs. Russell answered. He kissed his mom on the cheek and snitched a piece of bacon from a plate. She slapped at his hand playfully and told him to go tell the others to come and eat.

Danielle had noticed what a good relationship Bart had with his parents. He was sweet, attentive, and caring with his mother, and he and his father joked and talked like best friends. It seemed an ideal situation, certainly much better than Carson's. Maybe Roberta was right. She was seeing new sides of Bart and she liked them. Maybe her feelings towards him would change.

Within minutes the table was surrounded. The food was blessed and devoured, and with everyone pitching in, the meal was quickly cleaned up. In no time, they were back on the slopes, packing in as many runs as they could that day.

"Your ankle doing okay?" Danielle asked Bart on their fifth run.

"It feels great. I was worried I'd wake up this morning and find it stiff, but it really feels good."

She and Bart had split up from Lenny and Roberta and had taken some different trails. Danielle had been a little surprised at how comfortable she was with Bart now. He was attentive and kind, and she enjoyed his company. When she'd talked to him before this, he'd seemed kind of nerdy and weird, but seeing this outdoorsy, fun side of him made her realize that Bart was a nice guy. And, she wondered, was it her imagination or did he seem to get better-looking the more she got to know him?

They stopped at the lodge for lunch and ate with his parents, Lenny, and Roberta. Danielle enjoyed watching how cute his parents were together. They were almost like newlyweds the way they joked and teased each other, held hands, and even stole kisses now and then. Danielle liked the relationship they shared and could see that Bart had grown up in a home with loving parents and family and a good example. She had no doubt that any wife of his would be treated like a queen, with love and respect.

"So, you're studying psychology, huh?" Danielle asked him as they rode the lift to the top of the mountain. "What do you want to do when you finish school?"

"I'm interested in sports psychology. I'd like to work with athletes, you know, help them overcome mental hang-ups they have specific to their sport, help them to enhance their performance and become better athletes physically by improving their mental performance."

Danielle hadn't known this about him. "Sounds fascinating," she said.

"It is," he said. "What about you? You're working for Creative Display, but Roberta said you have a degree in business."

"I didn't really know for sure what I wanted to do when I went to college so I studied business because it was so general," she explained. "I'm thinking of going back to school and getting a degree in interior design. This job has shown me what I'm really interested in and actually have a talent to do."

Bart expressed a desire to see Danielle's tree, saying his mother had helped out with the Jubilee of Trees every year for as long as he could remember. "In fact," he added, "my dad and the other orthodontists in his practice buy a tree every year."

"They do?" She wasn't surprised, knowing his father. "You really have neat parents," she told him.

"Thanks," he said. "They are pretty cool. You should see my dad on the tennis courts. He beats me three out of four games every time."

"Wow, either he must be really good," Danielle began, "or you must be—"

"—pretty bad," Bart finished her sentence for her, laughing. "Actually we're both pretty good, but he's much better. Of course, he has more time to play than I do. But when I was on the tennis team in high school, I could give him a pretty good game."

"I like tennis, but it's been a while since I've played," Danielle admitted. When Bart suggested a game sometime, Danielle agreed, surprised to realize she'd actually enjoy a game of tennis with Bart.

Arriving at the top, they skied smoothly off the chairlift. Snow swirled around them as afternoon clouds moved in and dropped low onto the mountain.

"This will probably be our last run," Bart said. "Which trail do you want to take?"

"That one." Danielle pointed to a trail head behind him. It was hard enough to be challenging but easy enough to be fun. And it was long. She didn't want the skiing to end yet.

Together they wound their way down the trail through snow-laden pine trees. Bart was terrific on skis, and she felt she had improved just skiing with him that day. At odd times during the day, she'd thought about Carson, and couldn't help but compare the two men. Bart had such a wonderful background and home life. He was focused on his future, secure in himself and his decisions, and open with his feelings. Danielle didn't feel she had to guess where she stood with him or figure out any secret feelings he had. Carson was closed and private about his feelings, and she wasn't sure where she stood with him. Plus he had plenty of issues with his home life and family.

But it wasn't Bart she thought about the last thing at night before she fell asleep, and it wasn't Bart she thought about first thing in the morning when she woke up.

It was Carson.

··· ✦ ···

"Danielle, you're wanted on the phone," Dorothy Camden hollered to her daughter, who was watching the six o'clock news with her father. It was Wednesday, her day off, and she'd spent it doing absolutely nothing.

"Hello," she answered, hoping Roberta had called to make plans for the evening. But she knew better than to expect Roberta on the other end. Ever since she and Lenny had become engaged, she never had any free time anymore. She was as good as married already, Danielle sighed. She didn't resent Lenny, but she did wish she and Roberta could spend some time together before the big day.

"Danielle, it's Bart," the voice on the other end said.

"Hi, Bart," she answered enthusiastically. She was glad to hear from him. She'd decided that he was a nice guy, and she liked the fact that she knew exactly where she stood with him—on a ten-foot-high pedestal!

Still, he seemed to have so many stars in his eyes for her it would take months, even years, for him to see the "real" her. But far be it from her to convince him otherwise. She didn't mind it that he thought she was so wonderful.

And it wasn't as if Carson had even called to see how she was—if she'd had fun skiing or if she was even alive. Her mother had noticed a few calls on their answering machine, but the person had just hung up without leaving a message. Danielle was too much of a realist to think they could be from Carson. But she couldn't help hoping.

"I've got a tennis court reserved at the club tonight. I wondered if you'd like to go play tennis and then go get a bite to eat or something," he invited her.

*Beats sitting home watching television*, she thought. "Sure, that sounds fun. What time?"

She wondered if he called from a car phone since he was at her door in just under ten minutes. She was still in her room changing her clothes when the doorbell rang. When she went downstairs both of her parents were sitting with Bart in the living room, talking.

"Hi, Danielle," he said, jumping to his feet as she entered the room. He had impeccable manners and she could tell he was obviously thrilled to see her. After assuring her parents she wouldn't be late, she left with Bart in his Outback, which was just like the one she'd had before she lost her job at Turner Consulting.

"How do you like your Outback?" she asked, reaching for the door.

"Here," he said, "I'll get that." He opened the door for her. "It's great, especially in bad weather."

She wondered if Bart would pass the toilet seat test. She didn't doubt it really. She hadn't noticed while they were in Sun Valley, but wished she would've paid attention. As dumb as her mother's test was, she was curious to know how Bart would fare.

"I had one for about a month," she told him when he climbed inside. "I had to sell it when I lost my job."

She told him all about her experience at Turner Consulting while they drove to the racquet club where Bart and his parents were members. When they got inside, Danielle could tell that Bart was a familiar face around the club. He was greeted by nearly every person they passed as they made their way to their court.

For the first half hour they volleyed the ball, warming up and letting Danielle's tennis muscles get used to playing again. Danielle knew from Bart's first serve that she was toast.

"Did you say you played on your high school tennis team?" she asked breathlessly as she ran for a stray ball.

"Yeah. I was All-State my senior year. I lettered in tennis."

"Now you tell me?" She swatted the ball over the net to him.

"My game's gotten pretty rusty since then. I don't play as much as I should." He stretched his racquet over his head with both arms, loosening up his shoulders for the serve.

"Coulda fooled me," she said, getting ready for one of his searing serves. He found out early that her weak spot was her backhand. She knew that was exactly where he was going to place the ball, right inside the center line.

*Focus*, she told herself. *You can do this.* She studied his form, watched, and waited.

Then, off like a rocket, the ball sped toward her. Pivoting to her left, she swung her racquet and to her surprise connected with the ball, sending it across the net to the opposite corner, catching Bart completely unaware.

He lunged for the ball, but it was too late.

"Whoa!" he hollered. "Where'd that come from?"

"I don't know," she yelled back, "but I hope there's more."

"Nice return," he complimented.

"Thanks," she replied, standing a little taller. She'd returned one of his "ace" serves. Not bad for a novice.

They continued playing, Danielle's game holding steady with bursts of good luck occasionally. Still, she was no match for Bart. He beat her hands down every time. When they finished, she was gasping for air and sweating. He was breathing moderately hard.

"This is definitely not good for my ego," she told him.

"Hey, I thought you did a great job. You were doing pretty good there for a while."

"Thanks. You sure you didn't play pro or something?"

Bart laughed and offered to carry her gym bag for her. "They make great strawberry smoothies at the snack bar. Want one?"

"Sure," she said, noticing once again how friendly everyone was to Bart as they walked down the hallway toward the snack bar. She was seeing Bart through completely different eyes. She still wished it was Carson by her side, but she was beginning to be glad that if it couldn't be Carson, at least she had Bart.

That Sunday in Young Women Danielle approached her Laurels about helping at the homeless shelter on Thanksgiving morning. She knew they wouldn't all jump for joy at her invitation, but she'd hoped they'd at least be open to the idea.

"Oooh, no," Allie said. "I don't like being around people like that."

"Me either," Erin answered. "Besides we're going to my grandma's in Idaho for Thanksgiving."

"I'm sorry. We're going out of town, too," Chloe told her. Danielle knew if Chloe could be there, she would.

"What about you, Lucy?"

"I, um, I'd have to ask my dad first, but I probably could," she answered with some reluctance.

McCall said nothing. Danielle still felt like there was a wall between them and had tried to find common ground between them, but McCall just wouldn't give her a chance. "How about you, McCall? What is your family doing for Thanksgiving?"

"I don't know yet," she answered, without offering more information.

"How about if I call you Wednesday?" Danielle offered.

"You can if you want," McCall answered, not even looking at her.

Danielle was puzzled by this young woman. She was pretty and Danielle was sure she was popular, but she acted like a cross between a spoiled brat and a pampered princess. Danielle wished the young girl would give her a chance, but she wasn't about to jump through hoops for her. McCall needed to learn somehow that the world didn't revolve around her.

Somehow Danielle had to get her to go to the homeless shelter with her.

# CHAPTER THIRTEEN

The week before Thanksgiving, Vincent and his crew spent most of their time decorating the governor's mansion. From the breathtaking gold and crystal decorated Christmas tree, to Cassie's stunning wreath masterpiece, to the enchanting present-filled sleigh, the mansion was transformed into a Christmas wonderland. Vincent had pulled out all the stops on this project, and in the end it had been worth all the work and worry.

The governor and his wife were ecstatic about the results and raved about Vincent's creations. There was a full-page article in the newspaper about Vincent and Creative Display's efforts with several color photographs. Vincent was in media heaven. He loved the attention and the exposure.

The day before Thanksgiving, Danielle's Christmas tree and the other two trees being donated by Creative Display were transported to the convention center where the Jubilee of Trees was held. Since theirs were the first trees to arrive, Vincent made sure they were given prime spots in the lineup.

"It turned out great," Cassie said, pausing to give Danielle a hug as she helped with last-minute touch-ups. "Your idea was a stroke of genius."

"You think?" Danielle scrutinized the tree, hoping it really did look as good as she wanted it to. Her family was coming to see it, and so were Lenny, Roberta, and Bart. She wanted it to be just right.

"Marvelous, girls," Vincent exclaimed as he came to check on their progress. It was getting late and everyone was exhausted. It had been a long week. "This one will be a favorite, I'm sure."

"Thanks," Danielle said, suddenly feeling tired. She'd worked until almost midnight every night that week and was exhausted. It didn't make her feel any better knowing she'd committed to volunteer at the homeless shelter early in the morning. But since Roberta's dad's company had donated the funds to decorate her tree and was sponsoring the dinner, Danielle thought it was the least she could do to show her appreciation. Besides, with Lucy going and maybe McCall, she couldn't back out now.

"Are you sure people are going to figure out that it's a family tree?" she asked.

Vincent looked at her with one eyebrow raised. "I'd say it's pretty obvious, wouldn't you, Cass?"

Cassie nodded. "I don't think you have anything to worry about," she agreed. "Oh, look, here comes Abby."

"Hello," Abby called as she approached. "The tree looks beautiful. I think we should get some spotlights on it to help it stand out. I want everyone to be able to see each detail of the ornaments." She turned to Vincent. "Honey, we need you over by the snack bar. I can't decide how to arrange the tables."

"I'll be right there, love." He gave her a kiss on the knuckles.

Before unplugging the lights, Danielle took one final look at the tree and thought about Carson and his family tree. His family would fit on one branch, she thought sadly. But still, even though he didn't have grandparents, or a lot of aunts and uncles, or a huge pack of nieces and nephews, he still had a father and some distant relatives. He did have family. He just wouldn't put aside his pride long enough to take the first step. She still felt he needed to do that, even though telling him had obviously cost her their relationship.

But the loss of a family was a terrible price to pay for one's pride.

❧

That night Danielle made the dreaded phone call to the Blakely home to see if McCall was going to join them in the morning. McCall wasn't home so Danielle talked to her mother.

"I wondered if McCall was planning on going with me and Lucy in the morning. We're volunteering at the homeless shelter for Thanksgiving dinner," she said.

"What a wonderful service to give this time of year," her mother said. When Danielle had met McCall's mom at church, she had been amazed at how different she was from her daughter. While pleasant looking, Sister Blakely wasn't knock-out gorgeous like her daughter, and she didn't wear ultra-fashionable and expensive clothing. She was also as sweet and humble as a saint.

"Has McCall said anything about going?" Danielle asked and wasn't surprised at Sister Blakely's negative response. A deep voice in the background on the other end of the phone caught Danielle's attention.

"Just a moment, please," Sister Blakely said into the phone.

There was a pause and the muffled sound of voices, then Brother Blakely came on the line. "This is Ted Blakely. Are you McCall's Young Women teacher?"

"Yes, Danielle Camden." Had McCall complained to her father about her teacher? Danielle caught her breath as the man spoke.

"I know your dad, Earl," he said in a deep voice. "We worked together in Scouts a few years back."

"Really?" Danielle remembered how much her father had loved working with the Scouts. He had been in charge of merit badges as the boys worked toward their Eagles.

"He's a good man," Brother Blakely said. "Sue tells me you've invited McCall to go to the homeless shelter tomorrow to serve Thanksgiving dinner."

"Yes, has she mentioned it?" Danielle asked.

"Nope," he said briskly. "But that doesn't mean she isn't going. I can't think of anything that girl could use more than to see how other people live and how blessed she is. You can plan on her going."

Danielle heard McCall's mother in the background, saying how upset McCall would be if they didn't ask her first. Brother Blakely grumbled something back to his wife, then came back on the phone. "What time do you want her to be ready?"

"We have to be there by seven-thirty."

"She'll be ready by seven," he promised.

Danielle hung up, wondering what to expect from McCall. She hated to think what was going to transpire at their house that night when her parents told her that she was going to the shelter.

A smile lifted one corner of her mouth. What she would give to see the look on McCall's face when her parents told her she was going!

⁕⁖⁕⁖⁕

McCall didn't say one word on the way to the shelter. Danielle hoped her car door would still open after the way McCall had slammed it shut. In contrast, Lucy happily talked nonstop the whole trip, telling Danielle all about the dress she had borrowed from Chloe for the Christmas dance. Danielle could tell that Lucy could hardly wait for the big night.

Making sure her car doors were locked, Danielle led the girls to the building where the shelter was located. Glancing around uneasily at the cluttered alley and crumbling brick building, Danielle and the girls hurried to get inside. Even at seven-thirty, the area didn't look too safe.

Several people were already at work in the kitchen, putting cubes of margarine in dishes and quivering mounds of cranberry jelly into bowls.

"Hi," Danielle said uncomfortably, looking around. "Is Roberta here?"

"She's in the storage room," a man answered. "She'll be right back."

"There are some aprons in that drawer over there," an older woman said, jerking her head toward the back. "You can put on some of those plastic gloves, and empty those bags of dinner rolls into these baskets."

"Okay," Danielle said. "Come on, you guys. Let's get to work."

"Put your purse in that cupboard," the older woman said. Danielle saw that her name tag had "Judy" written on it. "Walter will lock it up before we open up the doors and start serving."

"How many pounds of potatoes do you think we should mash?" Roberta entered the room, dragging a fifty-pound bag of potatoes behind her. "Hi, Dani," she exclaimed when she saw her friend. "Hi, girls."

"Roberta, this is Lucy and McCall. They're in my Laurel class."

Roberta smiled at each of the girls. Lucy smiled back, but McCall just folded her arms over her chest and looked bored. "I see you got an apron and some gloves." Roberta let the bag rest on the floor.

Three more people from Roberta's dad's office arrived to help.

"Okay, people," an older gentleman wearing the name tag "Walter" said. "Let's get organized here." Roberta told them that Walter ran the shelter. He himself had been homeless at one time, but with the help of a shelter in Chicago where he'd lived, he'd managed to get a job and become self-sufficient. He still worked as an insurance adjustor but devoted his life to keeping the shelter going.

More people arrived, and under Walter's direction, the place began to hum like a well-oiled machine. Each volunteer had an assignment. Danielle and Roberta worked on the mashed potatoes, peeling so many spuds Danielle thought she'd practically peeled the skin off her thumb. Lucy and McCall were assigned dining room duty, covering each table with white paper and setting out napkins and utensils, salt and pepper, and cups of ice water.

"Hey, look," Danielle said, seeing an older volunteer with white hair and a bushy white beard helping to set up chairs. "That guy looks like Santa Claus."

Roberta followed her gaze. "Kind of, but he's too skinny to be Santa."

"But the beard and the hair sure look real," Danielle defended her statement.

"I guess," Roberta said. "Too bad he doesn't have a little red hat to wear. That sure would help."

"And too bad we don't have a little red hat for Lucy and McCall," Danielle said, adding humorously, "I'm sure that would really make McCall's day."

"What's up with her anyway?" Roberta asked.

"She's spoiled," Danielle said. "She's the youngest out of five and the only girl."

Roberta nodded knowingly. "And she's not really thrilled about being here, is she?"

"Her parents forced her," Danielle told her friend. "She hasn't said a word to me yet this morning."

Roberta shrugged. "Maybe it will be good for her to see how homeless people live."

"That's what her parents are hoping."

"How's everything coming?" Walter asked as he walked around the kitchen checking on the progress of the meal.

"The potatoes are just about ready to start mashing," Roberta reported. "How soon do you want to open the doors?"

"In about an hour," Walter said. "We'd better put on another pot and get some more cooking. I expect an even bigger turnout this year than we had last year."

Danielle pulled a face when he said to peel more potatoes, and Roberta said brightly, "I know. Let's get Lucy and McCall to peel for a while."

"Good idea," Danielle agreed, "but you get to ask them. McCall already hates me."

McCall's expression was nothing short of murderous in response to Roberta's request. But everyone was busy with their own assignments, and there was still much to be done before the doors opened.

After a while Danielle started to feel sorry for her Laurels so she offered to trade peeling for serving when it came time to serve dinner. It didn't take much coaxing. Both girls dropped their potato peelers and ran before Danielle changed her mind.

Walter was right about the turnout—the line of people waiting for Thanksgiving dinner went down the street and around the corner. The Santa Claus man had put out a small five-foot Christmas tree and thrown several strands of colorful lights on it. The woman named Judy helped him hang ornaments and candy canes on the tree. They turned on Christmas music, and Danielle noticed the white-haired man setting up an old ceramic nativity scene on top of a broken-down piano in the corner of the room.

"Look." Danielle nudged Roberta. Both girls watched as the man gently arranged each piece in a traditional nativity fashion, setting the manger and baby Jesus directly in the middle with Mary and Joseph on either side.

"It's like watching *Mr. Krueger's Christmas*," Roberta said. The man didn't appear to be poor or needy, but he did seem to carry a sadness about him, a loneliness that showed on his wrinkled face.

Danielle and Roberta continued staring at him as he stepped back and viewed his arrangement. Then Walter announced that he was opening the doors. The room immediately filled with people, some quiet and scared-looking, others loud and laughing. Some of them were dressed in dirty, misfitting rags; others looked presentable but shabby. All were very grateful for the meal.

Lucy was asked to refill butter dishes and water glasses, so Danielle took her place next to McCall, serving potatoes.

"Thank you, girls. Thank you, thank you," an older woman said as she accepted a generous dollop of mashed potatoes and gravy. She was missing most of her front teeth. "I can't eat the meat, but I love the potatoes 'n punkin' pie."

Danielle felt her heart growing inside her chest as each humble soul filed past, filling a plate with a warm, home-cooked meal. In their eyes she read pain and sorrow, loneliness and hardship. Was this all she could do? Give a couple of hours of her time and feel it was enough? These people had no one to turn to, nowhere to go. They lived on the street or wherever they could find shelter. Some died of illness or were killed for their shoes. What difference did one measly meal make to them?

Yes, it was something, but it was nowhere near enough. And what about the children? How could they live a life like this? What did they call home? Where did they lay their heads at night?

Danielle felt a tightness in her chest. How did this happen? How did people end up with nothing?

She longed to tell them about the Church, about the welfare system. The gospel could help them, give them a chance in life, a new beginning. But as each person shuffled by with outstretched hands, she realized the problem was much bigger than her and her desire to help them. Where did one person even begin to make a difference?

But someone had to help. Someone had to try.

Danielle watched as a tiny, hunchbacked man made his way slowly down the line. He mumbled to himself as he made his way, barely able to lift his plate. When he stopped in front of McCall, he looked up, the blank look in his eye turning to one of delight. "Sophie?" he said to McCall. "Sophie, is it you? Is it really you?"

McCall looked at him, speechless. The man got so excited he dropped his plate. People behind him in the line shouted and swore at him for holding up their progress.

"Sophie!" He reached toward her. "My sweet little daughter. Where have you been?" McCall stepped back, not knowing what to do. Thankfully the white-bearded man rushed over and wrapped his arm around the tiny man. Leading him away to a table in a far corner of the room, the older volunteer spoke softly to the other man as they went. The little man turned and cried for "Sophie" once, but the white-bearded man kept talking to him and leading him away. Someone else quickly cleaned up the mess, and the line moved on.

McCall was too shaken to serve, so Roberta took over while Danielle took McCall to the back room. Practically hyperventilating, McCall leaned against the wall in Walter's office. The young girl was visibly shaken.

*These poor, helpless people,* Danielle thought. *That poor, lonely little man.* Tears filled her eyes and fell down her cheeks.

*"Inasmuch as ye have done it unto one of the least of these my brethren, ye have done it unto me."* The scripture from Matthew came to her mind, alive and powerful. These were God's children, lonely and lost. *"For I was an hungred, and ye gave me meat: I was thirsty, and ye gave me drink: I was a stranger, and ye took me in."*

Her parents had always told her that aside from raising their family, their greatest joy in life came when they were serving others. A yearning, warm and strong, filled her, a desire to help these less fortunate, lonely souls. But what could she do? How could she alone make a difference?

"Hey," Danielle said to McCall, "are you okay?"

"He thought I was his daughter," McCall said, looking up at her, her bottom lip trembling. "That poor, poor, man." Without warning, McCall broke into tears.

Danielle hugged her to her chest, holding her close, and let her cry.

# CHAPTER FOURTEEN

After McCall's tears stopped, Danielle stepped back and gave her a warm smile. "Are you okay?"

McCall wiped at her eyes and sniffed. "I just don't understand how these people end up on the streets. Don't they have anywhere to go? Isn't there someone who can help them?"

"I guess not," Danielle said. "I guess it's up to us to help them."

"Everyone okay in here?" Danielle turned to see the white-haired man at the doorway.

"Oh, hi. Yes, we're okay." Danielle gave McCall a reassuring smile.

"The old man thought you were his daughter, Sophie. She died fifty years ago," the white-bearded man explained. Danielle noticed how tired he looked, saw the dark circles under his eyes.

"How sad," McCall whispered. "Is he going to be all right?"

The man shook his head. "Hard to say. Winter on the streets isn't easy on an old guy like him."

"Danielle," Roberta called. "We need more gravy."

Danielle gasped. "Oops, I'd better get back out there and help." She looked at McCall. "You feel like helping some more?" she asked.

McCall nodded. "Do you think they might need help in the kitchen? Washing dishes or something?"

"Here," the white-haired man said. "I'm going that way. We'll find something for you to do."

Danielle smiled her thanks and rushed to the stove, picking up the pot and carrying it to the food line. "Sorry," she told Roberta. "I got hung up."

"That's okay. The line's slowing down." Roberta took a deep breath and looked at Danielle. "How's McCall?"

Danielle ladled a stream of gravy onto a mountain of potatoes for a wild-eyed woman who had pink sponge curlers in her hair, and ten to twenty plastic bead necklaces around her neck. "That old guy really upset McCall. This whole thing has been such an eye-opener for her. And for me. It's hard to believe these people don't have anyone they can turn to."

"I know," Roberta said. "It's sad, isn't it? Makes you feel kind of guilty to go back to your house, where it's warm and dry, and eat a huge Thanksgiving dinner."

"Then sit around and watch ball games and eat some more," Danielle added. "Then go to sleep in a soft, comfortable bed."

The white-haired gentleman walked by. Danielle smiled at him, hoping he knew how much she appreciated his kindness. "What do you think his story is?" she asked Roberta when he got out of earshot.

"Who knows? Maybe he's all alone himself. I think it's neat he's here helping."

"Me too," Danielle said. "All these people here today—it's incredible. I've never realized how good it feels inside to give service, to know you've actually helped someone else."

"It's going to be kind of hard to just walk away and forget about it, isn't it?" Roberta said.

"I'll never forget about today. I'm so glad you talked me into helping. But you know what? I want to do more," Danielle declared. "I can't just leave today and feel good about myself. Especially with Christmas coming. What will these people do for Christmas?"

"Walter has dinner for them on Christmas Day also. Usually people donate coats, blankets, and boots, which he gives to them."

"What about all the children?" Danielle thought about her former Primary children and imagined any of them suddenly without a home, without clothes or food. Without presents at Christmas. "The children ought to wake up to some kind of Christmas."

"A lot of organizations rally at Christmas to give kids presents," Roberta reminded her.

"But what about the rest of the year? Who helps them to change their situation? Who helps them to improve their lives?"

"The state has programs; the Church helps these people, too. And there are a lot, like Walter, who have places where they can come for food and shelter."

But Danielle wanted to do more. Especially for the children. Especially at Christmas.

*~·~ 🐚 ~·~*

Many of the people who came for dinner had eaten and gone on their way. Others stayed inside and just sat, looking around the room. Others clustered into groups and talked, like old friends. Danielle was grateful that the good weather had held out for their sakes. The warmer weather and lack of snow didn't make it seem like the holidays, but she was sure it made sleeping on the streets more bearable.

As Lucy and Roberta pitched in to help put away leftovers, and McCall finished cleaning up the kitchen, Danielle noticed the man with the white hair and beard mingling with the guests. He took time to shake their hands, learn their names, and show them that they mattered to him.

"Walter," Danielle asked as she dried pots and pans, "who is that volunteer over there with the white beard?"

"His name is Harry. He's been volunteering for about six or seven months. He comes in every Saturday and Sunday and on holidays. He knows a lot of these people by their first names. He's very generous and helps a lot of these folks, especially when they need medical care. He's a good man. Doesn't talk about himself at all; he's very private. But he's been a great blessing to me. I've learned to rely on him for his help."

Danielle marveled at these volunteers who served so cheerfully and gave so willingly of their time. Why hadn't she figured out before now how important it was to serve others? Had she been so selfish with herself and her time that she hadn't ever bothered looking beyond her own needs to see the needs of others?

McCall and Roberta finished drying the pots and pans and putting them away while Lucy and Danielle went into the dining area to wipe off tables and sweep the floor. A few guests remained, visiting or sleeping with their heads resting on their folded arms on the table. Danielle just wiped around them, not wanting to disturb them. Again her heart filled with compassion. Where did they sleep at night? How did they survive?

As Lucy swept the floor, Danielle's thoughts wandered as she looked outside at the clouds, which had begun to gather. She could donate more time here, helping Walter. He could use all the help he could get. But what about Christmas? And again, she wondered, what about the children?

Her attention drifted to Harry, who was walking one of the guests to the door. She saw him take something out of his pocket and slip it into the man's hand. The homeless man looked down to see what it was, and Danielle could see the green bills in his hand. Her heart grew warm as she wondered how many other people Harry had slipped a few dollars to.

She'd never seen anyone as kind and gracious as this man was. He was like a real-life Santa Claus, giving, loving, and serving.

Santa Claus. Children.

*Omigosh! That's it!*

What about a Sub-for-Santa with a real live Santa? She and Roberta could organize it. It would be a perfect project for her Laurels. They could gather toys for Walter to give away at Christmas and could even find out names of inner-city families who would otherwise not have a Christmas. "Santa" could actually deliver the toys.

Her fingers, toes, and scalp tingled with the thought. That was it. A Sub-for-Santa. After what Walter said about Harry, Danielle was sure he would be willing to help.

"Roberta." Danielle caught her friend as she came into the dining room to help wipe off tables. "I have an idea, but I need your help." McCall was still in the kitchen, so Danielle motioned to Lucy to join them. They sat down and Danielle told them about her idea—gathering the gifts and arranging the Santa deliveries.

"It sounds great, Dani, it really does." Danielle sensed hesitancy in Roberta's voice. "I mean, sure I'd love to help out any way I can, but . . ." she paused, ". . . it's just that we've set our wedding date for

February fourteenth, and I'm going to be kind of busy getting ready for that. I don't know how much help I can really give you."

At first Danielle couldn't believe her friend wasn't as excited about the idea as she was; then she realized that she was expecting too much. Of course, right now her wedding was the most important thing to her. It should be.

"I understand," Danielle said, patting her friend's hand. "Maybe you can spend a few hours when you have time."

"The other Laurels and I will help," Lucy offered. "It sounds neat."

Danielle smiled at Lucy, grateful for her willingness. "Thanks, I know we'd be doing something really wonderful for others."

"I'll do what I can to help, too," Roberta added.

"Thanks." Danielle gave her friend's hand a squeeze.

"We just have to get Harry to play Santa," Roberta said. "Can you imagine the look in those kids' eyes when they see him come to their house with presents? Look—" she showed Danielle her arm, "—it gives me goosebumps just thinking about it."

"You guys come with me to ask him," Danielle said.

Harry was putting away chairs in the dining room, and he glanced up as they approached him.

"Excuse me, Harry," Danielle said. "Could we talk with you for a moment?"

He nodded and Danielle motioned toward some chairs. "Do you mind if we sit?"

After they were seated, Danielle explained her idea, hoping she was saying the right words to convince him to agree to help. Harry appeared to listen carefully, but kept his gaze lowered while she spoke so that she couldn't read his expression.

"You see," Danielle went ahead with her sales pitch, "Being here today has really helped me realize just how much people need our help. And with the holidays and Christmas . . . I just want to find a way to do more. Especially for the children." She paused, but Harry remained silent. What was he thinking? What if he said no? Danielle felt a flash of panic. She exchanged a worried look with Roberta, then tried to continue calmly.

"Anyway, I was thinking that I'd like to organize a Sub-for-Santa. I know that the people I work with would be very generous with their donations and so would the people in my church. I'm LDS and we have several organizations that would get involved."

Harry scratched his bearded chin. At least he seemed to be thinking about her offer.

"Maybe you'd like to think about it for a while," she said after a few moments of silence.

Harry spoke at last. "I'd be happy to help," he said softly.

Danielle wasn't sure she heard him correctly. "Did you say you'd be happy to help?"

He nodded. "Yes."

Danielle clapped her hands together. "I'm so excited. This is going to be great, I just know it." She quickly collected her thoughts. "Could I have your home phone number so I can contact you? I thought I'd get a volunteer list together and then have a meeting at my house. My parents will be thrilled to help with this."

"You can contact me through Walter. Leave a message with him and he can get it to me."

Before Danielle could broach the next subject and learn how Harry would feel about playing Santa Claus for her project, her attention was caught by the laughter coming from the kitchen. When they walked back to see what all the commotion was about, Danielle saw McCall laughing at sixty-five-year-old Marvin, one of the volunteers, who was dancing around with a dishtowel wrapped around his head like a turban, and several dishtowels tucked into his belt like a skirt, which he removed one at a time in a mock belly dance. After his song, Marvin removed the last towel from his waist and snapped it at some of the other volunteers, sending them running and giggling around the room.

It was an entirely different McCall who rode home that afternoon as she and Lucy giggled over Marvin's "Dance of the Scarves" in the kitchen.

After dropping Lucy at her house, Danielle and McCall rode in silence to McCall's house.

"Thanks for your help today," Danielle said, pulling up in the driveway. McCall looked down at her hands, scraping at the light purple fingernail polish on her thumbnail. Danielle was afraid that she was still upset about what the old man had said to her. "Are you okay?" she asked.

McCall nodded, then looked at her. "What's going to happen to that old man?"

Danielle sighed. "Well, there are a lot of places he can go for food and shelter during the night. As long as he doesn't get sick, I'm sure he'll make it through the winter."

McCall nodded thoughtfully. "I wish I could get him a better coat, though. Did you see how many holes his had in it? It was all torn and worn out."

Danielle realized that McCall had just given her the opportunity of a lifetime. "Well, it just so happens that I'm putting together as Sub-for-Santa, and we'll get donations for the homeless shelter as well," she said. "Coats, blankets, boots, gloves, that kind of thing. I'm sure we could get him a new coat."

"Really?" McCall lit up at the thought.

"In fact I've been hoping that you girls would help me out with this project. I've got a lot to do before Christmas if I'm going to pull this off." Danielle held her breath, waiting as McCall pondered for a moment.

"I can probably help," she said finally. "I'd like to see that man get something warm for Christmas."

"Great!" Danielle exclaimed. "I'll let you know when we have our first meeting."

McCall opened the door, ready to step out, but stopped. "Thanks," she said quietly.

Danielle said nothing as she studied the expression on the younger girl's face.

"I'm glad you took us with you today. It was . . . I don't know . . . neat, I guess. I didn't know there were so many homeless people in our city. All those people who volunteer are really cool."

"Yeah, they are, aren't they?" Danielle nodded in agreement.

McCall nodded. "I better go in. See ya, Danielle."

Danielle watched McCall walk away. The wall between them was still there, but brick by brick it was coming down. After their morning at the shelter, Danielle realized that she could spend hours and hours planning fun, entertaining activities for her Laurels, but the only thing that was going to have any impact on these girls and change their lives was service.

She found herself wishing she'd gone to Young Women when she was younger. She wondered how different her life would be today if she had.

⁂

Early the next day before the doors opened to the public, the employees of Creative Display and the crew and committee for the Jubilee of Trees were at the Convention Center working furiously to have everything ready for the rush of holiday shoppers.

"Put the spotlights on each side," Abby said as she stood back and took another look at Danielle's tree. Cassie and Danielle each positioned a spotlight to shine toward the tree from either side.

"There," Cassie said. "How's that?"

"Perfect!" Abby said, clasping her hands together victoriously. "What a show we're going to have this year."

Across the room, Vincent yelled for Abby to come and help, so she was off to help him create yet another masterpiece. Determined to make the Jubilee every bit as good or better each year, Abby had spared no expense. She had every sort of entertainment imaginable lined up to perform during each day, and the air was full of fragrant spices and the heavenly odor of fresh-baked goods.

Danielle had never felt the holiday spirit as profoundly as she did this year. Part of this, she knew, was because she was more involved preparing for the holiday than she ever had before. Between decorating the Christmas tree, volunteering at the homeless shelter, and now organizing the Sub-for-Santa, she'd honestly felt the spirit of Christmas as never before.

"Hey," a male voice said, "this tree is great." Danielle turned to see Bart, Lenny, and Roberta coming in her direction.

"Hi, you guys," Danielle said. "This is a surprise." She climbed down from the stepladder and greeted each of them with a hug. "Thanks for coming down."

"We wanted to see the tree and see what you're doing for the rest of the day. We're going to breakfast then to a movie or something," Roberta said.

"Would you like to come?" Bart asked hopefully.

"Sure," Danielle said. "I'm actually finished. I was just adjusting a couple of ornaments." She looked back at the tree one last time to make sure it looked just right.

"I'm through here," Cassie said, gathering up some snippets of ribbon and lace. "I think I'll go see if Abby needs my help."

"Okay, Cass," Danielle said. "Thanks for your help."

Cassie answered with a wave.

"So . . ." Danielle looked at her friends. "You really like it?"

"It's beautiful, Dani," Roberta said. "I think it's one of the prettiest ones here." Danielle was flattered. She knew Roberta had to say that, but she still liked hearing the words.

"My folks would love this tree," Bart said. "My mom should be here sometime this morning. I'll tell her to come and take a look."

"It's awesome, Danielle," Lenny said. "Good job."

"Thanks, you guys. I'm glad you like it," Danielle said, enjoying their praise. She hoped it brought a lot of money to the cause. That was all that mattered.

***

"Well," Danielle said out loud as she plopped down on her bed. "That was fun."

She kicked off her shoes and peeled off her stockings. Another Carson sighting. This time it had been at the movie. He was with a honey-colored blonde this time. He'd seen Danielle, he'd even waved, but that didn't do anything to stop the ache in her heart. Why did she care? Why?!

Bart had been attentive and generous, buying her a large box of Swedish fish because he knew they were her favorite. He was such a nice guy, she told herself for the hundredth time. Why didn't she like him more? She'd sat right next to him, their knees touching nearly the entire movie and she'd felt nothing. But there was Carson, the big idiot, clear across the room and she'd felt like there was a geyser inside her chest, ready to erupt. Darn him, anyway!

# CHAPTER
## ✤ FIFTEEN ✤

Saturday morning Danielle made calls for the first Sub-for-Santa meeting. Any snow that had fallen on Thanksgiving had melted, but Danielle still felt a warm holiday glow.

"Hi, Walter, this is Danielle Camden," she identified herself. "I helped out on Thanksgiving, remember? I wonder if you could get a message to Harry for me. We're going to have a meeting at my house on Sunday evening at seven to talk about the Sub-for-Santa." She gave him her phone number and address.

"I'll give him a call," Walter said. "His health isn't real good, and I have a feeling he's been kind of sick lately. I have his home phone number around here somewhere."

Looking down at her list, Danielle put a check beside Harry's name. Her ward Relief Society president was coming and also someone from the Young Women organization. Both were happy to have a Christmas project to lend their services to. The priesthood would also be represented, and even her sister Miranda was coming. Rachel was getting too close to her due date and too uncomfortable to do much, but she offered to make phone calls to solicit donations. And all five of her Laurels had said they would come.

Roberta and Lenny planned to drop by if they could and even Bart had offered to come to the meeting. Danielle debated over and over whether or not to invite Carson. It would not only help her out to have his participation, but it would give her a reason to call him and hopefully clear the air between them. As busy as she'd kept herself and as hard as she tried not to, she couldn't keep him off her mind.

Before she could talk herself out of it, she dialed his number, her heartbeat racing faster and faster with each ring. Just as she was about to hang up the phone, the answering machine picked up.

"Leave your message and we'll get right back to you," it said.

"Uh, hi, uh," she stammered. "This is a message for Carson Turner. This is Danielle Camden calling. I'm organizing a Sub-for-Santa and wondered if you have any free time or would be interested in helping me out. We're having a meeting at my house Sunday evening at seven o'clock. I hope you can be there. Mom's making her famous German chocolate cake to serve afterward. I'd love—"

"BEEP!" The machine clicked off and left her hanging in mid-sentence.

"—to see you there," she finished, then hung up the phone. "He won't come," she said and crossed his name off her list.

⋇⋇ ✦ ⋇⋇

"Okay, everybody," Danielle said to the small group of people gathered in her living room. Her mother had decorated the house beautifully with dozens of pots of poinsettias scattered about and a sparkling Christmas tree dressed in white lights with shiny burgundy ornaments. A spicy pumpkin scent from a burning candle filled the air.

"First of all, thank you for coming tonight. I know how busy you all are, and I know we really don't have that much time to pull this off, but if we work together I think we can really make a big difference to some less fortunate families for Christmas."

The doorbell rang and Dorothy Camden slipped out of the room to answer it. To Danielle's delight, Harry walked into the room and took a seat offered by her mother. Danielle gave him a warm, sincere smile and continued.

"Tonight I would like to present to you my plan of action, get your input and approval, and then make assignments. We'll meet again in a week and see how close we are to our goal. Keep in mind, the final goal is to donate used clothing and items to the homeless shelter and provide Christmas gifts and food for needy families on Christmas Eve. Of course, we'll be making the deliveries early enough in the day so you can still get together with your families, but we would like to encourage you to get your entire families involved in this experience. Everyone can help, even small children. The more the merrier."

Danielle looked around the room and waited for any comments. Bart, Lenny, and Roberta sat in one corner, the representatives from her ward were in the other. Straight ahead were Cassie and several others from Creative Display. Allie, Chloe, and Erin were there but Lucy was sick. Danielle didn't know where McCall was.

And of course, Carson wasn't there. Still hoping he might show up, she presented her plan, discussing the various needs and options for donations. Afterwards she opened the floor for discussion, and everyone had ideas to suggest and concerns to point out. Danielle soon realized how important each member of the group would be in making the Sub-for-Santa a success. The Relief Society president and Young Women counselor both felt they had the woman power and resources to gather donations with well over a hundred combined individuals working together. They would gather food items and blankets in addition to toys and clothes. The elders quorum president was eager to help organize and deliver the goods.

"What about getting a Christmas tree for each family?" Cassie offered. "I'll bet some families won't even have a tree." She and the other Creative Display volunteers committed to make sure each family would get a beautifully decorated tree.

Miranda would focus on obtaining food donations for each family.

"Now we just need to come up with names. I can think of several families here in our own neighborhood, but I'm sure there are many inner-city families who could also use our help," Danielle said.

"I can get some names from Walter," Harry volunteered. "There are a few families who come through the shelter."

"We'll work with Harry to get the names," Roberta offered in behalf of Lenny and Bart.

"That would be great, Roberta." With her wedding only a few months away, Danielle appreciated her friend's willingness to do anything at all.

Danielle looked down at her agenda to make sure they'd covered everything. "If it's all right with everyone, we'll meet again the same time next Sunday and report on each of our assignments."

When her mother invited the group into the kitchen for German chocolate cake and ice cream, the room emptied quickly except for Danielle and Harry. He looked at her apologetically. "I think I'll just go on home," he told her.

Danielle felt a stab of disappointment. "Can't you stay for dessert? My mother makes the best German chocolate cake you've ever tasted."

"Well, I don't—"

"Please. It's the least we can do to thank you for your time and willingness to help."

Danielle won out and escorted Harry into the kitchen where the committee was oohing and aahing over Mrs. Camden's delicious cake. Danielle cut a big piece for Harry, adding several scoops of ice cream to the side.

"Here," she said, showing him to an empty chair around the dining table. "Have a seat and I'll get you a drink of ice water."

As she went to get some water, Danielle wondered about Harry. What was his story? He seemed educated and despite a limp, carried himself with a sense of pride, but there was a loneliness and sadness about him that tugged at Danielle's heart. He seemed vaguely familiar, but Danielle couldn't imagine why.

"Danielle, I think the glass is full," her mother said as Danielle stood at the kitchen sink.

Danielle looked down at the overflowing glass. "Oh, I guess it is."

She carried the glass back to the table where Harry sat. Danielle's father had joined him, and the two men were talking about fly fishing and tying their own flies. The exchange between Harry and Earl Camden was the liveliest she'd seen Harry since she'd met him. Obviously fishing was one of his passions. As she set the glass on the table next to Harry's plate, her father launched into his explanation of how to get to his favorite fishing spot in Idaho.

"I'm telling you, Harry," he said, "I was pulling out bass this big." He held his hands two feet apart in front of him. When Harry described his favorite fishing spot, his face brightened noticeably as he spoke about standing thigh-deep in a rushing stream in the mountains of Montana. Leaving the two men alone to continue their conversation, Danielle returned to the kitchen to help Roberta, who was washing dishes.

Lenny came looking for Roberta, ready to leave as soon as Bart was finished in the bathroom. Danielle and her mother made eye contact. The toilet seat test!

"Dani, honey, can you hand me a pen?" Dorothy Camden asked her daughter. She was jotting down her frosting recipe for the Relief Society president.

One by one the guests thanked Dorothy for the refreshments and bid their good-byes. Before long, Bart joined Lenny and Roberta as they were getting on their coats. "Tell your mom that her cake was really good," Bart said to Danielle, who thanked him again for coming.

"Anytime," he smiled.

*Uh-oh*, she thought. *He's got that look in his eye.* It was obvious that his feelings were getting stronger. He took her hand, and she thought he was going to shake it. But he held it lingeringly.

*No, Bart. Don't do this.*

"Danielle, I really think it's great what you're doing here. I'm really proud of you for organizing this Sub-for-Santa. Call me anytime you need help." He pulled her closer to him.

"Thanks, Bart," she said quickly, pulling her hand back and grabbing his coat for him. "I'd better go help my mom clean up. I'll talk to you later."

As he pulled on his coat, he said, "Maybe we can get together and play tennis this week. Or go out to dinner."

"I'll have to see," Danielle said, her voice noncommittal. "I might be a little busy with all this organizing and stuff."

When Danielle returned to the kitchen, her Laurels were just getting ready to leave. "So, is that your boyfriend?" Chloe asked.

Danielle wanted to set Chloe's suspicions to rest immediately. "We're just friends," she said firmly.

"Too bad," her mother said. "I quite liked him."

"He's pretty cute," Erin said. "But he needs to lose the glasses. He'd be much better-looking if he did."

"Yeah," Allie agreed. "And maybe grow his hair out just a little. He looks like a missionary."

"Uh-oh," Erin noticed the time. "I gotta get home," she said. "I've still got homework."

Thanking Danielle's mother for the "yummy" cake, the girls pulled on their coats and gloves. "Bye, Danielle," Chloe said, slipping into her coat, then added, teasingly, "Maybe Bart can come to one of our activities sometime."

"Good-bye, you guys," Danielle said, irritatedly, and pushed them out the door. Shaking her head she went back to the kitchen to finish cleaning up. Harry was just getting up from the table to carry his plate to the sink.

"Here, Harry," Danielle offered. "I'll take that for you."

"The cake was wonderful," he said. "I haven't had a good piece of German chocolate cake for years."

As she watched him leave in an old nondescript Buick sedan, Danielle wondered why she felt drawn to him. She wasn't usually the type to get involved in other people's lives and problems, but she was curious about Harry. Maybe it was the loneliness that surrounded him or the sadness on his face that tugged at her heart, touching her deeply, moving her to reach out to him.

# CHAPTER
## SIXTEEN

That night before going to bed, Danielle organized her notes from the meeting and jotted down some ideas and thoughts about the discussion. She was pleased with the support and willingness everyone had shown to make the Sub-for-Santa effort a success. The only thing that could have made it better would have been Carson's presence.

*I guess I shouldn't be surprised he didn't show,* she thought as she kicked off her slippers and sat down on her bed. The last time she'd talked to him, he'd been clearly unhappy with her, and the only times she'd seen him since then, he'd been with a date.

"Good night, honey," Dorothy Camden said, peeking into her daughter's room.

"Good night, mom. Thanks for letting me have the meeting here tonight and for making refreshments. Tell me, what did you think about Roberta's fiancé, Lenny?"

"He seems like a nice boy," she said. "I didn't get to speak with him too much though."

"Yeah," Danielle said thoughtfully. She must have sighed without realizing it because her mother looked at her expectantly.

"What is it, sweetie?" she asked.

Danielle raised her shoulders and looked at her mother. "I don't know, Mom. I want Roberta to be happy. I just hope Lenny will be good to her, take care of her."

Her mother nodded in understanding. "His friend Bart certainly is a nice boy," she commented.

"Yes, he is," Danielle agreed. "He's polite and well-mannered, too. He treats me like a queen. I know he likes me . . . a lot," she ended on a sigh.

"Is that a problem?" her mother asked.

"Kinda," Danielle said, bending one knee up and wrapping her arms around it. "I just don't feel the same for him. I really do like him, I just don't *like* him," she said, emphasizing the word.

"Oh, Dani," her mother comforted her. "These things take time. If it's right for you to be with Bart, your feelings will change and grow."

Danielle looked at her mother in surprise. "They will?"

"Yes, honey, of course they will," she promised. "Love takes time. You have to get to know each other better. The more you get to know him, the more your heart will be able to tell if he's the one."

Danielle let her mother's words sink in. Then she remembered that Bart had used the bathroom before he left and asked her mother if Bart had passed the test. Dorothy Camden neatly sidestepped the question. "I regret even bringing up that silly test," she said. "Bart's a very nice boy."

Danielle stared at her mother. "I know that. But did he pass the test?" she repeated.

Mrs. Camden sighed with exasperation. "Oh, all right. No, he didn't. He flunked the test."

Danielle gasped. "You're kidding! Are you sure?"

She shook her head regretfully. "No one used the bathroom after him. Sure enough, he left the seat up."

Danielle shook her head with disbelief. "I'm shocked. Bart is like a walking manners textbook. I'm so surprised."

"I was too," Dorothy admitted.

"How about that?" Danielle said, relaxing back. Of all people to fail, Bart was the last one she would have expected. Then she had a thought. "Since I haven't known about this test until recently, I want to ask you something, Mom."

"I need to get up early in the morning, honey. I've really got to get to bed." She seemed strangely evasive, and Danielle wondered if her mother knew what she was going to ask.

"It will just take a second." Danielle's eyes narrowed in amusement. "Did you do the test on Todd?"

"Todd Hardaway?" her mother questioned innocently, too innocently, Danielle thought.

"You know very well I mean Todd Hardaway," Danielle said. "Mr. Perfect, remember?"

Danielle's mother looked away. "Actually, honey, I don't remember."

Danielle didn't believe her for a second. *"Really,* Mom."

"Well, it's been such a long time since he was here," she hedged. "Let me think."

"Mother. I'm sure you remember. Did Todd leave the toilet seat up or not?" She could tell by the closed expression on her mother's face that she didn't want to answer. Which meant that Danielle definitely wanted to know what she was hiding.

"Does it make a difference now?" Dorothy asked her.

"No, not really," Danielle said thoughtfully, then she changed her mind. "Actually, yes. I'd like to know."

"Well, you know I thought the world of Todd. In my opinion he was a perfect young man."

"Yes, I know. But—" Danielle prodded.

"Okay. No," she said frankly, "he didn't put the lid down." Her mother looked away quickly, as if she'd just revealed Todd's dark side as a serial killer.

"And you would have let me marry him? Mother, I'm shocked!" Danielle teased.

"Well, he was such a nice boy," Dorothy rationalized. "I guess I figured he made up for it in so many other ways."

"I'm really surprised, Mom," Danielle said, pretending to be horrified. "I mean, first it's toilet seats, then it's squeezing the toothpaste from the middle. Who knows what else it could lead to next?"

"All right Danielle, that's enough," her mother reproved her. Danielle stopped her teasing but was inwardly glad to hear that Todd "Perfect" Hardaway actually did have a flaw.

Danielle had one more question. "I'm confused, Mom. You told me you thought leaving the toilet seat up showed whether a boy was considerate or not. Does it or doesn't it?"

"Okay, yes, but I was willing to let it slide with Todd," Dorothy said in her defense.

"I can't believe you were willing to risk my happiness," Danielle said, half teasing. Still part of her was serious. She didn't put much stock in the toilet seat test, but her mother did. That's what bothered her.

Dorothy put her chin up. "I didn't see it like that."

"Mom," Danielle said, very seriously. "Do you still feel like I made a big mistake not marrying Todd?"

Her mother thought for a moment before she answered. "Honey, I thought the world of Todd and I would have been very happy if you'd have married him. But if you didn't love him and you didn't feel good about it—especially if you were prayerful about it and sought the Lord's help—then no, I don't think you made a mistake. I think you did the right thing."

Danielle grew teary-eyed. It was the first time since she stopped seeing Todd that her mother had shown her support for Danielle's decision.

"I guess the bigger question is, do you feel like you did the right thing?" her mother asked her.

"Sometimes when I see all my friends married or getting married, and having babies, or when people in the ward say things about how old I am and ask me why I'm not married or why I didn't go on a mission, I start to doubt my feelings. I wonder if I made a mistake. But Mom, I didn't love Todd. I tried to, I wanted to, but I just didn't."

Her voice broke and she realized that she still had some painful feelings to work through. Most of that pain had come from the fact that no one, except Roberta, had agreed with her, or understood why she broke up with Todd. Her sister, Miranda, had been the most understanding person in her family, but everyone else had thought she was stupid to end their relationship. Danielle had started to wonder if she possessed enough good judgement to recognize the right guy when she finally met him. Maybe she'd already met him and just didn't know it. Maybe Bart really was the right guy for her, but she was just too dense or out of touch with the Spirit to know for sure.

Seeing that her daughter was upset, Dorothy Camden put her arm lovingly around Danielle's shoulders. "Honey, I know you worry about this and you wonder if and when you're going to get married. But as long as you're living the gospel and doing the best you can, especially if you're staying close to the Spirit and letting the Lord direct your life, everything will turn out for you, you'll see. I know you'll find a wonderful man to marry. You just can't get discouraged. You have to keep yourself strong and ready for when it happens, because it will come when you least expect it."

"He'll just *waltz* right into my life, right?" Danielle said sarcastically.

"Exactly," Dorothy agreed. "And whoever does will be a very lucky fellow."

"Thanks, Mom," Danielle said. She got off the bed and hugged her mother, then she crawled into bed and pulled the covers up beneath her chin. Outside a bitter Arctic wind was blowing through the Salt Lake Valley. Danielle thought about the homeless people, the families, the children. Where did they sleep on nights like this? How did they stay warm?

She didn't know exactly what the Lord had in store for her, or if she would ever find her eternal mate, but she did feel good about her efforts to help the less fortunate. Even though she was lonely and very much alone, she felt somehow fulfilled inside with the joy that came from giving service. She was full of questions and didn't have any answers, but she did have faith that the Lord was aware of her and guiding her. For now that was enough.

And, she snickered, Todd Hardaway had flunked the toilet seat test!

*⋇⋇ ❀ ⋇⋇*

"Okay, Lucy, look down while I put this eyeshadow on you," Rachel Camden said. As Danielle had predicted, her sister had been more than pleased to help with Lucy's transformation. The dance was less than an hour away, and Lucy was a bundle of nerves.

The doorbell rang.

"Danielle," her mother called from the basement. "Can you get the door?"

"Sure, Mom." Danielle ran to the front door, wondering who it was. "McCall! What are you doing?" She could tell that the girl had been crying.

McCall tried to speak casually. "I, um, I just wondered if Lucy could use my help getting ready for the dance."

"I'm sure she'd love your help," Danielle said cautiously. She'd heard McCall talking about her own date some weeks earlier. "But don't you have to get ready for the dance yourself?"

"I'm . . . not . . . going . . . ," she said, fighting the tears that threatened to spill any minute.

"Do you want to talk about it?" Danielle asked.

McCall shook her head.

"Well, come on in," Danielle invited. "We'd love your help."

McCall followed Danielle to Rachel's old bedroom, where Lucy sat in front of a mirror, in one of Rachel's old robes with hot rollers in her hair, while Rachel applied her makeup. Dorothy Camden had stepped in as tailor and was taking the dress in at the waist and making some minor adjustments.

"McCall," Lucy exclaimed when she saw her. "What are you doing here?"

"Hold still," Rachel told her. "I don't want to get mascara all over."

"Sorry."

"I just came to help you get ready," McCall told her.

"What time is your date picking you up?" Lucy asked, keeping perfectly still.

"I'm not going to the dance," McCall said in a tone that let them all know she didn't want to talk about it. Danielle looked at Chloe, who looked back at her; neither of them said anything. They didn't dare.

"Okay," Rachel said as she gave Lucy's lashes one last brush stroke, as if finishing a beautiful oil painting. "Look up."

Slowly lifting her eyes, Lucy looked in the mirror and a smile grew on her face. Rachel had done a magnificent job—not too much makeup, just enough to bring out her beautiful, thickly lashed eyes and classic cheekbones.

"Lucy," Chloe said breathlessly. "You look beautiful."

Lucy blinked several times quickly, to clear the tears gathering in her eyes. "Oh!" she exclaimed. "Do you have a tissue? I don't want to ruin my mascara."

Danielle handed her a whole box. "Nice job, Rachel. Do you think you could do that for me?"

"Sure, but only if you'll let me pluck your eyebrows."

"No!" Danielle exclaimed. "I've told you a hundred times, it hurts too much."

"Then there's no point," Rachel said crisply. "Eyebrows are like a picture frame for the eyes. I'd be wasting my time unless you let me fix your eyebrows."

"Here you go," Dorothy Camden announced as she returned with the altered dress. "I think I got it." She looked at Lucy's reflection in the mirror. "Lucy, honey, you look so pretty."

"Thanks, Sister Camden. Rachel did it."

Rachel smiled proudly. "Let's hurry and do your hair, then I've got to get off my feet. I can feel them swelling."

"You know, I always wanted silky brown hair like yours," McCall said as she helped take the rollers out of Lucy's hair. She wound one of the ringlets around her finger.

"You did?" Lucy asked with surprise. "But you've got, like, the perfect hair. Everyone wants your hair, McCall."

McCall gave a wistful little smile, and Danielle wondered what had happened to her that evening. For the first time, she seemed extremely down and vulnerable.

"Okay," Rachel said, sweeping the curls up on top of Lucy's head. "How brave do you feel?"

"Brave?" Lucy asked.

"I'd like to pin most of it up and have these long pieces curl around your face." Rachel pulled out a few strands and let them spiral down the sides of Lucy's face. It was regal, elegant, and very feminine.

"Oh, yes," Lucy said. "I like that."

"Jake's going to flip when he sees you," Chloe said happily.

Rachel sprayed and teased, arranging and pinning curls here and there until the final look was achieved. "There," she said. "That's it."

Danielle was stunned at Lucy's transformation. She felt like she was watching a butterfly emerge from a cocoon.

"Put on your dress," Chloe said, clapping her hands together. "I can't wait to see you in it."

The others waited while Lucy stepped into the bathroom to put on her dress. Then, a few minutes later, the door opened. When she stepped out, everyone gasped. The deep purple velvet bodice complimented her creamy complexion and dark eyes and hair. She wore a tiny glittering diamond necklace and matching earrings, a gift from her father for her first date. Even though they weren't real diamonds, she still loved them.

"Lucy," Chloe whispered. "You're beautiful."

Danielle grabbed her camera. "Let's take your picture before you go home. I wish I could be there when Jake picks you up."

"Me too," Chloe said. "Maybe we could hide in the bushes," she said to McCall, who smiled for the first time that night.

"My dad's going to take pictures," Lucy said. She put her hand on her stomach and took several breaths. "Are you sure I look okay?"

McCall stepped up to her and fixed one of the curls clinging to her face. "Lucy, you look just like Cinderella."

"I kind of feel like her, too," Lucy said, then looked shyly at McCall. "Thanks for coming over to help me. I hope everything's okay."

"Everything's fine," McCall assured her. "Now you go have fun tonight."

"I can give you a ride home, Lucy," Chloe said. "I've got to be going anyway."

"I'll go with you," McCall said.

Good-byes were said and Danielle watched as three of her Laurels walked out the door together. She didn't know what had happened to McCall, but she seemed okay now. It gave Danielle a warm feeling inside to see the girls becoming friends. She was amazed at how much she was enjoying this calling. She never would have guessed she'd like working with the Young Women so much. She was glad she had the oldest group though. Those Beehives had way too much energy and the Mia Maids had too much PMS for her.

Offering a silent prayer that Lucy would have a wonderful evening and that McCall would be okay, Danielle joined her sister and mother in the kitchen for a cup of hot chocolate and some pumpkin cookies, thinking that Lucy looked so wonderful after Rachel's makeover, she might even consider letting Rachel go after her eyebrows with a pair of tweezers.

⋙ ⚙ ⋘

"Danielle, someone's here to see you." Looking up from the arrangement she was working on, Danielle saw one of the young girls who had been hired as extra Christmas help. Wondering who it was but half expecting Bart, Danielle poked one more silk poinsettia flower into the centerpiece and dusted her hands on her apron. Then she made her way to the front of the store as she hummed "Let it snow, let it snow, let it snow," along with the Christmas music playing in the background.

"Hi, Mrs. Whitworth," she called to one of their best clients.

"The wreath was a big hit at my Christmas party," the woman replied.

"I'm so glad to hear that," Danielle replied. "Have a Merry Christmas."

"I will," the woman said. "You too."

Spicy smelling candles burned and the twinkle of thousands of lights on displays filled the room. Outside the sidewalks were covered with a light dusting of snow. Shoppers and last-minute decorators packed the showroom with the excitement and bustle of holiday entertaining. It was intoxicating.

She nearly crashed into Vincent as he came around the corner. He was also humming along with the song, and they laughed, then sang together with the chorus, "Let it snow, let it snow, let it snow." Then he bounced away, the jingle bell on his red furry hat bobbing and tinkling. Vincent was a Christmas addict. Everything about the season thrilled him. Danielle found his enthusiasm contagious.

However, her smile froze on her face when she reached the front of the display room to meet her guest. It was Carson!

"Danielle, hi." He looked so handsome in jeans and a ski parka. His cheeks were rosy from being outside. Her heart leapt into her throat at the sight of him. *Stop that,* she tried to tell herself as she felt her whole being light up like a Christmas tree. *Don't lose your head.*

"This is a surprise," she said evenly, scarcely able to breathe. "How are you, Carson?"

"I'm great, especially now that finals are over." He looked uncomfortable, as if knowing she had every right to send him packing. With the hubbub and madness of the packed showroom, Danielle knew it would be difficult to have any sort of real conversation.

"Why don't we go into the employee lounge where we can talk?" she said and turned to lead him away from the showroom. She crossed her fingers, hoping they would find the employee lounge empty. It was, and she took a seat, looking up at Carson and trying to read from his expression why he had come.

At first, they chatted about the weather and her job and his classes at the "U," and again Danielle wondered silently why Carson was there. He seemed nervous and uncomfortable. What was going on? she wanted to ask him. Instead, she let him sweat it out. She wasn't going to pretend nothing had happened between them and that everything was hunky-dory. They hadn't spoken for a long time and she'd seen him on at least two dates. No—she'd let him stew in his own juices until he was ready to say why he was there.

Finally, he was ready to come clean. "Danielle," he said, "I, uh—" He cleared his throat. Danielle swallowed hard with anticipation. "I owe you an apology," he said.

Her first impulse was to say, "that's okay," or "oh no, you don't," but she bit her tongue. Because the truth was, he did owe her an apology. Raising one eyebrow with interest she looked at him square in the face and waited for him to go on.

Taking a deep breath, he continued. "I'm really sorry about the way I acted the last time we were together. You were only trying to help and I—" he paused, "—well, I guess I haven't completely sorted through all my emotions about my father. I don't know, maybe in time I'll feel a need to talk to him. Right now I don't." He swallowed. "I can't."

*So you'd rather let your unresolved feelings for your father slowly eat away at you, is that it?* she wanted to say. Didn't he realize he couldn't ever be truly happy until he confronted his father and worked through their differences? But she knew she couldn't say that. Carson could say whatever he wanted, but Danielle knew he needed his father.

"Anyway," he continued, "I feel bad that I was so rude and I wasn't sure you'd ever want to see me again. But the truth is," he said, reaching for her hand, "I've missed you."

Her expression must have shown her skepticism. Every time she'd seen him he'd been with a date. How much could he miss her? "Really?" she said, trying to keep the sarcasm from her voice as she pulled her hand from his and clasped them together in her lap.

"Really," he said. "I know you probably don't believe me, but it's true. It seems like everyone I know wants to set me up with their sister or their niece or somebody."

"Carson, you don't need to justify who you go out with to me." She tried to speak evenly but her throat felt dry and parched. Still, she didn't want him to think it bothered her that he'd been dating, even though it did.

His eyes met hers. "I know that," he said, "but I would much rather have been with you than with any of those girls." Again, he reached out, taking her hand in his. This time she didn't pull it away.

Danielle took a deep breath, trying to keep her heart from doing crazy flip-flops inside her chest. Her head told her sternly not to get involved with this guy; he had way too much emotional baggage to deal with.

"I also wanted to tell you I'm sorry I didn't make it to your meeting Sunday. I went to a Christmas concert with the family I live with, and we ended up going over to some relatives' house afterward. How did it go?"

"Good," she said, glad to be on a less personal topic. "I have a lot of support and help."

"I hope you'll still let me help. Now that I'm out of school, I'll have some free time."

"I can use any help you have to offer," she said, knowing she couldn't refuse an offer to serve.

"I was wondering if you needed some suggestions for names for the Sub-for-Santa. I've met some pretty great kids at the hospital, and I know they'll be spending Christmas there. Their families are really struggling with their medical bills. I know they could use any help you could possibly give them."

"That's a wonderful idea," she said. "We're still looking for families." She paused, considering. "We're having another meeting this Sunday. Do you think you could come?"

"Sure. I shouldn't have any conflicts this time." He smiled winsomely at her and she felt her heartbeat speed up. "Um," he started hesitantly, "I wondered if you're busy this Friday. We could go out for pizza or something."

Danielle felt her heart skip a beat. "I'd like that!" she exclaimed, forgetting completely to listen to the warning voice in her head. But then reason—and memory—kicked in. She'd completely forgotten she was going to the Nutcracker Ballet with Bart and his parents. "Oh, I'm sorry, I can't. I've got another date." His expression reflected disappointment. And she was glad. Maybe now he knew how she felt. "I'm not busy on Saturday evening," she suggested. "We could go out then."

His expression brightened, then his excitement vanished just as quickly. "I can't. I just about forgot. I'm getting together with some missionary friends—you know, the ones I went to Thailand with after my mission. We're going out for Thai food."

"Oh," she said flatly. Maybe their relationship just wasn't meant to be. "Maybe some other time then," she said with a shrug. *So much for that.*

He didn't say anything, and Danielle felt her heart thudding slowly in her chest. Twenty minutes before, she'd been just fine. Busy working, not thinking about Carson. Well, only now and then. She'd almost resigned herself to never seeing him again. Then, without warning, he'd popped back into her life, and in a matter of minutes her heart had flipped, then flopped. Maybe a nice boring relationship with a guy like Bart was a much better idea after all. A relationship with Carson was like a roller coaster ride, with dizzying heights and thrilling twists and turns, but it wreaked havoc with her emotions.

"Hey, wait a minute," Carson said, looking pleased with himself. "Why don't you come to dinner with me? I'm sure John will bring his wife and the other two might bring dates."

Seeing the sincere pleasure in Carson's eyes, Danielle felt her heart flutter. "I wouldn't want to impose," she said, wondering why she didn't leap at the chance to go with him.

"But I'd like to have you there," he insisted, then hesitated. "Unless you don't like Thai food."

"Actually I do," Danielle admitted. When she'd worked at Turner

Consulting, she and some coworkers used to go to lunch at a Thai restaurant near the office.

"I'd really like it if you'd come," he said, tightening his hold on her hand.

"If you're sure," she said slowly, feeling the warmth of his gaze and the touch of his hand on hers.

"I'll pick you up at six o'clock on Saturday then," he smiled.

✹

But he didn't pick her up at six. He picked her up at eleven—that morning. He called about nine, wondering if she wanted to go to the mall with him to look for a new watch. Danielle dropped everything and was ready in a flash, practically waiting on the curb, when he pulled up.

Helping her into his Jeep Cherokee, he thanked her. "I really appreciate your help. I'm not that great of a shopper."

Was he kidding? Being with Carson and shopping was the best of both worlds. "Well," she teased with a dramatic sweep of her hands, "it *was* a huge sacrifice to come shopping with you. I had big plans to help my dad straighten the garage."

"Hmmm," he answered with a thoughtful nod. "Tough choice."

It felt so good to be with Carson that Danielle wanted to laugh out loud with happiness. A bus went by, carrying a load of skiers up to the mountains.

"We haven't seen much snow down here in the valley, but the resorts are getting plenty," he said. "I've been wanting to go skiing all season, but I've had a hard time finding time. Maybe during the Christmas break we could go together sometime."

"I'd like that," she answered and could almost imagine them riding on the lift together, skiing moguls, and sitting by a cozy fire in the lodge. Even though they'd talked about skiing once before and nothing had come of it, at least now Danielle knew why.

At the mall, they combed stores looking for a good deal on a watch. Carson didn't have much money to spend and needed something dependable. He finally found a watch he liked and almost bought it, even though it cost a bit more than he'd planned on spending. Danielle suggested they wait until they'd looked at all their options first, having learned from Roberta to be patient and check as many stores as possible before making a decision. They continued shopping, but took a short break to enjoy a hot, buttery pretzel and creamy frozen yogurt at the food court. At the next store, to their complete surprise, they found the exact same watch Carson nearly bought in a previous store, for almost twenty dollars cheaper.

"I think you've found your watch," Danielle congratulated him.

Outside the store, Carson surprised her with a brief kiss. Breathlessly she asked, "What was that for?"

"For the twenty dollars you saved me. That's groceries for a week for me," he informed her solemnly, taking her arm as they walked toward the escalator. "I've never believed in good luck charms, but I think you are one."

"I don't think so," she laughed. "My own luck isn't so hot. How could I bring good luck to someone else?"

"I don't know, but you do. Good things happen to me when I'm around you. I even think my grades have improved this quarter." He winked at her. "And whenever I look at this watch, I'll think of you."

Danielle didn't answer. If she were honest with herself, she could tell she was falling for him, a little too far, a little too fast. But her rational side told her to be careful. It was all too good to be true. Carson still had to resolve some issues with his dad before he could start building other relationships. *Slow down,* she told herself.

His voice broke into her thoughts. "Do you want me to take you home or do you feel like walking over to Temple Square?"

The last time she'd been there had been with Todd. She thought she'd like to replace that awful memory with a good one. "Temple Square," she answered, looking up at him and smiling.

Hand in hand, they strolled onto the temple grounds. The day was unusually warm, and visitors and tourists filled the sidewalks.

Inside the North Visitors' Center, Danielle and Carson wound their way up a circular pathway that led to the statue of the Christus. It didn't matter how many times Danielle saw the statue, it always moved her to tears, especially this time of year. Carson noticed she was blinking rapidly, trying to clear the moisture from her eyes. Without a word, he wrapped his arm around her shoulders and held her close.

"Excuse me," a voice behind them said. "Is that Carson Turner?" Danielle thought the voice sounded familiar, but even so, she was astonished to see Jack Harris, her former supervisor from Turner Consulting, walking towards them.

"Danielle Camden?" Jack couldn't hide his surprise. "Is that you?"

Danielle laughed at his obvious shock seeing her with Carson. She stepped forward and gave him a hug. "It's great to see you."

"It's great to see you, too," he replied, looking first at her, then at Carson. "I must admit, I'm a little surprised to see you two together. How'd all this happen?"

Carson laughed and took Danielle's hand in his. "We met last year when I was here for Christmas break, then ran into each other again at a Halloween dance on campus."

"You're going to school here?" Jack exclaimed. "Why haven't you called? Maureen and the kids would love to see you again. In fact, the whole tribe's here somewhere." He glanced around the room. "What happened to Harvard?"

"I quit. I'm in medical school up at the 'U,'" he said. Danielle thought he sounded much happier identifying himself with medical school than he had sounded talking with her about Harvard when they had first met a year ago.

Jack nodded approvingly. "I'm proud of you, son. You'll make a fine doctor." Danielle knew how much Jack's approval meant to Carson. "And your mother would be proud of you, too," he added.

At that moment Maureen Harris approached him. "There you are, honey. The kids are starving." Then she stopped cold. "Carson? Is that really you?"

Once again Carson explained what he'd been doing over the past year and answered her questions. Maureen made him promise to come over for dinner some evening so they could catch up, then she left to find her children.

"Well," Jack said, "I'd better help round up the family. Who knows where they've all wandered off to?" He extended his hand toward Carson and the two men shook hands. "You take care and don't be a stranger," he said gruffly. "And next time you see your father, tell him I said hello."

"Okay," Carson said, not revealing that he and his father didn't associate any longer. "I'll be over to visit one of these days."

Even though their good-byes had been said, Jack didn't leave immediately. "I feel bad your dad had to sell the business," he said awkwardly, "but I have to admit, I wouldn't have had the courage to start my own business if I hadn't lost my job at Turner Consulting."

"You have your own business now?" Danielle asked.

"I have my own consulting business," he said proudly. "I work out of my home and I travel a lot, but Maureen and the kids love all the frequent flyer miles I get. We're going to Disney World for New Year's."

"That's wonderful," Danielle exclaimed, thrilled that her old boss was doing so well.

"In fact, do you remember Jenny Marshall?" Jack asked and Danielle nodded, remembering the day Jenny had been fired for taking so much time off from work due to a messy divorce.

"She works part-time for me, doing the books, making appointments, taking care of travel arrangements. She's even remarried and is expecting another baby in the spring."

Danielle shook her head in amazement. "Imagine that," she said. "Tell her hi for me and give her my best."

"I will," he replied. Hearing his youngest daughter calling to him from the other side of the room, he said hurriedly, "I'd better run. I'll see you two later. Merry Christmas to you both."

"Merry Christmas," they answered together.

They stood talking about Jack, saying how good it was to learn he was doing so well. Danielle wanted to mention Carson's father, but wisely restrained herself. Seeing a group of tourists enter a nearby auditorium, Danielle and Carson started toward them to see what was happening.

"*First Vision* starts in five minutes," said one of the sister missionaries as they walked past her.

"I haven't seen that movie in English since before my mission," he said. "You want to go in?"

"I haven't seen it since seminary," she confessed.

Finding seats toward the back of the auditorium, they settled in for the film. Carson reached over and took her hand in his, holding it gently. *This isn't a dream,* Danielle said to herself, forcing herself to remember to breathe. And yet it felt like a dream to be sitting with

Carson, feeling his hand on hers. A wonderful, glorious dream she never wanted to wake up from.

The lights dimmed and the movie began. Soon Danielle was caught up in the story of young Joseph Smith as he sought to find the true church of God. As he knelt in the Sacred Grove to pray for an answer, Danielle couldn't stop the tears that filled her eyes and the emotion that filled her heart. Never before had she been moved by the account as she was now.

When the show ended and the lights came on, she tried to hide her tears, but her face was streaked with moisture. She looked away, but Carson had already seen her.

"Hey," he turned her face toward him. "Are you okay?" he asked gently.

She nodded. "Sorry," she said. Her nose had started to run, so she sniffed, hoping it didn't run down her face, too. She searched in her purse for a tissue, relieved to finally find a napkin from the frozen yogurt place. Dabbing at her cheeks and wiping her nose, she composed herself.

"I don't know why I started crying," she said with an embarrassed laugh. "I don't usually fall apart in movies." She was glad to see the tourists had left, and they were the only ones left in the auditorium.

"I think I understand," he said. "My first day at the MTC, I think all the missionaries were nervous, a little scared, and totally overwhelmed," he explained. "I know I was and I admit, I wondered what I was doing there.

"But that night they took us to a room and showed us *The First Vision*. The movie started and the most peaceful feeling filled me, and it grew until I felt like my chest would burst. I knew without a doubt that it was the Spirit bearing witness to me that the Church was true and that the message of the restored gospel had to be spread to the rest of the world. I was so grateful I could be a part of that."

Hearing this, Danielle was fascinated. "So you were okay after that?" she asked.

"Oh, I still had rough days and hard times, like learning the language," he said earnestly. "I never thought I'd ever be able to communicate with anyone again. But the Lord helped me and blessed me." He smiled at her, his eyes warm and kind.

"Thanks," Danielle said.

"For what?" he asked.

"For helping me not feel stupid for crying. For understanding." She looked up into his incredible green eyes. "For being you."

He leaned toward her, ready to kiss her, when one of the sisters announced, "The next movie doesn't start for forty-five minutes."

"Oh," Carson said quickly to the sister missionary. "Thank you." A bit embarrassed, they quickly left the auditorium and made their way back outside. Finding a bench in the sunshine, they sat down. The sky was deep blue and cloudless; a few fall-colored leaves clung to the tree branches. Danielle watched a group of young girls, probably on a youth outing, walk around the square, laughing and giggling. They reminded her of her Laurels.

"Look at that cute baby," Carson said, pointing at a little girl who was probably not even a year old. She sat in her stroller, wearing a light pink coat and a matching bonnet. Dark, wispy curls framed her face and a pair of big brown eyes looked at them.

"She is darling," Danielle agreed, wiggling her fingers at the little girl.

Her parents had been standing nearby, their backs to Danielle and Carson, as they were looking at something. When they turned, Danielle nearly choked. It was Todd Hardaway and his wife.

Trying to duck behind Carson, Danielle attempted to hide, but it was too late, Todd had seen her and was pushing the baby stroller toward her.

"Oh, great," Danielle muttered, wondering what the chances of running into him were. *So much for being a good luck charm,* she thought wryly.

"Danielle," Todd exclaimed as he and his wife approached. "Hi there."

Danielle tried to smile. "Hi, Todd."

Carson immediately stood up, a sign of the good manners no doubt instilled in him by his mother. Reluctantly Danielle stood also.

"It's been a long time," Todd said, glancing at Carson then back at her. "How are you?"

"I'm great," she said with all the confidence she could muster, deeply grateful that Carson—gorgeous, wonderful, perfect Carson—

was at her side. "Todd, I want you to meet my good friend, Carson Turner. Carson, this is Todd Hardaway and his wife—"

"Shelby," Todd filled in the blank.

"Nice to meet you," Carson said, shaking first Todd's hand, then his wife's. He crouched down toward their baby. "Danielle and I were just commenting on what a beautiful baby you have."

Todd smiled proudly.

"Thank you," Shelby answered. "Her name is Victoria. We call her Tori."

"Cute," Danielle said, sincerely impressed by the woman Todd had married. She didn't know why, but she liked Shelby. She and Todd looked happy. She hoped that they were and she also hoped that Todd controlled his temper when he didn't get his way better with Shelby than he had with her.

"My mother's name is Victoria," Shelby explained. "She passed away when I was a little girl."

Danielle nodded, instantly grateful that her own mother was still living.

"So, what do you do, Carson?" Todd asked.

"Oh, I'm in med school. First year," he answered.

Danielle felt the need to brag just a little. "He was at Harvard getting his MBA, then decided to go to medical school." Looking toward Todd and Shelby, she said, "Todd has an MBA, don't you?"

"Yeah," he answered, "At BYU."

"That's a great school," Carson said. Danielle remembered that Todd had tried to get into Harvard. She knew it was immature, but it felt good to give him the message that she hadn't lived up to his prediction of marrying a loser. She didn't know who she was going to marry, but she wanted Todd to see who she was dating. She fought the urge to stick her tongue out at him.

Tori started to fuss in her stroller.

"Well," Todd said. "It's her nap time. We'd better get her home."

"Nice meeting you," Carson said.

"You too," Todd answered.

"Bye," Danielle said and waved at the little girl. "Bye, Tori."

They watched the family leave and just as Danielle feared, Carson asked, "So, how do you know Todd?"

She shut her eyes, wishing she could somehow be abducted by aliens.

"Danielle?"

"An old boyfriend," she said reluctantly.

"Oh," he nodded. "I take it, it was serious?"

"Kind of," Danielle answered.

"How serious?"

"He asked me to marry him, right here on Temple Square, almost two years ago," she admitted. "I turned him down."

"Ouch! Poor guy," Carson said.

"Poor guy!" she exclaimed. "What about me? It was hard for me, too."

"That's a pretty big blow to a guy's ego, though," he said sympathetically.

"Yeah, well, don't think he was very nice about it. He let me know that I would basically have a miserable life without him and that I would end up marrying a total loser, if in fact I ever did get married."

Carson was incredulous. "He said that?"

"He sure did," Danielle said, the memory still fresh and, in all honesty, a little painful.

Carson pulled her into a hug. "I can tell you right now, you will definitely not marry a loser, and any guy who marries you will be the luckiest guy in the world."

"Thanks," she replied, appreciating his vote of confidence.

"Come on," he said. "We've still got a few hours until dinner. Let's walk over to the Church museum or something."

As they walked to the museum, Danielle reflected upon their meeting with Todd. For months after their breakup, she'd lived in fear of running into him again, hoping to avoid an uncomfortable situation. But now that it had happened, she realized that Todd seemed perfectly content and happy with his wife and darling daughter, and Danielle felt like she was doing what she was supposed to be doing with her life.

With the release of guilt came relief as she realized she'd finally found closure to a part of her life that had never healed. Of course, it had helped, having Carson by her side. In fact, it went a long way toward giving her the strength to face Todd and his wife, which she wouldn't have wanted to do alone, even if it hadn't been as bad as she had once feared it would be.

# CHAPTER
## SEVENTEEN

Sunday morning Danielle awoke with the lingering taste of garlic and spicy Thai food in her mouth, and thoughts of Carson in her head. Their date yesterday had been perfect and last night had been perfect, too. Even though Carson had originally been invited to visit with old missionary friends and reminisce about Thailand, he and Danielle frequently became lost in their own conversation, separate and apart from the group. The more they got to know each other, the more they realized they had in common. Both had played clarinet in their high school bands, neither had ever been to Hawaii but wanted to go there, neither had ever broken a bone or been hospitalized, and both had had the chicken pox as children over Christmas.

They were silly things, Danielle knew, but it was exciting and fun to find things they had in common, to realize that they were more alike than she'd ever expected. Aside from their list of shared backgrounds and interests, they shared something even more important—the gospel. Carson was firm and steadfast in his testimony of the gospel and was committed to a temple marriage and raising his family in the Church. Even though Danielle hadn't always been a committed member—at times sleeping in and missing church and even skiing on Sunday occasionally—she'd never doubted that the Church was true. She knew the Lord loved her and that she was blessed beyond what she deserved. And now, having finally learned to lean on the Lord at all times, she'd grown even more committed to the gospel and stronger in her testimony.

Remembering the evening before, how Carson had held her hand or draped his arm around her shoulders at dinner, she stretched lazily in her bed, smiling dreamily to herself. She'd had a warm, protective feeling with him close by. A low, steady current ran between them, an electrifying spark she'd never felt with anyone else before. His brief but tender good-night kiss had turbo-charged her heartbeat and turned her bones to mush.

As she thought about her feelings, she made an astonishing realization. She didn't just *like* Carson, she *loved* him. Letting the revelation sink in for a moment, she wondered how that would change their relationship. For him, it wouldn't—because she didn't plan on telling him. But for her, it would—because it would mean that if nothing worked out between them, she was in for a whopper of a heartache.

But for now it felt so good to be in love. She loved being in love. Rolling over, she stretched her arms over her head. Every time the phone rang, she could feel her skin tingle, anticipating that it might be him. When they were together, just holding his hand sent chills up her spine. Even the most boring, mundane activity, like waiting in line at the movies or to be seated for dinner, didn't bother her—because she was with him. The worst part about loving a person, she decided, was being apart from him. She wanted to see Carson every night, be with him constantly, but that couldn't happen. Not with her job, and his classes and work up at the children's hospital.

Even if he never returned her love, even if she knew that loving him was setting her up for difficulty—especially with his estrangement from his father—she didn't know how to *not* love him. How could she turn off her feelings and tell her heart not to love him?

She couldn't.

She could only keep them to herself. She'd embarrassed herself once before, with Todd, telling everyone about him and their relationship. Then, when it hadn't worked out, everyone had wanted an explanation. Well, not this time. She would keep her feelings locked away in her heart. Only Carson held the key.

Finally Danielle pushed herself out of bed, knowing that if she didn't get moving she would be late for her nine o'clock sacrament meeting. Trudging sleepily into the bathroom to shower, she thought of the Sub-for-Santa meeting at her house that night, and mentally she reviewed the list of assignments and things to do to be ready for it. She'd touched base, by phone or in person, with each member of the committee to follow up on all their assignments. The Christmas spirit had moved each member to go far above and beyond their required assignment, and Danielle was touched by their willingness to serve and give to those families and children in need. Danielle herself was propelled by the vision she had in her mind of the children's faces as Santa Claus and his elves stepped inside their humble homes and delivered a very unexpected Christmas to them. To see the joy of Christmas and the miracle of the season shine in their eyes and instill hope in their hearts would be the only thanks she needed for her efforts.

But there was something she still needed to take care of.

She still hadn't been able to ask Harry about playing Santa Claus. She'd meant to at the shelter, then again, at the meeting last Sunday, but the timing hadn't been right. But she couldn't put it off any longer. She had to ask him today, before the meeting tonight.

"Mom," Danielle said as she grabbed her coat and scriptures off the chair in the hallway, "I'm going to drive separately. I'll meet you and Dad at church."

"Okay, sweetie," her mother called from the kitchen where she was putting a roast in the oven for dinner.

She quickly called the homeless shelter to see if Harry was there, but no one answered. Harry usually volunteered on Sundays, so she decided to drive to the shelter after church and see if she could catch him then and talk to him in person. She sent a swift prayer heavenward. *Help me, Father,* she said silently. *If I am to be an instrument in Thy hands to help others, I need Thy help.*

Her church meetings seemed to pass slowly, as Danielle anticipated her encounter with Harry. She hoped he would accept her invitation to play Santa Claus. She also hoped that she could help him somehow. She didn't know what the Lord expected of her, but she did know that she hadn't been able to stop thinking about Harry, feeling that somehow she was supposed to help him. But help him how, she had no idea.

There was only one way to find out.

There was still no snow on the ground but the day was bitter cold. The vibrant-colored fall leaves had faded with winter's chill. Danielle stepped inside the warmth of the shelter kitchen and glanced around for any sign of Harry or Walter. She didn't see either of them.

"Can I help you?" a large woman wrapped in a red and white checkered apron asked her. She was busy spreading mayonnaise on a counter filled with slices of bread to make sandwiches for lunch.

Danielle twisted the strap of her purse nervously. "Is Walter here today?" she asked.

"He's in his office," the woman said, picking up a bottle of mustard and squirting a yellow circle onto every other slice of bread.

Danielle tapped on Walter's office door and waited. At his invitation to "come in," she opened the door and poked her head into the cramped office. Seeing Danielle, Walter stood up and shook her hand. "Well, hello there. Did you come to help out today?"

Danielle shook her head. "Actually, I can't today. I've been spending a lot of time trying to organize a Sub-for-Santa and I was looking for Harry."

Walter's face lit up. "A Sub-for-Santa. That's wonderful."

Danielle appreciated his vote of confidence. "I need to talk with Harry before our meeting tonight, though. I tried to call you earlier but couldn't get through, so I came down. Is he here?"

"Sorry about that. We lost our phone service." Walter grimaced. "I wasn't able to cover all the bills last month."

"I'm sorry." Danielle's heart went out to him. Poor Walter, trying to keep the place going on less than a shoestring budget.

"Oh, it's not the first time it's happened," he shrugged. "The phone company's pretty good about it. I'll give Debbie a call down there in the morning, and she'll take care of it for me." He jotted a note to himself in his planner. "So, you're looking for Harry?" Danielle nodded and Walter scratched his chin, thinking. "I haven't seen Harry much this week. He wasn't feeling well when he was last here."

"Do you think I could have his phone number?" she asked hopefully.

"I don't see any harm in that," he said, running his fingers through a card file. He wrote the information on a piece of paper. "Here's his phone number. And his address, just in case you need it."

"As soon as I get this project completed, you'll see me a lot more often," she promised. She wanted to start volunteering at the shelter regularly.

"A pretty face like yours would certainly brighten up the place," he said with a warm smile. "We'll be glad to see you whenever you can make it."

When she got in her car, she used her cell phone to call Harry but got a busy signal. Glancing down at the address, she saw that it wasn't far from where she already was. His address was located in the Sugarhouse area of the city, next to the foothills and the University of Utah. She wondered if she really dared show up at his house, then decided to head that direction anyway, calling one more time along the way. But when she did call again, the phone was still busy.

"Don't people know about call waiting," she muttered. The day was sunny and bright, but still deceptively cold. Her breath fogged the car windows.

"Fine," she declared, "I guess I'll just pay him a visit."

Mustering up her courage, she read the address a second time and headed for his house. Once in the vicinity, she began searching for the name of his street.

She found Wildwood Lane and slowly drove up the street, admiring the lovely homes along the way. Branches from the trees along the curb stretched across the road, the remaining leaves forming a canopy of faded orange, yellow, and red. A few stray leaves dropped and fluttered to the ground like feathers.

Carefully watching the numbers on the houses, she finally located the one that corresponded to the address written on the paper. An intricate wrought-iron gate stood at the entrance of the large circular driveway. Vines of ivy wrapped their fingers around the gate and climbed the stone wall surrounding the home. The driveway swept in front of an expansive English Tudor-style home with two stories, a three-car garage, and two lion statues guarding the front door. Harry lived here? Could she have misread the address? But no, this was what Walter had written down from the card in his file.

The air was bitter cold as she walked to the front door, but her palms were sweating. *Heavenly Father, if I'm in the right place, help me to say and do the right thing to help Harry.*

The doorbell played a familiar tune when it rang. Was it Beethoven's Fifth? She shifted from one foot to the other to stay warm, waiting for someone to answer the door. If this was where Harry lived, she knew he was there; she'd called only three minutes earlier.

Ringing the doorbell again, she tucked her hands inside her coat sleeves and shivered in the cold. Finally, she heard a shuffling sound behind the door. Someone was there. Was it Harry? Was he looking through the peephole at her?

Just in case he was, she tried to smile pleasantly even though she felt like she was freezing to death. *C'mon,* she thought, *open the door and let me in.*

Another minute passed, but nothing happened. Frustrated, Danielle reached out and knocked loudly. The frozen skin on her knuckles felt like it would split open. To her relief, she heard the lock turning. Slowly the door opened. Harry stood there, clutching his robe to his neck. His face was pale and hollow.

"Hello, Harry. How are you? You look terrible. Are you okay?" she asked all at once, filled with concern for the frail, hunched-looking figure.

"What are you doing here?" he asked, coughing a little.

"I came to visit you. Walter said you weren't feeling well. May I come in for a minute?"

She could tell he was hesitant to let her inside. But she had come to talk to him about being Santa Claus and she didn't want to leave before she had done so.

"For just a minute, I guess." He stepped aside, coughing again.

The entry was large and spacious. The walls were covered in beautiful wood paneling, with lovely pieces of artwork hanging on them. A grand and sparkling chandelier hung above them. Beneath her feet was a gorgeous Persian rug.

"What can I do for you?" he asked, sounding a bit breathless and wheezy.

"I wondered if we could talk for a moment. I wanted to see how you were doing on the names for the Sub-for-Santa before the meeting tonight."

He led her into a formal living room and indicated that she should take a seat.

"About the meeting," Harry said, wincing as he settled into his chair. "I don't think I'll be able to make it tonight." He coughed again.

He was in obvious pain, and Danielle wondered exactly what was wrong with him.

"Is there something I can get you?" she asked. "Can I help?"

"No." He shook his head to emphasize the word. "There's nothing anyone can do." Shifting the conversation back to their original topic, he said, "I've got the names and addresses written down for you. They're in the other room." He leaned forward to get back up, but Danielle stopped him.

"I can get it," she told him. She looked at him closely, wondering what he meant when he said there was nothing anyone could do. Surely he could take medication if he was in pain or antibiotics if he was sick.

"You look like you could use a bowl of my mother's chicken soup," she offered.

"I'm fine," he said. "Really."

"Okay," she said, standing to go get the list. Something caught her eye. It was a portrait in the hallway. "I'll just go get . . ." she began, as she took a few steps closer to the picture, then stopped abruptly. *That can't be who I think it is.* She looked back at Harry, sitting in his chair, then at the picture again. There was no doubt in her mind. *It is. It's him!*

Now she knew why his eyes seemed familiar and why she had felt like she knew him. She did, at least, she had at one time. Harry was her old boss, Mr. Turner. Carson's father.

She whirled around to face him. "It's you!" she exclaimed, unable to hide her surprise. "You're Mr. Turner. Mr. Philip Turner. My old boss."

He opened his mouth as if to deny it, then let out a tired sigh.

"You are, aren't you?" she asked, bewildered at the drastic change in his appearance. What had happened to him, she wondered.

"Yes," he admitted. "I am Philip H. Turner."

# CHAPTER
## EIGHTEEN

It took her a moment to digest the fact that Harry was her old boss, a man she'd worked for but didn't care for in the least. His mere presence at work used to send an icy chill of fear to her bones, and yet the Harry she knew was one of the most kind, gentle people she'd ever met. She was utterly confused. How could the two men be the same person?

"I don't understand," she said, peering at him closely. "You've changed."

"Yes," he nodded. "Many things have changed for me."

He didn't go on, but she couldn't help wondering what he meant, what had changed for her old boss. And why had he changed his name? "Is the H for Harold?" she asked.

"No." He shook his head. "Harrison. That was my father's name." He looked down at his hands. The "H" could have stood for humble, Danielle thought, looking at him, because that's exactly what this man was, humble. He looked up at her again. "I prefer to go by my middle name now."

Danielle felt her scalp tingle. What did all of this mean? Here she was, in Mr. Turner's house, and she was dating his son. She *was* a connection between the two, the piece that linked them together. Was that what the Lord had in mind? Was she supposed to bring them back together somehow? If so, how?

"Wow!" She sat down in a nearby chair, shaking her head. "Carson will never believe this," she murmured.

"Carson? My son?" Mr. Turner asked anxiously.

Danielle looked at the eager expression on the man's face, the longing and loneliness in his eyes. "Yes," she said gently.

"Have you seen him? Spoken with him? How is he?" The topic of his son brought renewed life to his tired body. She worried that he might send himself into another coughing fit. She assured him that Carson was doing well, and she told him about his schooling, his joy at studying medicine, his love for children. "He's a good man, Harry," she said. "You have a fine son. But he needs you in his life. You two should be together."

Harry shook his head. "Carson is angry with me and I don't blame him. I was a terrible father and I don't deserve his forgiveness." He covered his mouth as he began to cough again, a rumble from deep inside his chest. Danielle wondered if he was seeing a doctor. When he was able to stop, Danielle spoke again.

"That's ridiculous. You two need each other. You're all you two have got. He should be here, at home, living with you, taking care of you."

"No, no," Harry said. "He's much better off without me. I . . . I nearly ruined his life. I can't blame him for not wanting to have anything to do with me. After all the years I forced him to do exactly what I wanted, exactly the way I wanted it, I don't expect him to ever have anything to do with me again."

"But you two have so much to give each other," she pleaded with him. "And I know that if Carson doesn't make peace with you, he will never be happy."

"I appreciate what you're saying, Danielle," Harry said softly. "Nothing would bring me greater joy than to have my son back . . . in my life." As emotion began to catch at his voice, he cleared his throat, pausing to gain control of his feelings before he spoke again. "But it has to be up to Carson. He has to make the first move. I've tried to reach out to him . . . I've tried to make amends, but he doesn't want anything to do with me." He sighed, his breath ragged. "I've hurt him so badly. As he was growing up, I could never take time for him. I neglected him for years, and I can't make up for that now."

"Of course you can," Danielle insisted. "I know he'd forgive you if he could just see what a changed man you are."

"No," Harry shook his head again. "It's no use. He refuses to have any contact with me at all, and I love him too much to go against his wishes. I've forced him to do things my way his entire life. If this is how he wants it, I have to respect that."

"That's a bunch of garbage!" Danielle said promptly. "He's just being pig-headed and stubborn, like . . . , like . . ." she grasped for the right word.

"Like me," Harry said sadly. "He's just like I was at his age."

Danielle let out a frustrated huff. "I want to help. If you love him as much as you say you do, then you need to find a way to get through to him. Don't you see, Harry, if you don't, he'll turn out—" She stopped, wondering if she dared to say it, but Harry finished her sentence for her.

"Just like me," he said again, looking at her thoughtfully.

Danielle let his words linger in the air between them for a moment.

"You know I'm right, don't you?" Danielle tried to persuade him.

He shook his head regretfully. "Even if you are right, he won't back down. I know him. He's not going to give in."

Danielle couldn't let it go. "But like I said, if he could just see you and how much you've changed, it would soften his heart I know it would." She prayed desperately for the right words, but they didn't seem to be there for her.

"You must care a lot about my son," Harry said to her.

She smiled shyly. "I do."

Harry coughed, then sat back, breathing heavily. "He's a lucky boy to have you then. In fact, you remind me a little bit of his mother when she was young."

Danielle was startled. "I do?"

He nodded. "I have some pictures . . . if you'd like to see them."

Danielle assured him that she did want to see them, and he slowly led her to an adjoining room. The effort got him coughing again, and it took a minute to get past the attack.

"I think you should see a doctor for that cough," she suggested.

"I have," he answered.

Danielle felt a little better, and she looked around the room where she and Harry now stood.

It appeared to be both an office and library, with one whole wall filled with shelves of books. Against another wall was a gorgeous cherry wood desk. On the wall facing the street contained a picturesque window flanked on either side by a collage of picture frames. Danielle was drawn immediately to the pictures. Harry stood beside her and they both gazed at the many photographs on the wall. Most of them were black and white; some were color portraits.

Carson's life spread out before her eyes: pictures of him as a toddler on the beach, dressed as a cowboy for Halloween, fishing with his father. Every year of grade school, middle school, and high school was represented. She smiled at his graduation pictures, noticing how much longer he'd worn his hair, how much he'd changed. There were a few more of Carson with his father, again fishing, or wearing backpacks as they stood along a mountain trail. And there was a picture of Carson in his missionary suit, wearing his name tag and a broad smile.

Danielle saw many pictures of Carson and his father, but not many of his mother. There were a few, mostly portraits, but not many photographs.

As if he read her mind, Harry explained. "My wife was the photographer in the family. That's why you don't see her in many of the pictures. I have stacks of boxes of pictures she took, a whole closet full. But she's only in a few of them," he said sadly. "I wish I would have thought to take some of her."

Danielle nodded slowly. How he must miss his wife. "She was a beautiful woman," Danielle said, looking at a family photo.

"Yes, inside and out," he replied.

Danielle noticed the strong resemblance between Carson and his mother. She had the same broad smile, golden wheat hair color, and green eyes. But she appeared to be quite a petite woman. Carson obviously got his build from his father.

Then Danielle got an idea. "Does Carson have a scrapbook with pictures like this in it?"

"No," he shook his head. "Not that I recall. His mother took a lot of pictures but she never had time to organize them into books."

"Do you think I could have some of those pictures?" she asked hesitantly. "I'd like to make Carson a scrapbook for Christmas."

"Certainly," Harry smiled and Danielle thought she saw a little of Carson in his smile, after all. "I think that's a wonderful idea."

He opened a closet door in the room and just as he'd said, there were literally dozens of boxes of pictures.

"Oh, boy," she said. How would she ever sort through them?

"You're welcome to work on it here in my home," Harry offered. "That way I could help you identify pictures and organize them."

"You wouldn't mind?" she asked.

"Actually, I think it would be good for me. I haven't been able to bring myself to look through these pictures since Laura's death. Perhaps it's time." He began to cough again.

"Can I get you a drink of water?" Danielle asked nervously, wondering if he were going to collapse in front of her.

"Please," he said between coughs. "In there." He pointed toward the kitchen. Racing to the other room, she found a glass in the cupboard, filled it with water, and quickly returned. He was sitting in a burgundy leather wing-back chair, looking more tired and frail than he had before, if that were possible.

After several gulps he seemed much better. "Thank you." He took another drink before setting the glass down.

"Harry, what exactly did the doctor say was wrong with you?" She knew she was being nosy, but the man needed help and had no one to turn to. Someone needed to care about him.

"It's just a nasty chest cold," he told her.

"That's all, just a chest cold?" she asked directly.

He met her eyes and appeared to see something there that refused to hear less than the truth. "It's a little more than that," he finally admitted. "I have cancer . . . I'm dying."

# CHAPTER
## NINETEEN

Danielle looked into Harry's tired eyes. "What kind of cancer? Are the doctors sure? What about surgery, treatment?"

Harry exhaled slowly. "I have lung cancer. I was finally diagnosed exactly a year ago, but the doctors think I've had the cancer a lot longer than that."

*About the same time Turner Consulting was going through all of its problems,* Danielle thought.

"I've been through surgery, radiation treatment, and chemotherapy. That's why my hair is white. It all fell out and when it came back in, it was like this," he told her.

That explained his drastic change in appearance, the weight loss, hair color, and even his low, gravelly voice from the constant cough. "Didn't any of that help?" She couldn't accept that there was no hope.

He shrugged. "Had I gone in when I first started having problems, they could have removed the tumor. But I ignored all the signals that something was wrong and waited until it was too late. The cancer has spread," he said matter-of-factly. "There's nothing anyone can do."

Tears stung Danielle's eyes. Why? Why would this man who had turned his life around to become a giving, caring, loving human being, who wanted to make a difference and serve others, have to die? "What do the doctors say?" she managed to ask.

Harry smiled gently at Danielle, as if he appreciated her concern, though he himself was resigned to his illness. "They've seen people in my condition last two weeks, two months, even two years. It's different with everyone."

She thought about him rattling around in the big house, sick and alone, with no one to take care of him, and her heart nearly broke. "Are you in pain?" she asked hesitantly.

"No." He shook his head. "It's just this chest cold that's giving me problems now. But I'm feeling better than I did a few days ago. A nurse comes by each day, and my food is brought in. I have a house-keeper three days a week. My physical needs are taken care of."

But what about his emotional needs? Danielle asked herself. What about his son? This could well be the last Christmas Carson and his father had. They had to be together. They just had to be.

"Let's talk about something else," Harry suggested. "How's the Sub-for-Santa going? The list of names of families is right there on top of my desk."

She found the list, which gave the names of about ten families and their addresses. Each family member was listed by name and age, and identified as a boy or girl.

"This looks wonderful," she said. "Thank you."

"I'm happy to help," he said. "I'd like to do more."

"But what about your health? Are you up to doing more?" She didn't want him to overdo, especially with his health as it was.

"I'm feeling better each day. I would like to help if I could. In fact, I've always had a secret desire to do something. " He paused and Danielle waited, wondering what he would say. "Of course, maybe you wouldn't want to bother."

She would've done anything she could for Harry. "What is it?" she prompted.

"Well, I've always wanted to play Santa Claus. I never did that for Carson, you know—dress up and hold him on my knee, try to make the holiday special for him."

She hadn't had a chance to ask him to play Santa for their service project and here he was, volunteering. Not only did he look the part with his white hair, white beard, and kind blue eyes, he definitely had what it took to be Santa on the inside—a pure heart and a desire to serve.

She looked at him warily, "Did Walter call you and tell you why I was coming over today?"

"No," he answered with some confusion. "Why?"

"Harry," she said, watching his expression, "I came over today specifically to ask you if you'd dress up and be Santa."

Surprise and delight filled his face. "You did?"

She nodded, still amazed at the coincidence. But maybe it wasn't just a coincidence. She was positive there had been some divine intervention in the Sub-for-Santa project. So far everything had gone so well, everyone had worked so hard. And now this.

He must have had the same thought because he said, "Perhaps there's more to this service project than we understand."

"I believe there is," Danielle replied. "This will be something special and unforgettable, not only for the children, but for the volunteers, too."

"Then I'm grateful to be a part of it," he said kindly.

The thought of Harry showing up to a family with small children, when they least expected it, seeing their eyes light up, their faces full of joy, made Danielle's heart swell. "So am I," she said.

"I'll take care of getting a Santa suit," he said.

"Let me know if you need any help," she offered, noticing the lateness of the hour. "I'd like to come back and work on the scrapbook soon. I don't have much time before Christmas."

"Anytime you'd like."

With the meeting already planned for that night, Danielle suggested Monday night and Harry looked pleased. "If we can wrap things up quickly at the meeting," she said, "maybe I could come back here after and get a head start on all this."

"Well, then," she said, wishing she didn't have to leave him alone, "I guess I'd better get home before my parents wonder what happened to me." Then she had an idea. "Hey, why don't you come home and have dinner with me and my family? You can ride with me and we'll bring you home."

He quickly declined. "Thank you for asking but I don't think so."

"You need to eat," Danielle said firmly. "My mother made a huge pot roast, and she makes the best mashed potatoes and gravy you've ever tasted."

Harry didn't have to say anything. She could tell by the look on his face that he wanted to, and struck with inspiration, she smiled persuasively. "Besides, my dad would love to take you out to his workbench and show you all his fly-tying equipment."

Struck with a double whammy like that, Harry didn't have a chance. "If you're sure your parents wouldn't mind having me . . ." he said slowly, a slight smile tugging at his lips.

Danielle clapped her hands together. "They'll be thrilled. Is it okay if I use this phone? I'll call my mom and let her know you're coming."

Harry excused himself to go change while she made the call, and was nearly to the door when he stopped and turned back to face her. "Danielle, I know it's much too late for apologies, but I'm sorry you were laid off last year. I wish there was some way I could make it up to all the employees who lost their jobs because of me. I've hurt so many people through the years. I've treated them so badly. And I know I'll be held accountable for the things I've done to others."

It was clear that he felt truly sorry for what had happened. This was what a broken heart and a contrite spirit looked like, Danielle thought, her heart deeply touched.

"That's all in the past now. It doesn't matter anymore," she told him.

"It's hard, knowing how many lives were affected by my own selfish acts," he said, obviously full of remorse. "I'm sure many people hated me for what I did."

"I'll admit, I was angry when I lost my job," Danielle said honestly. "I had just bought a new car and was trying to move out on my own." His expression grew even more pained at her words. "But, Harry, losing that job was a blessing in disguise. It opened doors of opportunity for me that I would have never pursued on my own. I love my new job and the people I work with, and I've been thinking about going back to school in a new field. My life is so much better than it was. So I can't help but think that maybe all of this was supposed to happen."

He shook his head slowly. "I wish I could take back so much."

"But, Harry, you've changed. That's what matters." Danielle could see that he had been carrying this burden of guilt for a long time and wished she could say something to help ease his sorrow. "What's important is what you're doing now. And what you're doing now is very important. Your volunteer work is helping so many other people."

He nodded, acknowledging the truth of her last statement, at least. "I know it won't change the past," he said, "but I find that the only pleasure I have in my life is when I can give to others. I finally feel like I've discovered what truly brings joy to a person. Nothing makes me happier than working at the shelter. You know," he said thoughtfully, "I've learned that you gain a greater love for people when you serve them. I admit, when I first lost my business and was diagnosed with cancer, I was very angry at God. I figured, I might as well die, because there was nothing left for me. I had focused my entire adult life on making money and gaining power but it never brought me the happiness I wanted. Then, one day on a visit to my insurance agent, I met Walter. We started talking and I found myself telling him my life story. I know God sent him to me, because Walter helped me realize that I still had so much to be thankful for. He's the one who talked me into volunteering at the shelter. Now, I finally know what true happiness is. I feel it every time I'm helping others. I just wish," he cleared the emotion from his throat, "I just wish I would've learned all of this before I lost my wife and son."

<hr />

At dinner Harry and Earl talked like old friends. They looked at the photo albums showing Earl's fishing trips and then went to the garage where Earl showed him the fishing flies he had created.

After dinner was cleaned up, Danielle and her mother whipped up a batch of chocolate and butterscotch chip cookies for the meeting that evening. But as the time for the meeting grew near, Danielle could tell Harry was tiring. His cough was getting worse and his face was pale and hollow. Before he found it necessary to ask, she offered to take him home. Dorothy wouldn't let him leave without a plate of food and a bag of her homemade dinner rolls. Although Harry was clearly worn out, Danielle could see that he was very grateful for the home-cooked meal and friendship.

Danielle was back in plenty of time to bring chairs into the living room for her guests. She wondered if Carson would come as he had

promised and thought it was better that Harry wasn't there. Their
first meeting ought to be more private, she thought. Certainly there
would be a lot of emotion when they finally did see each other face to
face. But how was she going to bring the two men together, and how
could she get Carson to quit being such a hardheaded nincompoop
about his father?!

Roberta, Lenny, and Bart were the first to arrive, and seeing Bart,
Danielle felt her stomach curdle. What had she been thinking? It
could get very sticky having Bart and Carson both there.

"Roberta," Danielle said as the guys took off their coats and
found a seat, "can I talk to you for just a minute?"

"Sure," Roberta said, handing her coat to Lenny. They walked
into the other room. "What's up?"

"You have to help me," Danielle said.

Roberta sensed Danielle's anxiety. "With what? Is something
wrong?"

"I'm worried that tonight could get uncomfortable with both
Carson and Bart here. It didn't even occur to me until just now."

"Ooooh, you're right." Roberta pulled a face. "This could get
tense." She thought for a moment. "I guess Lenny and I will just have
to run interference. You know, be prepared to create a diversion or get
Bart distracted somehow."

"Would you?" Danielle cried with relief. "I would really appreciate it."

"Sure," Roberta patted her friend on the shoulder. "Don't worry
about anything. By the way," Roberta remembered, "where did you
go earlier? I called but your mom said you were out."

"Oh," Danielle exclaimed. "Have I got something to tell you!"

"Danielle," her mother called, "could you get the door?"

"We'll have to talk later," Danielle said.

"I can't wait till later. I'm dying to know now." Roberta took
Danielle's arm, refusing to let her leave until she had learned the
news.

"I can't now," Danielle laughed at her friend. "I've got to get this
meeting going."

Roberta went to find Lenny and Bart, and Danielle answered the
door. She was thrilled to find Carson on her doorstep. He had come

directly from a church meeting in his student ward and was still in his suit and tie. Danielle couldn't help staring, he looked so handsome.

"Is it all right if I come in?" Carson asked after a few seconds. A cold winter wind swept into the entry through the open door.

"Oh, yes," she said, "of course." She stepped aside. "I'm glad you made it."

"Me too," he said. "My Jeep broke down so I had to borrow my friend's car. I think the clutch has gone out."

"I'm sorry," Danielle empathized, knowing how expensive car repairs could get.

"Yeah, me too," he echoed her sentiment. He slid off his coat and added it to the others hanging on the hall tree. "Maybe Santa will bring me a new one for Christmas," he joked.

*He could if you'd let him!* she thought. If Carson would only let his father help him, he wouldn't have all his financial worries on top of everything else.

Carson found a seat, Danielle noticed gratefully, on the opposite side of the room from Bart. The rest of the committee arrived soon after, and Danielle went ahead and started the meeting.

Just as she'd anticipated, everyone on the committee had done an outstanding job with their assignments. Harry's list was added to the list of names Roberta, Bart, and Lenny had compiled. Roberta briefly told about each family on her list. Each situation was desperate, and the Sub-for-Santa was the only way these people would have any kind of Christmas.

Danielle introduced Carson to the group, and he told about the many children who would be spending Christmas at the hospital. A visit from Santa Claus and a small gift would do much to brighten their holiday, he assured them. Which led Danielle to the next topic.

"I'm pleased to announce that we found someone to play Santa Claus. He's a member of our own committee. You met him here last week," Danielle explained. "Harry's volunteered."

The others exclaimed their approval.

"His health isn't very good, so it might be a good idea to have a standby just in case he isn't able to do it. So you might be thinking of someone else." Danielle glanced down at her notes. "Okay, how are the donations going?"

There was a brief accounting from the Relief Society and from Chloe, Lucy, and Erin, who were there as Young Women representatives, the two groups in charge of donations. They reported that the ward had been very generous—donating more than enough clothing and household items, children's toys and gifts, and large sums of money—to meet the needs of the people on their lists. And there was more rolling in each day. Danielle's sister Miranda added that the food donations had been very generous, and she would use some of the donated money to buy the rest of the needed items.

Cassie reported that there were plenty of decorated Christmas trees for all the families, and she could get more if needed.

A time was planned for the committee to get together and organize the gifts and wrap everything. Roberta volunteered to set up the delivery schedule and make arrangements with each family to have Santa and his helpers drop by.

Sister McKay volunteered to make elf hats for all the members of the committee. While they probably wouldn't look like elves, they could certainly look like Santa's helpers.

With all the business taken care of, Danielle offered her sincere thanks to everyone for their hard work and support, then closed the meeting, repeating words she'd heard just that afternoon from Harry.

"I know what a busy time of year this is for everyone, especially those of you who have your own families to provide Christmas for. But it is touching to see so many of you being so generous with your time and energy. I know that we become more Christlike when we serve others. What we are doing is going to make a difference to many people. It will touch their lives forever and hopefully, touch our own, too. I couldn't do this alone, and I can't thank you enough for sharing this vision with me."

Danielle couldn't help the emotion that crept into her voice. She had felt the promptings of the Lord giving her the drive and desire to push this project through to completion. Just as she had said, many people would benefit and be touched by what they were doing, not just the recipients but also those on the committee. They would be sharing gifts with those less fortunate, but even more important, they would be sharing the love of Christ.

"I hope you don't mind if we leave a little early," Roberta said to

Danielle, with Lenny and Bart flanking her on either side. "We're going to my house to compile our wedding guest list. Bart's coming over to help. Do you want to come over later?"

She knew Roberta was helping her out by getting Bart out of the house. "I'll have to see how late it is by the time everyone leaves. I still have some work to do on this project."

Bart stepped up and said, with a pleading note in his voice, "I hope I'll see you at Roberta's."

"I'll try," she said, forcing a smile, even though she didn't think she'd have time to go over. If she went anywhere it would be over to Harry's to look at pictures. But judging by how tired the man was when she took him home, she guessed he had probably already gone to bed.

She felt bad that Bart was feeling something she couldn't return, but she had tried to like him—and she did, as a friend—but that was all it would ever be. There just wasn't anything more.

When the three found their coats and left, Danielle gave a sigh of relief. *I owe Roberta a huge favor,* she thought to herself. *Huge!*

Everyone else had gathered in the kitchen for hot chocolate and cookies, which was where Danielle found Carson, leaning against the counter holding a plate of cookies and a mug of cocoa.

"These are great," he said, holding up a half-eaten cookie. "Are you as good a cook as your mother?"

"Who do you think made the cookies?" she asked, feigning offense.

Carson looked impressed. "You?"

"Yes, me," Danielle answered loftily.

He nodded his approval. "Very good."

The committee members finished their refreshments, then called their good-byes as they left. Chloe, Lucy, and Erin came by to say good night, but as she thanked them, Danielle noticed they were all looking past her into the dining room.

"Hello," Danielle said, realizing that they weren't listening to her. "Hey, you guys. What's with you?"

"We just wanted to get a better look at him," Chloe whispered.

"Him who?" Danielle asked, amused.

"The cute guy at the table. Who is he?"

Danielle realized who they were looking at and chuckled. "That's a friend of mine. His name is Carson Turner. I can introduce you to him if you want."

"NO!" Chloe said louder than she wanted to. "I mean, no, that's okay. My hair's all stupid."

"And I'm in sweats," Erin added.

"Maybe next time then." Danielle offered, smiling at them. Just being around Carson had them all flustered. Of course, she knew how they felt. He had that effect on her, too.

"So," Danielle said, taking advantage of the opportunity, "how was the dance, Lucy? Did you have fun?" Earlier that evening, Danielle had noticed that Lucy wasn't quite as reserved as usual and she'd been wondering about Lucy's first dance. She'd also noticed that Lucy's hair was curled and pulled back with clips, instead of her standard pony tail. She wore a light dusting of eyeshadow and blush, and even a touch of mascara.

Lucy smiled broadly. "It was awesome," she said. "We had so much fun."

"And what did Jake say when he first saw you?" Danielle asked. The other girls giggled. Obviously they'd already heard the details.

"I was upstairs in my room when he came to pick me up so my dad answered the door. I came down the stairs, just like in the movies, and when Jake looked up and saw me his mouth dropped wide open. It was so funny," Lucy giggled. "He just stood there; he couldn't even speak. My dad got it all on video."

"Did you ever find out what happened to McCall? You know, why she didn't go to the dance?" Danielle asked.

"Oh, yeah, her dad found out that the guy she was going with had some trouble with drugs and stuff," Chloe explained.

"And that he got a girl pregnant last year," Erin added. "Her dad didn't feel good about her going so he made her cancel the date."

"Wow," Danielle said, shaking her head with disbelief. "I don't blame her dad for being worried, but McCall must have been pretty disappointed."

"She was very upset," Chloe answered. "You know, I'm glad I'm not popular like she is. There's too much pressure." The other girls agreed.

"I think I'll give her a call later," Danielle said, making a mental note to do just that. As she told "her girls" good-bye, she realized again just how much she enjoyed being with them. She was their advisor, but they in turn, seemed to do a lot of the teaching, to her and each other. She had to admit that the bishop had been inspired, giving her this calling. She was grateful she'd had enough sense to accept it.

By nine o'clock the last of the committee members had headed home, and Carson was just getting ready to leave.

She and Carson walked together to the front room where he'd left his coat. Except for the light from a small lamp in the corner, the room was dark.

"I haven't really been involved in many service projects since my mission, so I'm glad to have a chance to be a part of this one," he said.

"So am I," she replied, not mentioning that aside from his help, she was glad it gave them another reason to be together.

"I know I don't fit the mold very well," Carson said, "but I'd be happy to fill in as Santa if that other guy isn't able to do it."

Really?" Danielle asked with delight.

"Yes, really," he said. "I could pull it off as long as I have a few pillows and a fake beard."

She smiled up at him, amazed that both he and his dad had volunteered. "I think that's wonderful," she said. "And I'm sure you'd fit the suit just fine. Harry's quite tall, too." *Like father, like son.*

"Great," he said. The room was silent except for the ticking of the clock. A flash of light from a pair of headlights caught Danielle's attention. She glanced outside and saw that snow had begun to fall.

"Look," she whispered, "it's snowing." Big, fluffy flakes floated gently from the sky, filling the air with winter magic. Carson slid his arm around her waist and pulled her close. They watched in silence as the world outside became a sparkling wonderland.

"Isn't it beautiful?" Danielle asked softly. Carson didn't answer, and Danielle sensed a sadness about him. "Carson, are you okay?"

He cleared his throat. "Yeah."

"You don't seem okay. Something's wrong. Please tell me," she persisted. She stepped back so she could see his face.

He hesitated a moment, then said, "I was just thinking about my mom. She loved the snow. Every year when the first snow fell, she would play this old Bing Crosby Christmas album, and we'd make sugar cookies together. She'd let me have the last bit of dough to make any shape of cookie I wanted. Then we'd get all bundled up and go out and make a snowman together. We'd put it right by the driveway so my dad could see it when he came home from work."

Danielle had a knot in her throat. He missed his mother so terribly. She wished she could say something to make him feel better.

"I miss her the most this time of year. Even though it's been several years, it hasn't gotten any easier."

Reaching up, Danielle stroked his face, wanting somehow to ease his pain.

"Sorry," he said abruptly, shaking his head as if to clear the memories away. "I didn't mean to get all serious on you."

"It's okay. I like hearing about your mother. I wish I could have known her."

"You would have liked her," Carson said with a gentle smile. "And she would have liked you, too."

Danielle smiled back, pleased that Carson thought so. She liked thinking that Laura Turner would have liked her. She hoped that his father did, too.

His father.

Some of the emptiness Carson felt could be replaced by the love of his father. If only he'd let his father make up for his mistakes in the past.

Looking into Carson's eyes, Danielle felt as though she could see deep into his soul. He was such a good person. He had a strong testimony and was focused on what he wanted to do with his life. But he'd taken some of the misfortune he'd grown up with and allowed it to blur his eternal vision. And if Carson didn't make peace with Harry before he died, she knew he would suffer the rest of his life. *What can I do to get through to him,* she wondered.

"What?" he said finally.

"What, what?" she answered.

"You look like you're very deep in thought," he observed.

"I was just thinking about how great it is that you're so focused with your education and your future," Danielle hedged.

"Well, it's taken me a while, but I think I'm finally where I should be." There was a sense of satisfaction in his voice. "I really needed your encouragement last year when I was trying to decide what to do about school. It helped me have the courage to make some big changes in my life."

"Really?" she exclaimed. "I did that?"

"Yes," he said, leaning closer to her. "You did. See, I told you. You're a good luck charm for me." Like a magnetic force pulling them together, their lips met for a quick but very sweet kiss. Danielle decided she liked being his good luck charm. She felt the words, "I love you," bubble just below the surface, but she forced them to the back of her mind. Just because she loved someone didn't mean it was right. She knew that her heart couldn't be trusted when it didn't agree with her head. And her head told her to be very careful.

"Guess I'd better get going," he said reluctantly, pulling away. "As pretty as the snow is, the roads are going to be slick."

"Thanks for coming tonight," she said, hating the evening to end.

"I'll call you soon," he promised, and was out the door. Danielle watched as he got in the car and pulled away. She watched until his tail lights disappeared into the night.

Carson was a warm and tender person, caring and kind. So how could he not care about his own father?

# CHAPTER TWENTY

Danielle stood on Harry's doorstep waiting for him to answer the door. It was a bone-chilling cold Monday evening, and she hoped to get a jump on the scrapbook she was making for Carson's Christmas gift. For a moment she wondered if Harry wasn't home, then the door finally opened.

"Hi," she said brightly. "Is this a good time for me to get some pictures?"

"Of course," he said graciously. "Come in."

She handed him a loaf of bread that was still warm from the oven. "Mom sent this over for you. It's her famous honey and whole wheat. And this—" she held up a Tupperware bowl full of chicken noodle soup, "—is some soup. I think you'll like it."

He smelled the loaf of bread appreciatively. "Tell her thank you for me. I can't remember the last time I had homemade soup and bread."

Danielle removed her coat and hung it on the coat rack.

"How did the meeting go last night?" he asked.

"It went great. Things are really pulling together. Carson stayed after for a while."

"How is he?" Harry asked.

"He's doing well," she told him. "He's putting in a lot of hours at the children's hospital during the winter break. His car broke down so he's trying to get that fixed."

A pained expression crossed Harry's face. No doubt he was thinking that he could help Carson if his son weren't so stubborn.

"Well," Danielle said, trying to stay upbeat, "I've been looking forward to seeing all these pictures." She noticed that Harry had a little color in his cheeks, and he didn't appear to be coughing quite as much either.

"They're in here," he answered, walking to the study, which was warmed by a cozy gas log. "Since I knew you were coming tonight, I went through the closet and started to sort through the boxes."

She followed him into the room and noticed soft Christmas music playing in the background. It dawned on her that it must be the Bing Crosby Christmas album Carson and his mother had listened to. Apparently it meant something to Harry as well.

When she commented on the music, he looked somewhat surprised that she had recognized the singer.

"Carson told me that his mother used to play this each year when it started to snow," Danielle said. She watched as Harry's face softened with the memory. "He misses his mother very much," she told him. Her heart ached for both of them.

Harry nodded. "I do, too, although you'd think after all these years it would get a little easier. Well, I guess it's to be expected for us to remember more at this time of year. She died on Christmas Day when he was on his mission, you know." Danielle nodded.

Taking a deep breath, he sighed and patted her hand. "Why don't we get started with these pictures?"

The study was strewn with boxes and photos. There were a few picture albums, but mostly stacks and piles of photographs, some in color, some in black and white.

"Wow," Danielle exclaimed. "Where do I begin?"

Harry indicated a box on a coffee table. "I gathered as many of Carson as a baby as I could and put them in this box."

Danielle picked up a handful of pictures and sifted through them. Carson was a beautiful baby, with big eyes and a head full of blonde, stick-straight hair. He had chubby cheeks and pouty lips. "What a cutie," Danielle said.

Harry looked longingly at the pictures. "He was such a good baby. Slept through the night from the day he came home from the hospital. Such a sweet disposition, too. He'd play for hours with his toys; he loved Legos and little race cars the most."

"He looks a lot like his mom, doesn't he?" she commented, looking at a picture of Carson sitting on his mother's lap. "But he definitely got your height."

"His mother used to say that we were lucky," Harry reminisced. "If we could only have one child, then at least we got one who inherited all our best qualities."

Danielle laughed at some of the pictures. Carson standing in a wading pool with his bare bottom turned toward the camera. Carson and his father standing side by side, holding up rainbow trout. On a bike with training wheels. Wearing cowboy boots and a cowboy hat.

Together Danielle and Harry rifled through most of the boxes, arranging and organizing the pictures into chronological order. Several times Harry stopped to tell a story about a special picture. His voice was thick with emotion as they discovered photographs of Carson and his mother embracing at the airport before Carson left on his mission. Danielle felt tears sting her own eyes as Harry shared with her the strength it had taken for his mother to send him on a mission, knowing she might never see her son again.

"I wish I could have known her," Danielle said softly as she gazed at the lovely woman.

"You would have liked her," he said. "And she would have liked you, too."

Danielle smiled at him, remembering Carson had said the same thing. "I hope so," she said.

When the clock struck nine o'clock Danielle realized she'd been there almost three hours. She could tell Harry had hit his limit. He seemed very tired.

"I think I ought to get going," she said. "Do you want me to help you put all this away? Or I could come back tomorrow and finish looking at the pictures and we can put everything away then."

"We can leave them out," he said. "I stayed up until two in the morning last night looking at them." He ran his finger gently across a picture of his wife. "I haven't had the strength to look at these since she passed away. It's been hard," he said, "but I think it's been good for me." He looked at the picture again. "I don't think I'm afraid of dying because I know she's going to be there on the other side." Then he chuckled, "Not that I'll be going where she is, though."

"What do you mean?"

"Oh, you know," he said, with a shrug. "I've made far too many mistakes here."

"Harry, you're being too hard on yourself," Danielle scolded him. "You're a good man, and I know the Lord loves you. Of course you'll be with your wife again. I haven't the slightest doubt." She was amazed to hear herself speaking to her old boss this way, but she felt this was what the Lord would want her to say to Harry. It was almost as if she had been given the necessary words to offer comfort to a dying man.

Harry's eyes were bleak but he gave her a faint smile. "I'd like to believe you. I certainly aim to do everything I can in the time that's left me so I can be worthy of Laura. I can't imagine anything better than being with her for eternity and anything worse than not being with her." He paused for a moment and added, "And having Carson with us would truly be paradise."

"He will be," Danielle said. "You can't give up hope." She gathered the pictures together and put them in a bag. "I'd better get going," she said. They both stood up and Harry led her to the entry.

"Thank you for everything," he said. Danielle looked at him, not sure what she'd done to be thanked for. Without warning he gave her a brief hug. "I think if I could have had a daughter, I would've wanted her to be just like you."

"Thank you," she said, unable to find any other words that seemed appropriate at the moment. "I'll see you tomorrow, okay?"

Danielle hummed one of Bing's Christmas melodies as she drove home. She was so very glad she'd met Harry and could spend some time with him and, she hoped, in some way, help him. He was so alone and so lonely.

⚜

Danielle felt a sense of accomplishment as she pulled into the driveway. She felt good about her visit with Harry, but she was glad to be home. It had been a long day and she was tired. But before she could even turn off the engine, her father came running out the front door.

"Dani, Sister Blakely just called looking for you!" he explained as she rolled down her window.

"McCall's mom?" Dani's heart skipped a beat. "Is something wrong?"

"McCall's run away from home. Her mother wondered if you could help them look for her. She's really worried. They think she might be with the boy who asked her to the Christmas dance—the one they didn't let her go with."

Danielle shifted the car in reverse then pulled back out onto the road. She could remember times growing up when she'd disagreed with her parents' rules, when she'd been so mad at them that she'd honestly thought she hated them. But she would have never run away. Sure, she'd thought of it, but she would have never actually done it.

"McCall," she said out loud, shaking her head. "Where are you and what are you doing?"

Within minutes she was at the Blakely home, where she found McCall's mother in tears, pacing the floor with worry over her daughter's disappearance.

"What can I do to help?" Danielle offered.

Sister Blakely gave her a grateful look. "I've made a list of places I thought she might go. Her father's checking with her friends right now to see if any of them know anything. But these are the places where the kids like to hang out. Maybe they've gone there." She sniffed and wiped her nose and eyes with a tissue.

"Are you sure she's with this boy?" Danielle asked.

McCall's mother nodded then started crying again. "He drives a black truck. And has those speakers, you know, the kind that rattle your windows. I was so afraid something like this might happen. She's been so difficult lately. She just seems to hate us. I'm sure she's trying to hurt us and get back at us for not letting her go to the dance. I'm just so afraid for her. This boy is mixed up with so many bad things."

Danielle took the paper and glanced over it. "I'll go look at these places and ask around if anyone's seen her. Do you know what she was wearing?"

"Just jeans and a long sleeved t-shirt. I don't even think she took her coat," her mother choked out.

"Don't worry," Danielle tried to soothe the frantic mother. "We'll find her."

The older woman's eyes were full of gratitude. "McCall really thinks the world of you. She's told me several times how much she likes you."

"That means a lot to me," Danielle said. "I think the world of her, too. Here's my cell phone number if you need to reach me." She handed the woman the piece of paper she'd scrawled her name and number on.

Inside her car she glanced at the list and realized that her stomach was in knots. McCall wasn't even her own daughter, and Danielle was consumed with worry. She wondered if there could be anything harder than being a parent—especially at times like this.

⋇⋇ 🕮 ⋇⋇

After each place she checked, Danielle phoned McCall's mother to let her know she'd had no luck. Sister Blakely told her that McCall's father and brother both hadn't had any luck either. They'd even gone to the boy's house but no one was home.

"I'm on my way to the bowling alley," Danielle told her. "And the pizza place is just down the street from that."

"It's after midnight," Sister Blakely said. "I think you should let Jim take over. He can keep looking."

"I'm almost there," Danielle said. "I'll just give these last two places a try, then I'll stop." Pulling into the bowling alley, Danielle could tell the place was closed. There was a car in the parking lot, but the lights were off and it was dark inside. The sign on the door told her that the bowling alley had closed almost an hour earlier.

Disappointed, Danielle drove to the pizza place. It, too, looked empty, but the lights were still on. Danielle made sure to lock her car doors before she went inside.

"Hi," she said brightly to the middle-aged woman counting money at the register.

"We're closed," the woman told her flatly, not even looking up.

"Oh, I don't want to get something to eat. I'm trying to find my friend. I thought she might be here with her boyfriend getting pizza." The woman didn't say anything; she just kept counting bills.

"She's got shoulder-length blonde hair and she's about my height. She was wearing jeans and a long sleeved t-shirt."

The woman stopped counting and looked at Danielle. "Was she with a guy—black hair, earrings, an attitude? Driving a pickup?"

Danielle's heart leapt for joy in her chest. "That's them."

"You tell your friend that her boyfriend's cheap," she scowled. "He didn't even leave a tip!"

Why wasn't Danielle surprised? "How long ago did they leave?" she asked.

"You just missed them."

"Dang it!" Danielle said under her breath.

"But I think you might be able to find them. He said something about getting some gas when they left. Don't know what a pretty girl sees in a slimy kid like that," she grumbled to herself. "I wouldn't trust my daughter with him."

Danielle dug into her pocket and found a five-dollar bill. "That's for the tip they didn't leave you." The woman tried to protest but Danielle cut her off before she could speak, "You've been a lot of help. *Thank you!*" she said as she flew out the door to her car.

Her car screeched out of the parking lot as she made a quick left hand turn onto the road and headed for the nearest gas station. As she pulled onto the black-top, she was nearly sideswiped by a black truck tearing out of the gas station. She caught a brief glimpse of McCall sitting on the passenger side. McCall didn't appear to have seen her, and Danielle figured it was just as well. They wouldn't be suspicious when she started following them.

She turned around and sped down the street to catch up with the black truck. She wanted to keep them in sight, but not give herself away. Praying that they didn't head for the Interstate, Danielle continued to follow as the truck wound its way through dark, empty streets. It was late; kids their age should be home, asleep. Heck, she thought, people *her age* should be home in bed asleep.

Danielle slowed as they approached a red light. The last thing she wanted was to pull up beside them. Staying in the far right lane,

Danielle was grateful when another car pulled up in the center lane between them. But when the light turned green, Danielle was caught off guard as the truck suddenly made a left-hand turn.

"Shoot!" she muttered, searching for a place to turn around. She was tempted to jump the median, but decided it wasn't wise. Instead she sped to the next intersection and made a U-turn. Racing back, she turned at the corner where the truck had and searched frantically for any sign of it. There was nothing.

She banged the steering wheel with her hand. Following the road, she drove slowly, wondering what to do next. She might have been able to prevent something from happening, but she'd lost them.

"Darn it!"

A light snow had started to fall, and she pulled over to call McCall's parents and tell them what had happened. She hated to say what she would have to tell them. If only she'd anticipated their move, if she had only been watching more closely, been on her toes . . .

She was just about to push "send" when the movement of a vehicle caught her eye. It was the black truck, pulling out of a driveway. With a screech of tires, it rocketed down the street, away from where they'd come, running a stop sign at the intersection.

Ramming her car into drive, Danielle stomped on the gas and took off after them. Exceeding the speed limit by at least twenty miles per hour, Danielle did her best to keep up. The snow fell faster and the wet roads turned slushy.

Judging by the way the truck's speed increased with every mile, Danielle figured she'd been discovered. Staying on his tail, Danielle squealed around corners and skidded through stop lights with him. She was sure a cop was going to be around every turn, but she couldn't let McCall out of her sight.

Finally the truck pulled into a 7-Eleven parking lot and stopped. Danielle's heart nearly stopped, too. The driver got out of the vehicle and stood, waiting for her, with his feet spread wide, his arms folded defiantly across his chest. Danielle couldn't see McCall inside the truck. Where was she?

Approaching cautiously, Danielle stopped her car a safe distance from the boy. Leaving the engine running, she stepped out and said as boldly as she could, "Where's McCall?"

His language appalled her, but she got the basic gist of his message. Who was she and what did she want?

"I know she was with you," Danielle said. She didn't want to anger him further; he seemed mad enough as it was.

"Well, now she's not!" His spiky, gelled hair and black leather coat made his defensive demeanor appear even more threatening.

"Do you know where she is?" Danielle brushed the snow away from her face.

The boy swore and called McCall several unflattering names. He didn't have a clue where she was nor did he care.

Danielle fought the urge to tell him what she thought of him, expecting that he could easily recruit a few friends to come and kick the daylights out of her. Jumping back into her car, she sped away, keeping an eye on the rearview mirror, just in case he decided to follow her.

Relieved that he didn't seem interested in continuing their conversation, she retraced their route, wondering where McCall was and how she was going to call the Blakelys and tell them what happened.

Driving slowly in the snow and peering through the windshield, Danielle strained to make out a shadow on the other side of the road, not far from the street where the truck had pulled out of the driveway. Could it possibly be McCall? Making a quick U-turn, Danielle doubled back, driving even more slowly, so she could check every inch of the side of the road.

Whatever she'd seen a moment ago was apparently gone now. But she could have sworn—

Wait! What was that?

Danielle stopped the car and hit reverse, sliding a little in the snow. Sure enough, huddled beneath the protection of a garage overhang was a slight figure. It was too dark to see for sure, but Danielle took a chance and pulled her car into the driveway, the headlights beaming directly onto the person.

It was McCall!

Danielle jumped out of the car and ran toward her. McCall bolted away, but Danielle called after her. "McCall, it's me, Danielle. Wait!" McCall stopped when she realized who it was and turned toward Danielle, who held out her arms toward the sobbing, freezing young girl and pulled her into a hug. "It's okay," Danielle soothed. "Everything's okay."

She slipped out of her parka and wrapped it around McCall's shivering body and gently guided her toward the car. Danielle helped her inside, then hurried around the car and got in herself. Cranking up the heat, she turned the vents toward McCall, who huddled in her seat, silent tears running down her face.

Danielle power-locked the doors of her car, just in case, and started down the road. Grabbing her cell phone, she made a quick call to the Blakelys to tell them their daughter was safe and on the way home.

In the fifteen-minute drive home, McCall sobbed for at least ten minutes of it. When the younger girl's tears finally waned and she quit shivering, Danielle spoke. "Did he hurt you?"

McCall shook her head.

"Do you want to talk about it?" Danielle asked. McCall shook her head again.

Danielle reached over and patted the girl's hand. Wanting to convey her concern and love, she also wanted to shake some sense into the girl, but knew it wasn't the right time.

After a few minutes, McCall finally spoke. "Thank you," she said quietly.

Danielle nodded and gave her young friend a smile. "I'm glad I could be there."

"He just pulled over and told me to get out," McCall said in a hollow voice, as if shell-shocked.

"For no reason?" Danielle asked, trying to get the story, but without seeming to pry.

"He took me to a friend's house," she said. "He wanted to me to stay the night there with him."

Danielle caught her breath but held her tongue, letting McCall continue.

"When I told him I wanted to go home, he got mad at me and called me all kinds of names. He told me that I was on my own. I could go home, but I'd have to find my own way."

Danielle shook her head in disbelief. What a jerk! How could anyone leave a young girl alone on the dark city streets at night, in the snow without a coat? What had McCall ever seen in this guy anyway?

McCall's next words echoed Danielle's thoughts. "I can't even remember what I ever saw in him in the first place."

Realizing they were almost to McCall's house, Danielle asked, "Were you really going to run away from home?"

"I don't know," McCall said, exasperated. "My parents just don't seem to understand. They won't let me do anything. First, they didn't let me go to the dance; then tonight, they told me I couldn't have my car for a month because I was late getting home two nights in a row."

"I remember thinking the same thing about my parents when I was your age," Danielle said. "Now that I'm a little older I've learned something."

McCall sounded vaguely interested. "Yeah? What's that?"

Danielle looked over at her. "I learned that they did what they did because they loved me."

"But—"

"McCall, let me just ask you something," Danielle interrupted. "Why didn't your parents let you go out with what's-his-name?"

"With Kyle? Because they didn't *feel good* about him." Her tone was mocking.

"And why didn't you want to stay with Kyle tonight?"

McCall grew quiet then answered slowly, "Because I didn't feel good about it."

"Maybe your parents know what's better for you than you give them credit for. You think?"

McCall looked down at her hands.

"I know they've been frantic with worry all night," she went on. "Your dad and brother were looking all over for you, too."

"They were?" She looked up at Danielle with a penitent look in her eyes. Then her head dropped back against the head rest. "I'll probably be grounded until graduation."

"Do you blame them?" Danielle said, half joking.

McCall shook her head. "No, I guess not." When Danielle pulled up in front of McCall's house and turned off the engine, McCall looked at her pleadingly. "Please come in with me," she said. "I'm scared."

"Just remember," Danielle reminded her, "your parents do love you, and they want what's best for you."

McCall nodded. "I will."

"Ready?" Danielle asked.

"Ready."

No sooner were they out of the car than McCall's parents came running, showering her with hugs of love and relief. Not one word of scolding or anger was spoken. Right now all that mattered was that McCall had returned to them safely.

# CHAPTER TWENTY-ONE

Danielle worked furiously on Carson's scrapbook. Between the Sub-for-Santa project, the scrapbook, and her job, Danielle was starting to feel worn out.

"Danielle," her mother called up the stairs to Danielle, who was sitting on the floor in her room, surrounded by photographs. "Someone's here to see you."

She shut her eyes and prayed for strength. She was never going to finish the book in time. With a sigh she stood up and went downstairs to see who it was.

She didn't expect to see the young girl who stood shyly in the entryway. "McCall!"

"Hi," McCall said. "Are you busy?"

Danielle didn't even think twice. Even though she was swamped, she was more than willing to make time for one of her girls—especially after what had happened last night.

"Not at all. Come on in," Danielle invited. "Let's go into the living room where we can talk."

One of the first things Danielle noticed about McCall was that she looked different. Danielle had never seen her without makeup worthy of a magazine cover, but tonight she wore only lip gloss. Instead of her usual perfectly styled hair, she wore it naturally curly and pulled back into a pony tail.

"So," Danielle asked when they got seated. "How are you?"

"Oh, I've been better," the girl answered with a shaky laugh. "I sure messed up."

Danielle gave her a sympathetic smile, not wanting to say anything to add to the girl's misery.

"I, uh, wanted to thank you again, for . . . you know, for coming to find me the other night."

"I'm glad I did," Danielle said fervently. "It wasn't a good night to be out in the cold without a coat." She didn't mention that it was never a good time to be with a guy like Kyle.

"I know," McCall admitted. "I was so stupid."

"Hey, we all do stupid things sometimes," Danielle said. "Believe me, I know."

McCall shook her head. "I can't picture you doing something dumb, especially as dumb as what I did."

Danielle smiled ruefully. "Well, I did and sometimes I still do." But since she didn't want to have to give an account of one of her less-than-brilliant antics from her youth, she decided it best to change the subject. "Are you hungry? I think my mom just made some brownies."

But McCall was not easily distracted and pursued Danielle's comment. "No, really, tell me. What kind of things did you do when you were my age?"

Danielle wished she'd never mentioned it, especially when McCall insisted that she'd feel better if Danielle would tell her at least one stupid thing she had done.

Exasperated, Danielle said, "It's not like there's one isolated incident, just dumb stuff like borrowing my parents' car before I got my driver's license and getting in a fender bender—with the bishop!"

"You didn't!" McCall giggled. "What else?"

Danielle wanted to drop the subject entirely. But McCall pleaded so she gave in, admitting that she used to tell her mother she was going to Young Women, but would meet her friends and go to the movies instead.

McCall looked down, embarrassed. "I've done that before."

"You haven't lately," Danielle commented. "You've been to almost all of our activities since I've been your advisor."

"That's because you're cool. Our last advisor was mean," McCall scowled.

"Sister Bradshaw? She was mean?" This was news to Danielle, who had always liked the soft-spoken woman from Georgia who seemed to personify Southern hospitality and charm.

McCall groaned. "She was fine until she got pregnant, then she turned into this witch person. She was all sorts of ornery."

Danielle chuckled at the image of the poor woman who'd looked like she was ready to deliver a small elephant. In her opinion, Sister Bradshaw had every right to be ornery.

"See," McCall said. "I don't know what all the fuss is about. You did stuff when you were a kid and you turned out fine."

"Ha!" Danielle scoffed. "Look how I turned out. I'm twenty-seven and unmarried and don't have any prospects of getting married. My life is so dull I may even go back to college and get another degree. I've gotta do something fast or the bishop's going to get the idea to call me on a mission."

McCall didn't look convinced. "But look how cool you are. Don't you think it's because you did normal kid things when you were my age—instead of being Miss Perfect?"

Danielle thought about McCall's question. There had been a time when she'd tried to rationalize her years of rebellion as an important, even necessary, stage of finding out who she really was and discovering her "real" self. But if she was honest, she had to admit it was really a matter of poor choices and dumb mistakes.

"No," she told McCall. "I'm not proud of how I acted and the things I did. All those mistakes, all that time I spent being stupid—it was really a waste of time. Most of the people I knew in Young Women and high school are way ahead of me. Some of them went on missions and they're in really great shape, spiritually. They have families, they own homes; some even have their own business. Then there are the friends I hung out with. They're either stuck in dead-end jobs or bad relationships with guys who are losers, and getting nowhere."

Danielle didn't know what McCall was thinking, but at least she was listening to what she had to say.

She went on. "I've learned a lot from my mistakes, thank goodness, and I'm a lot happier now than I used to be. The main thing I've learned is that it's better to do the right thing and get the blessings, and the sooner you start, the better shape you'll be in."

McCall stared out the window as she pondered Danielle's words.

"How do you feel about running away from home?" Danielle asked, hoping to end their conversation on a positive note.

"Embarrassed, ashamed," McCall answered.

Danielle nodded, knowingly. "Was it worth it?"

"Hardly!" she snorted. "Kyle's such a jerk, he was totally not worth it. And now I'm grounded until after Christmas. The only things I can do is go to church, school, and our mutual activities. In fact, my parents almost made me quit the cheering squad."

"Good," Danielle nodded in approval.

McCall stared at her. "Good? How can you say that?"

Danielle smiled. "Because I need lots of help on the Sub-for-Santa, and it sounds like you have lots of time on your hands."

"Great." McCall rolled her eyes.

"Hey, I thought you wanted to help. Remember the homeless shelter, how much you liked that?" Danielle reminded her. "This will be the same. You'll enjoy it."

"I guess," McCall said unenthusiastically. "I haven't got anything else to do." She was quiet, thinking. "I wonder whatever happened to that old man. His coat was full of holes."

"The one who thought you were his daughter?"

McCall nodded

"Hopefully he's spending a lot of time at the shelters with the cold weather. But I'm sure he could still use some help. They all need our help."

McCall's eyes gleamed with genuine interest. "You really think we could help him?" she asked. "I mean, really help him. Find him somehow and give him a warm coat and some food or something." McCall looked up at Danielle, her face alive with interest.

"I'll ask Walter at the shelter," Danielle said. "He might know how we can get some stuff to him."

To her surprise, McCall threw her arms around Danielle's neck and gave her a hug. "Thanks, Danielle. That'll be cool. And thanks from my parents, too. They couldn't quit talking about how great you were last night."

"Just don't pull a stunt like that again." Danielle wagged a warning finger at her. "No boy is worth it. Got that?"

McCall looked embarrassed. "Yeah."

"You need to talk, you call me," she said sternly. "Deal?"

McCall smiled. "Deal."

_,.,_ &&& _,.,_

Carson surprised her Wednesday afternoon when he called to invite her for dinner. He took her to a charming Italian restaurant near the University. They talked about his classes and her Sub-for-Santa project, about his mission, and her calling in the Young Women. They'd finished their dinner and were sharing a piece of cheesecake when Carson surprised her with a question out of the blue.

"So . . . what do you see yourself doing in five years, Danielle?" he asked.

"Um, well . . ." She halted, trying to think. She hadn't really mapped out her future. Her hands were full just dealing with the immediate issues. "I guess I'll sign up for some classes at the 'U' and start working toward an interior design degree. I don't know what else."

"What do you mean, *you guess?*" Carson asked.

Danielle sat back, thinking about what she had said and why she had said it as she did. It wasn't that she was hesitant to speak honestly to Carson; he was so easy to talk to. She just needed to think it through so she could say what she really meant. She wrinkled her brow in thought. "It's just that all my life I was raised with the expectation that I would graduate from high school, go to college, get married, and have a family," she said. "That's the pattern everyone I knew followed."

He nodded, listening, and she continued.

"So I just wasn't prepared in the event that it didn't happen that way. I mean, I graduated from high school, then did the college thing, and when I didn't get married, I got a job. And now here I am, twenty-seven years old, and I'm just barely deciding what I want to do with the rest of my life because my life didn't follow 'the plan' the way I thought it would."

"I can relate," he said. "When I was ready to come home from my mission, my mission president interviewed me and said that the first thing I needed to do after I got enrolled in college was to start looking for a wife. Do you know I haven't dared go to any of our mission reunions because I'm not married."

"Really?" Danielle said, looking at Carson in surprise. She hadn't really realized that a man might feel caught by the same expectations as a woman.

He took a bite of his cheesecake and swallowed it, then said frankly, "Plus, I have to admit, I'm not real proud of the fact that I finished college, then went to a year and a half of graduate school, only to scrap that and start all over again. By the time I'm through with med school and start practicing, I'll be in my thirties."

Danielle thought of the two of them, both starting down one path, then realizing it wasn't what they wanted and starting down a different road. They'd found what they wanted to do; they just had a late start. A thought suddenly occurred to her.

"Do you ever think that maybe it was supposed to happen this way?" she said. "Maybe we each had things to learn, things to experience that will make us better people. I look back on what I've done so far with my life, and even though I have some regrets, I feel like at least I've learned and grown through the process. I think I'm a better person for it all."

Carson looked at her admiringly, then smiled and reached for her hand. "You're a wonderful person," he told her, "and I think you're right. I've learned a lot and grown a lot from the things I've done."

"See," she smiled back. "We're doing okay."

He smiled at her, looking deeply into her eyes. "We sure are."

❧❧ ❀ ❦❦

After dinner they went back to her house. Her mother met them at the door, completely beside herself with excitement.

"Miranda and her family are on the way over," she said, nearly bursting at the seams. "Adam got his mission call. He's going to open it here. Rachel and her family are coming over, too."

When Carson excused himself with the comment that this was a family event, Danielle took his hand. "You don't have to go," she said, not ready for their evening together to end.

"We'd love you to stay," Dorothy added. "They'll be here any minute, and since you served a mission yourself, it might be nice to have you here, just in case Adam has any questions."

With this encouragement, Carson might have agreed to stay, but since Miranda and her family pulled into the driveway just then, he didn't have any choice. Miranda's daughter, Ashlyn, ran in the house, eager to see Danielle. Since they were only six years apart, they'd grown up more as sisters than as niece and aunt. Ashlyn had been away at school and had just come home for the Christmas break. The two girls hugged, then Danielle turned around to introduce her niece to Carson.

"Ashlyn's down at SUU in Cedar City, working on a degree in journalism," Danielle told Carson, who reached out and shook the younger girl's hand. "She'll graduate this summer at the top of her class."

Ashlyn blushed. "Geez, Danielle, you don't have to tell everyone."

"Hey, you can't hide your light under a bushel, you know," Danielle teased.

"Obviously not with you around I can't," Ashlyn retorted.

Rachel and her family arrived soon after, and everyone gathered in the living room, where they waited for the exciting news. Earl Camden stood in front of everyone and invited his only grandson to stand beside him.

"This is a very special occasion, Adam," he said, one arm around his grandson. "We are very proud of your decision to go on a mission."

Danielle remembered the struggles her nephew had gone through as a teenager. After the death of his father, he'd lost his desire to excel in school, to play basketball, or to hang out with good friends. Instead, he'd turned to drugs, trying to escape the pain of losing his father, and in the process, lost touch with himself. It had been a long road back for him, but he'd turned his life around. His senior year, he led his high school basketball team to the state championship. He also graduated with honors, after serving as senior class president.

"Thanks, Grandpa," Adam said. He held up the envelope so everyone could see, then slowly and carefully, he opened it. Unfolding the letter, he started to read the contents aloud. No one in the room said a word. Danielle squeezed Carson's hand tightly with excitement.

Suddenly Adam stopped reading and stared at the letter. Then he looked up and smiled. "I'm going to the Czech Republic."

Miranda gasped and jumped up to hug her son, tears running down her face. When she finally released him, her father hugged his grandson. Then Garrett, Adam's stepfather, stepped forward to give him a hearty hug.

"I leave February 29th," Adam announced. Then it dawned on him, "That's leap year. Cool!"

Ashlyn was next to hug Adam, then the rest of the family crowded in. Tears, laughter, and excitement filled the room.

"I can't believe it," Adam kept saying as family members hugged him. Danielle gave him a hug and kissed him on the cheek. "I'm so proud of you," she said.

"Congratulations." Carson shook his hand. "That's a great mission. My friend Chad went there. He loved it."

"He did?" Adam asked excitedly. "Does he live around here? Do you think I could talk to him?"

"I'm sure he'd love to. I'll give him a call," Carson offered.

"Thanks," Adam said. "I can't believe this," he said for the hundredth time that evening.

Rachel insisted on hugging her nephew also even though she was barely a week away from her due date and could barely move. She was retaining a lot of water and was very uncomfortable.

"Let's go into the kitchen for some cake," Dorothy announced to her family. Hearing that Adam's mission call had arrived, she'd quickly whipped up a treat to serve in honor of the occasion.

Danielle and Carson stayed behind until the crowd in the kitchen had gotten their cake and settled down to eat.

"This brings back so many memories," Carson said to Danielle. There was a faraway look in his eye. She couldn't tell him that she'd seen a picture of him the day he received his mission call or that his father was trying to find the actual mission call so she could include it in the scrapbook she was making for Carson.

He told her about his mission call and the day he'd received it, how excited he was and how much his mother had cried. He'd had no idea at the time that she'd received the devastating news about her cancer only days earlier.

"Would you have gone on your mission if you'd known about your mother's condition?"

He took a deep breath, then answered. "Before I left my mother told me that my going on a mission was something she'd hoped and prayed for since I was born. She told me that my serving a mission was more important than anything else to her. I couldn't let her down. I know it was what she wanted me to do."

"Dani," her mother called, "do you and Carson want some cake?"

Hoping they could talk more later, Carson and Dani went into the kitchen and joined Adam at the table.

"So, has it sunk in yet?" Danielle asked Adam.

He shook his head. "No way," he said. "I'm still in shock. I just can't picture myself over there, actually speaking these people's language, being a missionary. This is so weird."

"You're going to do a great job," Carson told him. "You'll learn to love these people as much as you love your own family," he said. "You'll be amazed at how much you can love them. That's what happens when you dedicate your life to the Lord and serve others."

*That's almost exactly what Harry said,* Danielle thought. *But if that's true, and Carson believes it, why can't he use that same principle with his own father?*

By the time Carson and Danielle finished eating their cake, nearly everyone had migrated into the family room where Adam was looking up information about the Czech Republic on the Internet.

"I guess I'd better get going," Carson said. "Thanks for letting me be here tonight. It was really great seeing Adam get his mission call like that."

"It was, wasn't it?" Danielle said, stacking her empty plate on top of his, then they both stood and walked to the front door together. Carson took his coat from the coat rack.

"You've got a great family," he said. "I really like them."

"Thanks. They like you, too." *And my mother was very impressed when you passed the toilet seat test.*

"Danielle," her mother hollered from the other room. "Don't forget to ask Carson about Christmas Eve."

"Oh yeah," Danielle said. "My mother was wondering—actually we were both wondering—if you'd like to come over for Christmas

Eve. We usually have a little program of some kind and eat clam chowder and orange rolls. This year I'm thinking of asking Harry if he'd mind popping in to play Santa Claus. We've never done that, and I think it would be fun for Rachel's girls. He's all alone and I'd like to invite him to spend the evening, too."

"Sounds great," Carson smiled his thanks. "The family I'm staying with is going to Idaho for a few days, and I was just going to go up to the hospital and volunteer or something."

"And if it's not too much, we'd like to have you eat dinner with us on Christmas Day, too," she added.

Carson looked at her questioningly. "What do you mean 'too much'?" he asked.

"I don't want my family to overwhelm you," Danielle said, almost apologetically.

"Are you kidding?" he said, surprised. "I've never really spent time with a group of people like this for holidays. You guys have so much fun together, I like being around all of you." Taking both of her hands in his, he stepped closer to her. "In fact—"

Danielle felt tingles crawl up her back.

He pulled her into the living room, lit only by the soft glow of the Christmas tree.

"Danielle," he spoke softly, "I think you have a wonderful family. They've been so good to me."

"They really like you," she told him. "They like having you around."

"That means a lot to me," he said, brushing his hand across her cheek. Then he leaned in closer to her and kissed her softly. Enfolding her in his arms, he held her gently. Warmed by his embrace, she leaned against him. She could tell he was trying to say something, but couldn't seem to get it out. So she waited.

But when he didn't speak, she finally asked, "Are you okay?"

He gave her a squeeze before letting her go. "Yeah," he whispered. "I'm okay, I just . . . Uh, there's something . . ."

Danielle waited, not knowing how to make it any easier for him to say whatever he was trying to say.

"Danielle, I . . ." He swallowed. "I love you."

Danielle felt lightheaded and breathless. A million feelings flooded her; relief, excitement, happiness, even disbelief. Circling her arms around his neck, she stood up on her toes to give him a tender kiss before she replied, "I love you, too."

When they drew apart at last, both were smiling.

"Well," he said, looking at her, his eyes gleaming.

"That was hard for you to get out," she teased.

"I've never told a girl that before," he replied honestly. "I wasn't sure what you were going to say back to me."

"I guess you have to take a risk now and then, don't you?" she said lightly, reminding herself that Carson's life was very complicated. And she was now a part of it.

"I guess so," he said. "But it was definitely worth it."

"I think so, too," she told him. Maybe this was a step in the right direction for Carson. Maybe as he opened his heart to love her, he would be able to find a way to let his father back into his heart and his life. They would all be at her house on Christmas Eve. She hoped that would be the time they could patch up their differences. Perhaps the spirit of Christmas would bring about a healing miracle between father and son.

Carson's voice broke into her thoughts. "What are you thinking about?"

"Oh . . ." She turned her attention back to him. "I was . . . , well," she hesitated.

He raised an eyebrow, waiting for her to speak. "Yes?"

"Well . . . ," she swallowed. "I was thinking about your dad."

"My dad!" He let go of her hands.

She could tell he was angry, but it was too late to back out now. "I don't know," she said. "It's the holidays, and that's the time you spend with family and loved ones."

"He'll be with his loved ones," Carson said dryly. "Every crisp, green one of them."

"Carson!" she said in a scolding tone. "You don't know—"

He cut her off. "Danielle, I don't want to ruin a wonderful evening talking about my father. I know you don't understand, but believe me, if my father's lonely and unhappy, it's his own fault. He deserves everything he's got and then some."

*He deserves cancer? He deserves to be dying? He deserves to be abandoned by his only child, a son who can't find a place in his heart to forgive?* Tears stung Danielle's eyes, and she quickly blinked them away.

"You really can't understand, Danielle," he said, his voice tight with emotion. "Your family is normal and happy. Your parents love you. Maybe if my father had spent some time with me, actually shown me that he cared about my life, my happiness, and not his money and business, maybe things would be different. But they aren't. I can't change the past and what he did. But I can change the future—by keeping him out of my life."

Danielle couldn't believe that the warm feelings between them could turn cold and harsh so quickly and without warning. "But you can't go through the rest of your life never speaking to him again, never seeing him," she said pointedly. "I know he was wrong, but you have to forgive him. For your own sake as well as his."

He shook his head. "Maybe I do, but I can't right now. I'm just not ready. And I don't know when I'll ever be ready." He grabbed his coat that was hanging over the back of a chair. "You know what, I gotta go." He turned and walked toward the door.

Danielle didn't want him to leave like this. "Carson, I'm sorry, I know it's none of my business," she pleaded, "but can't you—"

Carson's look stopped her cold. "You know, you're right, Danielle," he said curtly. "It isn't any of your business." Opening the door, he walked out the door. The frigid winter air wasn't nearly as freezing as how cold he left her heart.

# CHAPTER
## TWENTY-TWO

"What's wrong, Dani?" Miranda asked when Danielle stumbled blindly back into the kitchen. She still stung from Carson's last remark. Why couldn't she just leave it alone? She had known it would upset him to bring up his father. And it really was none of her business. Yet she was positive that she had to do something to bring them back together. She knew the Lord hadn't brought Harry into her life for no reason.

Harry wasn't the same man as Philip Turner had been. Harry was a kind, caring, loving, and Christlike person. Somehow she had to help Carson see that side of his father.

Danielle didn't even dare to look at Miranda for fear she would start crying. "Oh, nothing," she said, slumping down into one of the kitchen chairs. Right now she didn't want to talk about it. She didn't even want to remember the conversation she'd just had with Carson. Even if they did love each other, that didn't mean she could just forget that Carson had a father who needed him.

"Did you and Carson have an argument?" Miranda asked gently. "He sounded a little upset in there."

"Upset?" Rachel walked into the room at that moment. "Who was upset?" She opened several cupboards and looked inside. "Does Mom have any Tums? I've got horrible heartburn from that cake."

Danielle didn't answer, not wanting Rachel to get involved in the conversation.

Rachel looked over her shoulder at Danielle. "You were talking about someone when I came in. Is it Carson? Is something wrong?" she insisted.

Danielle rolled her eyes and slumped down even further in her chair, and Rachel continued her search even as she waited for Danielle to answer her questions.

"Ahh, I knew they had some." Rachel found a container of the antacid and popped several into her mouth. She pulled a face as she chewed them and swallowed. "I'm so sick of these."

"Are you still having contractions?" Miranda asked.

Rachel's voice was filled with disgust. "No, the stupid things stopped. I swear if I don't have this baby soon, I'm going to scream." She sat down with her two sisters at the table. "Now, what were you talking about?"

"I was just asking Danielle about Carson," Miranda said, looking at Danielle apologetically, as if she regretted asking about him just in time for Rachel to intrude on their conversation.

"He is such a cutie," Rachel said. "Has he kissed you yet?"

"Rachel!" Danielle exclaimed, sitting up in her chair with an exasperated huff.

"I bet he's a good kisser. He's got really nice lips."

"Oh my heck," Danielle complained. "I can't believe you sometimes."

"I'm sorry, just because I'm big, fat, and pregnant doesn't mean I can't see. Don't you think he's cute, Miranda?"

"He's very nice-looking," Miranda agreed. "But that has nothing to do with what we were talking about." Danielle glared at her sister, not wanting to reopen the door to their earlier discussion.

"So what's going on, Dani?" Rachel asked.

"Nothing really," Danielle answered lightly, hoping to discourage further conversation.

"But I heard you and Carson talking," Rachel said. "He's sure unhappy with his father."

Danielle should have been surprised, but she wasn't. "You heard us?"

"I was coming out of the bathroom when he was telling you that he didn't think he could ever forgive his father," Rachel defended herself, adding that she thought Carson sounded pretty upset.

Danielle sighed, realizing that there was no keeping it from her sisters now. "He is."

"What happened between them?" Miranda asked.

Danielle found herself explaining the whole situation to her sisters, starting back at the beginning when she worked for Mr. Turner and first met Carson. Then she brought them up to date with her Sub-for-Santa and Harry.

"The whole situation does seem more than a coincidence," Rachel declared, as if having discovered it all by herself.

"Forgiveness can be hard for some people," Miranda said thoughtfully. "It took me over a year to even begin to come to terms with Tom and what he did to me. I never thought I'd be able to forgive him."

Danielle remembered when Miranda's first husband, Tom, had died in a plane crash. For months, no one, except Miranda herself, knew that the woman who was with him in the plane was someone he'd been having an affair with. Miranda hadn't even planned on telling her family, but when the children had begun talking about getting sealed to their father in the temple, Miranda finally had to tell them the truth. Danielle knew it had nearly torn Miranda apart inside to tell her children that she didn't want to be sealed to their father. It had taken time, but Miranda had ultimately found the strength to forgive Tom.

Miranda always credited the Lord with giving her the strength to forgive Tom. It was the Atonement, she said, that had worked a miracle in her life. She could never have done it alone.

"It is so very difficult to forgive," Rachel said, breaking into Danielle's thoughts. "But we need to rely on the power of the Atonement. The Lord can lift anyone's burden. But if Carson isn't ready, it won't happen. He has to ask for the help; he has to want it. I know for myself how hard it is to put pride aside and admit you can't do it alone."

Rachel had experienced her own share of heartache due to some poor choices her husband had made. Nevertheless, Doug had regretted his actions and admitted his wrongdoing. Rachel hadn't wanted to forgive him at first, but she, like Miranda, had learned to seek the Lord's help in letting go of her anger and hurt. Danielle could see that since going through that difficult time, Rachel had become a more loving, compassionate person. She and Doug had been able to survive the damage done to their relationship and had actually built a stronger marriage from it.

"Carson is a good person, Dani. He just needs time and understanding," Rachel declared.

"But he doesn't have much more time," Danielle explained. "I don't know how long Harry can hang on."

"Then all you can do is fast and pray for him," Miranda said. "Somehow the Lord will soften his heart."

"We'll pray for him, too," Rachel said.

As she looked at her sisters, Danielle realized that she was glad she'd talked to them. Each had personal experience on the topic of forgiveness, and she was grateful for their words of wisdom.

"You really care about him, don't you?" Rachel said more than asked.

Danielle shrugged, still reluctant to open up to her sisters. "I don't know." But she knew she was lying. She loved him, and it was even worse, knowing that he loved her, too.

"Okay. Yes," she confessed. "I do care about him. I love being with him. But I've made so many mistakes when it comes to guys and dating, I don't trust my own instincts anymore. I mean, look at what happened with Todd."

"Well," Rachel said as she rubbed her round stomach, "as much as I liked Todd, I think you made the right choice."

"You do?" Danielle was shocked at this revelation. Rachel had been Todd's biggest fan.

"Yes, I do. You've really changed in the last two years. You've had to struggle and grow, and I think you're a much different person than you were when you were dating Todd. You're stronger and more independent. Todd's the type of guy who wants a wife who will adore him and worship the ground he walks on and do his every bidding. Personally, a guy like that would make me crazy. I don't think you two would have been very happy. Plus," she added, lowering her voice. "I didn't find this out until the other day, but did you know he didn't pass the toilet seat test?"

"*He didn't?*" Miranda pretended she was going to faint.

"Mom just barely told me," Rachel said.

"But she was going to let Danielle marry him!" Miranda exclaimed, giving a wink to Danielle.

"I know," Rachel said, shaking her head. "I'm as surprised as you are."

"You know," Miranda confided, "Tom blew the test, too. That should have been my first clue."

"Well, Doug passed it," Rachel boasted.

Danielle looked at her sisters and asked, "So you guys really believe in this test?"

"Yes!" they chimed together.

"I know it sounds silly," Miranda went on, "but I'm convinced it works."

"Carson passed the test," Danielle told them proudly.

"There you go." Rachel waved her hands grandly to punctuate her words, then rested her hands on her swollen belly. "Then he's worth hanging onto, Dani. I think things will work out between Carson and his father, and you and Carson. You just need to have faith, and pray your heart out. The Lord has brought you into these men's lives for a reason. Just follow the promptings in your heart."

Danielle swallowed the lump in her throat. "Thanks, you guys," she said. "I'm glad we talked."

Rachel slapped the table. "Good! Now that that's settled, I'm hungry. Does Mom have any pickles and bologna? And Cheez Whiz. Mmmm, that would be perfect."

❦

"Danielle?" The voice on the other end of the phone was barely audible.

"Hello? Who is this?" Danielle asked. She could tell it was a woman's voice, but it didn't sound familiar. "Hello?" she repeated when there was no response, only the muffled sound of sobs.

The sobbing paused momentarily. "Dani, it's me . . . Roberta," the caller choked out.

Danielle felt a stab of alarm. "Roberta! What's wrong? Has something happened?"

"It's Lenny," she sobbed. "He . . . he . . ." Roberta burst into tears again.

"What, Roberta? What about Lenny?" Danielle pulled in several large breaths to remain calm. Was he sick? Was he dead? What?!

"He broke . . . our engagement. It's over," she wailed. Danielle's heart went out in sympathy for her friend, but she found it necessary to hold the receiver away from her ear while Roberta vented her emotion.

When she quieted down after a few moments, Danielle asked, "What happened? Why did he break off the engagement?"

Roberta sniffed and cleared her throat. "He said he needed more time. He's not ready to settle down yet."

Danielle wanted to throttle Lenny for all the times she'd heard of men using that line. "I am so sorry," she said. "I don't know what to say."

"I'm just so stunned," Roberta told her, her voice still shaky. "I didn't see this coming at all. I mean, one minute we're picking out china patterns and planning our honeymoon, and next he's telling me that he's changed his mind and doesn't want to get married."

"Do you feel like some company? Do you want me to come over?" Danielle asked, wishing she knew what to say.

Roberta sniffled again. "Bart just called. He said he talked to Lenny, and then he called to see if I was okay. He offered to take me for a ride. We could come and get you," she added hopefully.

"Sure. If you want to. I'll be here." Danielle herself knew the pain Roberta was feeling. It wasn't hard to recognize.

"Thanks," Roberta said gratefully. "I don't know what I'd do without you."

⊱⊹⊰

Sitting at the table in a pizza parlor, Roberta told Danielle and Bart about the last conversation she'd had with Lenny. As she talked, she morosely picked the green peppers off her pizza and made a little pile by the side of her plate. Bart and Danielle listened quietly, letting her unload her feelings. Occasionally Danielle caught Bart's eye, his expression asking her what they should do to help. Danielle could only shake her head. Roberta was still in the "processing stage" of the breakup. Danielle realized that her friend couldn't hear any advice or encouragement how to survive and go on; all she could do was try to digest the magnitude of what had just happened to her. The hole left by Lenny's departure was just too gaping to fill right now.

"I've got 750 wedding announcements at home, half of them addressed and ready to send," Roberta moaned. "My mother's been baking banana bread and making mints for the last month. I've got a freezer full of this stuff. What am I going to do with it now?"

"Maybe you could donate the bread to the Sub-for-Santa," Danielle suggested.

Roberta nodded and blew her nose on a napkin. "Good idea. I'd like to do that." She pushed her plate away. "I guess they can't use one thousand 'Lenny and Roberta Forever' napkins, could they?" She laughed sardonically, then started crying again.

"Hey, honey." Danielle put her hand over her friend's. "It's going to be okay."

"We'll help you through this," Bart said, placing his hand over Roberta's other hand.

"Thanks, you guys." She looked at Bart with red-rimmed eyes. "Bart, did Lenny tell you he was having second thoughts? Did you have any idea he was thinking about breaking up with me?" she asked.

"No." Bart shook his head. "Not a clue. He talked a lot about wanting to take off and go backpacking in Europe, you know, go skiing and tripping around and stuff. I didn't think anything of it at the time. But then, he never said he was going to break up."

Roberta listened quietly, not speaking, as if shell-shocked.

"Listen, Roberta," Bart said, "Lenny and I are good friends, but in all honesty you're much better off without him. Being married to him would have been hard on you. He's not really very responsible, and he doesn't like to work hard. You probably would have had to work the rest of your life to help support your family. He was telling me just the other day he wanted to drop out of college and start a landscaping business."

"He did?" Roberta asked, her eyebrows scrunched together in confusion. "He's never even done landscaping, has he?"

"No," Bart said. "He just thought it sounded like fun. He decided it was the perfect job, so he'd have winters off to go skiing."

Danielle was so mad at Lenny she thought she would have been tempted to punch him if he'd been within reach. "I don't believe this," she said, looking from Bart to Roberta.

"Me either," Roberta said. "What a jerk." Her bottom lip quivered. "Now what do I do?" She closed her eyes and swallowed, her face naked in its suffering. "It hurts so bad," she choked out.

"I know," Danielle patted her hand. "I know."

Roberta covered her face with her hands. "I feel so stupid and ugly and worthless," she moaned.

"Roberta," Bart said, leaning toward her. "You are not stupid and ugly. And you're certainly not worthless. I always thought you were much too bright and beautiful for Lenny. A lot of times I wondered how he got lucky enough to get a girl like you."

His words seemed to break through Roberta's grief. "You did?" she asked. She did not look up, but Danielle sensed that Bart's compliment offered a soothing balm to her aching heart.

"Oh, yeah," he said, still looking at her although she kept her face in her hands. "In fact, I was thinking of asking you out first, then Lenny beat me to it."

Lowering her hands, she looked at him. Her eyes were red, her cheeks still wet with tears. "Really?" she whispered.

"Really," Bart told her, smiling.

Roberta sighed. "I just don't know what to do now."

"Just take it slow and easy," Danielle told her, laying a hand on Roberta's and giving her a comforting squeeze. "You need time to let this settle, then you'll begin putting your life back together."

"And we'll help you," Bart said, taking her other hand. "Won't we, Danielle?"

"Anytime you need us," she agreed.

Roberta's eyes filled with tears, which she blinked quickly away. "Thanks," she said. "You guys are the best." An anguished look passed over her face and she looked at Danielle. "What will I do with our tickets for a Caribbean cruise in February?"

"You should still go," Danielle said and Bart nodded.

Roberta looked unsure. "You think?"

"Absolutely," Danielle smiled sweetly, then added with an inno-cent look, "and I think you should take a friend with you."

Roberta smiled for the first time that night. "Me and you?"

Danielle nodded. "Who else?"

"It would be fun," she said uncertainly.

"It would be a *blast,*" Danielle assured her.

Roberta thought about it for a minute, then smacked the table with her fist. "You're right. It would be a blast. Promise you'll go with me?"

Danielle crossed her heart. "Are you kidding? Of course I will."

It was barely noticeable, but along with the smile on her face, there was a glimmer of hope in Roberta's eyes.

# CHAPTER
## ❧ TWENTY-THREE ❧

"Are you sure you want to do this?" Danielle asked McCall as they drove down the back streets of downtown Salt Lake City. It was the first day of Christmas vacation for McCall and she wanted to spend it looking for the old man from the shelter who'd mistaken her for his daughter on Thanksgiving day. The area around the railroad tracks and under the freeway was cold and unwelcoming. McCall had been haunted by the experience and felt that somehow this was a sign she was supposed to help him.

Danielle wished they had someone else with them to protect them. Someone big and strong and scary-looking.

"McCall, I'm nervous," she confessed. "I think we should just leave the blanket and coat at the shelter with Walter. He said the old guy would show up eventually."

"But what if he doesn't? They said on the news that we were having record-breaking cold temperatures that are supposed to last all week. Can we just try for a few more minutes?" she begged.

Danielle looked at the clock. It was eight-fifteen in the morning. She hoped that any dangerous people or bad guys would still be sleeping after a night of carousing.

"Okay, we'll look until eight-thirty, then we're going home." Walter had told her that they needed to look for the old man early in the morning, because once he woke up, he'd spend the rest of his day out looking for food or clothes and wouldn't return until nightfall.

Satisfied, McCall peered out the window looking for the viaduct where Walter said they could find the old man.

"Wait," McCall said excitedly. "I think that's it."

Sure enough, there, where the railroad lines crossed and the freeway passed overhead, was a sheltered area. They didn't see anyone moving around, but there were telltale signs of inhabitants: firepits, garbage, cardboard boxes, even some movement.

Danielle wasn't sure they should even get out of the car. What if some crazed lunatic attacked them? But McCall wasn't about to give up. She grabbed the wool coat and a few bags of food items, leaving Danielle to carry the other bags of groceries and the warm blanket. Danielle locked the car and followed McCall toward the spot Walter had described.

Shivering against an icy wind, and stepping as quietly and carefully as they could, they made their way to the sheltered area and began looking. The place was barren except for several piles that looked like they belonged to someone. Most likely, those who had slept here the night before were already up and gone, probably in search of something to fill their empty bellies. Danielle's heart clenched inside her chest to think of anyone having to sleep here, especially in below freezing weather.

McCall tripped on something and cried out, her voice echoing through the emptiness. "What was that?" she screamed, then clapped her hand over her mouth to muffle the sound. From underneath one of the boxes, someone's hand protruded. A sickening wave washed over Danielle. She didn't want to, but she knew she had to look.

"Do you think . . . ?" McCall looked at her with frightened eyes.

*Just do it and get it over with,* Danielle told herself.

Reaching toward the box, Danielle gave it a strong push, then stepped back to McCall's side, where they huddled in fear. The box tipped on its side then fell back and settled into place. But Danielle had glimpsed a body—a tired, old body—lying curled up on the ground.

She lifted the box again, slowly, watching for any movement. She let the box fall away and peered closer. "It's him," she told McCall.

McCall approached her reluctantly, her face pale. "Is he dead?" she whispered.

"I don't know." Danielle shook her head slowly. How anyone could survive sleeping outside at night in this weather was beyond her. She pushed away several liquor bottles with her feet, and the smell of alcohol rose up to assault her nostrils. Finding his wrist, she searched for a pulse and found none. She glanced up at McCall. "Help me roll him over."

"No," McCall recoiled in fear.

"Darn it, McCall, help me!" she demanded.

"Okay, okay." The girl dropped her load and knelt down quickly at Danielle's side. Together they rolled the man's rigid body onto his back; his face was white and still. Danielle felt his throat.

"Can you feel anything?" McCall asked anxiously.

"Shhh," Danielle said, straining to detect any sign of life. She wasn't sure if it was her own pulse or his, but she felt something.

She pulled his threadbare jacket back and rested her head on his chest. Ever so softly, she detected a very slow, faint heartbeat.

Moving quickly, Danielle jumped to her feet, scaring McCall to death. "We need to call 911 now!"

Racing back to her car, Danielle grabbed her cell phone and placed the call. In the meantime, McCall had the coat and blanket over the old man, trying to keep him warm until help arrived. She looked up as Danielle hurried back, a mix of concern and gratitude on her face.

"Hey!" someone shouted, as the girls stood over the old man, huddled together against the cold. "What are you doing?"

Danielle looked up to see a man with long wild hair and a bushy beard coming at them. "Leave Evans alone. He's not doing anything."

"We're not hurting him," McCall cried. "We're trying to help him."

"Get away from him, I said!" the man yelled, his rheumy eyes burning with rage.

"He's dying," Danielle tried to explain, but the man was livid. Danielle was frightened for both of their sakes. He was out of his mind enough to do something crazy. He was ready to come at them, swinging his fists, but the sound of a siren, wailing in the distance, caught his attention.

*Thank you,* Danielle prayed. Help was on the way.

Within minutes the paramedics had loaded the old man into the ambulance. By then over a dozen other homeless people had gathered to watch their friend being taken away. Intending to follow them to the hospital, Danielle grabbed McCall and pulled her to the car.

"Wait," McCall cried. "What about all this stuff?"

"I'm sure these people can use it," Danielle told her.

McCall looked after the ambulance sadly. "But I want him to have it," she mourned aloud.

"We can get him another coat and blanket," Danielle suggested reasonably.

McCall looked at the haggard, pitiful group in front of her and motioned toward the bags of food and the coat and blanket. "This is for you," she said, then added, "Merry Christmas."

They ran for the safety of their car and locked the doors. With the heater blasting, they raced to the hospital, but they didn't get there in time. The old man had died of exposure while en route. McCall dissolved into tears when the paramedic told them.

"I knew he needed a warm coat," she sobbed. "If only we'd found him sooner."

The paramedic was compassionate but practical. "Things like this happen far too often," he told her. "Some of these homeless folk who live on the streets make the mistake of drinking until they pass out, then they don't think to go inside somewhere for shelter from the cold. Eventually they freeze to death."

It was a sad truth, but an awakening for both of them. Danielle knew that neither of them would ever be the same again.

⚜

Haunted by the old man's death, Danielle was driven more now than ever to help people who needed it. She spent the next afternoon with her mother organizing toys, gifts, and donations in their basement for the families on their lists. There was also a huge pile for the shelter—old coats, gloves, boots, and blankets. Each time she looked at it, she thought of the old man. She wondered how many would meet the same fate unless someone helped them.

Danielle and her mother each took a list, and one family at a time, began a pile for each member of each family. Danielle found comfort in taking positive action and in doing something she knew would make a difference. She enjoyed picking a special Barbie doll for a six-year-old girl named Emily. She found a Jazz basketball for Emily's nine-year-old brother, Jason. She added clothes, socks, underwear, and pajamas to each of their piles.

In the middle of their organizing, the phone rang. It was Roberta. "Danielle, I know I told you I'd come over and help you organize the Sub-for-Santa stuff, but do you think we could do it later?"

"What's up?" Danielle asked.

Roberta spoke quickly. "Bart and I were talking about all the new movies that are out right now and we decided to catch an afternoon showing of the new Harrison Ford movie. I said I'd ask if you wanted to come, too, then we could work on the Sub-for-Santa stuff after."

Danielle looked at her mother, who was busily putting gifts into neat piles and checking names off her list. "Mom's here right now helping me, and my Laurels said they'd come and help, so I really can't. Why don't you two go ahead without me. We're getting so much done I hate to quit right now."

Roberta offered to call when they got out of the movie and help Danielle finish the work.

"Sounds good," Danielle answered as she eyed a fleecy red University of Utah sweatshirt and added it to one of the piles. "You doing better today?"

"A little," Roberta said. "After we dropped you off, Bart and I talked until about one in the morning. He helped me see a lot about Lenny that I'd never seen before. I'll tell you about it later."

Danielle was smiling as she hung up the phone, glad to hear that her friend was feeling better. She updated her mother on Roberta's progress while they continued working on family lists until every gift was distributed into nice large piles. They'd already created a separate list of things they needed to buy to complete some of the wish lists. With the large amount of money that had been donated, they had plenty to cover the expense. Sister McKay from the Relief Society had brought over red stocking caps with white pom poms on the ends for the volunteer elves, and large cloth bags she'd sewn for the gifts. Danielle could hardly wait to see the look on the children's faces when

Harry rang their doorbell, cried, "Ho, ho, ho," and delivered bags full of gifts and food, as well as a Christmas tree.

That evening, after she'd finished organizing the Sub-for-Santa gifts, Danielle drove to Harry's house to finish getting the rest of the pictures for Carson's scrapbook. She actually felt like collapsing into bed, but knew she had to spend every spare minute working on the scrapbook if she wanted to have it finished in time and exactly right.

"Good evening, Danielle," Harry greeted her warmly when she arrived. "I was hoping you'd come tonight."

"How are you feeling?" she asked, seeing the brightness in his eyes and color in his cheeks.

"Much better, thank you." He offered her some hot chocolate, which she accepted gratefully, chilled to the bone from the bitter cold.

"And this should go perfectly with it," she said, handing him a plateful of gingerbread her mother had baked.

He leaned down closely to the plate and took a whiff of the spicy cake. "Mmmm, smells just like the kind my grandmother made when I was a little boy."

Danielle asked him about his Christmases as a youngster, and over the next two hours Danielle learned that Harry had grown up in a very poor home, without a father. His mother took in sewing and waited tables at a diner near their home. Harry had spent a lot of time with his grandmother while his mother worked nights, weekends, and holidays. In fact, she wasn't able to spend Christmas with him until she started working as a maid at a hotel. When he was old enough, Harry got a paper route and gave his mother everything he earned. He also bagged groceries at a nearby supermarket and mowed lawns in the summer. All his money went to help support his mother and himself. He vowed as a teenager to get an education so that when he grew up, he would make enough money to buy his mother the home she always dreamed of.

He spoke fondly of the day he was able to give his mother that special home, how she'd cried and cried when he'd given her the key to her new house. After only nine months, though, she'd had a stroke and had to live in a nursing home. But she was proud of her son and his successes, and when she died, he knew she was pleased with him.

Harry showed her the pictures of his mother on the day he surprised her with her new home. She was happy and glowing and full of smiles.

"I admit," he said, "I got carried away with success. It just seemed to fuel my fire. The more money I made, the more I wanted. I was older when I married Laura. How I wish I could do it all over." His voice became sad and melancholy. "All that time I spent at the office, I would spend with her and Carson. I had no idea she would be taken from me so soon. I thought we'd have the rest of our lives together."

He found a picture of Carson as a five-year-old, sitting on Santa's knee, the young boy wide-eyed and smiling, holding a candy cane up to the camera. Looking at the picture wistfully, Harry said, "It seems like yesterday that he was a little boy." He shook his head. "Time went so quickly; he grew up so fast."

Before long they had organized the pictures, and Danielle had another large pile of pictures to use for the scrapbook. The rest they put back in boxes.

As Danielle finished stacking the boxes neatly in the closet, she turned back to Harry. "I've been wondering if you had any plans for Christmas Eve and Christmas Day this year."

"Plans?" he asked. "No, I don't have any plans."

"I thought you might like to spend Christmas Eve with my family," she invited him. "We have a program and eat clam chowder, and it's really fun. My folks would really like it if you'd come, and I would, too."

When he didn't answer, but only looked at her silently, she added, "We'd also like you to join us for turkey dinner on Christmas. Please say you will."

"Are you sure it's no bother?" he said slowly.

"No," she said quickly. "Not at all. We want you there. And," she paused, "if you aren't too tired after all the Sub-for-Santa deliveries, I thought maybe you could come dressed like Santa. My sister's daughters would get such a kick out of it. It would really be fun for them."

It was the chance to be of service, Danielle thought, that finally won him over. "I would love to," he said.

"You will!" she exclaimed. "That's great! Thank you. It will be so fun to have you."

She gathered her pictures to take home, then Harry helped her on with her coat and walked her to the door.

"You'd better take good care of yourself," she said. "I don't want you getting sick again." She gave him a warning tap on his shoulder.

"Be careful driving home," he said in return, and with a smile, added, "Thank you for everything, Danielle."

Danielle stepped toward the older man, raised up on tiptoe, and gave him a quick kiss on the cheek. "You're welcome," she said. Then, suddenly feeling shy, she turned and hurried out the door.

�™⋘ 🕸 ⋙™

Cassie looked up at Danielle as she walked through the front door at Creative Display. It was less than a week before Christmas and the crowds at the store had finally subsided. They were finishing up a few orders then getting ready for their after Christmas clearance sale.

"Vince," she called. "She's here."

"What?" Danielle said, checking her watch. It was five minutes to ten. She wasn't even expected until ten.

Vince rushed down from his office, his footsteps tapping a staccato rhythm on the stairs. "Danielle, darling, I'm so proud of you!" he cried.

Danielle didn't understand the fuss. What was going on?

"Your tree," he said, "Your beautiful, clever Christmas tree. It sold for the highest amount of any tree at the Jubilee of Trees this year."

"Mine?" she cried. "Really?" She was dumbfounded.

"It's being donated to the children's hospital. They're delivering it tomorrow so the children will have it for Christmas. Isn't that marvelous?" He gave her a squeeze. "I'm so proud of you."

"But it wasn't even that fancy. It wasn't nearly as pretty as that crystal tree. Or that one with all the beanie animals on it," she said.

"But it was unique and beautiful and certainly meant a great deal to someone," he told her.

"Was it the Russell Medical group that bought it?" she asked.

"No," Vince answered, "they did bid on the tree, but an anonymous bidder got the tree and requested that it be sent to the children's hospital."

"Anonymous?" Danielle wondered who had bid on her tree.

Vincent nodded, smiling at her warmly. "As I said, something about the theme of your tree touched someone's heart. I'm so proud of you."

Danielle was completely blown away by the news. If Bart's parents didn't buy it, then who did?

⁂

Cassie and Danielle spent the rest of the day finishing the trees for the Sub-for-Santa. When a tree had been trimmed to perfection, it was loaded into the delivery truck, ready for Christmas Eve.

Danielle's heart filled to the brim with the generosity of friends, family, and even complete strangers who'd heard about their Sub-for-Santa efforts. They had received so much cash that they not only had enough to buy food for turkey dinners for each family, but they could also give each family some cash to use as they needed.

Danielle's sister Miranda and her daughter, Ashlyn, had done all the grocery shopping for the project. Poor Rachel was too miserable and uncomfortable to do much but complain. She seemed to need to let everyone else know just how miserable she was, even though there was nothing anyone could do to give her relief.

That night, Roberta came over to help Danielle work on Carson's scrapbook. They laughed, looking at a picture of Carson in junior high, with goofy-looking glasses and braces.

The telephone rang. Danielle was still laughing when she answered it. It was Bart. She hadn't spoken with him since the night of Roberta's breakup. "Hi, Bart. How are you?" she asked.

"I'm great, thanks," he said. "Is Roberta there?"

"Oh," she said, a little surprised. "Yeah, she's right here." Danielle handed the phone to Roberta. "It's for you. It's Bart."

Danielle busied herself arranging pictures on a page but couldn't help overhearing their conversation. Obviously they were making plans to do something.

"Hey, Dani," Roberta said, placing her hand over the receiver, "tickets go on sale tomorrow for End Zone. Bart and I were thinking about going. You want to come?"

Danielle appreciated the offer but she wasn't the least bit interested in going to the concert. Even more important, she was picking up some vibes between these two. Some very strong vibes.

Danielle had to admit, she'd been amazed at how well Roberta was doing after the breakup with Lenny. Now she was beginning to understand why.

"So, you two are going to the concert?" Danielle asked after her friend hung up the phone.

Roberta nodded enthusiastically. "He likes End Zone as much as I do. In fact, the more we talk, I'm amazed at how much we have in common."

"You two have been talking a lot?" Danielle asked, curiously.

"Well, not *a lot*," Roberta clarified, "but more than we used to. He's been so nice to go out of his way to keep me busy, you know, to help take my mind off Lenny."

"Seems like Bart has done quite a good job of taking your mind off Lenny," Danielle teased.

Roberta's eyebrows lifted in surprise. "What do you mean?"

"Come on, Roberta. What's up with you two?" Danielle demanded to know.

Roberta feigned shock, but she didn't convince Danielle.

"You two have something going on, don't you?"

"Of course not," Roberta denied. "We're just friends."

"You're busted, Roberta," Danielle exclaimed. "You two like each other. I can see it all over your face."

Lowering her eyes, Roberta placed her hands over her flushed cheeks.

"And you know what?" Danielle asked. Roberta didn't answer. "I think it's great!"

Roberta's eyes opened wide with surprise. "You do?"

"Yes! You've always spoken highly of Bart and you two make a great couple. I think you're perfect for each other."

"You do, really? I mean, you're okay with this?"

"I am so okay with this that I hope you two are very happy together," Danielle reassured her. "Heck, I hope you two get married."

Roberta clasped her hands to her chest and breathed a sigh of relief. "I'm so glad to hear you say this because I've been so worried. I didn't know how you felt about Bart, you know. I mean, you two have been out on a few dates, and I didn't want to get in the way of something between you two."

Danielle shook her head. "I do like him, but just as a friend. Bart's a great guy, but he's not for me. I'm really happy you two found each other."

Roberta closed her eyes for a second, then opened them and said, "I am too. Oh, Danielle, I can't tell you how wonderful it has been with him. He's been so supportive. I don't know how I would have survived all this with Lenny if it weren't for Bart. We have so much in common, and he's so sweet and thoughtful. And he's so focused. He knows what he wants to do in life, and he's got such a strong testimony. And," she said dreamily, "he's so handsome."

Danielle wouldn't exactly classify him as handsome, but hey, if Roberta thought so, that was all that mattered. "I think this is really great," she said sincerely.

"Thank you," Roberta said, leaning over to hug her. "You are the best friend ever. I was so worried to talk to you about this. But I shouldn't have been."

"You're over Lenny then?"

"I'm *totally* over Lenny," Roberta said with a wave of her hand. "In a way, I feel like all of this has happened for a reason. I thought having Lenny break up with me was the worst thing that could have ever happened, but it turned out to be the best thing that could have happened. Maybe I was supposed to learn something while we were together. And, of course, I feel bad about all the money that was wasted on pictures and wedding stuff. I'd like to hot glue every one of those stupid reception napkins to his bare skin, but other than that I'm okay."

She smiled proudly. "I mean, I hope he's happy and that he gets his life together, but I see now that we really weren't meant for each other. We didn't want the same things in life, and down the road we would have had some serious problems in our marriage." Roberta had a dreamy, faraway look in her eye. "I really feel good about Bart," she said. "I'm so much happier, and our relationship is so much more relaxed. I don't feel I have to push him to do anything, and he makes me feel like a queen."

"It's just like I told you," Roberta said. "When you least expect it, Mr. Right waltzes into your life."

"I guess I should've taken dancing lessons then," Danielle said, remembering how she'd thought Carson had "waltzed" into her life. She grimaced at the thought of their last date together, which had started out so wonderfully and ended so badly. He'd finally told her he loved her, but when she'd mentioned his father, he'd shut her out completely. Where did that leave them, she wondered.

"Don't you give up," Roberta encouraged her. "It will happen to you, too. You just have to have faith."

Danielle wondered if faith would be enough. She thought she had faith, but so far it hadn't produced any Mr. Right for her. Just a lot of Mr. Wrongs.

# CHAPTER
## TWENTY-FOUR

Christmas Eve morning, Danielle woke up before her alarm rang. Everyone was meeting at her house for freshly baked cinnamon rolls and hot cider before the deliveries began. There would be over thirty people and three delivery trucks involved in making the deliveries possible. She was more excited than she'd ever been as a child on Christmas morning. Never before had she felt the true meaning of the season as she had this year.

Arranging the Sub-for-Santa had taken every spare minute of her time. Time she should have spent shopping for Christmas gifts for her own family. Or working overtime to earn more money. Time she could've spent with Carson, except he hadn't called to ask her out.

She rolled out of bed and onto her knees to start her day with prayer. She needed the Lord's help and guidance to be with her and the others more than ever today. They were on His errand and she knew He would bless them. Especially Harry. Of all the volunteers, he needed extra strength the most to help him through the day. And she prayed for Carson. That his heart would be softened so that he and his father could finally become a family again.

After a quick shower she dressed, pulled on her elf hat, and joined her mother in the kitchen to help get the food ready for their guests. By seven o'clock volunteers had begun to arrive. The excitement in the air sparkled and cracked. Everyone was caught up in the spirit of the event.

Roberta and Bart arrived, and Danielle gave them each a big hug and wished them a Merry Christmas. They looked radiant together, and Danielle was thrilled for them. Lenny had called Danielle the night before and said he wouldn't be able to help out. He wished her well and she did the same.

Her girls—Lucy, Erin, Allie, Chloe, and McCall—all showed up to lend a hand. Giving each of them a hug, Danielle felt her heart expand inside of her chest. She loved these girls and felt their love and support in return. Pulling McCall aside, she asked, "How are you doing?"

McCall gave her a brave smile. "I still can't quit thinking about that old man, but you know what? Part of me doesn't want to. I think the more I remember him, the more I'll try to help other people. Just like today. I am so glad we're doing this Sub-for-Santa."

"I know what you mean," Danielle told her. If that old man's dying served a purpose in motivating them to help others, then his death wouldn't be in vain.

"I never knew giving service could be so neat," McCall said.

Danielle hugged McCall again. "C'mon, let's go see what everyone's doing."

The house was full of happy chatter, Christmas music played in the background, and the spicy, sweet smell of her mother's cinnamon rolls filled the room.

Brother Mitchell, from the elders quorum, arrived with his big delivery truck. He worked for a vending machine company, and his truck was perfect for hauling the many bags of gifts. He walked through the door wearing a wavy black wig and a rhinestone-studded cape.

"Brother Mitchell," Danielle said with surprise. "Uh . . . , you're . . ."

"Mornin' darlin'," he drawled in a Nashville accent. "Sorry I'm late but I couldn't find my blue suede boots." He struck a pose with one leg out and one arm raised in the air.

Danielle laughed. This guy was a kook, the ward comedian. All the youth loved him. He was the last person to go to bed at ward camp outs and the first one to wake up in the morning. He was also the first person to show up when someone was moving in or out of the ward, or when someone's roof needed to be reshingled.

"Interesting outfit," Danielle said.

"Thank you. Thank you very much," he said. He looked around at everyone else, then turned back to Danielle. "Hey, darlin'," he said, feigning dismay. "I thought you said you wanted us to dress like *Elvis,* not *elves.*"

Everyone busted up laughing and Brother Mitchell gave them all a quick rendition of "Jingle Bells" Elvis-style. Then he removed his disguise and donned his elf cap. His sweatshirt was the only one in the bunch with blinking lights and a Rudolf on it whose nose played a tune when it was pushed.

Danielle's stomach bunched up with excitement and nerves. Hopefully they were so well organized that everything would run smoothly. She'd gone over the day's events in her head a million times, and she'd prayed unceasingly for the Lord's help. Nothing could go wrong.

Everyone was there. Even the Vollmans from next door had come over to help send off the volunteer brigade. The only two people missing were those she was most anxious to see—Carson and Harry. While the others filled their stomachs, Danielle watched out the window for any sign of either of them. Maybe she should have offered to pick up Harry. Maybe something had happened to him during the night.

A car pulled around the corner and to her relief, she recognized Harry's car. Tears stung her eyes as he stepped out of his car, wearing his Santa suit. Reaching inside, he pulled out the white fur-trimmed hat and pulled it onto his head. In the red suit, with his white hair, beard, and mustache, the man looked just like the real Santa Claus.

Danielle had the door open before he got to the front steps. Rushing out to meet him, she gave him a big hug. "I'm so glad you made it," she cried. "Are you okay? Do you feel all right?"

Harry chuckled and patted her back. "I feel great," he said. "What a beautiful morning."

Indeed it was. The sun was rising up over the Rocky Mountains, lighting the clouds on fire with orange and pink, turning the heavens to a glorious blue.

"Come in, everyone's anxious to see you," she said, leading him inside, where Harry was greeted with a cheer and applause. The bells around his belt jingled merrily. People couldn't believe how authentic he looked in the Santa suit. Some who hadn't seen him before even tested his beard, unconvinced that it was actually real.

The ringing of the doorbell sounded, and Danielle's heartbeat took off running. *Please, oh please, oh please, let it be Carson.*

"I'll get it," Roberta called.

"NO!" Danielle exclaimed, then she quickly calmed her voice. "That's okay, I can." She hurried from the room, crossing her fingers on her way.

The anticipation almost killed her as she turned the door knob. Her knees nearly gave way when she saw that it was Carson, a huge, bone-melting smile on his face.

"Hi," he said.

"Hi," she answered. They looked at each other for several seconds before she finally said, "Come in. I'm glad you could make it."

"I wouldn't miss it for anything," he replied, then said humbly, "I'm sorry I was so rude the other night, Danielle."

"You were right, though. I shouldn't poke my nose in where it doesn't belong," Danielle apologized.

"But it does belong, and so does the rest of you," he insisted, looking deeply into her eyes. "I want you in my life, and that means the good and the bad. I shouldn't have been so upset with you. Will you forgive me?"

"Of course I do," Danielle said, moving easily into his arms. He pulled her towards the living room, where a pine garland adorned the top of the doorframe.

"That isn't mistletoe, is it?" he asked her.

"You know, I don't really know exactly," she said innocently. "But I think it just might be."

Giving her a sly smile, he wrapped his arms around her. "I'm not sure either, but I'm willing to take a chance that it is."

"You sure like to live dangerously, mister," she said, enjoying the feel of his arms around her.

He wrapped his arms around her and kissed her sweetly. The sound of voices coming their way forced them to step apart quickly. Danielle felt unsteady and lightheaded from the kiss. She teetered back on one foot and Carson wrapped one arm securely around her.

"There you are," Roberta exclaimed when she came around the corner and saw Carson and Danielle. Bart followed at her heels. "Your mother asked me to find you. Everyone's ready to get started."

For one brief moment, Danielle wondered if Carson and Bart were going to be uncomfortable around each other, but Carson stretched his hand toward Bart with a casual, "Hey, how're you doing?"

"I'm great, man," Bart said as the two shook hands.

When Roberta grabbed Bart's hand and towed him away to get the food ready, Carson looked at Danielle, his eyebrows raised. "What's up with those two?"

"I'll tell you later. You'll never believe it," she grinned.

Danielle heard the jingle bells on Harry's belt ringing above the chatter of voices. *Please, dear Heavenly Father, these two men need each other. Bless them and help me, I can't do it alone.* Drawing in a large breath of air, Danielle led Carson into the kitchen where the volunteers were finishing up their breakfast.

Seeing Carson, Mrs. Camden quickly pushed him toward the stove and gave him a large, frosting-dripping cinnamon roll on a paper plate. Danielle glanced around the room and saw Harry seated at the table. She wanted to keep them apart until the time was right for them to meet.

Earl Camden stood and clinked his spoon on his glass to get everyone's attention.

"Folks," he said, "this is a wonderful occasion that brings us all here, early on Christmas Eve morning. You have all worked hard and spent much time in preparation for this day. I want my daughter, Danielle, to know how proud I am of her for coming up with this idea, organizing the project, and seeing it through. Honey—" he looked at his daughter, "—this will be one Christmas a lot of people will never forget. What you folks are doing today will make a difference in a lot of people's lives. Giving service like this is truly what Christmas is all about."

Everyone in the room was silent.

"I think it would be very appropriate to start this event with a prayer. I've asked our good friend, Brother Mitchell, here, if he would say it." Brother Mitchell stood and removed his hat.

Danielle noticed Harry across the room, sitting at the table with his back to Carson, who was standing near the stove, still eating his cinnamon roll. She knew it would be tricky to keep them from running into each other this morning, but she had faith that the Lord would help her. Of course, there was a chance that Carson wouldn't recognize his father anyway. Harry looked nothing like the Mr. Turner she'd known over a year earlier. He probably weighed a good thirty pounds lighter than when she knew him. His face was thin and gaunt, and covered with his snowy white beard.

Although Danielle's nerves were on edge as she anticipated their first meeting, she felt a calming spirit as Brother Mitchell said a sweet humble prayer, full of thanks. Her heart felt warm as he expressed gratitude for the birth of the Savior and for the Atonement, the Lord's greatest gift to man. He asked the Lord to bless them that they would be safe and that they would be able to have His spirit with them as they visited each home and went to see the children at the hospital.

When the prayer ended, a sweet peace enveloped everyone in that room. They were joined together by one purpose, to serve the Savior. Hearts were full, words weren't necessary. Smiles, hugs, and handshakes were exchanged. The Spirit of Christmas had descended upon them. It was time to make the deliveries.

# CHAPTER
## TWENTY-FIVE

The procession pulled up to the first house by eight-thirty in the morning. Roberta, Danielle, and Carson rode with Bart in his Outback. Danielle could see that all the houses on the street were old, small, and falling apart. Shutters hung by one nail, fences leaned under the weight of snow. Yards were strewn with broken-down automobiles, wrecked bicycles, and old refrigerators.

A sea of red fur hats with white pom poms unloaded from cars and trucks. Harry marched toward the front door, a pack of gifts over his shoulder and several helpers behind him carrying more bags of gifts. Banging on the door, he bellowed, "Ho, ho, ho!"

"What a great Santa Claus," Carson whispered to her. "His beard and mustache look real. Where did you say you found him?"

"At the homeless shelter," Danielle answered. "He's a volunteer there."

"Wow," Carson said. "He's perfect."

Just as Danielle had expected, Carson didn't recognize his own father. But then she wasn't really surprised. Harry and Philip Turner weren't the same man, physically or spiritually.

Hearing the excited squeal of children inside the house and wanting to see the look on their faces when the door opened, she pulled Carson by the hand and hurried up the sidewalk. Someone handed her a cardboard box containing food and goodies.

"Ho, ho, ho," Harry called again, just as the door opened.

Three children, dressed only in oversized t-shirts, answered the door. The smallest, a little girl with her thumb in her mouth, froze with fear, then burst into tears. Her father came from behind and scooped her up into his arms, trying to soothe her, and invited their guests inside.

Santa stepped inside, followed by his helpers. Chloe, McCall, and Lucy held boxes and bags of gifts and food. In addition to a turkey, pies, and other dinner trimmings, there were boxes of canned goods and treats as well as basic items like milk, flour, sugar, and butter. Cassie and Jace, one of the delivery guys from Creative Display, carried in a beautifully decorated Christmas tree, found an empty corner of the room, and set it down. When Cassie plugged in the tree, it lit up the room with a warm, cozy glow. Everyone ooohed and aaahed, the children clapped with glee, and the mother, now holding the youngest daughter, began to cry.

Danielle looked around the room to see a ragged couch that sagged pitifully in the middle. A chair stood nearby, the upholstery worn through so that it was losing its stuffing; the orange crate next to it held a lamp. There were no pictures on the walls, no carpet under their feet. The only curtains were threadbare sheets thumb-tacked above the window. Catching McCall's eye, she saw the distraught look on her face. Danielle knew her feelings exactly. No one should have to live in conditions like this. Especially when there were so many with so much who could share and help them out.

Harry set the bag of gifts down next to the tree, then turned. He found the oldest child, a young boy about seven years old. He was missing his front teeth. The chair squeaked in protest as Harry sat down and patted his knee. The little boy knew just what to do and hopped up into his lap. Santa asked him what he wanted for Christmas.

"I would like a blanket and some socks. I know you didn't come to my house last year because I wasn't so good, but Santa, I've been really, really good this year, so if I could, could I please have a football?"

Tears stung Danielle's eyes, and a knot grew in her throat.

Harry gave the boy a hug and said, "I know you've been extra good this year. I think you'll like what you find in those gifts my elves packed."

"Your elves sure are big," the little boy said.

Harry chuckled. "Yes, they are. I have the smaller elves make the toys. The bigger ones help me make the deliveries," he explained cleverly.

The next child, a four-year-old girl, sat on his lap. All she wanted was a picture book and a pack of bubble gum.

Danielle couldn't believe it. These children didn't have lists as long as their arms, full of expensive toys. Theirs were meager requests, asking for things other children got on a simple trip to the grocery store.

The youngest little girl, barely two, wouldn't sit on Santa's lap, but her mother held her next to him. Harry stroked her rosy cheek with his finger and told her what a sweet, pretty little girl she was and that Santa had brought her something very special this year. She looked at him with wide, blue eyes and giggled when he tickled her tummy.

Danielle couldn't stop the tears from falling onto her cheeks. Harry was so loving and warm to the child that by the time he was done visiting with her, she'd wrapped her tiny arms around his neck and given him a hug good-bye.

"Thank you," the parents said humbly as one by one, the volunteers left the house. "Thank you so much."

Danielle glanced into their kitchen to see a card table and two folding chairs. A small television sat on a milk crate in the corner with a hanger bent and twisted for an antennae. Her heart ached. Couldn't they do more for these people?

Harry gave the children one last hug, and before he left he slipped an envelope to the father. Danielle didn't know how much, but she knew this was money from Harry himself. Tears streamed down both parents' faces as they shook his hand in parting.

The group left the house singing, "We wish you a Merry Christmas," but Danielle could barely get through the song because of the lump in her throat. The freezing cold air stung her wet cheeks.

Carson wrapped an arm around her and pulled her close. She rested her head on his shoulder, weeping softly. What if they hadn't decided to do this? What if no one had seen this family's need and found a way to help them? And, she wondered, how many families hadn't received help this year?

Each visit afterwards was as sweet as the first had been. Parents, crying and grateful; their children, squealing with delight and wide-eyed with wonder; their homes, ramshackle and sparse. Danielle's heart filled to the brim and overflowed with emotion.

What was wrong with the world? How could so many people have everything they wanted and not see those around them in such great need? Wasn't there some way to even it out? Couldn't the rich be a little less rich and the poor be a little less poor?

By the fifth house, Danielle noticed that Harry was losing some of his energy. He seemed to struggle carrying the bag of gifts into the house.

"That Harry is incredible," Carson said as Danielle and he watched the bearded figure approach the front door. "He's really into this Santa thing."

"I'm worried about him," Danielle said.

"Why?"

"He seems to be getting tired. I don't want him to overdo it."

Carson watched the man climbing the front stairs. "He does look like he's having some trouble. I wonder what's wrong."

"He's not well, but he insisted on playing Santa. He said he's always wanted to."

"What's wrong with him?"

"He's got cancer," Danielle choked on the words. "He's—" The front door opened at that moment, and she wasn't able to explain.

Harry did his best to "Ho, ho, ho" his way into the house, and the elves rushed inside behind him, carrying gifts, boxes of food, and the tree.

Danielle watched as Harry took each youngster on his knee and asked them what their Christmas wish was. He even got the older boy, probably thirteen or fourteen, to sit on one of his knees. The boy was embarrassed, but Harry managed to get him to laugh a few times. The boy said he wanted a watch for Christmas. Danielle scanned in her mind, trying to remember if she'd put a watch in one of the piles. She couldn't remember buying a watch or seeing one donated. At the first opportunity, she pulled the mother aside.

"When I called to get your list, did you tell me your son wanted a watch?" she asked the woman.

"No," the mother whispered frantically. "This is the first time he's said anything about it. I thought he wanted a pair of basketball shoes."

"That's right," Danielle remembered. "We got him shoes."

She was sick. She wanted these kids to get at least one thing they wanted.

"The basketball shoes will be wonderful. He'll be very happy with those," the woman assured Danielle.

But Danielle wanted the boy to have a watch.

"What's wrong?" Carson asked as they walked outside. "Are you still worried about Harry?"

"Yes, but I'm also worried about the boy in there. He told Santa he wanted a watch."

"Didn't you get him one?" Carson asked.

"No, his mom told us he wanted a pair of basketball shoes," she said glumly. "I want to get that boy a watch. He deserves one thing he wants for Christmas."

Carson stopped walking and lifted his arm. He pulled up his sleeve and exposed the watch on his arm. "Here," he said, "Let's give him mine."

"No, Carson, you don't need to do that," she protested.

"But I want to. I'd really like to give it to that boy. I can get another one sometime." He removed the watch and handed it to her.

She looked up into his face. "Are you sure?"

He smiled at her. "It would make me really happy to give it to him."

Lifting up on her toes, Danielle kissed him on the cheek. "I'll go give it to his mom." She scurried back up the steps just as Harry was making his exit.

"I just wanted to wish you a Merry Christmas," Danielle said to the woman, trying to keep the watch a secret from her son standing next to her. She hugged the woman and slipped the watch into her hand. "That's for your son," she whispered.

The woman glanced down at her hand, then gasped and quickly put her hand in her pocket. Fresh tears filled her eyes. "Thank you," she whispered.

Danielle walked down the stairs with Harry while everyone climbed back into their cars. "Harry, are you okay?" she asked.

He paused and gave her a tired smile. "Yes, dear, I'm fine. Just a bit worn out already. I don't have the energy I used to."

"I don't want you to overdo it," she said.

He started to speak then stopped, his eyes fixed on the person approaching them. "Is everything okay?" Carson asked.

Danielle's heart thumped wildly in her chest. This was their first meeting. She prayed desperately for the Lord to soften Carson's heart.

"I was just checking to see if Harry needed someone to take over for a while," Danielle said, watching Carson's face closely for any sign of recognition.

"I'd be happy to wear the suit for a while if you'd like a break," Carson offered the older man. "Your shoes will be hard to fill. I won't do it justice as you have, but I'll give it my best shot."

Danielle realized Carson didn't know who he was talking too, but his words had obviously touched Harry, who was blinking rapidly in an effort to clear the moisture from his eyes. He hadn't seen his son for months, and she could tell he was struggling to maintain his composure. He didn't answer right off, and Carson looked at Danielle with concern.

"Our next stop is a single woman; I think she's in her eighties," Danielle told Harry. "Do you want to visit her, then let Carson do the rest of the families?"

"Yes," Harry answered. "That would be nice." He looked at his son. "Thank you."

"Hey," Carson said. "No problem. I brought a pillow just in case."

One of the groups honked their horn, ready to head to the next stop. Danielle waved and said, "We'd better get going. We still have five more homes to visit."

They were halfway through, and it was almost eleven o'clock. Plus they still needed to visit the children's hospital.

"I'll be right there," Danielle told Carson. With a quick nod, he ran back to the car where Bart and Roberta waited while Danielle walked Harry to his ride.

"Are you okay?" she asked softly.

"He didn't recognize me," Harry said sadly.

"You are in a disguise," she reasoned. "And you're the last person he's expecting to see wearing a Santa suit." She didn't mention that his cancer and treatments had also taken a heavy toll on him.

"He seems so happy. Maybe it's a mistake to even tell him. Maybe I should leave before he finds out, and I ruin another Christmas for him," he said miserably.

Danielle was horrified. "Harry, no! It's time for you two to get this worked out. Everything will be fine, you'll see."

"I hope so," he said as the others in the car opened the door for him. Danielle watched him climb inside the vehicle, then took a deep breath of the icy cold air. She wasn't as sure as she wanted Harry to believe. Her nerves were strung tight, her muscles tense with anxiety and anticipation.

"Is the old guy okay?" Carson asked when she joined them.

"I think so," she answered, buckling up her seatbelt.

"He doesn't look so good," Carson observed. "You said he had cancer?"

"Yes. He got lung cancer from secondhand smoke," Danielle explained. "He rode in a carpool for years with a man who smoked. What's even worse, the guy who smoked is fine."

"I hate to see him take off the suit," Carson said. "He sure seems to enjoy playing Santa Claus. Those kids love him. He must have a lot of grandkids or something."

"No," Danielle explained. "Actually he's all alone. He doesn't have any family around here."

The conversation shifted as they passed a Christmas tree lot still full of trees and Bart commented on how upsetting it was to see so many trees were cut down and wasted. Settling back in her seat, Danielle agreed inwardly, but she had a more immediate problem on her hands. What was going to happen when Carson finally discovered who Harry really was?

# CHAPTER
## TWENTY-SIX

It took a while for Mrs. Parsons to answer her door. The elderly woman stood barely five feet tall and probably weighed only ninety pounds. She had a crocheted shawl around her rounded shoulders and a surprised look on her face.

Harry gave her a cheerful "Ho, ho, ho!" and led the group inside.

"Oh, my goodness," she said, placing one hand on her wrinkled cheek as the tree was placed in the corner of her tiny front room. "How lovely."

"Could we put these groceries away for you, Mrs. Parsons?" Sister McKay from the Relief Society offered. Erin and Allie were eager to help and smiled warmly at the elderly woman.

"Goodness gracious," the woman exclaimed, overwhelmed with the bags and boxes of food items. "Look at all of this. I had no idea you would do all of this. No idea at all."

She directed Sister McKay and the girls to the kitchen while the men set up her gift, a warm and sturdy space heater. Danielle had also wrapped a new winter coat for Mrs. Parsons. The poor woman was nearly freezing in the cold, inside and out.

"Oh, my goodness," she cried when she came back into the room. Tears of joy trickled down her face. "This is so wonderful. Thank you. Thank you ever so much."

Harry gave her a gentle hug and told her that a special van would come by that evening to take her to the senior center where a

Christmas Eve celebration would take place. She was also invited there for Christmas dinner the following day.

"Bless you," Mrs. Parsons said. "Bless all of you." She wept openly, mopping tears from her face with a crumpled handkerchief. "I just don't know how to thank you."

Roberta and Bart helped arrange the half dozen gifts underneath the tree that now lit up the room with its sparkling glow. Danielle felt the warmth of the heater replacing the cold as the group sang, "We wish you a Merry Christmas." Mrs. Parson continued to cry, and Harry kept his arm protectively around the tiny woman until the song ended.

As before, the group bid farewell and filed out the door one by one. Once again, Danielle saw Harry press an envelope into the elderly woman's hand.

"What's this?" she asked, looking down at the envelope.

"Just a little something to help you get by," Harry said. "Merry Christmas." Then he did something that made the woman's eyes shine brighter than all the lights on the Christmas tree. He kissed her on the cheek. She put her hand to her cheek and giggled like a school girl.

Danielle hated to leave, knowing that the woman was all alone and would be spending the holiday by herself. She hoped that somehow they'd helped her Christmas be a happy one.

Danielle and Carson followed Harry out of the house as he clung to the railing, slowly making his way down the front stairs. Seeing that he was having some difficulty, Danielle rushed up to help him. Carson followed her lead, supporting him on the other side, and together they walked him to the car.

"I think I'll take you up on that offer now, son," Harry said breathlessly.

Danielle froze, wondering if he realized he had called Carson "son." Carson didn't seem to even notice, but busied himself helping Harry remove the belt and jacket. Harry wore his regular clothes beneath the suit.

"Do you need us to take you home, Harry?" Danielle asked him.

"Not yet," he said. "I'd like to stay as long as I can."

"Okay," Danielle said in understanding. He wanted to see his son dress up like Santa Claus, she was sure of it. "You let me know as soon as you're ready."

He patted her hand "I will. Thank you." Danielle smiled and helped him into the car.

"I'll get dressed on the way," Carson said.

Danielle found the bag containing a beard and mustache and helped Carson get ready before their next stop. It was nearly noon and the group was getting tired and hungry. They decided that after doing the rest of the houses, they would stop for hamburgers before they went to the hospital.

Helping Carson secure the fur-trimmed hat and straighten his beard, Danielle couldn't help but laugh when his outfit was complete.

"You're not bad-looking for an old, fat guy," she flirted.

"Gee, thanks," he said. "Just for that you might get a little something extra in your stocking, young lady."

Danielle giggled, glad she'd brought along her camera. Her parents had given it to her for her birthday, a fancy hi-tech digital kind that let her make her own pictures on her computer. This way she could easily put one final photo in the scrapbook. She wanted to get a picture of Carson and his dad together for the last page.

⁂

The opportunity came just before they went to the next house. Carson was waiting for the volunteers to get the bags of gifts and boxes of food unloaded to take them inside while Harry stood in the background watching all the activity. Carson took advantage of the brief lull to walk over to Harry and ask him a question on playing Santa's role. Quickly Danielle grabbed her camera, took aim, and snapped several pictures of Carson and his father, facing each other, talking. They didn't seem to notice.

When the signal was given, Carson went to the front door and rang the bell. As the door opened he called out, "Ho, ho, ho," in a deep voice. "Merry Christmas!"

"Mama, mama," a little boy called. "It's Santa and a whole bunch of people."

A woman, carrying a baby on one hip and holding a toddler's hand, came to the door. "Come in," she welcomed them.

Danielle remembered this woman's situation. She was a single mother with six small children. She was on welfare but could barely provide the essentials for her family, let alone any extras like Christmas presents. Standing back, Danielle watched as Carson gathered the children around him and met each one. Danielle had prepped him on their names and ages, and he only got mixed up on two of them. But he was wonderful and the children loved him.

"I bet you'd like a few teeth for Christmas," he told six-year-old Melissa. She was missing her two bottom front teeth and giggled the entire time she was on his lap. "What else would you like?"

"A Barbie," she said, still giggling, her dark curls bouncing with her laughter. "And a jewelry box, with a ballerina that twirls around when you open the lid."

Then she stopped laughing.

"But, Santa—" she looked up at him with two of the biggest brown eyes Danielle had ever seen, "—most of all Santa, for Christmas, I want my daddy. If you see him, will you tell him to come home. Please?"

Carson pulled the little girl into a hug and held her for a long time. Throughout the room, Danielle heard others sniff and saw them wipe at the tears in their eyes.

In the car, they rode in silence to the next destination. They were almost through with their deliveries, but with each home they visited they realized that they should have tried to do even more. Some of these families lived in extreme poverty. They lacked furniture, some of them sleeping in sleeping bags on the hard, bare floor.

After a quick stop for some hamburgers at a drive-through restaurant, their final stop was the children's hospital. The convoy of volunteers pulled into the hospital parking lot and paraded into the building. Carson was a hospital employee, so he served as guide and led them through the large facility to the room where they would meet the children.

Danielle was impressed with how many nurses and other employees greeted Carson as he led them down the long hallways. Since he was still in the Santa suit, some of them joked and asked if they could sit on his knee. Even the doctors they passed knew him by name and wished him and the rest of the group a Merry Christmas.

"Do you know everyone here?" Danielle asked him as they waited for the elevator.

"Just about," he said. "It's a great place. Everyone's really friendly here."

Danielle glanced back to check on Harry. He seemed to be holding up well. He gave her a smile and a nod, knowing that she was concerned about him.

Carson led the group to a large gathering room, and when they walked inside, Danielle was thrilled to see, right smack in the center of the room, her Jubilee of Trees Christmas tree.

"Look," Roberta cried. "It's your tree."

Danielle felt a tingle of happiness. Her tree was perfect here. All the smiling, happy tole-painted ornaments hanging from each branch served as a reminder that everyone was a part of the same family, each a brother or a sister. The smiles on the ornaments brought warmth to the room and a feeling of universal love and caring.

She noticed Harry looking at the tree. "So, that's the tree you decorated?" he asked. She'd told him about the Jubilee of Trees during one visit to his home.

"Yes," she answered. "That's it."

He nodded his approval. "I'm glad I got to see it."

A thought came to her. "Harry," she asked, "you didn't happen to bid on this tree, did you?" It couldn't be just a coincidence that he bought her tree and donated it to the hospital where his son worked, could it?

"Me?" he said innocently, with a glint in his eye.

"Where do you want us to put the gifts?" Brother Mitchell asked Danielle.

"Oh, right over here," she directed. She wanted to talk to Harry some more, but it was almost time for the children.

The men distributed the gifts around the tree; the Laurels opened up the boxes of candy canes and other Christmas goodies that were to be passed around to the children. Carson took his place in a chair next to the tree, ready to brighten each child's day by hearing their wishes and Christmas dreams.

A nurse, middle-aged and nearly as round as she was tall, and full of smiles, entered the room.

"Carson, is that really you under that beard?" she asked when she saw him sitting in the chair.

"Hi, Betsy," Carson said, getting to his feet.

He hugged the rotund lady, who had to stand on her tiptoes just to put her arms around his waist.

"Everyone," he said, "this is Betsy Norton. She's the activities coordinator for the hospital."

She gave the group a wave and said, "The children are on their way. Is there anything you need?"

"I think we're ready," Carson said.

"The kids are so excited. This is really wonderful of you folks to take time away from your families to come and visit them," she said gratefully.

Danielle and the rest of the volunteers found chairs off to the side where they could wait until it was their part in the program. They were going to sing a few Christmas songs with the children, then let each child have a moment with Santa and receive their special gift and treats.

Sister McKay took her place at the piano and played some lively Christmas carols, as one by one, the children were rolled in on beds and wheelchairs, or carried in and placed in chairs. Only a handful were able to walk in on their own. Some were as young as two years old; others looked as old as twelve or thirteen. Several children were completely bald, Danielle guessed, from cancer treatments; others were bandaged or bound by some hi-tech medical device. But every one of the children smiled and exuded excitement. It was Christmas Eve and Santa had come to pay them a special visit.

Roberta led the volunteers in a rousing rendition of "Up on the Housetop" and then had the children join in doing hand movements with the words. McCall, Chloe, Lucy, Allie, and Erin handed out bells on ribbon necklaces to each child and everyone joined in while Brother "Elvis" led them in "Jingle Bells." The group sang "Rudolph" and "Frosty" and even found a couple of children in the audience missing teeth. They were brought up to the front with Santa and the group sang "All I Want for Christmas Is My Two Front Teeth."

Then it was time for the children to visit with Santa. Danielle stood back by Harry and watched as Carson took a turn with each child. Some were able to sit on his knee; others he sat by on their bed or near their wheelchair. But no matter what, he always managed to get a laugh or giggle out of them. Then, after telling him what they wanted for Christmas, they circled their frail little arms around his neck and give him a hug.

He was in his element. There was no doubt that Carson loved these children. Danielle's heart grew inside her until she thought her ribs would snap. Nurse Betsy, who stood right next to Danielle, leaned over and said to her, "I've never seen the kids so happy. Thank you again for coming today."

"I'm so glad Carson suggested it," Danielle said. "They really like him, don't they?"

"Oh, my goodness, yes," the nurse exclaimed. "He's everyone's favorite."

Danielle noticed Harry listening intently.

"He really cares about each of them and always takes time to learn each of the children's names," Betsy said. "They seem to know he really cares and they seem to take to him immediately." She smiled and waved at one little girl who held up a doll and candy cane for her to see. "He certainly seems to have a special way with them. He's going to be a wonderful doctor someday." She excused herself to check on one of the children.

Harry and Danielle watched Carson and the other volunteers interacting with the children, both of them silent for several minutes.

"Hey," Danielle said, noticing Harry wiping at his eyes. "Are you okay?"

The man put his handkerchief back into his pocket. "Look at him," he said proudly. "He's loving every minute with these children."

Danielle smiled and watched Carson playing airplane with one of the little boys. "He really does. Isn't it great?"

"I thought I knew what was best for him," Harry said. "Forcing him to study business, to follow in my footsteps. He knew all along where he belonged. I was so stubborn I couldn't see it. I wouldn't listen. No wonder he can't forgive me. I nearly ruined his life."

Danielle placed an arm around his shoulders and gave him a hug. She was glad Harry got to see how happy Carson was.

"I'm so proud of him," Harry said. He cleared his throat and got the handkerchief out of his pocket again.

"I think he'd like to hear you say that," Danielle said. "He's been waiting a long time to hear those words."

Harry looked at her and smiled. "I just hope he'll listen."

# CHAPTER
## TWENTY-SEVEN

The group gathered to bid their farewells in the parking lot outside the hospital. It was four o'clock in the afternoon, and it had been a very long, but very fulfilling day. Hugs were exchanged and tears were shed as a light snow started to fall. No one in the group of volunteers could deny the special spirit that had been with them the entire day. Each and every one standing there knew, without a doubt, they had made a difference in many people's lives that day. They all also knew their efforts couldn't stop there.

Scraping the snow from their windows, everyone piled into their automobiles and headed home to their families, eager to join in their own Christmas Eve festivities.

Danielle gave a special thanks to "her girls," who had been a tremendous help and a lot of fun. It had been a great sacrifice for them to come today, but she noticed that they'd formed a closer relationship since they'd been spending more time together. She was happy to see them comfortable and friendly with each other. Each of them expressed their thanks to Danielle for being their leader and for letting them help with the Sub-for-Santa.

McCall especially was moved. "I think Mr. Evans would be happy with what we did today."

Danielle knew she'd been thinking a lot about the old man who passed away. "I do, too," she replied. "So," she looked McCall carefully in the eyes, "are you okay?"

McCall smiled. "Yeah. You know, I almost don't want to open presents in the morning. I'm afraid it will ruin everything."

"It's been an incredible day, hasn't it?" Danielle agreed.

McCall nodded. The other girls were getting in the car, ready to get home to their families.

"I think we just need to try and keep this spirit with us throughout the entire year. Not just at Christmas," Danielle suggested.

"Could we do more service projects for our Young Women activities?" McCall asked. "Maybe spend more time at the shelter?"

"You bet," Danielle said, amazed at McCall's enthusiasm but very pleased.

Chloe honked the horn to hurry McCall along. "Guess I better go," McCall said. "Merry Christmas, Danielle, and thanks for being such a great advisor."

Danielle smiled and waved good-bye as a warm feeling washed over her. She never thought a calling could be so rewarding.

Carson and Danielle rode back to her house with Bart and Roberta. Harry rode back with Sister McKay. Danielle prayed constantly that the Lord would be with them. She didn't doubt that Harry's true identity would surface sometime during the evening.

*Please soften Carson's heart, Father. Help him to be able to forgive his father.*

The storm seemed to worsen with each mile they traveled. The roads grew icy. They could barely see beyond the hood of the car. Danielle was grateful when they arrived safely at her house.

Bidding Roberta and Bart good-bye, Danielle sent them on their way before the roads grew more treacherous from the winter storm. While Carson helped load empty toy sacks and food bags into Sister McKay's trunk, Danielle and Harry took refuge in the garage. She took advantage of a moment alone with Harry.

"How are you feeling?" She noticed that he'd coughed through the afternoon and seemed tired. The man who used to run a multi-million dollar company looked frail and weak in front of her.

"It's been a long day," he said. "I think I should just go home."

"Go home! But, Harry, you can't."

"I'm really worn out," he told her.

"Is that really what it is?" she questioned directly.

He sighed, his shoulders sagging wearily. "I'm afraid this is going to upset him and I certainly don't want to have a family blow-out at your house and ruin your family's Christmas."

"You're not going anywhere," she said. "My family is expecting you and it's time you and Carson worked things out."

"But—"

"Hey, Danielle," Carson called. "Do you want me to leave on the Santa suit?"

Danielle looked at Harry, and he returned her look.

"It's up to you," she said.

"He seems to really be enjoying it. Let's let him do it," Harry said.

"Yes," she called back to Carson. "Keep it on."

He waved back through the thick, falling snow then slammed Sister McKay's trunk shut. She maneuvered her way onto the street and drove away slowly.

"You'll stay, won't you?" Danielle asked. Carson had picked up a snow shovel and cleared a path to the front door.

He pressed his lips together, shut his eyes for a moment and took a deep breath. "All right," he finally said, "I'll stay. I just wish I had as much faith as you did. I'm not sure Carson's going to react like you're hoping he will."

"If you could have anything you wanted for Christmas, Harry, what would it be?" Danielle asked him.

He looked over at his son, who was still shoveling. "It would be to have my son back," he said.

"I believe that Christmas is a time for miracles," she said. "But sometimes we have to help make them happen."

He didn't reply but by the look on his face, Danielle knew he was considering her words.

"Let's get you inside," she said with a shiver. "I don't want you to catch pneumonia."

She led him to the door that connected the garage with the mud room. Dorothy Camden heard them come in and greeted them cheerfully.

"Come in, come in," she fussed. "You must be frozen to the bone. I've got some hot wassail on the stove." She took Harry's coat, hat, and gloves and hung them on hooks so they could dry. "Earl's in by the fire." With Harry in good hands, Danielle went back outside to get Carson.

"You don't have to do that," she called to him from inside the dry garage. "The snow's covering it up as fast as you clear it."

"I'm almost done," he answered.

He took up one last scoop of snow with the shovel and tossed it onto a mound of snow, then brought the shovel into the garage, where she helped him brush off the snow that covered his head and shoulders.

"Thanks for staying dressed up," she said. "Harry's really tired and I don't think he's feeling well. You only have to keep the suit on for another half hour or so, for Rachel's girls."

"I don't mind," he said. "Just let me fix my beard and hat before I go in."

"Why don't you wait here just a minute? I'll go in and find out what's going on. Rachel's van and Miranda's car are both here, so I'll see when they want you to make your appearance."

Once inside, the toasty warmth of the house stung her frozen cheeks and nose.

"Where's Carson?" her sister Miranda asked when she walked into the kitchen.

"He's out in the garage," she whispered so Rachel's youngest daughter, Hailey, who was sitting at the dinner table coloring a picture, couldn't hear. "He's still dressed up and wondered when we wanted him to make his appearance."

"Oh," Miranda exclaimed. "He's ready now?"

"Well, he can take the suit off and put it on later, if you want."

Danielle's mother stirred the pot on the stove.

"The clam chowder's not quite ready anyway," Dorothy said, putting the lid back on the pot. "Maybe we should go ahead with it since he's already dressed. Besides, we may not have much time anyway. Rachel's been having contractions all day."

"She has?" Danielle exclaimed. "Why isn't she at the hospital?"

"Don't say anything to her." Dorothy lowered her voice. "She's been to the hospital two times already and they keep sending her home. She's getting very upset."

"I can imagine," Danielle said.

"I'll gather everyone around, and we'll go into the front room around the tree," Miranda said.

"And I'll flick the porch light a few times to let you know when we're ready for Santa," her mother suggested.

Danielle's dad had already pulled Harry into the family room to watch some Christmas special on television. Rachel was sprawled on the couch, her husband, Doug, rubbing her swollen feet. Miranda's husband, Garrett, and children, Ashlyn and Adam, were playing a computer game in the den. Putting on her coat again, Danielle hurried out to the garage, feeling bad that she'd left Carson out in the cold.

"Hey," she called, "are you about frozen out here?"

"Nah, this suit is pretty warm. My toes are a bit frosty though."

"They'll be ready for us in just a minute," she said, looking out at the thick white falling from the sky. "Wow, it's really coming down."

"Yeah, we're supposed to get eight to ten inches tonight."

"You and Harry may end up staying here tonight," she said, half hoping that's exactly what would happen.

"Is Harry doing okay?" Carson asked.

"I think we wore him out today," Danielle admitted.

"He seems like a pretty cool guy. What's his story?" Carson leaned back against her father's workbench.

Danielle didn't know what to say. She certainly couldn't lie to him, but she didn't want to tell him about his father like this. Searching for something to say, she was relieved when the porch light flipped off and on several times.

"We'll have to talk later," she said. "They're ready for us." She grabbed a bag of presents her mother had wrapped in advance. "There's a gift in here for everyone. Do you want me to help you with people's names?"

"Could you? I think I've got most of them, but I get Rachel's girls mixed up."

"I do too, sometimes," she confessed. "I'll help you."

"How's my beard?" he asked.

She looked up at his face and adjusted one side just a little. "It looks great," she said. "You make a pretty attractive Santa Claus, you know that?" She reached up and stroked his beard.

"You keep talking like that, and you are definitely going to end up with a very special Christmas gift," he said.

"Really?" she said. "For me?"

"You've been a very good girl this year," he said, pulling her close. "Merry Christmas, Danielle," he said. "I love you."

"I love you, too, Carson," she answered. "It's been so wonderful that we've been able to share Christmas." *And I'm sure hoping it stays wonderful.*

With a glowing warmth filling her chest and flushing her cheeks, Danielle hurried to rejoin her family. She heard Carson jingle the bells around his belt loudly, then call, "ho, ho, ho," as he walked up the front steps.

Danielle entered the living room just in time to see Rachel's two youngest daughters light up when they heard the noise outside.

"What in the world?" Earl Camden said, getting to his feet. "Who's outside making all the racket?"

Hailey, the seven-year-old, giggled and said, "It's Santa Claus, Grandpa."

"Santa Claus?" Earl said, acting completely surprised. "At our house? I don't think so, honey. He has so many people to visit tonight."

A knock at the door set Hailey giggling even more. Her ten-year-old sister, Holly, was smiling, her eyes lit up with excitement. The oldest sister, twelve-year-old Hillary, rolled her eyes, feeling much too mature for Santa.

Sure enough, when Earl answered the door, Santa Claus came bounding into the living room, wishing everyone a Merry Christmas.

Danielle glanced over and saw the delighted expression on Harry's face. She wanted to make sure he had at least one last memorable Christmas. He was a good man; he deserved it.

"Well now," Carson said, "I just happen to have a little something here for each of you. I'd like to start with the youngest of the bunch. Who would that be?"

Hailey's hand shot up like a rocket. She waggled her hand trying to get his attention. Carson purposely overlooked her, teasingly asking others in the room if they were the youngest. Finally, he recognized Hailey, who was nearly ready to explode.

She climbed up on his knee and looked up into his face. As she spoke to him, she petted the fur on his coat with her hand, much as she would a dog or cat.

Rachel's husband stood in the corner videotaping the entire scene.

Everyone laughed when Hailey told Santa, "I sent you a letter with my Christmas list, but I wonder if it's too late to change my mind?"

"I'll see what I can do," Carson told her. "What would you like to change?"

"I was going to ask for a Barbie car, but I decided I would rather have Mommy have our baby. She's says she miserabobble."

"Miserabobble?" Carson asked, trying to keep a straight face.

Rachel shook her head and smiled at her youngest, who was known for her direct, and sometimes painful, honesty.

"Yeah, you know, her tummy's fat, and her ankles are swollen, and she has to go to the potty all the time."

"Oh," Carson nodded, having no idea how to reply.

Danielle tried to hold in the laughter. Carson's face had flushed a bright red that matched his Santa suit.

"I have a gift for you," he said to the little girl. "And I'll see what I can do for mommy, okay?"

Danielle handed him the brightly wrapped package with the girl's name on the tag.

"Thank you, Santa," she said. "Merry Christmas." She gave him a kiss on the cheek and a big hug.

Holly was next to sit on Santa's lap, then Hillary. Even though Hillary was embarrassed at having to do something so "juvenile," Carson still managed to get a giggle out of her.

Once the gifts had been distributed, it was time to eat dinner, which would be followed by their Christmas program. Danielle knew from past Christmases that her parents liked to keep the Santa part of Christmas separate from the spiritual part of the holiday. Later they would read the account of the birth of Christ from the scriptures and sing Christmas carols.

"Boy, look at it coming down out there." Rachel's husband, Doug, cast a worried look out the front window. "Honey, I sure hope these contractions aren't serious. I'd hate to try and get you to the hospital in a hurry on a night like this."

"Don't worry," she said, propping her feet up on the coffee table. "They've stopped."

"But isn't that what happened with Hailey?" Miranda reminded her. "You had all these contractions, then they suddenly stopped and you went into labor two hours later and delivered within forty-five minutes."

"Honey," Doug said, his face showing the alarm that Danielle heard in his voice, "don't you think we ought to take you to the hospital, just to be safe?"

"No, they'll just send me home again," Rachel said with a calm, even tone. "I'm fine, honey. I don't feel anything unusual happening down there."

"You're sure?" he insisted.

"Positive. I'll let you know if I have even the slightest hint of a contraction or pain." Rachel rubbed her hand on her rounded stomach. "I just hope I have room to eat some of that delicious clam chowder. It's a Christmas Eve family tradition," she told Harry and Carson.

Danielle looked at her sister, swollen with child, and uneasily thought of the icy roads outside. Of course, she'd never had a baby herself, but she hoped Rachel didn't put off going to the hospital too long.

# CHAPTER TWENTY-EIGHT

Rachel's three daughters were excited about the pajamas they'd gotten from Santa Claus. They went upstairs to Grandma's room to try them on before dinner.

"Carson, what kind of traditions did your family have?" Rachel asked.

Since the girls were out of the room, he slid the Santa hat from his head and removed the beard.

He shrugged. "We didn't really have any. A lot of times my father was out of town on business. He usually made it back Christmas morning, but sometimes he got stuck in airports and didn't even get home in time for Christmas."

Danielle noticed Harry looking down at his hands in his lap. She knew he was hurting inside. Her heart ached for him.

"My mom was good about making the holiday special, but there were many times I heard her cry in her room after I'd gone to bed. I know it was hard for her to have him gone."

The tone of the room was sober.

"Since she passed away, Christmas really hasn't been that big of a deal." He looked over at Danielle. "Until today. Doing the Sub-for-Santa, visiting all those families and the kids at the hospital, has really made this the best Christmas I've ever had."

He took one of Danielle's hands and gave it a squeeze. "I'm glad to be able to spend this night with all of you. Since I don't really have a family anymore, I appreciate you inviting me to be with yours."

Danielle felt tears sting her eyes. She knew Carson wasn't trying to be cruel, but each word had to feel like a knife going right through Harry's heart.

No one in the room had much to say. The moment was awkward. Danielle searched for some way to break the uneasiness.

"Ow!" Rachel said, sitting up suddenly on the couch. She leaned forward, both hands on her knees and drew in several deep breaths.

"Rachel!" Doug flew to her and knelt at her side. "Honey, what is it? Are you all right?"

But she couldn't answer; she was busy trying to breathe. After a very long minute, she relaxed. "That was definitely a contraction. Honey," she looked at her husband, "I don't want you to panic, but I think it's time. We'd better get to the hospital."

He jumped to his feet. "I'll grab your coat. Should I call the hospital? Or the doctor?"

"We can call from the car." She reached toward Doug, who took her hands and helped her to her feet. "I think we'd better hurry. I'm feeling a lot of pressure." She couldn't stand up straight.

"Holy cow, Rachel," Miranda exclaimed. "Don't have that baby in Mom's living room. Let's get you to the car!" She rushed to her sister's side and placed a supportive arm around her shoulders. "Doug, go get the car started. We'll help Rachel."

"Right," Doug said. "Where are my keys? Where's my coat?"

"I'll get them," Danielle said, rushing to the hall closet. Thankfully his keys were inside the coat pocket.

"I'll shovel a path," Garrett offered.

"I can help," Miranda's son, Adam, joined in.

"Hurry!" Miranda called, seeing how washed out Rachel's face appeared. "Rachel, honey, are you okay?"

"I feel another one," Rachel said with a groan. She leaned forward and moaned deeply. Tears came to her eyes. "Oh, no," she said, gasping. "I'm feeling a lot of press—" She couldn't finish.

"Oh my gosh!" Danielle exclaimed. "Mom! Dad!" she hollered.

They heard a crash in the kitchen, then Dorothy Camden came running down the hallway. "What in the world?" she said, then stopped dead in her tracks at the sight of her daughter. "Rachel, what is it?"

"I'm . . . ," she gasped and inhaled deeply. "The baby . . . Oh no!" She let out a cry, then began to bawl. "My water just broke."

"What do we do?" Dorothy looked around frantically. "Earl, do something!" she barked at her husband.

"What?" he cried.

"Call 9-1-1," Carson finally said.

"Right." Earl raced from the room.

"Mom," Danielle exclaimed. "What about the Vollmans? He's a doctor. Are they home?"

"I think so," Dorothy exclaimed. "I'll run next door and get him."

"Hurry, Mom," Rachel cried in agony. "Hurry!"

"Rachel." Carson knelt down beside her. "We need to get you comfortable. Danielle, help me. Rachel, can you walk to the other room?"

Rachel was crying and hunched over again as another contraction gripped her middle.

"She can't even talk!" Danielle said.

"We better lay her down right here," Carson said. "Someone get a towel or something to put underneath her."

Miranda ran out of the room to get a towel.

Carson and Danielle helped Rachel to the floor and propped pillows behind her. As the contraction eased, Rachel collapsed back and gathered her strength.

"Here," Miranda said breathlessly as she returned with an armload of towels.

The two sisters spread the towels beneath Rachel and tried to talk to her in soothing tones.

Danielle prayed desperately that Brother Vollman would hurry and that Rachel would have the strength to withstand the pain. She could hardly bear to watch her sister in agony, but she didn't want to leave her side. She wished she could do something to help her.

The front door burst open. "Where's Rachel?" Doug cried. He looked at his wife, lying on the floor. "What are you doing?"

"She's not going to make it to the hospital," Carson told him.

"Our neighbor is a doctor," Danielle told him. "Mom just ran next door."

"A doctor?" Doug asked, looking suddenly pale.

"Help him," Danielle ordered Miranda. "He looks faint."

Miranda leaped to his side. "Doug, you have to hang in there. Rachel needs you. Breathe, Doug. Take deep breaths."

While Doug got his bearings back, to everyone's relief Dorothy burst through the door with Brother and Sister Vollman behind her. Brother Vollman quickly assessed the situation. "We need more towels, many more towels," he directed. "And something plastic—a curtain for the shower, or table covering."

Dorothy ran from the room.

"If you need my help, doctor, I work in a hospital," Carson offered.

"Gut, gut. Stay right here, then." He knelt down next to his patient. "Hello there," he said to Rachel. "How are you doing?"

She began to cry. "I'm scared. I can't do this."

He patted her hand. "You're doing fine. Let's take a look and see what's going on, shall we?"

As he began his examination Rachel gasped in pain, another contraction was coming. She grabbed Doug's hand and squeezed with all her might. Danielle saw him wince in pain.

"Hilde," Brother Vollman asked, "have you got my bag?"

"Yes, Dieter." His wife handed him his doctor's bag, and he removed several items. "You," he spoke to Doug, "You are the husband?"

Doug nodded and jumped to his feet, ready to run for help.

"Sit down and let her lean against you," he directed. "She's going to need your help when she pushes."

"Pushes!" Doug exclaimed. "I don't believe this. The hospital's only fifteen minutes away. We can make it."

"Sit down, Doug!" Rachel yelled. Doug dropped to the floor.

Dorothy raced into the room with more towels. Earl Camden hurried behind her with a red and white plaid picnic tablecloth.

They handed the tablecloth to the doctor, who, with Danielle and Carson's help, spread the tablecloth then several layers of fresh towels beneath Rachel, who was writhing with pain, nearly twisting Doug's hand from his arm.

"The operator said the switchboard is going crazy," Earl told everyone. "There have been over fifty accidents in the last three hours. They'll get help here as soon as they can."

"I don't believe this," Dorothy Camden said, holding her face with her hands. "Rachel, are you okay?"

The contraction finished and Rachel fell back against her husband, exhausted.

Doug kissed the top of his wife's head. "I'm here, honey. Everything's going to be okay. Right, Dr. Vollman?"

The doctor nodded. "We hope the ambulance comes soon, but if it doesn't, we can do this. Okay?"

"Okay," Rachel replied shakily. "Keep the girls away. I don't want them to see this."

"Ashlyn's upstairs with them," Miranda told her. The doctor checked Rachel's pulse and felt her forehead.

"Oh, no, here comes another one," Rachel cried. "Ohhh!!!" She grabbed Doug's hand in a death grip and cried out in pain.

"Breathe, Rachel," Dr. Vollman commanded. "Focus and breathe."

"You can do it, honey," Doug told her.

"It hurts!" she cried. "OHHHH!"

Danielle felt tears fall from her own eyes. Harry and Earl stepped quietly from the room to give her privacy as the doctor asked Carson to help him prepare Rachel for the delivery of her child. Carson nodded his understanding of the instructions. They were ready.

"I need . . . to . . . push . . . ," she said, through pained gasps for air.

"Okay," Dr. Vollman said. "That's good. Take deep breaths and when you feel the contraction, push." He checked her and said. "The baby's right there. You're doing great!"

"I don't believe . . . this . . . ," Rachel said. "Ohhh! Here it comes."

With a determined groan, she clenched her eyes shut and bore down with the contraction.

"Gut!" Dr. Vollman cried. "Gut. The baby's head is crowning. Breathe, Rachel."

After the contraction subsided, Rachel pulled in several deep, shaky breaths. A few seconds passed. "Here it comes again," Rachel said, her voice raspy and weak.

"When I tell you," Dr. Vollman said to Carson, "clip the cord." Mrs. Vollman handed Carson a pair of sterilized scissors from the doctor's bag.

"What's going on?" Garrett said as he stomped through the front door. "Adam and I have got the walks—" Miranda grabbed him quickly and pulled him off to the side. A moment later he went back outside to watch for the ambulance.

"I can't . . . ," Rachel panted. "I can't!"

"Yes, you can, Rachel. You're doing great. The baby's on its way," Carson encouraged.

"Oh!" she screamed out in pain.

Danielle shuddered and twisted her hands together. She wanted to do something for her sister, but there was nothing she could do. She was helpless. So she prayed. She prayed with all her might, for Rachel, for the baby, for Dr. Vollman, and for Carson.

"There's the head," Dr. Vollman cried. "Push!"

Rachel screamed in agony as she pushed again with every bit of strength left. A shiver tore up Danielle's spine. She didn't dare look, but she forced herself. Her eyes took in a scurry of activity. Both men were hunched over, Rachel was doubled up and groaning as if the bowels of the earth itself were in anguish.

Every person in the room held their breath. Then Rachel collapsed back. And as clear and fresh as church bells on a frosty Christmas morning, a tiny infant cry was heard.

Rachel burst into tears and her husband collapsed, holding onto her with joy and relief. Danielle knew her own face was wet with tears. Everyone in the house came running to see, pausing just outside the entryway to the living room.

Carson held a clean towel out for the doctor to place the baby in. He wrapped the newborn baby in the fleecy softness. The infant whimpered as Carson cradled it in his arms. The sight of Carson, still dressed in his Santa Claus suit, presenting the child to his mother brought another rush of emotion to Danielle's heart. A symbol of a Christmas so long ago, the true meaning of Christmas.

"It's a boy," Carson said, cuddling the baby in his arms. He wiped the newborn's face with a cloth, then placed the baby in Rachel's arms. "You have a son."

In the distance the wail of a siren approached.

"A son," Rachel whispered. She looked up at her husband, peeking over her shoulder. Together they wept. Their precious, healthy baby had arrived in the world, safe and sound.

Doug kissed his wife on the cheek and on the forehead. "I'm so proud of you, honey. I love you."

"Mommy," seven-year-old Hailey asked from the doorway, "can I see my brother?"

"Sure, sweetie," Rachel said, extending her hand toward her youngest daughter. "C'mon, Holly, Hillary. Don't you want to see him, too?"

Danielle watched as the three sisters gathered around their tiny brother. He had a mass of dark, black hair, and his mouth was puckered and trembling.

The girls oohed and aahed over their darling baby brother.

Rachel looked up at the two men who had helped her through the ordeal. "Thank you," she whispered through her tears.

Dr. Vollman smiled. *Sehr gut,* he said. "I'm proud of you."

"Congratulations," Carson said.

"Thank you for your help," Dr. Vollman told Carson. "You will make a fine doctor someday."

Carson beamed. "Thanks, Dr. Vollman."

Flashes of blue and red lights strobed through the front window. Danielle heard Garrett hurrying the crew inside.

"They're in here," he said as he burst through the door. He stopped when he saw the bundle in Rachel's arms. A smile broke onto his face. "Did you . . . Is that . . . the baby?"

Rachel nodded.

"I have a brother," Hailey announced. "Just like the baby Jesus. Can we name him Jesus, Mommy?"

Rachel smiled. "We'll see, honey. We'll see."

The ambulance crew rushed inside. Dr. Vollman gave a quick report to them as they prepared to check the mother and baby, then transport them to the hospital.

Danielle was so proud of Carson. He'd actually helped deliver Rachel's baby right there in her mother's living room. She didn't even want to think what would have happened had Carson and Dr. Vollman not been there tonight.

Dorothy Camden followed behind as the ambulance crew prepared to wheel Rachel and the baby out to the ambulance. Earl stood close by. "We love you, punkin'," he said.

Miranda and Danielle peeked at the sleeping baby and gave their sister a quick hug. Doug followed behind the crew, ready to ride with her to the hospital.

It took a moment for all the talking and commotion to die down. Dr. Vollman and Carson had saved the day, and everyone in Danielle's family had to take a moment to thank them for what they'd done.

After the Vollmans left and the women had removed the makeshift delivery room, the family sat in silence, still trying to process all that had just occurred there in that very room a short while ago. There was great joy, but also great relief. The Lord had truly been with them that evening, there was no doubt about that.

Carson removed the Santa jacket, which was stifling hot by now. He was in the process of sliding off the pants that he had over his own jeans when the talking stopped and everyone watched as Harry approached Carson. The tired, old man extended his hand toward Carson. "Son, I'm proud of you."

"Well, thank you," Carson said, shaking his hand.

"No," Harry said deliberately, ready to end the charade. "Son, I'm proud of you."

"Thank you, Har—" Carson began, then stopped, bewildered, in midsentence. He looked at Harry closely. "What do you mean?" A curious, skeptical look crossed his face. "What are you trying to say?"

"Carson," Harry cleared his throat. "I'm your—"

"No!" Carson held up both hands and backed away from his father. "Don't say it."

# CHAPTER
## TWENTY-NINE

A pained look crossed Harry's face.

"Carson," Danielle said. "Please."

Carson looked at Harry again. "You're telling me you're my father?" An angry look crossed his face. He turned to Danielle and his voice was like ice. "You knew he was my father this whole time? How could you?"

"Carson," Danielle said, "I thought—"

Carson's eyes were hard. "You thought what? That you could get me and my father together again?"

"Please, son," Harry said. "Can't we at least talk?"

"No, I don't think we ever could," Carson said curtly. "At least, you could never be bothered."

Sensing that this was a private matter, Danielle's family tactfully slipped from the room.

"Carson," Danielle begged. "He's your father. He's changed."

"Maybe on the outside." Carson shook his head. "But not on the inside."

"I'm sorry. I know I was wrong to do this without telling you, but—" Danielle swallowed, "—I got to know Harry, not Philip Turner the businessman. He's a different man. He's a good, humble man."

Carson looked at his father, his eyes full of contempt. He didn't speak.

"Son," Harry said, "I know I can't erase the past. The Lord knows how I wish I could, but I can't. I was wrong and I was a terrible father. It breaks my heart to think what I put you through. But if there's any way I could make that up to you now, any possible way, I would."

"There's nothing you can do," Carson said evenly, taking a step back to increase the distance between them.

"I know." Harry's shoulders drooped and he looked at the floor. "You're right."

Danielle couldn't believe her ears or her eyes. Only minutes ago Carson had shared with them one of the most sacred experiences she'd ever been a part of in her entire life, bringing Rachel's baby into the world. Now he was as cold and unfeeling as she had once believed Philip Turner to be.

"I am truly sorry, though," Harry said. "I have tried to right my wrongs and do everything in my power to undo all the damage I've done in my life. I don't deserve your forgiveness, but I am sorry." Harry looked his son squarely in the eye. "I didn't handle your mother's death very well. At the time I felt like part of me died with her. Now I realize that you needed me even more after she died, and I wasn't there for you. I was too absorbed with my own grief to help you with yours. I didn't listen to you, I wasn't there for you. And what's worse, I decided I knew what was best for you. But seeing you tonight, with that baby—well, it was the proudest moment of my life. I know you aren't proud to be my son, but I am very proud to be your father. And I know your mother is proud of you, too."

Danielle was so moved by these words and the man's humble sincerity, that she could feel her eyes stinging with unshed tears. But her heart fell when she saw the cold, uncompromising look on Carson's face. When Carson looked at her, she didn't even try to hide her disappointment. As he looked away quickly, a thought occurred to her.

Maybe, just maybe . . . She walked over to the Christmas tree and found a wrapped package and a card with Carson's name on it. "Here." She handed him the present. "This is for you."

He looked at the gift, then back at her.

"I think this would be a good time to open it," she told him. She could tell he didn't want to, but he unwrapped the box, then lifted the lid, and took out the photo album.

Wordlessly, Harry and Danielle watched him turn to the first page. Carson's mouth dropped open when he saw the picture of himself as a baby. Holding her breath, Danielle prayed that Carson would be touched by the pictures of himself with his family, and that his heart would be softened and he would remember the power of the Atonement in providing the strength needed to forgive his father's shortcomings.

She was surprised when Carson chuckled at one of the pictures of himself as a young boy. Page after page, he looked over the pictures, his expression playing out the memories. Happy ones, sad ones, forgotten ones, all treasured.

He paused when he came to a picture of his mother and father, standing with him in front of the temple, the day he went through to receive his endowments before his mission. Whether he liked it or not, they were a forever family. Danielle knew he had a testimony of the restored gospel, that he believed in the sealing power of the priesthood and in the atoning sacrifice of the Savior. He just needed to put his pride and hurt aside and let the healing faith of that testimony rebuild and restore his relationship with his father.

When he came to the last page, he stared for a long time at the picture Danielle had taken of him and his father earlier that day. As soon as they got home that night she'd had Ashlyn help her download the picture onto the computer and print it, so she could slip it into the album before wrapping it.

Finally he looked up, and Danielle saw that the lines of anger which had been etched on his face had softened. His eyes held sadness instead of contempt, and his expression held a myriad conflicting emotions: pain, confusion, yearning, even homesickness. Her eyes filled with tears as she realized that he'd turned the corner.

Still, she didn't know what to say, and the silence was growing heavy and awkward.

"Thank you," he said finally, his words broken by the emotion caught in his throat. "How did you . . . ?"

"Your father helped me," she said. "We had a hard time deciding which pictures to put in; there were so many to choose from."

"There are more?" he asked.

"Boxes and boxes full," Danielle told him. "Your mother filled a whole closet with pictures."

"She didn't go anywhere without her camera," he mused aloud, his gaze drifting away thoughtfully. "I forgot about all the pictures."

"It was because of you that she took up photography," Harry told his son.

"Me? Why?" Carson asked, unconsciously holding the book against his chest, as if pressing the memories back into his heart.

"She took a photography class right before you were born because she wanted to record your whole life in pictures," Harry explained. "She went through several rolls of film a week right after your birth. We spent more money on developing film than we did on groceries." Even though it had been many years since she'd died, it seemed to Danielle as if the pain in his voice was still fresh.

"All those fishing pictures," Carson said slowly. "I'd forgotten."

Danielle had been amazed at how many fishing trips the family had gone on. Up until his mother's death, it seemed as though Carson and his father and mother had spent a lot of time together. Maybe even more than Carson remembered.

Or, maybe, Danielle thought hopefully, he was realizing that his father hadn't been such a bad father after all.

"Remember our trip to Montana when you were fourteen?" Harry offered.

"When I fell out of the boat?" Carson chuckled.

"You were soaked, but you weren't about to go back to camp."

"I caught the biggest fish I'd ever seen that day. It must've been this big." Carson stretched his arms wide to show her. "In fact, I think there's a picture in here." Looking down, he leafed through the pages until he found the exact photo. Sure enough, there he stood, holding the fish up by the gills, with his father smiling proudly next to him. He showed it to Danielle.

"He broke a record with that fish," Harry told her. "In fact, last time I checked, the record still held."

"Really?" Carson asked his father, pleased at the news. His eyes drifted back down to the album. The next photo showed a younger Carson on a motorcycle. "Remember my Honda 350?" he said softly.

"How could I forget it? Your mother nearly tanned my hide for letting you buy it. She was convinced you were going to kill yourself riding it."

"She sure hated that thing," Carson told Danielle.

Another picture caught his eye and again, he and Harry exchanged memories. Picture after picture, they compared notes, recalling the circumstances surrounding each photograph. Danielle felt like an intruder as they seated themselves on the couch and continued their journey to the past.

Before her very eyes, Danielle knew she was witnessing a miracle taking place. A miracle that only the redeeming power of the Savior's love could provide. Seeing Carson and his father laugh together at something funny, Danielle could feel the tears threatening once again as the bond between them appeared to be mending, one shared memory at a time.

"Whatever happened to that motorcycle?" Carson asked his father.

"It's still in the garage, covered up with an old tarp. I think it still runs, though."

Carson nodded, pleased to hear his old motorcycle was still around.

"'Course, your mom would probably find a way to send down a lightening bolt or something if you ever tried to ride it now," Harry said.

Carson laughed. "She probably would."

"You remind me a lot of her," Harry told his son. "You've always favored her, but in this last year you've grown to look like her even more. You have her eyes and her smile."

Carson looked at his father. "You've changed in the last year, too."

Harry didn't answer.

"You look like pictures of Grandpa, with his white hair."

Harry nodded.

"This year has been hard for you, hasn't it?" Carson said.

"Yes, it has," Harry admitted.

"It's true, then. You have cancer?" He could barely look at his dad.

"Yes, son, it is," Harry said gently.

"Are you going to die from it?" Carson closed his eyes, and a flash of pain crossed his face.

"I'm afraid so."

"How long do the doctors—"

"They don't know. It's hard to say. Six weeks, six months, a year."

"I had no idea you . . ." Carson's voice trembled. "That you . . . , uh . . ." His voice broke.

Harry patted his son's hand. "Not many people did. I kept my operation and chemo quiet. Of course, not many people cared anyway." Danielle couldn't swallow, there was such a big lump in her throat.

"I'm sorry, Dad," Carson said softly.

# CHAPTER THIRTY

Harry wrapped his arms around Carson in a strong hug, a father's hug. "No, son. I'm the one who's sorry. Sorry I wasn't a better father."

"I don't want you to die," Carson choked out. "I was wrong to shut you out. I'm sorry, Dad."

Harry nodded, tears streaming down his own face. "I know," he said. "Me too."

Wiping at the tears that streaked her own face, Danielle hurried across the room and grabbed a box of tissues off the piano. Taking several for herself, she set the box down on the coffee table in front of the two men. Carson took a tissue and wiped his own eyes and nose.

"I owe you an apology, too," he said to her. "This might never have happened without your help."

"You mean without my 'interfering'?" Danielle smiled at him.

Carson nodded apologetically.

"I just about gave up," Danielle said. "But the Lord wouldn't let me."

Carson raised an eyebrow, not sure of what she meant.

"I know it sounds weird, but I felt like the Lord needed a way to get you two together, and he chose me. I don't know why."

"I think I do," Harry said. He reached toward her, and she knelt down beside him. "Because you're the only one who could get through to a couple of numskulls like us."

"He's right," Carson said. "You're a pretty special girl. When I said you were my good luck charm, I meant it." He pushed to his feet and reached deep into his pant pocket. He looked up at her, suddenly looking nervous and awkward. "I, uh, was going to save this for later," he said uncomfortably, giving her a weak smile, "but I think I'd like to give you your Christmas present now."

He held out a small gift box, tied with a silver ribbon. Danielle stood and took the box and stared at it, then lifted her eyes slowly to meet Carson's apprehensive gaze. She didn't dare hope what it could be.

With trembling fingers, she took off the bow and wrapping paper and removed the lid, revealing a deep red velvet box. She took it out and opened it. Tucked between two tiny satin pillows was a sparkling diamond ring.

"Oh, Carson!" she exclaimed, breathless. "Is this—I mean, is it what I think it is?"

"Well, if you're thinking it's an engagement ring, then yes, it is," he answered.

"Oh, my gosh! Carson!" she exclaimed. Then bursting into tears and laughter, she wrapped her arms around him. He lifted her off the ground in an enthusiastic bear hug, and kissed her before setting her feet back on the ground.

"I want to do this right," he said and pulled the piano bench away from the piano. "Sit here." Kneeling before her, he took her hands in his. "Danielle, I don't have a lot to offer you right now. And even after I finish my schooling, I may not make a lot of money. You know I want to travel and help people in Thailand. It will be an adventure, that's for sure. But I can't think of anyone I'd rather have by my side than you." He bowed his head for a moment, then looked back up at her. "I know it may seem like I'm rushing things, but I love you, and more than anything I want to marry you."

Danielle smiled as fresh tears spilled onto her cheeks.

"Will you marry me, Danielle?"

Emotion flooded her, and she wasn't sure she could get the words out. "Yes, Carson," she choked out, looking into his hopeful gaze. Clearing her throat and taking a deep breath to slow her racing heart, she said, "I love you, too, Carson. And yes, I will marry you."

The explosion of applause and cheers erupting from the hallway startled them both. Neither had realized, they'd attracted a crowd, but the family had gathered quietly in the shadows to witness the event.

Carson and Danielle burst out laughing. Wiping her cheeks and eyes on her shirt sleeve, Danielle called out, "Oh, my heck, you guys! Get in here, will ya?"

When hugs and congratulations had all been given, Harry hugged Danielle once again. "I don't know how to thank you, my dear. This is truly one of the happiest days of my life. To have my son back and to know . . . that he will have you and your wonderful family . . . after I'm gone. I feel like I can die a happy man."

"Well, don't get any ideas about leaving us too soon," she warned. "I want you here for the wedding and to play with your grandchildren."

Harry placed a gentle hand on her cheek. "I'll do the best I can."

Suddenly Danielle was attacked by her three nieces, who had to see her engagement ring. Then her father at last approached her.

"It's not going to be easy giving up my baby," Earl said, squeezing his daughter tightly.

"Easy, my foot," Danielle exclaimed. "You've been harping about me not being married for the last six years. You're glad to get rid of me and you know it."

He laughed and hugged her again. "I'm happy for you, punkin'," he congratulated her. "Carson will take good care of you. He and I had a nice talk on the phone last night. I feel good about him."

"You knew about this?" she asked her father with surprise.

"Of course he did," Carson interrupted. "I wouldn't think about asking for your hand in marriage without talking to your father first." He and Earl exchanged satisfied looks.

Danielle looked at them and caught her mother's smile. "You knew, too, Mom?"

Dorothy nodded. "It's been hard to keep it in. But I'm very happy for both of you. I couldn't think of a more wonderful young man for my daughter to marry than you, Carson."

"Thank you, Mrs. Camden. I'm glad you approve," Carson said.

"How could they not?" Danielle told him matter-of-factly. "You passed the toilet seat test."

"The what?"

"The toilet seat test," Danielle said with a laugh. "I'll tell you about it later."

His face remained puzzled as he tried to make sense of her words.

"This has been quite a night," Dorothy Camden announced. "We have a lot to celebrate. Is anyone hungry?"

"Yes," the family chorused and allowed themselves to be herded into the kitchen, leaving Danielle and Carson to themselves for a moment.

"I'm so happy," she said, placing her arms around his neck. "I can't believe this is happening." Once she had thought she'd have to give up her dreams to travel and have adventure, for the sake of love and marriage. But it was just as the scripture in 3 Nephi 13:33 promised: "Seek ye first the kingdom of God and his righteousness, and all these things shall be added unto you."

How much easier her life would have been had she followed this counsel from the very beginning. If she would have just put the Lord first, everything else would have fallen into place for her. But how could she complain? The road had been long and rocky, but finally, finally, she'd made it. Of course, she knew there would be more stumbling blocks in the road; she didn't expect life to be trial-free. But somehow, knowing Carson would be at her side, she wasn't afraid to face those challenges.

"I'm happy you're happy," he said. "And I'm so relieved you said 'yes.'"

Danielle was surprised. "Did you even wonder?"

"I don't have much to offer. I'm just a poor medical student," he said frankly.

"Your love is all I need right now," she assured him. "Everything else we'll work out later."

"You may find yourself in strange countries, doing a lot of traveling. It could be quite an adventure at times," he warned her. But Danielle only smiled. She would tell him sometime that a life of adventure was a dream come true for her.

"As long as we're together, I'll follow you to the ends of the earth," she promised.

Carson kissed her and she knew she'd never been happier. "I don't know how to thank you," he said, his eyes aglow with gratitude.

"You've given me so much, especially something I didn't know I was missing. You gave me back my father."

"I only did what the Lord wanted me to do," she answered honestly.

"But the photo album," Carson said, shaking his head. "That must have taken so much time."

"It did," she agreed, remembering the hours sifting through photographs, "but I loved every minute of it. I spent a lot of time with your father, going through pictures, learning about you and your mother. It was wonderful."

Carson nodded thoughtfully. "I want to spend as much time with him as I can," he said. "Before it's too late."

"He's a different man," Danielle told him. "You'll need to get to know him all over again."

"I know. I can tell." He tucked her hair behind her ear.

She looked into his eyes and saw they were full of emotion. He'd received a pretty big shock that night, not only that Harry was his father but that he was also dying.

"Are you okay?" she asked out of concern.

He nodded. "Yeah, I just can't help thinking that cancer is going to end up taking both of my parents. Helps me realize just how fragile life is. And how important relationships with loved ones are."

Danielle listened, letting him talk out the feelings in his heart.

"There's not enough time to waste holding on to hurt feelings or foolish pride. Life is just too short, loved ones are just too precious." He pulled her close and held her tightly. "I'm sorry for the time I wasted being mad, when I could have been with my father. But, I'm just grateful to have some time left together. I'll never be able to thank you enough for giving that to me."

"It wasn't me," she told him. "The Lord knew how much you two needed each other right now."

"I feel so blessed right now," Carson said. "I get my father back and get engaged all in one night. This will be a Christmas I'll never forget."

"Me either," Danielle said, enjoying his strong, protective arms around her.

Outside the window, snow fell, bringing with it a silent, reverent hush, until the clatter of dishes in the kitchen broke the stillness. It was time for dinner.

"I want to take you for a ride on my motorcycle when the weather's good again," Carson told her.

Danielle frowned a little. "I don't know. I don't really like motorcycles. They're dangerous."

"Now you sound just like my mother," Carson complained teasingly.

"Well, they are," she defended herself.

"I promise, I'll be careful. I wouldn't want anything to happen to either of us," he said, looking deeply into her eyes before kissing her once more.

"Come on," Danielle said, taking him by the hand, the newness of the ring on her finger sending tingles through her body. "Everyone's waiting for us."

Dinner was a feast of fun and celebration. Doug called from the hospital to let everyone know that Rachel and the baby were doing great. He also thanked Carson once more for his part in bringing their son safely into the world. Carson told him the good news of the engagement, and once again, the family reveled in their joy and blessings.

After dinner the family gathered around the piano to sing Christmas carols. Standing beside Carson under the glowing lights from the Christmas tree, Danielle thought with wonder as she sang that although she had sung these songs many times before, they had never had the power and sweetness they did now. She found it nearly impossible to sing the last verse of "O Little Town of Bethlehem" as the spirit of love and Christmas filled her soul.

> How silently, how silently
> The wondrous gift is given!
> So God imparts to human hearts
> The blessings of his heav'n.
> No ear may hear his coming;
> But in this world of sin,
> Where meek souls will receive him still
> The dear Christ enters in.

The dear Christ had entered in—into their home and their hearts. It was a season of giving and caring, of loving and sharing. Tonight they had witnessed the birth of a baby, seen the power of the

Atonement, and felt the bond of love strengthened. The dear Christ had blessed them with his wondrous love.

Surrounded by the ones she loved most, wrapped in the cloak of the gospel, Danielle felt the great power and glory of the Savior. How grateful she was for his birth. How grateful she was for blessings she would never be worthy of nor able to repay. Blessings she sometimes didn't recognize because they were disguised by challenges, adversities, and trials. But when unveiled, they were beautiful manifestations of the Savior's love.

She knew that those challenges, adversities, and trials would always be present in her life, but her faith had been nourished by the miracles they had been blessed with that night. With that faith and the constant love of the Savior, as well as the help and support of her dear family and friends, she would have the strength to face whatever lay ahead.

Carson wrapped one arm around her shoulders and his other arm around his father's shoulders as together they sang from their hearts, *Joy to the world* . . .

When the song ended, Carson leaned over to kiss her, then he whispered into her ear, "By the way, what's the toilet seat test?"

## ABOUT THE AUTHOR

In the fourth grade, Michele Ashman was considered a "daydreamer" by her teacher, who wrote on her report card that "she has a vivid imagination and would probably do well with creative writing." Her imagination, combined with a passion for reading, has enabled Michele to live up to her teacher's prediction, and she loves writing books, especially books that uplift, inspire, and edify readers as well as entertain them. (You can also catch her daydreaming instead of doing housework.)

Michele grew up in St. George, Utah, where she met her husband, Gary, at Dixie College before they both served missions, his to Pennsylvania and hers to Frankfurt, Germany. Seven months after they returned they were married and are now the proud parents of four children: Weston, Kendyl, Andrea, and Rachel.

Her favorite pastime is supporting her children in all of their activities, traveling both inside and outside of the United States with her husband and family, and doing research for her books.

Aside from being a busy wife and mother, Michele teaches aerobics at the Life Centre Athletic club near her home. She is currently the Missionary Specialist in the Sandy ward where her husband serves as the bishop.

The best-selling author of *An Unexpected Love, An Enduring Love, A Forever Love,* and *Yesterday's Love,* Michele has also published children's stories in the *Friend.*

Michele welcomes comments and questions from readers, who can write to her at P.O. Box 901513, Sandy, Utah 84090, or e-mail her at GPBell@MSN.com.